MICHAEL CRAFT

desert summer

st. martin's minotaur ⚔ new york

www.minotaurbooks.com

Library of Congress Cataloging-in-Publication Data

Craft, Michael, 1950–
    Desert summer : a Claire Gray mystery / Michael Craft.— 1st St. Martin's
Minotaur ed.
        p. cm.
    ISBN 0-312-33423-0
    EAN 978-0-312-33423-9
    1. Gray, Claire (Fictitious character)—Fiction.   2. Motion picture producers
and directors—Crimes against—Fiction.   3. Women theatrical producers and
directors—Fiction.   4. Divorced women—Crimes against—Fiction.   5. Women
college teachers—Fiction.   6. Palm Springs (Calif.)—Fiction.   7. College
theater—Fiction.   I. Title.

PS3553.R215D474 2005
813'.54—dc22

                                                            2004066402

First Edition: August 2005

10 9 8 7 6 5 4 3 2 1

Une douzaine de livres,

un million de mots,

tout pour Léon

acknowledgments

The author wishes to thank Mark Fetko, James Shapiro, and Maureen Winkler for their generous assistance with various plot details. Mitchell Waters, the author's agent, and Keith Kahla, his editor at St. Martin's, have provided the ongoing support and enthusiasm that have made this series possible. Heartfelt thanks to all.

contents

PART ONE

improvisation

"Menacing. Psychotic." With a thoughtful nod, I added, "Depraved, certainly, but *pathetic* as well. She gives us chills, but at the same time, we need to feel *sorry* for the woman and ask, 'How did she get this way?'"

"Isn't she a lesbian, Miss Gray?"

"Probably," I allowed. "Does that explain her descent into madness?" My students answered with uneasy laughter.

One of them asked, "But why should we feel sorry for her?"

"Because Mrs. Danvers is a *character,* not a *caricature.* When portraying any character, the actor's challenge is to convince the audience they're watching a real person whose current behavior, however off-the-wall or seemingly inexplicable, is the product of a human, three-dimensional past. Otherwise, our efforts are for naught—we might as well be mounting a shadow play or a puppet show."

The scene we were rehearsing involved neither puppets nor shadows, but flesh-and-blood actors—albeit young ones, college students—who were struggling with the script of *Rebecca.* Although Daphne du Maurier's gothic potboiler is best known in its film version, directed by Alfred Hitchcock, the story was penned first as a novel, then as a stage play, the script of which was our current object of study. Predictably, the students in my summer theater workshop at Desert Arts College were most intrigued by the character identified simply as Mrs. Danvers, the demented head of the household staff at Manderley, ancestral estate of the de Winter family.

I snapped my fingers. "Improvisation. Let's take a break from the script and do some exercises. We've worked on projection, diction, and sound cover, but those are primarily vocal issues. It's time to delve deeper into the meat of acting—characterization. And the best way to get inside a character's head is through improvisation."

Through a comic groan, Paige Yeats asked, "Does that mean you're going to make us pretend to be butterflies?" She spread her imaginary wings.

"Or trees?" asked Cynthia Pryor, sprouting gnarled limbs. "Or ducks?"

Thad Quatrain, an earnest young man, answered for me. "I think what Miss Gray is driving at is that we're going to pretend to be Mrs. Danvers."

"*Guys too?*" asked Scott, one of their fellow students, sounding horrified.

"You're all actors," I reminded him. "The human experience is universal, crossing even the barrier of gender. So I want you to pair off for a few minutes and prepare a short scene between a *young* Mrs. Danvers and an even *younger* Rebecca, long before either of them first set eyes on Manderley. Don't rehearse the scene you invent; merely discuss the parameters of it. Then, in pairs, we'll have each of you improvise the scene, fresh, for the whole class. The point of this exercise is to fill in some of the 'backstory' that shaped these two enigmatic women prior to the time frame depicted in the play itself. Got it?"

"Sort of," said one of them with a note of skepticism.

"Uh-huh," said another without enthusiasm.

"But, Miss Gray," said Cynthia, "Rebecca herself doesn't even appear in the play."

"All the more reason we need to get to know her. Make sense?"

"Perfectly clear, Miss Gray," said Thad. Then he told the others, "Come on. Let's get to work." With a jerk of his head, he invited Paige to pair off with him.

And the others followed suit, drifting off to distant corners of the stage.

As they began to tinker with their scenes, I turned from the stage apron and looked out upon the row after row of empty seats that filled the auditorium with geometric precision. The plump crimson velvet cushions formed a pattern of vanishing points that reminded me of headstones in a military cemetery. Blinking away this morbid image (theater, to my mind, being the most life-affirming force that has ever sprung from the mind of man), I descended a short flight of stairs from the stage and retreated to my makeshift director's table, set up in the first few rows of seats.

On that Friday morning in late July, I shuffled a few papers and breathed a quiet, contented sigh, reflecting on the many changes that had recently reshaped my life. Not quite a year ago, I had moved from New York, where the theater circle seemed in general agreement that I had established myself as one of Broadway's most gifted directors. The reason for this career shift and change of venue—at fifty-four, no less—was that I had been irresistibly lured cross-country to chair the theater department of a new arts college in southern California, in the Sonoran Desert, near Palm Springs. The school had been built ("from the sand up," as it was reported in national news magazines) by D. Glenn Yeats, the software tycoon with a soft spot for the arts, who had decided to "give back" to society by founding the school he now served as president.

In wooing me westward, Glenn Yeats had dangled many entice-ments—artistic autonomy, boundless budgets, perks aplenty—but the plum I could not resist plucking was the opportunity to work with a world-class architect in designing and building the very playhouse in which I now sat, a state-of-the-art theater that Glenn never ceased to remind me was "mine."

Completing my first academic year at the college, I had decided to remain in my new desert home for the summer, conducting a work-shop that would suit several purposes.

First, it would allow me to lavish some intensive training on stu-dents returning to my program in the fall. Most notable of these was Thad Quatrain, a kid from Wisconsin who would soon enter his sophomore year. I had just lost the troupe's leading man, Tanner Grif-fin, to a blossoming career in Hollywood, and I was now grooming Thad to take his place.

What's more, the summer program allowed me to work with a few students outside our normal enrollment, putting them through something of an extended audition. Most notable of these was Paige Yeats, who happened to be the daughter of the school's founder. Paige lived somewhere in the Los Angeles area, where she would return to her junior year of college in the fall, hoping to establish a career in film. At her father's suggestion, she took advantage of the opportunity to study with me during the summer.

And finally, the workshop allowed me to experiment with various scripts I had been considering for production during the next season. *Rebecca* had been suggested by none other than D. Glenn Yeats. It was not a script I would have been drawn to on my own, but I found that Glenn's idea had merit. Noting the earlier success we had achieved with *Laura,* our premiere production at Desert Arts College, he felt we might build a tradition at DAC of mounting the stage versions of classic films. This struck me as a reasonable theme for a school in southern California, and working with the script, I found it to be a promising vehicle for my student troupe.

"Claire, darling!" The voice approaching from behind, accompanied by the jangle of armloads of noisy bracelets, was that of Kiki Jasper-Plunkett, the theater department's head costumer. "What's the verdict?" she asked, bustling toward me and plopping in the seat next to mine.

"Not guilty," I answered, having no idea what she was talking about. Having known Kiki for over thirty years, I was accustomed to her non sequiturs.

"I mean the script," she explained with a carefree laugh. "*Rebecca*—do you plan to produce it?"

Having not yet voiced this decision, I paused before answering, "I do. Yes, I think *Rebecca* will make a fine season opener. It has plenty of roles to go around, and we have plenty of talent to fill them. Season two—curtain going up."

Kiki rubbed her hands with glee. Over the clatter of her bracelets, she told me, "Wonderful choice."

I shrugged. "It was Glenn's idea."

"Talk about production values," she yammered. "What costumes! What a set! What a *spectacle!*"

"The play's not the movie," I reminded her. The play does not end with the spectacular burning of Manderley, as the movie does, but simply the resignation and departure of Mrs. Danvers. The entire action takes place in the main reception hall of the mansion, in England, sometime between the two World Wars.

"Yes, dear, of course," conceded Kiki, "but there's still *oodles* of delicious material for our designers and tech staff. When it was written, the play was contemporary, but now it's a *period* piece—replete with crusty accents—and a good dose of melodrama to boot." She flung her arms. "We'll have a *ball*."

Her enthusiasm was contagious. "We'll need music," I brainstormed. "Nothing conspicuous—just enough to set the mood and heighten tension."

"Done!" declared Glenn Yeats from behind. Turning, I saw him stride down the aisle from the lobby doors. At fifty-one (three years younger than both Kiki and I), the legendary e-titan was less imposing in person than his reputation would suggest. His vast wealth, his unrivaled business empire, would lead one to expect a commanding presence of heroic stature. In truth, Glenn Yeats was a bit of a nerd.

A computer wiz with a good idea and a keen sense of marketing, he had amassed untold billions but had never quite managed to slough off the image of a geek in designer clothing. That morning he wore a mint-green silk dress shirt with heavy gold cuff links (the long sleeves seemed wrong for the desert's brutal summer heat), tan gabardine slacks (nicely tailored, but sporting too many pleats), and shiny crocodile loafers with no socks (a look that seemed more evocative of Miami than southern California). Oiling his way into the row of seats behind us, he told me, "Your wish is my command. If the illustrious Claire Gray requires music for her next production—whatever it be—you have Lance Caldwell at your disposal." He was referring to the college's composer in residence, a prickly musician with abundant talent and no shortage of self-esteem.

"Why, thank you, Glenn," I said wryly. "I knew I could count on you."

Noting the lack of action onstage, he asked, "Taking a break?"

"I am, but the students aren't. They're preparing scenes for improvisation."

Kiki flashed me a grin, not seen by Glenn. She said, "Crack the whip, Glenn. No loafing—I wouldn't put up with it."

He laughed. "Claire's schedule is entirely her own. I wouldn't dream of interfering." His words, I'd come to understand, were sincere. While he took an active interest in my theater program—often popping in to visit rehearsals during the school year and workshops during the summer—his presence was always enthusiastic and supportive, never meddling. Even his suggestion that I consider the *Rebecca* script had been presented as "an idle thought—take it or leave it."

He jumped out of his seat, as if someone had goosed him. "Excuse me, ladies. I have a call." Pulling a vibrating cell phone from his belt, he flipped it open, jostled out to the aisle, and strolled into the shadows, gabbing into his palm.

Kiki sputtered, but dared not laugh.

"He means well," I said under my breath. "Besides, he's our employer."

"Besides," Kiki added, "he hopes to win your heart."

"Oh, Lord . . ."

Not long after I had arrived in California the previous September, Glenn had stunned me one evening with a profession—more a confession, really—of love. I was able to mutter honestly that night that this was "so sudden," that I needed "time to think," but I was not able to tell him that, in truth, I was buying time while sorting out my feelings for Tanner Griffin, my student and protégé. With Tanner now effectively out of the picture, if not entirely out of my heart, Glenn seemed to sense that it was time to renew his campaign for my affections. It was becoming clear to both of us that I owed him an answer, sooner rather than later. It was also clear to both of us that Glenn generally got what he wanted, but having never married and feeling comfortably independent, I was still hesitant to commit to him, despite the considerable dowry he could bring to such a pairing.

Fortunately, I didn't need to resolve any of this on the spot. My students had begun to drift downstage from the wings, some of them sitting at the edge of the apron, swinging their legs over the orchestra pit. I asked, "Everyone ready?"

"As ready as we'll ever be," said Scott. His tone of resignation made me wonder whether the hapless young actor would be portraying Rebecca or Mrs. Danvers in this exercise.

I asked the group, "Who'd care to go first?"

Scott and his partner didn't volunteer. But Thad and Paige exchanged a quick shrug and stood. "Sure, Miss Gray," said one. "We'll do it," added the other.

The students formed a loose circle on the stage floor, sitting to watch as Thad and Paige arranged a couple of chairs down center. Paige sat in one of them. Standing behind her, Thad told me, "We went back to when Rebecca was about twelve and decided to—"

"No preambles," I interrupted. "Begin the action, and let the scene set itself."

Thad nodded. Then he tapped Paige on the shoulder, saying, "Well, now, Rebecca, it's a lovely morning for your lesson, don't you think? What shall we practice today—croquet or tennis?" Thad's Mrs. Danvers spoke crisply, with the hint of an upper-class accent, at the higher end of Thad's natural register, but without a feminine falsetto.

"Oh, *Danny*," gushed Rebecca, hugging herself, "no more tennis, please, not today. It's ever so strenuous. I might chip a nail." With a pout, she added, baby-talking, "And we wouldn't want that, now, would we?"

"Of course not, my love. You're growing into a perfect young woman, and perfect you shall be. The day will come when all the finest gentlemen of Cornwall will beg for your hand."

"Oooh." Rebecca frowned. "I don't think I should like that, Danny."

"You *won't*," said Mrs. Danvers through stern, tight features. "But it's a game we all must learn to play."

"Can you teach me?" Rebecca bounced to her feet.

"You bet I can—eventually. For now, my precious, we must concentrate on croquet. Did you bring your mallet?"

From the look on Rebecca's face, she hadn't been expecting the question, but she quickly recovered, producing an imaginary mallet out of thin air, from behind her back. "Right here, Danny."

"Excellent." Mrs. Danvers stepped behind Rebecca. "It's important to remember that in croquet—as in life—posture is everything."

"Posture is everything," Rebecca repeated, making note of the principle.

"Let me demonstrate." Mrs. Danvers reached both arms around Rebecca's waist, guiding her wrists to form a proper grip on the mallet. "Keep your back straight!" she snapped.

"Sorry, Danny," Rebecca whimpered. "I can be ever so clumsy and stupid. But you know *everything*. I want to be just like you, Danny."

"Just like *me*?" asked Mrs. Danvers, flattered beyond measure. Leaning her head against Rebecca's cheek, she added suggestively, "Really . . . ?"

"Yes, Danny." Rebecca turned to face Mrs. Danvers, who still held the girl in her arms. "Really." She lolled her head backward, closing her eyes, parting her lips.

Mrs. Danvers hesitated, but not long, before pressing her own lips to Rebecca's, engulfing her in a passionate embrace.

The other students broke into lurid hoots and fevered applause. Kiki and I laughed openly and joined in the clapping. Glenn Yeats snapped his phone shut and joined us again in the row behind my table, wondering what he had missed. Thad and Paige emerged from their roles, joined hands, and indulged in an elaborate bow to their classmates.

"Not fair," said Scott. "You guys stole all the good stuff."

Thad reminded him, "You could have gone first."

Leaning over my shoulder, Glenn said into my ear, "What was that all about? Thad and Paige really looked 'into it.' Were they acting?" His tone carried no alarm. To the contrary, he seemed pleasantly intrigued by the prospect of romance between his daughter and the troupe's most promising young actor. Thad was not only talented, intelligent, and well mannered, but over the past year, he had grown into an exceedingly handsome and mature nineteen year old. What's more, he was the nephew of a renowned journalist, Mark Manning, which carried considerable cachet with Glenn, who was a publicity hound to the core.

"Of *course* they were acting," I told Glenn, finding a measure of amusement in bursting his bubble. "Thad was playing Mrs. Danvers.

So unless he's been fooling us and his true but hidden identity is that of a cross-dressing lesbian, I don't—"

"Sorry I asked," said Glenn.

I turned to the class. "Who's next?"

Cyndy Pryor wagged her hand. "We are, Miss Gray." Nabbing Scott by the arm, she dragged him to center stage and rearranged the folding chairs, setting up their scene.

Poor Scott. I cringed as he began the improvisation, assuming the role of Rebecca on her wedding night. The young bride's painful falsetto brought my hand to my throat as she begged Cyndy, portraying an aloof Mrs. Danvers, for advice on her conjugal appointment with Maxim de Winter, who was said to be awaiting her visit in the next room like a pent-up stallion.

"You need do it only once," Mrs. Danvers assured her young charge. "It's a filthy business, and you won't enjoy it, but it's the price one pays to become mistress of Manderley."

"But, Danny, I don't know *how*."

"*He* does—you can be sure of that. Try to clear your mind and draw a blank. If you think about what you're doing, you're apt to laugh, which will only slow him down and prolong the dirty ordeal."

"Ughhh." Rebecca shuddered.

Glenn's hand tapped my shoulder. "Claire," he whispered, "might I have a word with you? I'm due at a meeting, but there's something I wanted to ask you."

I hesitated; after all, my class was in session. But Scott's high-pitched wailing was reaching an annoying crescendo, so I decided to defer to the wishes of my employer. Telling Kiki, "Keep it moving," I rose from my seat and followed Glenn out to the aisle and up to the lobby doors.

Stepping from the semidark auditorium into the glare from the lobby's two-story wall of windows, I paused as my eyes adjusted to the assault of light.

Glenn said, "Claire, dear, I'm terribly sorry to interrupt your work, but something came up this morning, and I could use your help."

His deferential tone and serious features made me wonder aloud, "That phone call—what's wrong?"

"No, no," he assured me, strolling me to an upholstered bench near the windows, "the phone call was nothing, but the reason I came over here this morning . . . well, I'd like to ask you a favor."

We sat. "Yes . . . ?" My uncertain inflection conveyed only that I was inquiring about the nature of the favor, not that I was agreeing to oblige.

"I'm hoping you might drive up to the house tonight. I'm having a few people in for cocktails, and no party would be complete without you."

For me to attend a cocktail party seemed an odd request for a "favor." I'd enjoyed many lovely events at Glenn's spectacular mountainside home. If he wanted me to attend another, why not just invite me rather than tell me he could use my help? What was I missing? And why hadn't he mentioned this earlier?

Sensing both my hesitation and my confusion, he explained, "I know this is short notice, especially for a Friday night, but the purpose of this gathering is not entirely social. In fact, my reason for asking a few friends to join me is to defuse a situation that I fear could be potentially awkward—if not downright hostile."

Eyeing him askance, I admitted, "I'm intrigued, Glenn, if not entirely inclined to accept an invitation laced with caveats."

He smiled, reached for my hand, and held it in his lap. "Sorry. Perhaps I overstated the situation, but there's just no telling what may develop at a party crashed by Felicia."

The name was familiar. My brows pinched in thought. "Who?"

He actually gulped before clarifying, "My ex."

Aha. "Paige's mother is visiting the desert?"

He shook his head, dropping my hand. "Paige's mother, Madison, was my first wife. She still lives up in San Jose."

I thought aloud, "In the so-called Silicon Valley, where you first developed your software business."

"Correct. Madison keeps her distance. She's still bitter that I left her, so I'm grateful that she hasn't poisoned Paige's view of me. Paige is content to blame everything on Felicia, my second wife."

In the interest of precision, I elucidated, "Your second ex."

"Yes. She lives in LA and has another home in Santa Barbara." The man who had voiced his intention to win my heart apparently saw nothing damning in his failed record as a husband. "Tonight," he continued, "Felicia will be paying a visit."

"Oh," I asked vacantly, "is she on vacation?"

"No"—he stood—"she's on a mission. She's on the warpath. God knows what else she's on."

I rose as well. "What's this all about, Glenn? What's the problem?"

"That second home in Santa Barbara—that's the problem. There are some legal issues regarding the house, some covenants she disputes. It's a *significant* house, Claire, the first in California designed by I. T." He was referring to I. T. Dirkman, the renowned architect who had also designed Glenn's home in the desert, my theater, and in fact, the entire DAC campus.

Pacing a few steps in the yawning, empty lobby, Glenn explained, "Felicia has been hounding me about the house for several months now. Yesterday, she phoned to say that she was driving over from LA and that we had to meet and hash things out tonight. I fibbed"—Glenn may have been a business genius, but he was no wordsmith—"telling her that I already had plans tonight, hosting a party at my home. She called my bluff by inviting herself and telling me to expect her and her 'escort' at seven. Cripes. What's she up to?" Glenn ran a hand through his hair.

"So now you're scrambling to patch together a cocktail party so Felicia can crash it."

"Exactly," he said, tossing his palms. "Can I count you in? Felicia is bound to be testy at best, so I'm hoping to soften the encounter with a party atmosphere. Others are coming as well—the more the merrier."

Though my instincts were mixed, I answered, "Sure, Glenn, I'll be there. What time?"

"No later than six-thirty."

"Shall I bring someone?"

"Well, actually"—he stepped close and placed his hands on my shoulders—"I was hoping you and I might be 'together' tonight."

Shifting my weight, I backed off a fraction of an inch. "I don't know, Glenn." I shook my head. "If Felicia is as nasty as you say, I'd rather not put myself in the line of fire as your 'date.'"

"Very well." He laughed softly. "Bring someone."

Thinking a moment, I suggested, "Kiki?"

Glenn repeated, "The more the merrier."

2

Kiki and I had known each other most of our lives, having both attended Evans College, a small but respected school nestled in an idyllic setting back in Massachusetts, in the foothills of the Berkshires. Thirty-odd years ago, on the same day, we both graduated with theater degrees that would eventually lead us along different paths, mine to New York as a director, hers back to Evans as a costume designer and, ultimately, head of our alma mater's theater department. Like me, she was wed to her work.

Decades later, when Glenn Yeats was completing his plans for Desert Arts College, his determination to snare me for his faculty led him first to Evanstown, where he lured Kiki to commit to his ambitious project. Kiki's friendship then became the bait he would use to lure me as well—that and a visit from I. T. Dirkman, who unfurled his breathtaking plans for "my" theater building and sought my input on an array of issues, most of them technical, but others purely aesthetic. With both Kiki and I. T. Dirkman, Glenn had packed a one-two punch I was powerless to resist.

"Christ, it's hot." Kiki's eyes were fixed on the readout of the ceiling-mounted thermometer in my silver Beetle as we puttered up the steep roadway to Nirvana. It was after six that evening, but the temperature still topped a hundred ten.

"You're truly a master of understatement," I noted, glancing over from the driver's seat. The mountains surrounding us baked in the desert heat, their craggy shards of granite glowing a hellish shade of orange against a deceptively cold blue sky. I asked my old friend,

"Do you ever miss the greener, softer setting we knew back in Evanstown?"

"Not a bit," she said without hesitation. "I love it here. It's like a new life, every day a new adventure, even in the summer."

"Yeah, but thank God for air-conditioning."

She sputtered with laughter. "You got *that* right."

We were perfectly snug and cool inside my car that late afternoon. As the summer months had intensified, I had even come to enjoy midday strolls from the car to whatever chilled building was my next destination. The intense heat, coupled with the low humidity, had a penetrating quality that felt therapeutic and comforting, rather than hostile or dangerous. Of course, those were short strolls.

"And there's a lot to be said for the off-season," Kiki was saying. "No crowds. The slower pace. No need to phone ahead for restaurant reservations . . ."

"At the ones that are still open," I added. Many restaurants in Rancho Mirage and in neighboring Palm Springs, particularly those favored by tourists, simply shut down for the summer.

So did many of the more lavish homes, left in walled and guarded developments while their residents fled to cooler climes. Driving through the turns that led up the mountainside, past the Regal Palms Hotel, and onward to Nirvana Estates, I would have been hard-pressed to conclude that these luxurious surroundings had been abandoned for the season. Fountains and man-made waterfalls still gurgled and glistened; palms and ornamental grasses were perfectly pruned. These imaginary oases offered welcoming vignettes as we entered Nirvana itself and cruised past the tasteful homes with walls of glass peering out over expansive vistas of the surrounding mountain ranges and the valley below.

The most spectacular of these houses was at the top of the roadway, beyond a final turn. The estate designed by I. T. Dirkman and built by D. Glenn Yeats was without question the largest and most daring architectural statement to grace this rarefied village of extravagance. Its angled walls of stone cast sharp-edged shadows across the road. Driving through these slim patches of darkness, I blinked as each gave way again to dazzling sunlight.

Rounding the bend of a steep driveway, I turned into Glenn's parking court, a large paved area, gracefully landscaped, behind the house. A slit of the valley view could be seen between the building and a sheer wall of mountain that abutted the far end of the courtyard. As there was no parking valet that evening, I assumed this would be one of Glenn's smaller gatherings. I pulled my car to a shaded spot well away from the main door (the Beetle's cartoonish design seemed a bit too whimsical for the severe architecture) and cut the engine.

Opening the door, I was taken momentarily breathless by the rush of heat that seemed to suck every molecule of cool air from the car. Kiki had the same reaction. Getting out of the car and thumping her door closed, she admitted, "I guess you never do completely adjust to this." Jerking her head toward the house, she added, "Let's get inside."

As we crossed the courtyard, all was quiet, save for the perpetual jangle of Kiki's bracelets and the peck of her spiked heels on the granite pavers. Her passion for costuming was reflected not only in the direction of her career, but also in her habit of changing clothes several times a day. She had chosen basic black for this evening's event, though the sun would not set for another two or three hours. Her flowing gauze tunic conjured the bizarre image of a nun in naughty lace. As for me, I wore dressy cream-colored slacks and a silk blouse of deepest crimson; my affection for red could not be dampened, even by the desert's torrid days of summer.

The dramatic entry to Glenn's home was designed to blur the distinction between the outdoors and the interior space. On many prior visits, I had marveled at the artful, seamless transition from the courtyard to the inside lobby without the expected barrier of a door. But not this time. It was simply too hot for such fanciful contrivances, and I now saw that discreet tracks underfoot and above allowed a glass wall and door to slide into position. While the door had hinges, it had no handle, and as we approached, I wondered how to open it without smearing the glass with my palm. My question was answered when we drew nearer and a sensor swung the door open for us.

We no sooner stepped inside when Tide Arden, Glenn's executive secretary, bolted toward us with a broad smile. Her thighs flexed beneath a tight leather miniskirt as she strode forward on long, muscular legs. A black woman in her late twenties, she always struck me as fiercely amazonian—until she spoke.

"Ms. Gray . . . welcome . . . ," she cooed, her velvety voice sweet as saccharin, but not artificial. She carried an acid-green acrylic clipboard that presumably held the guest list. "And Ms. Jasper-Plunkett," she added, clicking a pen and checking both our names off the list.

I asked, "Expecting a crowd tonight?"

She clicked the pen again as a faint frown crossed the mannish features of her face. "Not many, no. Mr. Yeats will be happy you're here. He's in the living room. This way, please?" Spinning on her heel, she led us through the cavernous front hall. From the heights hung an enormous chandelier of modern design; its irregular crystal prisms dangled overhead like icy daggers.

"Claire, doll!" called a familiar voice as we passed the side hall where a small catering crew was stocking the service bar. Grant Knoll, a nice-looking man wearing an elegant nubby-silk sport coat the color of sand, rushed out to greet me with a kiss on the cheek.

"Awww, good evening, love." I returned his kiss. "I might have guessed you'd be here." A high-end real-estate broker who ran the sales office at Nirvana, Grant often oversaw the staffing of events at residents' homes. At Glenn Yeats's prompting, Grant had also helped me get settled when I'd moved from New York. In the process, he had become my best friend.

Almost as an afterthought, he added, "Hi, Keeks," pecking her as well.

"Howdy, neighbor." She mimicked a cowboy accent absurdly unnatural to her. Grant had sold her a condominium in nearby Palm Desert, in the same six-unit complex where he himself lived. I too had purchased a unit there, but had recently moved to larger quarters, a house in Rancho Mirage also brokered by Grant. Though Kiki and Grant thought of each other as friends as well as neighbors, I knew that Kiki harbored a grain of resentment that Grant and I had grown so close. "Claire, darling," she often reminded me, "you're my *oldest* friend," relishing the double entendre.

I asked Grant, "Everything set for next Saturday?"

With an exaggerated sigh, he seemed to wilt before us. "Don't ask.

I hate to come across like some drama queen, but this simple little commitment ceremony is turning into a full-blown wedding."

"Ideally, wouldn't it be exactly that?"

With a snort of laughter, his mood instantly lifted. "If the legal thicket over same-sex marriage ever gets resolved—*favorably*—you can bet Kane and I will be the first in line to make it official. Meanwhile, it's important for us to make our commitment as formal and as public as the law allows. So next Saturday, we'll do the I-do's."

At forty-nine, Grant had fallen in love with a much younger man, Kane Richter, shortly after my arrival in the desert. Having now lived together for most of the past year, they were ready for some knot-tying. The ceremony would be held at the luxurious Regal Palms Hotel, halfway down the hill from Nirvana.

With a snap of his fingers, Grant said, "Kane and I need to nail down some details at the hotel tomorrow morning. Why don't you come with us, Claire? We can do lunch afterward."

I considered his suggestion for a moment, then answered, "Sure, it's Saturday, and I have nothing planned." My summer schedule was a light one—the workshop met only on Monday, Wednesday, and Friday mornings.

In a well-enunciated whisper, Tide reminded us, "Mr. Yeats is waiting."

Flashing me a grin, Grant skittered back to the bar like a chastised puppy. From Kiki's expression, I could tell she was on the verge of making a crack that Tide would not find humorous, so I shushed her with a subtle shake of my head while saying brightly, "Let's go greet our host."

Though both Kiki and I had visited often enough to find our way, Tide was determined to escort and announce us, so we followed as she strutted the long hallway that opened into the main space of the house. Every time I entered Glenn's "living room," I was struck anew by its theatrical design, by its sumptuous use of materials, by its total integration of furnishings and art, and most impressively, by its sheer scale. A composition of spaces—solids and voids—defined areas meant for conversation, for reading, for gathering around the hearth of a gargantuan fireplace, and for simply appreciating the heart-stopping view that began with a wall of glass and stretched past the surrounding mountains to infinity. From the spot where I now stood, countless photos had been snapped, then published in oversize glossy magazines, but none had even remotely captured the actual experience of entering this space, which was in itself, in every sense, art.

Tide cleared her throat. "Mr. Yeats? Ms. Gray and Ms. Jasper-Plunkett have arrived." Then she disappeared into thin air, leaving but the slightest wisp of smoke. Or so it seemed, given the magical quality of our setting.

"Ah, excellent!" said Glenn, turning from the dark fireplace, where he stood in conversation with another man, whom I recognized as the creative genius who had erected these walls, I. T. Dirkman himself. Glenn stepped toward us, his sockless loafers clacking on the stone floor. "Claire, Kiki, do come in and join our little gathering. Can I get you a drink?"

I gave him a hug, then a chaste kiss on the lips, before answering, "A martini seems to be in order."

Kiki greeted him as well, saying, "Let's keep it simple. Ditto that martini. Breathlessly dry—up, naturally."

"Naturally," agreed Glenn with a playful grin.

I had expected one of the tuxedoed waiters to be summoned, who would then fetch our cocktails from the service bar, but Glenn announced, "I'm mixing tonight—seems more friendly—whatever it takes to keep Felicia in good humor." And he moved to a small drinks table that had been set up as a bar on the far side of the room. Over his shoulder, he said, "You ladies already know I. T., of course."

"Of course," we chorused, meeting the architect near the center of the room.

He extended his hand. "Good evening, Claire. Always a pleasure. And good to see you again, Kiki." A man of about sixty, he wore his silvering hair cropped short in a severe style that resembled a modified Caesar cut. Despite the summer heat and the casual mode of dress generally deemed appropriate for the desert, he wore a dark business suit, black oxfords, and a black knit shirt, buttoned to the throat. Completing this picture was his trademark eyeware, heavy black-framed glasses with round lenses. It was a look that conveyed an inescapable message: he was a man who didn't follow fashion, but forged his own style.

"So nice to see *you* again," I said uncertainly, groping for a name. I couldn't call him Mr. Dirkman, as we were too well acquainted. Nor was I inclined to call him I. T., which struck me as guy-talk. Unfortunately, I had never heard what his initials stood for, and although I kept hoping he would suggest, Do call me Ignatz (or Ingmar or Ira), he never did.

"My *God,* I. T.," gushed Kiki (who felt no compunction about guy-talk), "after a year working on the DAC campus, I have nothing but kudos for the theater, the classrooms and offices, the whole concept. And this *house*"—she twirled an arm—"well, I can appreciate why Glenn has such discerning taste in architects."

"*Architect,*" said Glenn, stressing the singular. Pouring martinis from the shaker into two sizable birdbaths of Mexican cobalt glass, he added, "There may be any number of 'name' architects, but the only one who truly matters, at least in my book, is I. T. Dirkman." He punctuated his statement with a sharp nod.

"The esteem is mutual," said Dirkman, spreading the flaps of his jacket and thrusting his hands into his pants pockets. "Without your early support, the initials *I. T.* would merely stand for—" He stopped himself short. "Well, let's just say they wouldn't mean at all what they mean today." I wasn't sure what he meant, and I doubted if even he understood what he was saying, but I was fairly certain he'd gotten a head start on his cocktails. Glancing toward the mantel, I spotted an empty glass, which confirmed my hunch.

Nabbing Dirkman's sleeve, Kiki burbled, "What those initials mean today is 'integrity' and . . . and . . . 'talent,'" and she hadn't even sipped her first drink yet. Eyeing her next to the architect, both of them dressed in dark, outlandish clothing, I was struck by the unlikely notion that they might be mistaken for a couple—at least visually.

He took off his glasses to study Kiki's face for a moment. "I had no idea your waters ran so deep."

"Oh, *pish,* darling!"

"Teeny time," announced Glenn, scooting toward us with the two drinks, trying not to spill them, but without success.

Kiki and I accepted the martinis, then skoaled. The clink of our glasses ricocheted about the room, magnified by the lofty space and stone surfaces.

"I. T.?" asked Glenn. "Another?"

"Most kind of you," the architect answered with a courtly nod.

Glenn returned to the drinks table and twisted the cap off a fresh bottle of Scotch. Though not a whiskey drinker, I recognized the bottle's blue label—and its two-hundred-dollar price tag. The liquor glugged from the mouth of the bottle as Glenn poured a hefty serving into a crystal glass containing a single ice cube.

"Hey, Pops, can I have some of that?"

I turned to see Paige Yeats enter the room from the direction of the kitchen. Trailing her was Thad Quatrain, who carried a small napkin bearing a shrimp as big as a lamb chop.

"Hi, baby." The billionaire turned from the bar, greeting his daughter with a warm smile. He reminded her, "It's a year till you're twenty-one."

"Nine months," she countered. "Besides, I'm not driving." She was living with her father while attending my workshop that summer.

"Well," he allowed, "you were good enough to stick around tonight—I know this isn't your idea of a good time."

"Felicia? I can think of better ways to start the weekend."

"All right, you can have a little something if you want, but *mix* it, and go easy."

"Sure, Pops." Paige beelined toward the bar.

Glenn stepped to Dirkman with the Scotch, telling Thad, "Thanks for keeping Paige company tonight. Hope you won't find this too dreary."

Paige said, "I wasn't about to face that woman alone."

"I don't mind," said Thad. "Thanks for inviting me." He took a bite out of the shrimp.

Glenn said, "You're welcome to a drink as well." Then, remembering that Thad was a year younger than his daughter, he added, "That is, if your uncle wouldn't mind."

"Mark wouldn't mind. He drinks all the time." When the rest of us laughed, Thad practically blushed, explaining, "I didn't mean it *that* way."

Through a lingering chuckle, Glenn told him, "Help yourself."

"Thank you, sir." And Thad joined Paige at the bar, concocting something that looked like mostly fruit juice.

A waiter appeared, circulating with a tray mounded with cracked ice and piles of the colossal shrimp. I accepted one and chomped off the fat end—*perfect* with my dry martini. Dirkman also took one, then held it up, feeding it to Kiki, who nipped and bobbed at the saucy crustacean like a trained seal.

Not much of a party person, Glenn poured himself half a glass of white wine and joined the rest of us in conversation. We spoke of the weather, the shrimp, the workshop. But eventually our discussion came back to I. T. Dirkman, his architecture, and the connection to Glenn's second ex-wife, Felicia.

I recalled, "This afternoon, Glenn mentioned a house of Felicia's—in Santa Barbara, I believe?"

"Yes," said Dirkman, nodding, cupping his glass of Scotch with both hands, "the Santa Barbara house was my first in California—thanks entirely to Glenn's patronage and foresight."

Glenn said, "I loved working on that house with you."

"Yes, it was a labor of love."

"Small, but it's truly a jewel box. It's . . . well, it's *art*."

"It's perfect," Dirkman concluded.

"And"—Glenn winked—"it's protected."

Tide Arden appeared. "Sorry to interrupt, Mr. Yeats. But *Mrs.* Yeats just drove up with her guest. Shall I greet them, or do you—"

"Thanks, Tide, but I'd better take care of this myself." Glenn started toward the front hall.

With mock disappointment, Paige told him, "No fair, Pops! Why not let *me* extend the royal welcome?"

"Just try to be civil," he said under his breath. Pausing outside the room, he told his secretary, "Get Grant, would you? I told Felicia there was a 'party' here tonight. It'll help set the scene if you and Grant could mingle with the other guests." And he moved off toward the front door.

Kiki had by now finished her second martini, and it was doubtless the liquor that emboldened her to ask Paige, "Do I detect a note of hostility toward your stepmother?" Well, duh.

" 'Stepmother'?" asked Paige, setting down her drink and crossing her arms. "I prefer to think of her as the bitch who wrecked my mother's life."

"Oh," Kiki mumbled through a grimace. "Sorry."

Paige flopped a palm to her chest. "Gosh, Kiki. No—*I'm* sorry— I shouldn't have snapped at you like that. I was only twelve when Pops left Mom for Felicia. It hurt, but I knew it wasn't his fault. I mean, Felicia *stole* him from my mother."

Though I was tempted to remind Paige of the number required to tango, the moment seemed wrong for such honesty.

Thad tried to lighten the tense mood by offering, "Can I get anyone another drink?"

"*Thank* you, dear," said Kiki, handing him her empty glass.

"My pleasure, Professor." Though DAC's students were welcome to address faculty by their first names, Thad seemed more comfortable maintaining a more traditional, respectful distance—a throwback of manners I found both refreshing and endearing.

". . . so it turned out to be a fortunate coincidence that the party is the same night as your visit." Glenn's voice approached from the front hall, along with his footfalls and those of his guests.

"A fortunate coincidence? Serendipity? Glenn, you truly *are* full of crap." And with those words, Felicia Yeats strolled into our midst.

A striking woman of confident bearing and cool manner, she would fit anyone's definition of "beautiful." I had read that she was a year or two younger than Glenn, in her late forties, but thanks to her pampered lifestyle, exquisite taste, processed hair—and surely a few nips and tucks—she looked nearer thirty. It was easy to see how Glenn may have considered his second spouse a stereotypical "trophy wife," and it was equally apparent that Felicia had proudly played that role. Tonight, that role was altered some, as her sophisticated black attire suggested she was not just Glenn's ex, but his widow.

Accompanying Felicia was a handsome man of about forty, no stranger to the gym, with wavy blond hair going gray and a tan that seemed a shade too dark to be healthy. Wryly, I wondered if he might be a gigolo. Like Felicia, he wore a dark, dressy outfit—a statement of urban chic that seemed wrong for the desert, especially in July. They looked as if they had compared notes on what to wear that evening. They looked like a couple.

Studying their clothes, I noticed the sharp contrast to Glenn's attire. In addition to his usual crocodile pumps and bare ankles, his outfit consisted of white pants and a billowy, blousy shirt that looked like something a pirate might wear, except that no pirate would be caught dead in red silk. Not only did these sartorial choices reinforce my opinion that Glenn was no clotheshorse, but I realized with a start that tonight's outfit made him look like . . . well, like *me*.

I had specifically not wanted to appear to be "with" Glenn that evening, hence I'd recruited Kiki as my "date." But Kiki and Dirkman now seemed to be joined at the hip. Felicia and her manfriend were cut from the same cloth. By virtue of their age, Paige and Thad were clearly together. And just now, gay Grant walked in with Tide the miniskirted amazon on his arm; though an odd couple (Tide was a good eight or nine inches taller than Grant), they made a couple nonetheless. Which left Glenn and me in our red silk blouses.

I cringed as Glenn said, "Felicia, let me introduce you to everyone. First and foremost, the toast of Broadway and the crown jewel in our fledgling faculty, the illustrious Claire Gray." His loafers slapped the floor as he pattered toward me with the dragon lady in tow. Smiling too broadly, he flung an arm around my shoulder. We must have looked like a pair of refugees from some cheesy operetta.

She extended her hand regally, sizing me up with a wary eye. "Felicia Yeats."

I could play this game. "Claire Gray," I told her. "My pleasure."

"I've heard so much about you, Claire." She left her statement hanging, as if daring me to ask exactly what she'd heard.

But I didn't bite. "Likewise," I told her.

"Glenn," she said, turning to him (I'd ceased to exist), "I'd like you to meet Peverell Lamonte." Her manfriend stepped forward. "Peverell is director of the Southern California Conservancy for Homes of Historic Interest."

"Of course!" said I. T. Dirkman, joining us. He looked a bit wobbly as he continued, "So nice to meet you at last, Peverell. The SCC does marvelous work. Marvelous!" They shook hands.

"Thank you, I. T., the honor is entirely mine. The conservancy exists for the express purpose of preserving the unique architectural heritage of our state. Among contemporary contributors to that heritage, your role has been unique."

"I am but one of many," Dirkman protested, but the false modesty of his stuffy tone was loud and clear. "Especially here in the desert. Palm Springs was a hotbed of the modernist movement."

"And still is," noted Peverell.

"Precisely."

"But even here in Rancho Mirage, the conservancy has its challenges. For instance, as recently as 2002, a pristine Richard Neutra house dating from 1962—one of only three in the Palm Springs area—was unexpectedly demolished by new owners within a month of paying over two million dollars for it. The permit required only an asbestos review and was issued over the counter."

Glenn piped in, "It was lamentable, a travesty."

"Truly tragic," echoed Dirkman.

"But," said Peverell, raising a finger and sounding a brighter note, "working with the planning committees of the various desert cities, we're attempting to raise the collective consciousness of the need to protect significant architecture—both residences and public buildings—with designated landmark status and historic-preservation ordinances."

With a thoughtful nod, Glenn added, "I'm a laissez-faire sort of guy, but when it comes to architecture, individuals can't always be trusted to act in the public interest. The restrictions that accompany landmark status are a necessary evil."

I nearly choked on the last sip of my martini.

"It's common sense," Dirkman agreed offhandedly.

Noting my empty glass, Glenn asked, "Another?"

"Not yet, thanks. I'm driving."

As a waiter began moving among us, offering shrimp, Glenn said to Peverell, "How clumsy of me—can I get you a drink?"

"Some Scotch would be great."

From the side of his mouth, Dirkman told him, "It's fabulous." He was beginning to slur his words.

As Glenn moved to the drinks table, Paige strolled forward with Thad, saying, "Nice to see you again, Felicia." Her flat, ambiguous tone was unconvincing.

Felicia eyed the young woman curiously for a moment, then it clicked. "Paige?" she asked. "Your father didn't mention you'd be here. It's been years."

"Yes, years." Was a blowup brewing?

"Are you, uh . . . living here now?"

"No, I'm still in LA, but here for the summer taking a class. This is Thad Quatrain. We're in Claire's workshop together."

Felicia looked adrift, having clearly forgotten who I was.

Thad gave her a smile. "Pleased to meet you, Mrs. Yeats."

Groping for something to say, she asked Paige, "Living in LA, do you ever run into Dustin?"

Now it was I who was confused.

Paige answered, "I wouldn't recognize him. Haven't seen him since the wedding." Then she turned to explain to Thad, "Dustin Cory is Felicia's son by a previous marriage."

Thad gave an uncertain nod, trying to keep track of the mingled bloodlines.

Glenn returned with Peverell's Scotch, telling Felicia, "I know you rarely imbibe, but can I get you something?"

With a cool gaze, she responded, "I thought you'd never ask."

"Juice? Perhaps a bit of wine?"

She eyed my big dark-blue glass, looking interested.

I told her, "It was a martini." With a smile I added, "Glenn's bartending skills are marvelous—who'd have thought?"

"Who'd have thought?" she repeated through a crooked grin.

"Well," Glenn asked her, "martini?"

"Yes, thank you. Worth a try. In the same pretty glass, please."

Glenn crossed to the drinks table, opened the shaker, and added some ice. Grabbing the gin and pouring, he noted, "Almost empty. Should I get a fresh bottle?"

"I thought you'd never ask," said Felicia as Glenn left the room.

During his absence, we made sure that everyone was introduced—Grant, Tide, and Kiki had not yet met Felicia and Peverell.

Kiki, well beyond tipsy by now, entertained us with a theater story (dealing with a sensational "wardrobe malfunction") as Glenn returned from the service bar with a full bottle of gin. He had already removed the metal cap, bouncing it in his free hand. Arriving at the drinks table, he emptied the shaker and started over, pouring a liberal amount of gin from its blue bottle. Capping the shaker, he shook it hard, then strained the icy liquid into one of the cobalt birdbaths. He joined us again in the middle of the room as Kiki was concluding, ". . . and the doctor said she had frostbite!"

Amid the general laughter, Grant asked, "Did they have to amputate?"

More laughter.

"Here you are, my dear," said Glenn, handing Felicia her cocktail.

Hoisting the glass, she said without enthusiasm, "Cheers, everyone." Then she sipped. Wrinkling her nose, she said, "It tastes like perfume."

I allowed, "Gin *is* an acquired taste."

When she took a second sip, her brows arched—she liked it. Then she slurped a mouthful, grabbing a plump, pink shrimp from a passing waiter.

Glenn suggested, "If everyone is taken care of, why don't we all sit down?"

"I thought you'd never ask," said Felicia through an airy laugh. Her catchphrase was wearing thin.

There were ten of us in the room, plus the catering staff who breezed through now and then, but we didn't even begin to fill the vast space, which had taken on a golden cast as the sun slid nearer the mountains. The room provided seating for at least twice our number.

"Perhaps over here," said Glenn, leading us to a grouping of furniture near the glass wall, where we could all enjoy the view.

A massive cocktail table of black granite, easily eight feet square, was surrounded on three sides by two sofas and a long leather bench; the fourth side was open, facing outdoors. As we arranged ourselves around the table, settling in with our drinks, I studied the dynamics of the jockeying—who would pair with whom? Not surprisingly, Kiki and I. T. Dirkman, who by now could barely stand, were first to sit together. Felicia took the center position on the bench, patting the cushion for Peverell to sit next to her. Paige stuck close to Thad, sitting in the position farthest from Felicia. Grant lounged elegantly on the sofa opposite them; his "partner," Tide Arden, declined to sit, standing behind him, as if preparing to take notes.

Which left Glenn and me. He sat at the corner of the sofa nearest Felicia's bench, saying, "Join me, Claire?" Reluctantly, I settled next to him. A spark snapped as the sleeve of my red silk blouse brushed his.

An awkward silence fell over us. Felicia had come to discuss something deemed touchy, and the rest of us knew we had been invited only as a distraction—we were pretend guests at a pretend party. Someone commented on the view. Someone else mentioned the heat.

Grant said to Felicia, "I understand you live in Santa Barbara. With those lovely sea breezes, you must find our little desert getaway downright oppressive, at least in July."

"Actually," she told him, sitting stiff-spined on the bench, "I spend most of my time in LA. I find the house in Santa Barbara rather uncomfortable, though the setting is sublime, and—"

"Another martini?" said Glenn, eager to switch topics. Peeping into her empty glass, he added, "It seems you enjoyed it."

"Whatever." She sighed.

Tide offered, "I'll take care of it."

"Nonsense," Glenn told his secretary, standing and taking the glass. "I'm more than happy to see to the needs of my guests." The e-titan's servile attitude was way over the top. We knew him better than that.

Felicia watched as he crossed to the bar with her glass and mixed a fresh drink. She told us, "If Glenn had behaved so nicely while we were married, we might still be together. Perhaps I wouldn't have been forced to dump him."

Paige came to life. "Really, Felicia? The way I heard it, Pops dumped *you*."

"Is that what he told you? There are two sides to every story, I suppose. We really *should* get to know each other better, Paige. I could fill you in on plenty. Perhaps tomorrow morning?"

"That might be interesting," said Paige, sounding not the least interested.

"It seems your father has yet to deal with his control issues. Simply put, he insists on having his way." Sagging some, she braced herself on Peverell's knee. For someone who rarely drank, she had emptied that first martini far too quickly.

From the bar, Glenn reminded her, "That's how I built an empire, Felicia."

"Bravo, Glenn. How clever of you. I admit, your strong-willed nature may be an admirable trait in an entrepreneur, but"—Felicia's gaze drifted to me—"it's ultimately what drove us apart. Life with Glenn Yeats would be excruciating for any woman with even a trace of independence."

For a moment, I was caught in a state of suspended animation. The earth stopped spinning; my heart skipped a beat. Had Felicia learned that Glenn had now set his sights, romantically, on me? Had she sensed my reluctance, based on the very control issues she had just raised? Or had she simply made a presumed connection between Glenn and me, based on nothing more substantive than our gaudy silk pirate shirts?

With a soft laugh, Glenn returned with Felicia's second drink, telling everyone, "I've always admired this lady's sense of theatrics." He handed her the glass, sat next to me again, and leaned to say into my ear, "But when it comes to theater, no lady alive could capture my affections as you have."

I tried to lick any last drops of gin from my glass, but it was dry. I grew all the more thirsty watching Felicia sip the ice chips from the surface of her frosty glass.

After she swallowed, she said, "Okay, Glenn, we've been dancing around a subject that needs to be addressed. I hate to ruin your little party, but we need to talk. May I have a word with you privately?"

"We're all friends here," Glenn said blithely. "Think of us as family. What is it you need to discuss?"

If he thought the group of listeners would cow Felicia with a sense of restraint, he was wrong. "What *we* need to discuss," she said, almost spitting the words, "is the future of that fucking little house in Santa

Barbara." She slammed her drink on the table, sloshing much of it on the black granite.

Dirkman gasped.

Peverell wrapped an arm around Felicia's shoulder, explaining, "Not to disparage the house itself. It's a work of art, but—"

"But it's unlivable!" blurted Felicia. "It's small. It's precious. It's *glass,* for Christ's sake. You can't even piss without—"

"What Felicia is trying to say," Peverell continued, "is that the house may be a bit impractical for day-to-day living."

"So?" said Glenn. "She also has the house in Los Angeles, which is immense. The Dirkman house is merely a getaway, a retreat." He repeated, "It's *art.*"

Felicia reminded him, "And it's sitting on some of the most valuable land in the country. Do you have *any* idea what Santa Barbara real estate is worth?" She took the martini from the table and drank another swallow or two.

Grant Knoll acknowledged, "She's right, you know. That's some of the priciest property anywhere."

With a frustrated sigh, almost a growl, Glenn asked, "So what's your beef, Felicia? Exactly what do you want?"

She shot off, "I want to *sell* it, *remodel* it, or tear it *down* and start over."

Dirkman gasped.

"That's ridiculous," said Glenn. "Out of the question."

"But it's *mine,*" she insisted.

"By the terms of our divorce," Glenn corrected her, "you now have possession and use of the house, but you are prohibited from selling it or substantially changing it. To ensure its architectural integrity, we've petitioned the local planning commission to confer landmark status on the Dirkman house, which would protect it with the force of law."

Grant, who often assisted Glenn with real-estate matters, confirmed, "The petition is moving through committee, a mere formality, I'm sure."

Peverell heaved an airy sigh. "I'm so conflicted." Was he gay? The body, the clothes, the hair. Not that it mattered, but I needed to revisit my original theory that he was Felicia's plaything. He continued,

"Felicia and I have been corresponding with regard to the house for some time. Obviously, the conservancy has an interest in the property's preservation, and I'm grateful to learn of the petition for landmark status. But if Felicia were permitted to *sell* the property, the SCC could possibly—"

Glenn demanded, "What's the bottom line, Felicia? What's behind all this? You've already got the much bigger house in LA. You have no financial need whatever. Why these sudden issues with the Dirkman house?"

She paused before answering, finishing her cocktail. "The house is mine, and that's that. The restrictions are unreasonable, and I'll be damned if you think I'll live the rest of my life bowing to the wishes of some prissy control freak."

"Prissy?" asked Glenn. Apparently he had no problem being known as a control freak.

"Don't forget"—she gave him an icy stare—"selling or remodeling aren't the *only* options. As you've already learned, Glenn, I can be surprisingly vindictive."

Dirkman piped in, "You'd *never* get a permit to raze that house."

Felicia stood, looking very wobbly. She slurred, "Who said anything about permits?" Fishing a cigarette out of her tiny handbag, she asked anyone, "Got a match?"

Dirkman, Glenn, and Peverell stood in unison. "Felicia!"

"After all, the land is worth far more than the house itself. If the house were to . . . disappear, the land could be sold, unrestricted." She turned to Peverell. "I think it's time to go now." Then she reconsidered, turning to Glenn. "Or perhaps another martini—one for the road, as they say."

Glenn grabbed her glass. His voice was heavy with cynicism as he told her, "Madam's wish is my command." And he stepped to the drinks table.

Peverell told her, "I think I'd better get you back to the hotel."

"Well, then, maybe I'll just take it with me."

Glenn stopped pouring. "You'll have to forgive me, but I'm afraid I'm fresh out of 'go cups.' Would you care to take the bottle?"

She grinned. "I thought you'd never ask."

Disgusted, Glenn capped the blue gin bottle, wiped it with a towel, marched it over to Felicia, and thrust it into her hands. "Enjoy."

"I'm sure I will." She made a step toward the front hall, but almost collapsed, saved from falling by Peverell.

Glenn asked him, "Where are you staying? Not far, I hope."

"We're just down the road at the Regal Palms."

"Regal Palms." Felicia snorted. "La-di-da. It's a dump."

"I'll see you out," said Glenn. And he escorted them from the room.

As soon as they were out of earshot, the rest of us were on our feet, comparing notes in excited whispers—like kids whose teacher had just left the classroom.

"Poor Mr. Yeats," said his secretary. "He's been through so much."

Paige acknowledged, "He's been through hell with Felicia, that's for sure."

Thad pointed out, "She was drunk. It was just the booze talking."

With a wink, I told him, "Most charitable of you."

Indignant, Dirkman said, "The nerve of that woman—what audacious threats."

"Audacious?" said Kiki, barely able to stand. "I thought she was rather fun—in a grim sort of way."

"Yes," allowed Grant, "most amusing—for a pampered old shrew."

Kiki asked, "She's not *that* old, is she? She looked fabulous."

Grant countered, "She looked well preserved."

We all turned as Glenn stepped back from the hall. Rubbing his hands together, he seemed oddly pleased. "Well," he told us, "I'm glad *that's* over."

To my way of thinking, his battle with Felicia had barely begun.

He continued, "And I'm glad you were all here. Without you, it would have been far worse."

"Really?" I asked. How could it have been worse?

"Oh, yes," he assured me. "Felicia can be a real hellion. I don't know about the rest of you, but I could sure use a drink."

As he moved toward the bar, Kiki suddenly burst into manic, drunken laughter. "My God!" she said, rushing to Glenn, fingering the big goofy buttons of his shirt. "Where *did* you get this? It looks like Blackbeard's pajamas."

We froze.

D. Glenn Yeats was not accustomed to insubordination, and it seemed inconceivable that he would tolerate a critique of his wardrobe from a wacky costume designer whose tastes could be politely described as eccentric. I held my breath as he stared at Kiki for a moment, then looked down at his shirt.

Scratching behind an ear, he breathed a soft laugh.

"You know, Kiki," he said, "maybe I *could* use a little help."

"A *little?*" she blurted.

"Don't press your luck."

3

Saturday morning sometime after eight, while the heat was still bearable, I decided to lounge outdoors with the local paper and a tall glass of iced tea. Having not yet put myself together for the day, I schlepped outside in a pair of flip-flops, shorts, and an old, oversize T-shirt, once red but now barely pink from years of washing—how very ladylike. Choosing a chaise that was positioned squarely in the shade of a giant bearded fan palm, I arranged the paper and the tea on a little glass-topped side table, slipped off my thongs, and stretched out on the long circus-striped cushion. I then adjusted the back to a comfortable angle, relaxed for a moment, and gazed serenely over the surface of my pool.

My pool. The very idea still gave me a rush of excitement. More than anything else, this shimmering blue patch of water—an icon of paradise—represented the enormity of the transition my life had made during the past year. The three thousand miles from my stodgy little apartment in Manhattan felt more like a million. The desert setting with its agaves and mesquites, the jaw-dropping mountain views at every turn, the relaxed pace—all these exotica had served to remind me, since the day of my arrival, that I was now far, *far* off-Broadway. But it wasn't until I had moved into my recently acquired "vintage modern" home in Rancho Mirage (with its triangular living room, boomerang coffee table, and ubiquitous banana-leaf motif adorning curtains, upholstery, and wallpaper) that I had fulfilled the lifelong fantasy of owning my own swimming pool.

Reigning over this private, secluded oasis from the plump cushions of my wrought-iron recumbent throne, I felt like the lord of a peaceable kingdom. A hummingbird—a flash of iridescence—skipped over the surface of the water, then disappeared into a radiant red clump of bougainvillea that climbed a stucco wall at the edge of my terrace. Overhead, perched somewhere in the bark of the towering shady palm, a mockingbird regaled me with its ecstatic trills and goofy chatter.

Ho hum, I thought. Just another day in my own little Eden.

Reaching for the glass of iced tea, I drank a few swallows, savoring the perfect combination of sugar and lemon that suffused the tea itself. Refreshed, I then set aside my sunglasses, unrolled that morning's issue of the *Desert Sun,* and glanced through the front-page headlines—trouble in the Mideast (naturally), sex scandal involving an archbishop (hardly news anymore), impending teachers' strike somewhere (cry me a river). I tossed aside the front section.

The entertainment section was dominated by movies, so I pitched that as well.

The sports section—well, why soil my fingers?

The real-estate section was always an eye-opener, and it was fun to note the escalating prices, but now that I was so contentedly settled in my new digs, poolside, I had little interest in trading up. So the mound of rejected newsprint continued to swell.

There was little left but the "People" section, with its society pages, labeled "Desert Scene." The area had an inordinate number of wealthy residents, many of whom were retired, so philanthropy was among the valley's favorite pastimes, even in the dead of summer. And the most popular excuse for writing fat checks was participation in all manner of charity functions—luncheons and balls, mainly.

Lined up with drinks in their hands, ladies (some in hats) and gents (many in tuxes) stared up at me from the group photos that tiled the pages in seemingly endless succession. The events benefited causes ranging from literacy and the arts to battles against AIDS, ALS, MS—a veritable alphabet soup of maladies.

Most of the photos focused on pretty people in their pretty clothes, but a few featured speakers at podiums addressing the events' varied purposes. In one picture, the head of a prestigious nearby medical center gesticulated with one raised arm—a pose that bore an unfortunate resemblance to that of Lady Liberty—while saying, "ALS need not be thought of as a death sentence. Recent research into Lou Gehrig's disease offers hope on many fronts." In another photo, the director of a local arts group lamented, "With state funding at an all-time low, it falls to us to bear the noble burden of securing a firm footing for the arts in our society, not only for our own edification, but for the enrichment of generations to come." And on and on.

Peering at the faces and skimming the captions, I noted that I was still new to the community, recognizing no one. The names meant nothing, a blur of type.

"More tea, Miss Gray?" Oralia Alvarez, my housekeeper, was crossing the terrace from the kitchen with a fresh pitcher of iced tea—of her own making. I had often watched her prepare the tea, and I had attempted to mimic her technique, using the very same ingredients, but my brew was always cloudy and rancid, while hers was consistently perfect.

"With pleasure," I told her, setting the newspaper beside me on the cushion.

"It is a lovely day," she mused, filling my glass. Though Mexican-born, she had lived in the area for many years. Her English, though fluent, was a bit stilted and proper. I noticed that she never used contractions in her speech. Cocking her head, she added, "Is it not?"

"It's always lovely here," I agreed. "Even when it's hot."

"Hot?" She chuckled. "This is nothing." She wore long pants, a loose smock, and tennis shoes. Oralia did not normally work for me on Saturday; her midweek visits were occupied by routine cleaning. As I had recently moved into a new house, however, there were a number of special projects that still needed attention, so she had agreed to work an extra day over the weekend. Preparing to get started (first on the list was a total rearrangement of the kitchen cabinets), she asked, "May I bring you anything else?"

"Thanks, Oralia, I'm fine."

With a slight bob of her head, she took the pitcher and headed back toward the kitchen. She had no sooner stepped inside when the phone rang.

I was tempted to shout, Tell them I'm not home.

Oralia peeped from the doorway. With the wireless phone in one hand, she said, "It is Mr. Griffin." Her tone asked whether I wanted to take the call.

"Oh?" I perked up. "I'll be right there."

She rushed out. "Stay put, Miss Gray. Here you are." She handed me the phone, then headed back indoors.

"Tanner?" I said, sounding a tad giddy, swinging my legs from the chaise and sitting up straight. "What a nice surprise."

"Why?" He laughed. "Did you think you'd never hear from me again?"

God, that voice. Tanner Griffin was the actor I had mentored during my previous year at the college. At twenty-six, he was not only an extraordinary talent; he was also young enough to be my . . . well, my nephew. That hadn't stopped us, though, from exploring an intense attraction that had been based upon professional expediency as well as passion and, ultimately, love. We had shared the same dream for his career, and that dream had been realized a few months earlier when he was discovered in one of my plays and whisked away to Hollywood.

Echoing his laugh, I answered, "Of *course* I expected to hear from you, but I know how busy you are these days. Tell me about *Photo Flash*."

He taunted, "You're not interested in movies, remember?"

Granted, my predilection for the legitimate theater was well known. In fact, my attitudes toward filmmaking could sometimes be downright peevish, even in print. But I explained to Tanner, "I was asking about *your* movie, not some cheesy blockbuster."

"Are you saying *Photo Flash* won't be a blockbuster?" He was still teasing me.

"It might be a blockbuster," I allowed. "But I doubt it'll be cheesy."

"I certainly hope not."

We gabbed on in this manner for many pleasant minutes, he supplying production details of his film, I telling him about my decision to produce the stage version of *Rebecca* that coming fall. The morning was heating up, and each time Tanner spoke, I drank more of Oralia's iced tea.

At a pause, I added, "Did you hear about the wedding?"

"Hm?"

"Grant and Kane, they're tying the knot. Big commitment ceremony next weekend—at the Regal Palms, no less."

"Hey, that's great. Good for them." Tanner's words answered my underlying question. I had wondered if he'd been invited to the event, but it seemed to be news to him. "I hesitate to broach this," he added, "but speaking of commitments, how are things going with you and Glenn?"

"Ughhh." Flumping back on the chaise, I explained, "He's still more than interested, and he's showing subtle signs of upping the pressure. But, Tanner, I just don't know . . ."

"Most women would jump at the chance."

With a snort, I reminded him, "Several already have. And where did it get them?"

"I'm sure they've been well provided for."

"I'm sure. But here's the point: If I entered into . . . 'something' with Glenn, and then it soured, our working relationship at the school would suffer as well. I love what I'm doing here, and I don't want to jeopardize that."

"Yeah, that's an important consideration. You'll sort it out, Claire."

Wryly, I told him, "I admire your faith in me."

"You've always had faith in *me*."

"Yes, love. I have."

We exchanged a few more tender thoughts, promised to keep in touch, then hung up.

Oralia must have been watching from the kitchen. As soon as I set down the phone, she was darting out with more tea. Just in time—my glass was empty. "I do not wish to pry," she said with a sweet smile, pouring for me, "but is everything going well for Mr. Griffin?"

"It seems so, yes. Production of his film is moving along nicely."

"Will you see him sometime soon?"

"I'm not sure." Dismayed, I realized that I had no idea when Tanner and I might again spend some time together.

"When you do, I hope you will please greet him for me." Oralia knew the extent of my relationship with Tanner, as any housekeeper would. Before leaving for La-La Land, he had practically moved in with me, and Oralia had grown fond of him.

"Of course, Oralia. I'll be happy to say hello for you."

Setting down the pitcher of tea, she stooped to gather the loose sections of the newspaper, cradling the bundle in her arms like a baby. "If you are finished," she told me, "I can take these before they blow into the pool."

"Good idea. Thank you, Oralia." Swinging my feet off the cushion, I sat upright again and handed her the society pages I had been perusing. "These women," I said, pointing to the photos, "have you noticed how they all look alike? The hats, the glitzy dresses, the frosted-blond hairdos—it's as if they're all in uniform."

With a soft laugh, Oralia told me, "These are the women I work for. Yes, they do look alike."

The shade of the towering fan palm had crept away from my chaise, so I put on my sunglasses again. Feeling hot, I drank another swallow of the cold tea. "Last night," I said, "I was visiting Glenn Yeats at his home in Nirvana. His wife was there—well, one of his two *ex*-wives—and she looked just like these women." I tapped the folded sheets of newsprint Oralia held, adding, "Felicia could have been any one of these gals."

Oralia's brow twisted in thought for a moment. "Felicia Yeats?"

"Yes. Though the marriage is finished, she still uses her ex-husband's name. Guess she enjoys being a Yeats."

Oralia nodded knowingly. "But it was her *given* name that I found strange. For a woman named Felicia, she did not seem at all happy." Oralia was connecting the name to the Spanish *feliz*.

Now it was *my* brow that twisted. "You know Felicia Yeats?"

Oralia shrugged. "I have met her."

I must have looked bewildered, as Oralia then explained, "She is a friend of a lady I work for in Indian Wells. It seems they all move in the same circles."

I noted, "But Felicia doesn't live here. She's from Los Angeles."

Grinning, Oralia reminded me, "They all have cars, Miss Gray."

I laughed heartily, then drained the last of the tea from my glass.

Oralia reached for the pitcher and poured yet another refill. "It was a week or two ago. Felicia Yeats came to the house where I was cleaning. She and my employer drove off to pick up another lady-friend, and they were going to some fancy lunch together. All dressed up"—Oralia shook her head—"but not a happy woman."

"No," I agreed, "from what I saw of Felicia, she doesn't fit the name at all."

Oralia heaved a sigh, uttering something in Spanish that seemed to say, Other people's problems . . .

I mopped my brow. Even with the steady supply of iced tea, the sun's march noonward was taking its toll on me.

"Perhaps you should go indoors, Miss Gray."

I stood. "Yes, I should. Besides, it's time to put myself together for the day." I looked a fright, and I was due to meet Grant and Kane at the hotel in an hour or so. Picking up the phone and the glass, I told Oralia, "I'll be away for lunch. But do help yourself to whatever you can find. Will you be here when I return?"

"Of course, Miss Gray." She walked to the house with me, carrying the pitcher and the newspapers. "When I finish in the kitchen, I want to clean the garage. The last owners . . ." She grimaced.

"Oh, Oralia," I protested. "It'll be far too hot to work in the garage this afternoon. It needn't be done today."

"Nonsense, Miss Gray. I do not mind."

With a wink, she added, "The heat—it is in my blood."

4

By ten-thirty, I had showered, dressed, and driven the mile or two from my relatively modest neighborhood on the valley floor to the snazzy mountainside development known as Nirvana. Stopping my Beetle at the gatehouse, I informed an avuncular guard of my appointment to meet Grant Knoll at the Regal Palms. Without checking (either he had already been coached regarding my arrival, or security was lax that morning), the guard admitted me, and I sputtered up the winding roadway to the hotel.

Pulling in beneath the giant shaded portico at the hotel's main entrance, I was greeted by not one parking valet, but two—one to open my door and assist me out of the car, the other to drive it away. Their natty summer uniforms included tan Bermuda shorts and crisp military-style shirts adorned with epaulets and arm crests. Grant and Kane, who had just arrived (I saw Grant's big white Mercedes being whisked away as I had turned into the curving entry drive), were waiting for me at the double front doors. Leaning together, they were engaged in an energetic but whispered conversation. From Grant's sly grin, I assumed they were discussing the considerable assets of the beefier car parker who had escorted me from my Beetle.

"Now, now," I said to Grant, drawing near, "you're married, remember."

"Not yet, doll. I've still got a whole week on the loose." Wrapping me in a big, happy hug, he stage-whispered, "I've always had the hots for a man in uniform." He was referring not to marines or policemen, but parking valets—that's how he'd met Kane, who used to work at one of the trendier restaurants in Palm Springs, but now worked in the publicity office of the DAC art museum while pursuing a graphic-design degree at the college. Not coincidentally, Grant served as president of the museum's board of directors.

With a smirk, Kane told Grant, "A week on the loose—that's what *you* think." Then Kane nudged him aside so that he too could give me a hug. "Morning, Claire. Glad you could join us today."

It wasn't difficult to see why Grant was infatuated by his young live-in. At twenty-two, Kane Richter had barely entered his prime. His good looks were complemented by an earnest but sweet personality, and his compatibility with Grant was intellectual as well as physical. On top of which, they were simply, hopelessly in love—a passion that had diminished not a jot in the ten months since they'd met. Though occasionally mistaken for father and son, both men reacted to these faux pas with a carefree humor that seemed to say, The joke's on you.

When the three of us passed the doorman and entered the hotel together, I was momentarily stunned by the thirty-degree drop in temperature; the morning had already heated up to over one hundred. Walking through the main lobby and under an opulent chandelier (very traditional, not at all like the crystal-daggered specimen in Glenn Yeats's front hall), we stopped at the front desk and asked to see the events manager.

"I'll let her know you're here," said the clerk, eyeing Kane while placing the call. A moment later, he told us, "Miss Conner will be with you in a moment."

So the three of us settled in the lobby, sitting in overstuffed armchairs upholstered in glazed chintz. Crossing his legs, Grant told Kane with a wink, "I think he likes you."

Kane glanced at the desk clerk. "Not my type."

"Good."

As Miss Conner's "moment" stretched on to several minutes, we gabbed of this and that, but mainly the ceremony. A few hotel guests came and went. Then Grant interrupted his own patter to tell us, "Look who's here."

Looking to the front doors, we saw Paige Yeats enter with Thad

Quatrain. Both were dressed for the heat in shorts and sandals, but with dressier shirts for their visit to the posh hotel. Paige carried a canvas tote slung over one shoulder. The informal bag, which served as a large purse, looked heavy on her, weighted by something bulky that made it bulge. As surprised to see us as we were to see them, they strode in our direction, beaming smiles as we rose to greet them.

After an initial round of hellos, I said to my two students, "*We're* here planning a wedding, but what brings you to these ritzy surroundings?"

"Well . . . ," said Paige with an awkward pause, "it was something Felicia said last night. There were conflicting stories about why she and Pops split, and she said she could fill me in. So I decided to take her up on her offer."

Thad added sheepishly, "I drove."

I asked Paige, "Is Felicia expecting you?"

"She invited me."

I recalled that at the previous night's gathering, Paige had referred to Felicia as "the bitch who wrecked my mother's life." This morning, however, Paige's tone was reserved, but not openly hostile. She was hard to read. Taking her words at face value, I assumed she was curious about the broader view of her family history.

Kane was saying, "You guys still up for that blues concert tonight?"

"Wouldn't miss it," said Thad. "Paige and I will pick you up at seven and head over to campus."

"Ahhh . . . ," said Grant with a wistful sigh, "the young ones are going out for a Saturday night on the town. How . . . *collegiate.*"

Paige told him, "And next Saturday, it's *your* big night. The commitment ceremony sounds like a blast. Thad and I will be attending together." She reached for Thad's hand, and he returned a gentle squeeze. By all appearances, their interaction qualified as something beyond "hanging out." They did indeed appear to be nurturing a budding romance.

Grant sniffed comically. "*Really,* young lady, our blessed commitment is an occasion of solemn dignity—hardly what I'd call 'a blast.'"

Kane assured everyone, "It'll be *plenty* of fun."

Thad gave him a reassuring cuff on the shoulder.

Watching these two dashing young men, Thad at nineteen and Kane just three years older, I noted that they would make a dandy couple, if so inclined. But Kane was betrothed to an older man, while Thad was warming up to a billionaire's daughter.

"Well," said Paige, rolling her eyes, "duty calls."

"I'll wait here," Thad told her as she took off down a hall toward one of the guest wings. Then Thad took a seat near a table that displayed a selection of magazines.

Grant, Kane, and I were about to resume our seats when the peck of heels on the marble floor announced the arrival of Miss Conner. "Hello, everyone," she said, moving toward us. A smartly groomed professional gal of around thirty, she wore a dark, tailored skirt and jacket and carried a bright red file folder. "Sorry to keep you waiting. Ready to put the finishing touches on the Knoll-Richter extravaganza?"

"You bet, Crystal," said Grant, who had worked with the woman before.

She greeted Grant with a hug, then Kane, and then she turned to me, offering her hand. "I'm Crystal Conner. This must be such a happy occasion for you."

Who did she think I was—mother of the groom? And if so, which one?

Grant rescued me with a proper introduction, concluding, "Claire is not only my dearest friend, but one of *the* great directors in the American theater."

"Now, Grant, *really,*" I said through a modest titter.

"Of *course,*" said Crystal, palm to chest. "I've always been a *huge* fan of your work, Miss Gray." She had no idea who I was. "So let's get started. Follow me, please?" And she led us down a hall toward the ballrooms, in the direction away from the guest rooms.

Walking the hall, we passed a few administrative offices and a row of little shops. Grant reviewed, "Now, the general plan is for the evening to progress through three distinct events, each in its own space— a cocktail hour prior to the ceremony, then the ceremony itself, then dinner."

Crystal flipped open her notes, confirming, "Exactly." Rounding a bend in the wide hall, she announced, "And here we are in the prefunction area, where cocktails and hors d'oeuvres will be served as your guests arrive."

We stopped in the middle of the sprawling space. Though there were windows at the far end, most of the light came from row upon row of chandeliers, mini-versions of the big one in the main lobby. Grant scowled. "Needs some dressing up. I mean, all these bare walls." They weren't really bare—with heavy wood molding and wainscoting, inset panels of tufted moiré silk, and handsome metal sconces. But there was a lot of unbroken space.

"There'll be a bar," Kane reminded him.

"And a grand piano," added Crystal.

"Oh." Grant nodded, satisfied. "That'll do it."

"Cocktails from seven till eight, then . . . ," said Crystal, walking to one of the wall panels and sliding it open, "then your guests can assemble in this smaller ballroom for the ceremony."

We followed her in. It was an attractive room, nicely proportioned, with a wall of French doors leading out to a terrace, elevated just enough to obscure the huge hotel swimming pool while framing the mountain view beyond. Crystal asked, "Did you decide if you want to take your vows in front of the window? Or on the far side of the room?"

"We'll go with the window," said Kane. "The sun will be getting low by then on the opposite side of the building, so the east view should be colorful, but not dazzling. Wouldn't want the guests to be squinting during the I-do's."

"God forbid," Grant seconded.

They discussed the details of the dais, a podium, the flowers, and lighting. I tuned out during most of this—what could I possibly contribute with Grant present? He could plan a party in his sleep. And Kane's design skills had been put to use producing the printed materials required for the event; his work was done, and the invitations had been mailed, but the programs and menus were still being printed.

We then moved to the main ballroom, where the dinner reception would be held. A good deal of time was spent discussing the meal, wines, and flowers. A seating plan had been developed, and place cards had been sent to a calligrapher. While the others talked and compared notes, I strolled the wall of French doors (like that in the other ball-room, but longer), looking out over the terrace.

This was the same terrace, I realized, that extended from the hotel's main dining room, where Grant and I had often lunched while admiring the view. On that late Saturday morning in July, however, heat waves rose from the limestone pavers as they baked under an intense white sun in a delusory blue sky. No one had ventured out, and all was still.

Crystal asked, "Do you want lobby signs on stanchions, directing guests to the event?"

"Good idea." Grant laughed. "There might be a few in our crowd who'd be embarrassed to step up to the main desk and ask, 'Where's the gay wedding?'"

"Consider it done," said Crystal—but not before she and Kane had compared notes regarding the type font to be used for the signs.

"Ughhh!" said Grant, feigning exhaustion. "Anyone ready for lunch?"

I perked right up. "Sounds good to me."

"Will you be lunching at the hotel?" asked Crystal.

"Where else?" replied Grant.

"Then you needn't walk all the way back through the lobby. We're closer than you think." And she scooted us through a service hall that opened into the dining room's reception area.

Though the restaurant was open for lunch, it was barely eleven-thirty, so no one else was seated yet and Crystal had to find the hostess for us. "Ah, Mr. Knoll," said the young lady as she approached us with her clipboard. "Good afternoon."

Grant checked his watch. "Still morning, actually. Oafishly early for lunch, but it seems we're all hungry."

"Our pleasure to serve," she said, escorting us into the formal dining room, which yawned before us like a sea of white linen, with its well-polished silver and precious little arrangements of cut flowers. "I assume you won't be needing your usual terrace table today."

We all laughed in response—it was simply too hot to eat outdoors.

So we ended up at a prime table near the center window, where we could enjoy a view almost as spectacular as that from the terrace, which was only a few feet away on the other side of the glass. A busboy brought water. A waiter brought menus and took our drink orders— iced tea all around.

We fell momentarily quiet while opening the menus and considering our options. Fingering his chin, Grant muttered, "Field greens with balsamic vinaigrette and shaved carpaccio . . ."

"Sounds wonderful." I closed my menu.

Watching Grant, Kane fingered his own chin. With a soft laugh, he noted, "Speaking of 'shaved,' it seems I forgot to this morning."

Grant's eyes slid in Kane's direction. "I would have mentioned it, cupcake, but I didn't notice till we were in the car." He gave me a wink.

"Does it really show?" asked Kane, a tad alarmed.

"Not at all," I assured him, reaching to pat his arm. His light-colored hair would make a pale beard at best.

"It may not show," said Grant in a mock-lecturing tone, "but you can feel it, can't you? Your internal self-image is as important as the face you show to the world." Reconsidering, he added, "Well, *almost.*"

With a grin, Kane told me, "Grant's notions of good grooming are fairly rigid."

"So I've heard." Recalling a previous discussion along those lines, I asked Grant, "How on earth do you spend twenty minutes shaving?" Though I had never shaved my face, I'd seen it done in commercials, and the process appeared to take all of thirty seconds.

"It's a matter of preparation," Grant explained wearily. "You don't just grab a razor and start hacking."

"I admit," said Kane, "when Grant first showed me his method, I thought it was nuts."

"The kinder word would be *obsessive,*" said Grant.

"Whatever. But after trying it a few times, I had to admit, there *is* a difference. A close shave is its own reward."

I laughed openly. "You two really *are* a match made in heaven."

Other patrons began to fill the room as we gabbed about nothing of consequence, simply enjoying each other's company, the lavish surroundings, and a light midday meal that was beautifully presented and eagerly eaten.

An hour or so later, we considered dessert, but decided against it.

Then Grant signed the check (he was there often enough that he ran a monthly account) and asked, "All set?"

"All set," I said, rising. "I ought to get home and see how Oralia is doing. She was preparing to clean the garage—in this heat, if you can imagine. If she finishes before I get back, I'm afraid she might retile the roof."

Grant and Kane rose as well. With a sigh, Grant noted, "Good help is *so* hard to come by, but that Oralia—she's a peach."

Strolling from the dining room, I thanked Grant for lunch and told Kane how much I looked forward to their ceremony the following Saturday. Recalling the society pages I'd browsed that morning, I asked, "Think it'll make the papers?"

"It *ought* to," said Grant, "but we've decided to keep the whole affair low-key and private—no press allowed."

With a smirk, Kane added, "As if they'd be clamoring at the door."

Passing by the hostess stand, Grant paused, saying he needed to confirm a reservation for an upcoming business dinner. A nicely dressed man and woman were standing with their backs to us; he was telling the hostess, "So I'm afraid we've been stood up. We'll be a party of two instead of three."

"With pleasure." The hostess crossed something off her list and prepared to escort them to their table.

As the couple turned, the man stopped short. "Oh, my. What a coincidence." It was Peverell Lamonte, director of the architecture conservancy, whom we'd met the previous evening.

Grant and I greeted him, introducing Kane.

Referring to the woman at his side, Peverell asked, "Does everyone know Lark Tutwiler?"

Though she looked familiar, I was sure we hadn't met, as her name was one not easily forgotten. Stylish and bejeweled (a bit much for a summer afternoon, to my way of thinking), she looked a few years older than Peverell, perhaps forty-five. Her frosty blond hair and creaseless features were interchangeable with those of any of the desert doyennes I'd seen in that morning's "People" section.

Even Grant, whose social connections were extensive, did not know the woman, so Peverell made a round of introductions, explaining,

"Lark is an old friend, and it was through her that I first met Felicia Yeats."

Gifting each of us with a regal little handshake, a mere waggling of fingers, she told us, "Felicia and I have been running in the same circles lately, and when she mentioned her issues with the Dirkman house in Santa Barbara, I thought she might like to meet Peverell." With a grin that was hard to read, she added, "It seems they've hit it off quite nicely."

Peverell nodded. "Which is precisely why I asked *both* ladies to lunch today."

"But," said Lark, stiffening her spine, "can you imagine? We were stood up."

My head ping-ponged as they took turns with their story. Peverell took up the volley, telling us, "We've phoned her room several times from the lobby, but she seems to be out."

"That's Felicia for you. She's a hell of a gal, but a little scatter-brained at times. She probably just . . . *forgot*."

"Either that," suggested Peverell, "or she hasn't crawled out of bed yet. She was a bit—shall we say—'under the weather' when I drove her back to the hotel last night."

I blurted, "She was *bombed*."

"Really?" asked Lark. "Felicia? I've never seen her even *touch* a cocktail."

"She was touching them last night," Grant assured her.

"Oh, well." Lark shrugged. "Poor lamb."

Peverell said to her, "Speaking of cocktails, would you care for a little something to start lunch?"

"*Wonderful* suggestion." She patted his arm.

Then they wished us farewell and, following the hostess, disappeared into the dining room.

Walking the hall to the main lobby with Grant and Kane, I wondered aloud, "How do women like that while away their days?"

"Shopping and drinking, I imagine," said Grant. Offhandedly, he added, "And charity luncheons, of course."

"Of course." Though we were being flip, I sensed there was a disturbing nugget of truth to Grant's words.

Entering the lobby, I noticed that the chair where Thad Quatrain had been sitting—reading magazines while Paige went to visit Felicia—was now empty. "Maybe Felicia went out with the kids," I suggested.

Kane countered, "Or maybe she and Paige never connected."

Suddenly curious, I noted that the same desk clerk was still on duty. As he was momentarily unoccupied, I crossed the lobby, with Grant and Kane in tow, and asked him, "Did you happen to notice the young man who was sitting in that chair? It was perhaps an hour and a half ago. He was waiting for a young lady while she went to visit a guest."

The clerk eyed Kane again, still interested. "Sure, I noticed him." His grin suggested that he had found Thad as attractive as Kane.

Clearing my throat, I recaptured the clerk's attention, asking, "Do you recall when he left—and with whom?"

Pausing in thought, scrunching his brows, the clerk replied, "Sorry, I don't remember seeing him leave. I must've been busy on the phone or the computer. That chair has been empty for quite a while, though."

I asked whether "quite a while" was closer to an hour or only fifteen minutes, but he couldn't say.

I turned to Grant. "If you guys need to run along, feel free. Maybe I'm unconscionably nosy, but I'd like to try talking to Felicia."

"Uh-oh," Grant said to Kane, "milady sniffs a plot in the works."

"I beg your pardon?" the clerk asked with a blank expression.

"Nothing, just being dramatic," Grant told him. "Could we have the room number of Felicia Yeats, please?"

"I'm sorry, sir, but we never give out the room numbers of our guests. If you like, I could connect you with her room on the house telephone." He gestured to a fancy French-style phone on a nearby side table.

Pulling Grant aside, I told him, "No point in that. We know she won't answer."

Then Grant pulled Kane aside. His eyes slid toward the desk clerk. "He's hot for you."

"He's ready to eat me alive."

"Work your charms. We'll wait over here." And Grant escorted me to the center of the lobby, where we perched on a settee and flipped open some magazines.

Kane sidled back to the desk and struck up a conversation with the clerk, leaning near and laughing softly. Within two minutes, Kane turned and walked over to us, sporting a broad grin. As we stood, he told us, "Mission accomplished. Room two-sixteen."

Stepping into the hall that led to the guest wing, Grant told Kane, "That was quick work. What'd you promise him?"

"Wouldn't *you* like to know."

Grant stopped in his tracks. "As a matter of fact, I would."

"Actually," I added with a chortle, "so would I."

Kane paused, relishing the moment before explaining, "I didn't have to promise anything. I just batted my eyes and played dumb, asking questions about his computer, as if I'd never set fingers on a keyboard. He lapped it up and finally swung the monitor around so I could see it. Pointing to the screen, he said, 'See? Here's the lady your friends were asking about.' In addition to her room number, I saw her credit card info, billing address, and a complete accounting of every cent she's spent here."

"Really?" I asked eagerly, a glutton for detail.

With a laugh, Kane raised his hands. "Hold on. All I got was a glimpse. I was lucky to decipher the room number."

"Good boy," said Grant, patting his partner's head as if rewarding a puppy for a newly learned trick.

So we took an elevator up to the second floor, and when the doors slid open again, we followed an arrow directing us to a turn in the hall. Another set of arrows directed us to another turn. Walking this hall, we passed a cleaning cart that blocked the open door to a room where a chambermaid was busy with a vacuum, apparently finishing her duties there. With her back to us, she neither saw nor heard us.

After a final turn of the hall, we located Felicia's room just a few doors away. A "do not disturb" sign hung from the knob. Direct commands from authority figures have always made me bristle, so it should come as no surprise that an arbitrary command from a flimsy sheet of plastic struck me as laughably lame and meaningless. Raising my hand, I gave the door a good rap with my knuckles. Then we waited.

Leaning near the door, trying to hear any noise within over the distant roar of the vacuum cleaner, I grew frustrated with waiting and knocked again, louder.

Noting my scowl, Grant said, "She's just not in. Peverell said he tried phoning several times."

The vacuum cleaner stopped. Then I heard the chambermaid loading her whatnot back onto the cart. With a dull thud, the door shut behind her.

"Come on," I said, taking the sign from Felicia's door, slipping it into my pocket, and leading Grant and Kane back down the hall.

When we turned the corner, the maid was trundling toward us with her cart. "Oh!" I said with a look of surprise, stopping. "I wonder if you could make up room two-sixteen, please. I'm having guests in right after lunch."

Grant took out his wallet and slipped her a five.

"My pleasure," she said in broken English, practicing her drill from the hotel phrase book.

Thanking each other with a mutual bobbing of heads, I clarified slowly, "Room two-one-six."

"Yes, ma'am." And she pushed her cart around the bend.

Grant, Kane, and I retreated a few steps toward the elevator hall, then waited. Craning our necks in the direction of Felicia's room, we heard the maid's cart creaking along, then stop. We heard the key in the lock and the squeak of the door opening. We heard the maid gather a few buckets and bottles from the cart before entering the room.

And then we heard her scream.

5

We rushed down the hall, turned the corner, pushed the cleaning cart aside, and piled into room two-sixteen, finding it to be a sizable suite. We were in the sitting room, where the chambermaid stood a few feet in front of us, hands to her mouth, trembling.

On the wall opposite the door was a wide window with a postcard-perfect mountain view. Exuberantly floral tieback curtains fell to the sides, framing a camelback sofa upholstered in a classic silk rep bearing bold, alternating stripes of emerald and burgundy. Sprawled before us on its down-filled cushions was Felicia Yeats in a bulky bathrobe of pink chenille.

Her face had taken on a pallid hue, as had the long expanse of her inner thigh that peeped immodestly from the robe's slit. Emanating from her blue lips and caked on the front of her robe was a stale stream of vomit. Unless I was mistaken, it contained chunks of undigested shrimp.

"*Dios mío,*" mumbled the maid.

"Holy shit," whispered Kane.

With a tisk, Grant noted, "Those curtains are a *fright.*"

"Perhaps someone should phone nine-one-one," I told them.

"Sure thing, doll," said Grant, pulling a cell phone from the inside pocket of his sport coat. Punching in the number, he added, "I hope they don't expect me to give mouth-to-mouth."

Eyeing him with an impatient gaze, I said, "Call an ambulance."

I added, "Then call your brother."

Within half an hour, a crew of emergency personnel had arrived, including Detective Larry Knoll of the Riverside County sheriff's department. "When I got Grant's call," he said, meeting me in the hall outside the suite, "I could hardly believe it."

Confused, I asked, "Did you know the victim?"

"Nope, never met her. Never even heard of her."

"So why were you surprised? Unexplained death is fairly routine in your line of work, isn't it, Larry?"

"Exactly. But it shouldn't be routine in *your* line of work. You moved here to teach college less than a year ago, and already you've stumbled on how many corpses—three?"

"Four, actually." I had to admit, my new life in paradise had a distinctly curious—and morbid—twist. During my decades back in New York, supposedly a crime-ridden metropolis, I had never so much as witnessed a mugging, but here in the resort communities near Palm Springs, where violent crime was rare, I seemed drawn like a magnet to cases of mysterious death. Trying to downplay the coincidence of my repeated discovery of murder victims, I suggested to Larry, "Maybe she just choked."

"Maybe," he allowed, "but I doubt it." Slipping a notebook out of his pocket, he said, "Tell me what happened."

The hall outside the suite was getting crowded, not only with the police crew and emergency techs who filed in and out, but with other hotel guests who were both curious about and alarmed by this unseemly development at the serene Regal Palms. So I stepped Larry down the hall to a little alcove where a bay window looked over a craggy ravine. Away from the bustle, I related to Larry the events that had led us to Felicia's room after lunch.

As I spoke, Larry took notes, and as he wrote, I observed Larry.

I had come to know him within weeks of my arrival in the desert, the previous September when a fellow member of the DAC faculty, a sculptor, and I had found his wife dead at their home. I had recalled that my new friend and neighbor, Grant Knoll, had mentioned having a brother who was a detective with the sheriff's department, which provides police services for some of the smaller desert communities. Larry was assigned to the case, and thus we met.

At forty-six, Larry was three years younger than Grant, but in many ways he seemed the older of the two. Perhaps it was the rigors of police work that gave him a sober, almost weary, edge; or perhaps *anyone* would seem to lack oomph and verve, juxtaposed with Grant's buoyant gayness and his witty joie de vivre. Larry was a family man—with wife, kids, dog, and a home way out in Riverside. He was a plainclothes cop, with the emphasis on *plain,* sharing none of his brother's sense of style. On that hot afternoon in July, he wore a light brown business suit, a starched but wrinkled white business shirt, and even a necktie (virtually unknown in the desert at *any* time of year).

Still, getting to know both of them, I understood that their superficial differences were shallow. Inside, they were clearly brothers, mutually respectful, even affectionate, sharing a deep concern for each other. In fact, Larry had eagerly consented to stand as Grant's witness at next week's commitment ceremony. They were not only brothers, but friends. I myself had come to think of Larry as a friend, and it's safe to say he felt the same about me—despite his razzing about my occasional skirmishes with suspicious death.

Running a hand through his hair, he struggled not to laugh while reading from his notes, "And you bribed the maid to open the room?"

"Well, the bribe was Grant's doing."

"Why were you so curious in the first place?"

Good question. "Let's just say I sensed something was wrong. I first met Felicia last night, and my impression was anything but favorable." I related the premise for the impromptu cocktail party at Glenn Yeats's home and the ugly scene Felicia had caused regarding the Dirkman house in Santa Barbara. "Grant was there too," I told Larry. "You should ask him about it."

"I intend to. Let's find him."

Larry escorted me from the hall, through the crowd at the suite's door, and into the sitting room, where the medical examiner and his team hunkered around Felicia's body. I now noticed that her fingernails, as well as her lips, had turned a frightening shade of blue. In the adjacent dining room, a deputy sat with Grant and the chambermaid, taking notes. Kane had already been dismissed; I'd noticed his departure while standing in the hall with Larry. Beyond the dining room, through the open door to the bedroom, other officers photographed the bed, looked through drawers, and seemed to be taking an inventory of God-knows-what.

Seeing Larry enter the room, another detective rose from the huddle at the body and stepped over to us.

Larry asked him, "First impressions?"

"Doc says she died just a few hours ago, earlier this morning. Her bedding was rumpled, but not slept-in, so she must have been up all night. There's puke all over the bathroom, so whatever hit her, hit her hard. Her airway was clear, so she didn't choke on it."

I wondered, "If she was so sick, why wouldn't she call a doctor?"

Larry speculated, "Sometimes when you vomit, you assume the worst is over."

The other detective nodded. "Or she was just too drunk to call for help."

I recalled, "She was well on her way when she left Glenn Yeats's home last night. Her escort, Peverell Lamonte, said he had a rough time getting her back to the hotel." I gave them what background I knew of Peverell.

Larry confirmed with me, "When the three of you followed the maid into the room today, you didn't touch anything, did you?"

"Of course not, Larry." I caught myself rolling my eyes—by now, I'd grown only too familiar with crime-scene protocol.

"So," Larry surmised, "by all appearances, she was up drinking all night, at least until she passed out." He indicated the single empty on-the-rocks glass that sat on the cocktail table in front of the sofa where Felicia still sprawled. "Fingerprints?"

"Only the victim's," the other detective answered. "And we found no other used glassware anywhere in the suite. It seems she was alone last night; there's no evidence of forced entry or struggle."

Considering these conclusions, Larry asked, "Any liquor bottles?"

"One empty. Bagged as evidence."

"Can I have a look?"

As the detective went to retrieve it, I told Larry, "Felicia started drinking martinis at Glenn's last night. She'd never done much drinking, but she took a quick liking to the gin. Glenn offered to let her take the bottle when she left."

The detective returned with a light blue gin bottle in a tagged evidence bag, apparently the same one Glenn had given her. I told Larry, "That's the brand."

As the bottle and its cap were bagged separately, Larry was easily able to expose the neck of the bottle and take a sniff inside.

I told him, "When Felicia took her first sip, she said it tasted like perfume. I assured her that gin is an acquired taste."

Larry's brow wrinkled, "It doesn't *smell* like perfume—*or* gin." Handing it back to the other detective, he ordered, "Usual analysis." And the bottle was taken away.

On the basis of all I'd seen and heard, I asked Larry, "Alcohol poisoning?"

"Good theory at this point, but we won't know for sure till we do some testing. A complete medical-legal autopsy is obviously in order."

I was well aware that such an autopsy would be ordered for any such death, even if presumed accidental, but something in Larry's tone prompted me to say, "Somehow, I get the impression you suspect this may not have been an accident."

With a soft smile, he told me, "You *are* getting good at this."

"Oh, nonsense." Though I tried, I could not conceal that I found his compliment enormously flattering.

"Now, then," he said, "let's talk to Grant."

As we stepped into the dining room, the maid was just getting up from the table, bobbing her head at the officer who had been questioning her, taking his card. Dismissed, she skittered from the room, passed through the sitting room without looking at the commotion around the sofa, and fled out into the hall just as a gurney was being wheeled in.

With a grin, Larry told the officer, "Watch out for *this* guy—he's a slippery one," referring to Grant.

"Your brother and I have finished, Detective."

"Thank *God,*" said Grant, rising. "Talk about the rubber-hose treatment."

I told the questioning officer, aside, "He tends to exaggerate."

"Yes, ma'am. Thank you, ma'am. I gathered that."

Larry asked him, "Have you questioned any other hotel staff who were on duty last night?"

"Yes, Detective. The housekeeping log noted a 'do not disturb' sign posted sometime before ten last night, and the records confirm that no staff entered the room after that."

"Oops." I felt the sheet of plastic through the pocket in my slacks. All heads turned to me.

I explained, "In order to trick the maid into opening the room, I had to hide the sign." Spreading the flap of my side pocket and peering down into it, I added, "I hope I haven't contaminated any evidence."

Unfurling a handkerchief, Larry used it to grab the edge of the sign and pull it from my pocket. "It's a safe bet that *hundreds* of people have handled this. But it's worth checking. If we can identify Felicia's prints on it, that will essentially confirm that she put the sign on the knob herself."

"Meaning," I elaborated, "someone outside the room wasn't playing tricks—deadly or otherwise."

"Exactly." Larry bagged the sign, which an officer took away. Turning to Grant, Larry said, "Claire tells me you were at the party last night when she met Felicia."

"Yup. Ironic, isn't it? We shared both our first and our *last* glimpse of her." As if on cue, Grant's statement was punctuated by the zip of Felicia's body bag.

"Sorry, dear," I told him. "I can't help feeling I've had a negative impact on your peaceful existence—like a serpent in Eden."

"Not at all, doll. Sort of spices things up. Besides, it's not as if it's *your* fault—Felicia's untimely demise, that is."

"I certainly hope not."

Larry asked his brother, "If you helped set up the party for Glenn Yeats, can I assume you were among the last to leave?"

"The very last, in fact. I gave a complete timeline to your charming deputy." The officer in question was well out of earshot, working with one of the evidence techs. Recalling Grant's earlier comment about men in uniform, I had to admit, this one looked exceptionally studly in his khakis.

Larry glanced over his notes. "So Felicia Yeats was the first to leave, accompanied by Peverell Lamonte, and everyone else left shortly thereafter."

"Actually, the other guests weren't that quick to leave. With Felicia gone, the mood improved, and there was plenty to talk about. I believe I. T. Dirkman, the architect, was last to leave, around nine-thirty, and I got out with the catering crew sometime after ten."

"Glenn was the only one left in the house at that point?"

"Yes." Then Grant reconsidered. "Well, Glenn and his daughter, Paige, both remained—she's staying there for the summer."

I added, "She's enrolled in my workshop." Mention of Paige reminded me that I had not told Larry about encountering her in the hotel lobby earlier that day.

But those thoughts were interrupted by a commotion in the hall. Loud and agitated, a man's voice asked, "Can't you at least tell me what *happened*?"

The deputy (the studly one) rushed over to Larry. "Detective? There's a man in the hall who claims to be the victim's son."

Recalling some conversation from the previous evening, I asked, "Does his name happen to be Dustin?"

"Yes, ma'am. Dustin Cory."

I gave Larry a nod.

"Bring him in," said Larry. "Let's have a talk with him."

An officer escorted Dustin through the sitting room just as the medical team ratcheted up the gurney, preparing to wheel away Felicia's body. Dustin stopped in his tracks. "Is that . . . ? It *can't* be . . ."

Larry stepped over to meet him. "Mr. Cory? I'm Detective Larry Knoll. I'm sorry to deliver such painful news, but I regret to inform you that your mother died unexpectedly this morning. It seems she had way too much to drink last night."

"Mom . . . *died*?" A big guy in his late twenties, perhaps thirty, Dustin Cory wore a heavy gold watch and flashy, expensive-looking golf attire, though he didn't look the least athletic. In fact, he had too much of a paunch for his years, and his pear-shaped torso bore an unfortunate resemblance to that of Baby Huey. With a sputter, he added, "She *drank* too much?"

"At least a liter of alcohol, apparently."

"But Mom *never* drank. Well, almost never."

Larry nodded. "Then her tolerance was lower than it would have been for a regular drinker." He paused, then asked, "Would you care to have a look, Mr. Cory, before we take your mother away? I have to warn you—she's not looking her best."

Grant muttered to me, "*That's* an understatement."

My elbow jabbed his ribs.

"Of course, Detective," said Dustin through a breathy sigh. "Let me see her."

So Larry escorted him over to the gurney, zipped open the bag a foot or so, and said, "I'm sorry."

Dustin peered inside for a long moment, as if in a daze, seeing nothing. Then he raised his hands to his face, wailing, "Mommy!"

Larry closed the bag, and a pair of deputies wheeled away the gurney.

When Dustin had composed himself, Larry suggested, "Let's sit down. I'd like to ask you a few questions."

Having not seen the room in its previous state, Dustin sauntered to the sofa and sat in the spot where his mother had died. Larry sat facing him on the edge of the cocktail table, took out his notebook, and leafed to a fresh page. Grant and I instinctively backed off—but listened to every word.

Larry said, "I know your mother was the ex-wife of Glenn Yeats, but I assume Glenn is not your father."

Holding his head, Dustin nodded. "Yes, Detective. My father was Felicia's *first* husband. Glenn came into the picture long after I was born. He was Felicia's second husband, and she was his second wife."

"Where do you live, Mr. Cory?"

"LA, like Mom. I mean, not *with* her. There's plenty of room at her place—it's a big house—but I prefer my independence and have my own digs in a high-rise."

"Married?"

Dustin managed a grin. "Like I said, I prefer my independence."

Flipping a page of his notes, Larry asked, "May I ask where you work?"

With a shrug, Dustin answered, "Self-employed."

"Doing what?"

"This and that. I'm sort of 'between projects' right now."

Grant and I glanced at each other. We silently agreed that Felicia's orphan struck us as little more than a pampered playboy.

Larry asked him, "Were you sharing this suite with your mother?"

"Of *course* not," said Dustin, aghast.

"I mean"—Larry gestured at their surroundings—"it's a nice setup. I'm sure it's expensive."

Dustin grinned. "That's not an issue, Detective."

"Ahhh . . ."

"No, I have a suite of my own on another floor. We drove out together from LA yesterday; she said she wanted the company." He paused in thought for a moment, then said, "What still has me stumped is, why would Mom go on a bender last night?"

"I understand she was angry. People often act out of character under such circumstances." Then Larry turned, gave me a quick look, and stood, telling Dustin, "Let me introduce you to Claire Gray, the director, and Grant Knoll, my brother, who both happened to be at Glenn Yeats's home last night when your mother paid her visit. They can tell this story better than I can."

Grant and I stepped forward as Dustin stood. We offered a predictable round of condolences, then described the confrontation regarding the house in Santa Barbara.

Dustin nodded as he listened. "Yeah, that's what I expected. Mom was on a rant about it all the way over in the car. I assumed there'd be fireworks last night; that's why I went out on my own."

Larry asked, "Where did you go?"

"Just out on the town. Stopped lots of places, wherever I could find some action. Started early, got back late."

I told him, "That was probably a good idea, Mr. Cory. The exchange between your mother and Glenn turned surprisingly bitter, and surprisingly fast. It was most unpleasant for everyone there."

Dustin wagged his head. "I never knew Glenn very well, so I don't know his side of the story, but Mom was hostile toward him since the day they split. She was so vindictive, I can't imagine what drew her to him in the first place."

I could. Was Dustin really that naive, or was he acting? And if so, why?

Larry handed his business card to Dustin. "I'll probably need to talk to you again, Mr. Cory. Will you be in town for a few days?"

"I imagine so—after what's happened. I mean, what about the body?"

Larry explained the need for an autopsy. "When the medical examiner has finished and when the coroner has issued a report, the body will be released to you. Meanwhile, you might give some thought to the arrangements."

"Of course, Detective. Thank you."

We again expressed condolences. Larry encouraged Dustin to phone with any questions or concerns. Then Dustin made his way out of the room and disappeared into the hall.

With Felicia's body gone, the activity in the suite had calmed considerably, and the physical investigation seemed to be wrapping up. Larry told Grant and me, "Thanks for your time. I think I owe you dinner or something."

"Nonsense, Larry. I feel guilty for putting you to work on the weekend."

"You know what they say: the law never rests."

"That's right, bro," said Grant, clapping Larry on the back. "No rest for the weary."

With an awkward hesitation not typical of Larry, he said, "I was serious, though—about dinner. Turns out, I'm sort of 'baching it' this weekend, so if you guys are free tonight, I'd be happy to take you out. Bring Kane too, of course."

Turning to Grant, I said, "I know this sounds pathetic, but I'm not too proud to admit it—there's nothing on *my* calendar for tonight."

Grant thought. "I've got something, but it's just a drop-by, nothing

I can't graciously cancel. And Kane is going to a concert on campus, so sure, I'm free. Let's do it."

"Great." Larry broke into a broad smile, an expression I had rarely seen on him. In that same moment, as if with fresh eyes, I realized what a handsome man he was. He asked Grant, "Can you set it up? You're so good at that."

"Sure, bro. Happy to. I'll phone you later with logistics."

"Great," repeated Larry. "Well, if you'll excuse me, I need to wrap up some details here." And with a little salute, he retreated to the dining room.

Stepping out to the hall with Grant, I said, "What a nice idea, dinner with Larry. Glad he suggested it."

But Grant had paused in the doorway and was looking back into the room, gazing at the sofa where we had discovered Felicia's lifeless body.

He shook his head woefully.

"Those curtains," he said. "They really *are* a fright."

6

By the time I left the hotel, drove down the mountain, and headed home across the valley floor, it was well past two. The afternoon heat would continue to rise for another two or three hours, but it was already well beyond the limits of my previous experience. I passed few other cars—and certainly no golfers—as I zipped past golf courses that had fallen into quiet hibernation. Sprinklers (big ones, with nozzles like those on fire hoses) shot giant fans of water over the thirsty greens, which withered beneath a taunting, laughing sun.

Or so it seemed. Suffice it to say, it was darn hot.

Turning off Country Club Drive onto my quiet side street, I reached to press the button of my garage opener, but as the house came into view, I noticed that the door was already raised. As I braked the Beetle and sputtered into the driveway, I saw Oralia standing inside the garage on a stepladder, rearranging items on the metal shelving that stretched the full length of one wall. At the sound of the car approaching, she turned and waved.

She had already cleaned the cement floor, miraculously removing several decades' worth of accumulated oil drips. I felt guilty pulling in, as if traipsing on clean white carpeting with dirty feet. When I switched off the engine, the air conditioner stopped, and when I opened the door, I gasped while inhaling my first lungful of the blistering, hellish air. "My God, Oralia," I said, bracing myself against the car door, "how can you stand the heat?"

She gave me a curious blink, then answered with a smile, "It is nothing, Miss Gray. I am not frightened by ladders."

"Not the height, the *heat*."

Backing down the ladder, she laughed merrily, as if I'd been joking. When her feet were firmly on the floor, she clapped some grime from her hands, asking, "Everything at the hotel, it went fine?"

"Lunch was lovely, thanks." I wasn't ready to tell her the rest—it seemed too abrupt, like opera before noon. Mustering a fevered but grateful smile, I said, "You've made some real headway out here. I'm impressed."

She shook her head, frowning. "They were not very clean, those people." She was referring to the previous owners of the house. "But we will manage. I have thrown away some things you will not need. I hope you do not mind." She gestured toward a large trash caddy, brimming with assorted junk, next to the newspaper recycling bin.

"I don't mind at all," I assured her. "Thanks for taking the initiative."

"Still, I would feel better if you looked through it. There might be something you want." She turned back to the shelves and resumed her project, arranging some gardening products, swimming-pool chemicals, hand tools, and car-cleaning supplies.

I wanted to get indoors, so I made a quick check of the trash. Piled in the caddy were empty boxes of insecticide, dirty rags, a cracked and sun-bleached garden hose, and useless cans of paint thinner and rust remover. Digging deeper, I found a dead potted cactus, a broken mousetrap, and an almost-empty jug of antifreeze. "I won't miss *any* of this. Good job."

Turning, I headed for the kitchen door, then paused. "Oralia?"

She looked over her shoulder. "Yes, Miss Gray?"

I turned back. "Why on earth would *anyone*—here in the desert, in this climate—bother with antifreeze?"

She turned to me with a confused look, as if I had asked a hopelessly foolish question. "People use antifreeze," she said, hands on hips, "so their engines will not freeze."

I rattled my head, as if we were speaking two different languages, hearing only gibberish from each other. "Here?" I asked. "How could *anything* freeze here?"

She explained, "The desert rarely freezes, but cars can go where

66

they want. You do not need to travel far to find cold weather in the mountains."

"Ahhh." Silly me. So myopic.

"So most people here put antifreeze in their cars. You can buy it anywhere, just like windshield-washing fluid." She patted a fat plastic jug of blue liquid on one of the shelves.

I must have looked befuddled again because Oralia added, "We do not get much rain in the desert, but windshields, they still get dirty."

I laughed. "I suppose you're right. In fact, I *know* you're right. Just look at my car." The windows had gotten dusty, and I had tried using the wipers, which only made it look worse. "I guess I ran out of fluid. I'll get it taken care of next time I have the car serviced."

Struggling not to laugh, Oralia didn't know what to make of me. "I will do it for you, Miss Gray. There is nothing to it."

"I didn't drive at all until I moved here," I tried to explain, feeling helpless, "and I'm afraid automobile maintenance is beyond my realm."

Though impeccably polite, Oralia couldn't help snickering. "Watch, Miss Gray. Watch, and learn." And she went to it, opening the hood (I'd never even done *that*), locating the correct reservoir, snapping the lid open, then filling it with fluid from the plastic jug. "As long as I am in here," she asked, "would you like a tune-up?"

Peering over her shoulder, I asked, "Does it, uh, *need* one?"

She looked back at me. "Just joking, Miss Gray."

And we both burst into laughter.

She closed the jug, snapped the reservoir shut, and slammed the hood. "Now, then," she said, replacing the jug on the shelf, "where was I?"

"Oh, Oralia," I whined, "I'm *wilting* out here. You must be too." Though of course she wasn't. "I need some iced tea. Won't you come in and join me?"

"It is your nickel, Miss Gray." She was a sweet woman, but she really did need to get the hang of contractions.

"Besides," I told her, swinging open the door to the back hall, "I could use the company." Truth was, I needed company more than

I needed tea. The discovery of Felicia Yeats—who was not only dead, but caked in her own vomit—had not sat very well on my emotions, to say nothing of the carpaccio I'd had for lunch. I needed to talk, and Oralia was a good listener.

I breathed a huge, relieved sigh upon entering the air-conditioning of the back hall. Oralia hugged herself, grabbing a sweater as we passed through the laundry room and into the kitchen.

"I made a fresh pitcher for you," she said, opening the refrigerator and removing the tea, along with a bowl of lemons.

"I wish you'd teach me how to do that. Yours is the best iced tea I've ever had; mine is terrible." I took a pair of glasses from the cupboard and set them on the counter by the tea.

"Do not even try, Miss Gray. That is why I am here." She poured for us.

Putting my arm around her shoulder, I gave her a hug.

She handed me my glass, and we both took our first sips. There was no need to add sugar; Oralia always sprinkled a smidgen into the pitcher, and it was perfect. The moment was so pleasant, I almost forgot my reason for asking her to join me.

Setting her tea on the tiled countertop, she asked, "Is something wrong, Miss Gray? You said you needed company."

"Oh—that. Let's sit down." I patted her hand.

She picked up the pitcher, and we moved to the small round breakfast table that looked out over the terrace. Through double-paned glass, the outdoor setting looked sublimely lazy, with cool ripples playing across the surface of the pool. As we sat and I drew another long sip of Oralia's tea, the sweltering afternoon temperature ceased to concern me. But the developments in room two-sixteen were still heavily on my mind.

I said, "You were asking about my visit to the hotel, and I told you I had a lovely lunch. But there's more, Oralia. Something happened there, and it's most disturbing."

"Yes, Miss Gray?" The concern was evident in both her voice and her eyes.

"This morning, I mentioned meeting Felicia Yeats last night, and you said you had also met her."

Wryly, Oralia noted, "We were never introduced, Miss Gray. I was washing windows, but yes, I was aware of who she was. As I said, I do not think she is a happy woman."

"No"—my tone of understatement was only too apparent, almost flippant—"Felicia Yeats is anything but a happy woman, not now. After having lunch with Grant and Kane, my neighbors from the condo, I decided to pay a visit to Felicia, who was staying at the hotel. When we entered her room, we found her, well . . . *dead,* lying on the sofa."

Oralia's fingers drew to her mouth as she whispered, *"Santa Maria. No."*

"Sí," I assured her.

"Oh, Miss Gray, that is so sad—an unhappy ending for an unhappy woman. I am sorry to learn this. Do you know how it happened?"

"Detective Knoll, Grant's brother, came to the hotel with the other police. The cause of death is not yet known. It might have been acute alcohol poisoning, or it might have been something else altogether. The investigation has just begun."

Oralia slowly shook her head. "Those women—who have lost their husbands and go to the parties together—it seems they all drink too much. Perhaps they find no other joy in their lives."

"But that's the irony. From all reports, Felicia hardly *ever* drank—though she certainly got a snootful last night."

"I suppose she must have." Oralia arched her brows and drank some tea.

Pondering her comment about women who go to parties together, I asked, "The woman you work for in Indian Wells, the one who went to lunch with Felicia, may I ask her name?"

"Of course, Miss Gray. That is Mrs. Coleman—Adrienne Coleman. I work for her on Thursdays."

"Is she a widow? You implied she lost her husband."

Oralia grinned. "She lost her husband not to the grave, but to divorce."

"Same as Felicia," I noted. "Birds of a feather." Then something occurred to me. I reminded Oralia, "We were saying this morning that all the women on the charity circuit seem to look alike. Maybe they go to the same hairdresser. Does Adrienne Coleman happen to have frosted blond hair?"

"Why, yes!" said Oralia with a little laugh. "She does. You are right about them—they are all alike—same hair, same expensive clothes."

"Not to mention the face-lifts."

Oralia nodded knowingly. "Yes, that too."

Reaching for the pitcher, I refilled her glass, saying, "I met another one at the hotel today—a friend of Felicia's, same look, same hairdo. She could have been any one of those gals from the society pages of the *Desert Sun.*" Then I stopped short as something clicked. The woman who was lunching with Peverell Lamonte had looked familiar to me, and now I understood why. With a finger snap, I told Oralia, "I think she *was* in the paper this morning. Did you throw it out?"

"Yes, but it is still in the garage. Let me find it for you." She slid back her chair, rising.

I also stood. "Relax, Oralia. I can get it." I felt guilty enough that she did most of my dirty work (even though I paid her to do it and she seemed happy in my employ), but I simply couldn't expect her to go digging through trash to satisfy my regal whim. She was my house-keeper, not my serf.

She grinned. "You will *never* find it by yourself. I will help."

So we both went.

The moment I opened the back door and stepped into the garage, I had second thoughts about my egalitarian social conscience. The assault of hot air nearly took my breath away. I had to stop a moment while my senses cleared.

But Oralia beelined for the recycling bin, saying, "Today's paper may be on the bottom instead of the top. I decided the plastic box could use a good cleaning, so I took everything out, then put it all back. I think the pile is upside-down now." Squatting, she began heaving stacks of newspaper out of the bin and, checking datelines, tossing them aside.

The mere sight of her working so feverishly—in a sweater, no less—made me break into an instant sweat. Dabbing perspiration from my eyelids, I could barely see as I staggered across the garage to join her. While she continued to rummage, I picked up a section or two, breezed through a few pages, then added them to the pile she had already placed near my feet.

"Here we are," she said, raising that morning's newspaper in triumph.

Taking it from her, I turned to the society pages and began perusing the photos. Though many of the faces were similar, one looked especially familiar. Checking the caption, I proclaimed, "Aha! Lark Tutwiler, that's the name. I met her at the hotel today." She was shown at a literary luncheon held a week earlier.

Pointing to a woman next to Lark in the photo, Oralia told me, "That is Adrienne Coleman. They must have all ridden together that day, with Felicia." But Felicia was not in the photo.

Taking a closer look at some of the other photos on the page, I realized that many of the same people had attended the same round of functions; perhaps during the hotter weather, the charity pool experienced some shrinkage. I noticed another photo of Lark at the ALS luncheon. In yet another, at the Desert Arts League, she was pictured with none other than Peverell Lamonte at her side. Peverell also appeared in a tuxedoed lineup at an AIDS event. And I spotted more photos of Adrienne Coleman, one at the Desert Arts League and another at a fund-raiser for MS.

"Oralia," I moaned, "my head is swimming. These photos are so confusing—who could possibly keep track?"

"It is not the photos that confuse you, Miss Gray. It is the heat."

With a giddy laugh, I admitted, "I think you're right."

"We should go inside and get you some more iced tea."

"My thought exactly."

And in we went.

7

Driving into Palm Springs that evening, Grant looked over from the wheel to ask me, "Don't you feel it?"

I paused before answering, hoping to feel something—but what?

He explained, "The sense of déjà vu. It's hanging in the air so thick, you can practically reach out and touch it."

With dawning insight, I said, "Don't tell me you expect to find true love tonight."

"Nope. I already found it, and I found it under remarkably similar circumstances. Have you forgotten?"

"No, love. How could I forget?"

It had been a hot night the previous September when Grant had first taken me to Fusión, a trendy new restaurant in downtown Palm Springs, where we had arranged to meet his brother, Larry, for dinner. Grant had driven my new Beetle that evening, and waiting for us at the curb in front of the restaurant was a young parking valet who would not only catch Grant's eye, but win his heart. Weeks later, Kane would move in with Grant, and a week from now, they would wed.

Tonight we were headed to the same restaurant to join Larry for dinner. Once again, Grant was driving my car, this time because he had lent his big white Mercedes to Kane, who was attending a blues concert at the college with his friends Thad and Paige, my theater students.

I patted the back of Grant's hand on my steering wheel. "It was sweet of you to send the kids off in style tonight."

"Bighearted—that's me. But *please* don't refer to them as 'kids.'

That makes me sound so lecherous. One of them is the man in my life, my spouse-to-be, my friend and soul mate, my—"

"Understood," I assured him with a laugh. Then a thought wrinkled my brow. "Grant? I couldn't be happier for you and Kane. Really."

Sensing something in my voice, he turned to me with a look of concern, asking, "But . . . ?"

Did I really want to talk about this? "Oh, crap. This sounds so juvenile—so needy and insecure. Grant, you know how much you mean to me. I can't help wondering whether your commitment to Kane will somehow, well . . . change what *we* have, you and I."

He reached over to give my hand a squeeze. "Nonsense, doll. Don't give that angle a second thought. Come next Saturday, nothing will really change. You and Kane play different roles in my life."

Exactly, I thought. Had I ever expected otherwise from Grant? Glancing out the side window, I noted that Indian Canyon Drive was eerily quiet. One of the main drags through downtown Palm Springs, it seemed to bustle on nearly any night of the year, but not on this torrid Saturday in late July.

Slowing at an intersection, we turned onto a side street—quieter still—and cruised to the curb, where a parking valet looked up from the book he was reading, surprised to get some business. He jumped up from his canvas chair, opened my door, then trotted around the car to open the driver's door, handing Grant a parking stub. As the kid drove my car away, Grant escorted me across the sidewalk and under the tidy awning that marked the entrance to the restaurant.

Things hadn't changed much in the year since the trendy bistro had opened. Its sleek decorating style was not everyone's idea of "fine dining." There were no chandeliers, no velvet-upholstered banquettes, no lush arrangements of flowers. Rather, pinpoints of light shone from a black ceiling on tables surrounded by black leather chairs. In the small entryway, a single stalk of pink ginger protruded from a tall glass cylinder on the hostess stand. Black-garbed and sunken-cheeked, the young lady greeted us, "Welcome to Fusión. So nice to see you again, Mr. Knoll."

"Thank you, our pleasure. Ahhh, it's nice and cool in here."

It was. The dark surroundings felt like a cave, a welcoming retreat from the extended summer daylight and the hot night to follow.

Grant continued, "My brother will be meeting us—"

"He's already here, Mr. Knoll. Would you care to join him in the bar?"

Silly question. We were well into the cocktail hour, and my lazy Saturday had proven far more harrowing than expected. A drink was definitely in order.

The small bar area was not much wider than a hallway. As Grant and I ducked in, Larry rose from the stool where he had been seated, nursing a short glass of something brown. He wore the same tan suit from earlier that day, but had changed into a more casual shirt, a soft, fuzzy polo of baby blue. In the dim light of the bar, I noticed that the shirt seemed to amplify the color of his gray-blue eyes.

"Claire! Grant!" Larry's upbeat tone seemed to suggest we were unexpected.

Grant backed off a step. "Now, you *can't* be surprised. This was *your* idea."

"Not surprised—just glad you're here." He offered each of us a little hug. "You're both looking great, as usual."

"I do try," said Grant, primping. He always looked perfect for any occasion. Having noted this many times previously, I was skeptical of the claim that his sense of style had been learned. Rather, I assumed it was genetic. It was in his bones.

Though I was not nearly so fashion-conscious as my gay friend, I did look good that evening. Despite the heat, I could not resist the urge to wear a flame-red blouse of crushed silk. Dressy black slacks and a simple gold chain completed my ensemble.

Tapping the rim of his glass, Larry noted, "You've got some catching-up to do. What can I get you to drink?"

Turning to me, Grant arched a single brow. "Martini, doll?"

"Need you ask?"

"Apparently not." And he signaled the bartender, who had been listening.

A beefy bald guy in a black leather vest—and nothing underneath, save a few strategic piercings—the bartender was a real bruiser, incongruous with our chic surroundings. But despite his fearsome look, I had earlier discovered that he had mastered the knack of mixing a delicately sublime martini, shaking the daylights out of it. He suggested, "If you'd care to go to your table, I'll have these brought in for you—they're easy to spill."

"Well, we wouldn't want *that,*" I agreed with a chortle.

So Grant led us back out front, and the gaunt hostess took us into the dining room.

"Uh-oh," said Grant, "we must be unfashionably early." There was no one else in the room.

"Hardly," said the hostess with a smile in her voice. "Your timing's perfect. The summer crowds tend to be on the thin side, so we're doubly happy to have you." She seated us at a spacious round table in the center of the room, telling us, "Karissa will be right with you."

Karissa must have been waiting in the wings, listening for her cue, for she appeared the moment the hostess had left. I recognized her from an earlier visit, despite her resemblance to all the other women I'd seen working there. Impossibly thin, wearing the same nondescript black clothing, she looked like a clone from some depraved perfume ad.

But her manner was pleasant enough. "Welcome back," she told us, twisting the cap from a bottle of water and pouring for us. "Chef has no specials this evening, as the off-season can be rather unpredictable, so I'll present our usual menu after I get your drinks." And she disappeared.

For a moment, we seemed at a loss for words. There was no music in the dining room, creating an ambience I generally appreciated—all the better for conversation—but just then it seemed all too quiet. The lull was soon broken by the sound of our friend in the bar shaking a double order of martinis. "My," I said with a wistful sigh, "what a comforting racket."

Grant said to his brother, aside, "Milady's tongue is hanging out. She has a hankering for hooch."

"I don't blame her," said Larry, giving me a wink. "She had a rough day."

"Rough day?" countered Grant. "She stumbled on a corpse. Sounds fairly humdrum—for *her.*"

I admitted, "I do seem to have fallen into a disturbing pattern."

"An unfortunate chain of coincidences," Larry assured me.

Karissa appeared with a little silver tray and two enormous martinis in classic stemmed glasses, serving first me, then Grant. Then she vanished.

Larry reached to touch his glass to both Grant's and mine, which we barely lifted from the table, trying not to spill them. A thin layer of ice shavings still clung to the surface of the gin, which was so cold it was thick. Placing my lips at the edge of the glass, I drew the frigid liquid into my mouth, then swallowed with a rapturous groan.

"Uh-oh," said Grant. "I think milady might be content to *drink* her dinner."

"Now, *there's* an idea," I said through a facetious grin.

With a mock tone of warning, Larry said, "And may I ask who's driving?"

"Grant is."

"Well, then—drink up."

And I did. The three of us fell into comfortable chitchat, speaking of nothing of consequence—the weather (I learned that a hundred days of hundred-plus heat was typical), my workshop (they learned that I had decided to direct *Rebecca* that next season), and previous meals we had enjoyed at that very table.

Continuing in this amiable vein, Grant asked, "So tell me, bro—how is it you happen to be loose on a Saturday night? What are Hayley and the kids doing?"

Larry seemed unprepared for the question. "They're, uh . . . spending the weekend with her parents." Turning to me, he explained, "Her folks have a nice place near San Diego. They've got a pool. The kids love it."

"Ah."

Karissa appeared again. "Sorry to interrupt, but I thought you might want to look at menus."

As she offered the first to me, I said, "Thank you, dear, but we've decided to drink our dinner this evening."

"Oh?" she asked, blinking.

"No, just kidding, of course. Thank you." I took the menu and opened it.

"Of course, ma'am." She didn't know what to make of me.

When she left, the three of us studied the selections, which had by then grown familiar to us. The fusion-style cuisine, with its odd melding of ingredients and cultures, had once seemed outlandish, but I had come to appreciate the chef's inventiveness, and I had never been disappointed by even my most adventurous choices. No question—tonight I would have the rack of lamb with sautéed artichokes. Similarly, both Grant and Larry had no hesitation in making their choices, and before long, we had placed our orders with Karissa, who gathered the menus and again left us to converse in our private dining room.

Perhaps it was the sense of quiet intimacy, or perhaps because an obvious topic had been looming but not yet broached—whatever the reason, I could not resist asking Larry, "Do you know anything about Felicia Yeats? What happened?"

Fingering the rim of his whiskey glass, he nodded. "The medical examiner has some initial findings."

"Anything you can . . . share?"

Grant laughed. "Oh, Lord. Here we go again."

"Well"—I wriggled—"I'm naturally concerned. I met Felicia last night, and today I found her dead. You did too, Grant."

"What *I'm* still concerned about is those *curtains*—hardly up to snuff for the Regal Palms."

"Now, stop that." I patted his hand. "You're not *that* shallow."

Larry eyed me with a grin. "Isn't he?"

Grant seconded, "Listen to this man. He grew up with me."

"Be that as it may," I said, trying to refocus the discussion, "I can't help wondering about Felicia's death. Whatever the circumstances, it was clearly tragic and unexpected." Lifting my glass, I added, "Sorry if I seem nosy." Then I sipped more of the martini.

"Claire," said Larry with a soft smile, "you don't need to justify your questions about the case—not to me, not anymore. I've learned by now to trust your hunches. You seem to have a knack for this."

I felt smugly self-satisfied that Larry was validating a contention I'd previously voiced to him—and to Grant and to Kiki and to Glenn Yeats. My decades of theatrical training had equipped me with a fair share of insight regarding character, motivation, and plot, all of which were as useful in Larry's realm as in mine.

"In fact," he continued, "I'd hoped to discuss the case with you tonight, so I'm glad you brought it up."

This was a switch. During my previous brushes with the inexplicably deceased, I had felt I was wheedling my way into his confidence. Too eagerly, I asked, "How can I help?"

Grant lolled back in his chair. "Milady turns sidekick—again."

Larry came to my defense. "I can't say I mind. As sidekicks go, Claire is not only helpful, but charming."

Grant shot me a sidelong glance with arched brows.

"Specifically," Larry told me, "it's fortunate, from the standpoint of the investigation, that you were present last night when Felicia visited Glenn Yeats. We don't know yet, of course, whether there's any connection between her death and the confrontation at the cocktail party, but it's a reasonable theory and a good place to start."

From my martini, I plucked the olive on its toothpick and twirled it between my fingers. "I take that to mean you've determined Felicia didn't die by accident."

"If it was an accident, it was bizarre at best."

"What happened, Larry?" I ate the olive.

"This afternoon at the hotel, when I sniffed the gin bottle, you mentioned that Felicia had said it tasted like perfume."

"And you said it didn't smell like perfume—or gin."

"Correct. Judging by the smell, I suspected the presence of methanol, also known as methyl alcohol or wood alcohol. It's a colorless, volatile liquid with a distinct odor. You'd recognize it—it's commonly used in paint removers, varnishes, windshield washing fluid, and antifreeze. As you can probably guess, it's extremely toxic."

Sitting there at the table, I was instantly transported back to my garage, where that very afternoon I had seen most of the products just mentioned by Larry. Oralia had replenished my windshield washer, and now that I thought about it, I had indeed noticed its distinctive odor.

Larry continued, "Working on my hunch, the medical examiner has confirmed the presence of lethal levels of methanol in Felicia's body. Her blue lips and fingernails, as well as the vomiting, are consistent with methanol poisoning. Naturally, foul play is suspected. So the working premise of the investigation is now murder."

Sobered by Larry's conclusion, Grant set down his cocktail. "Good God. I just assumed, well . . . I'm not sure *what* I assumed, but antifreeze poisoning?"

"Most likely."

Karissa entered the room to ask, "Another round of drinks while you're waiting for dinner?"

"Sure," said Larry. "Bourbon, please."

Martinis had suddenly lost their luster, so Grant and I ordered wine.

When Karissa was gone, I said to Larry, "Poisoning by antifreeze— I've heard of that. It seems to pop up in the news from time to time."

The detective nodded. "Antifreeze is commonly available, and it's very effective. Ingestion of just two to eight ounces can be fatal for an adult, with symptoms developing anywhere from forty minutes to seventy-two hours after ingestion. The usual period is twelve to eighteen hours, which is consistent with Felicia's case."

Grant made a dry, sticking sound with his tongue. "Sounds ghastly."

"But remember," said Larry, "the victim *is* drunk, just as with ethanol—that is, booze. As Felicia got more and more intoxicated, she lost all judgment. Chances are, she was feeling no pain."

"Ethanol or methanol," I pondered aloud. "It's strange they should sound so similar, yet methanol is so deadly."

"They're chemically similar," Larry explained, "but methanol is deadly because of the formation of toxic metabolites when it's ingested. Specifically, methanol is metabolized to formaldehyde, which is then oxidized to the principal toxin, formic acid. When methanol is used as a poison, the trick is to mask its flavor, smell, and color. Antifreeze is typically a bright color, so victims have sometimes been duped into drinking spiked Gatorade, for instance."

"I'll make a note to avoid it in the future," said Grant, who, I was reasonably certain, had never in his life drunk Gatorade.

Before addressing the obvious implications of Felicia's nasty encounter with Glenn Yeats the night before she died, I wanted to clear up a few lingering questions. I asked Larry, "Were you able to learn anything from the 'do not disturb' sign?"

"We were. As expected, the plastic sign contained numerous fingerprints, but we were able to confirm that a couple of them were in fact Felicia's. Which means it's highly likely that she herself put the sign on the knob sometime before ten last night, and it's highly *unlikely* that anyone else entered the suite until the maid opened the door and discovered the body."

"Did you analyze the contents of the gin bottle?"

"There wasn't much in it, but it was enough to work with. Initial testing confirmed the presence of methanol. We presume it was antifreeze, but we'll need to send out a sample for detailed analysis in order to determine the specific compound."

"What about fingerprints?"

"Felicia's prints were on the bottle. There was another clean set that we haven't identified. Oddly, there wasn't much else."

"I assume you checked the suite for any other container that might have held methanol."

"Sure. Other than the gin bottle, we discovered nothing suspicious in the suite. We also checked the hotel trash from the previous night for any obvious containers, such as an antifreeze jug, but nothing turned up."

Karissa returned with our fresh drinks, distributed them, and bowed out.

Larry swirled the ice in his bourbon, took a taste, then set down his glass. "Since Felicia's death appears anything but accidental, and since she was apparently alone last night after returning to the hotel, I'm interested in learning more details about the confrontation at that party—and specifically, the sequence of events leading up to the point when Glenn Yeats sent her home with that gin bottle."

Bug-eyed, Grant asked his brother, "You mean, you suspect Glenn Yeats—of *murder*?"

"Don't jump the gun. Let's say he's at the top of my list for questioning."

Larry, Grant, and I all understood that Glenn Yeats was not only one of the community's most generous benefactors; he was also the valley's most wealthy, powerful, and "connected" resident. So this was a case that even the most justice-driven lawman would need to handle with kid gloves.

Larry took a notebook out of his breast pocket and set it on the table. Clicking a ballpoint, he said, "Tell me what you know, Claire. I'll sort it out later. And don't worry—I won't do anything stupid."

I took a deep breath, exhaling noisily. "Well, it was quite an evening."

"I'll tell the world," said Grant.

"You're welcome to jump in anytime," I assured him. "Two heads are better than one at remembering details."

Larry said to me, "I guess it's your theatrical training, but I've always been impressed by your memory for detail."

Karissa returned and, with the help of a hunky busboy, delivered our first course. I had ordered a simple salad, while the brothers Knoll had each selected hot appetizers. When Karissa and her helper left, I told my companions, "Bon appétit, boys. Please, begin."

I could easily catch up with my salad later. So while Grant and Larry began eating, I began my story. "Glenn and Felicia's marriage ended several years ago, and as part of the settlement, Felicia got a house in Santa Barbara that had been designed by the renowned architect I. T. Dirkman, who was also present last night. Because the house has considerable design significance, Felicia was restricted from selling it or substantially changing it. An architectural conservancy has gotten involved, with an expressed interest in preservation of the house. Its director, Peverell Lamonte, was at the party last night as Felicia's escort. He drove her back to the hotel, and this afternoon, we saw him there preparing to have lunch with another woman, Lark Tutwiler. Felicia was supposed to join them, but they were inexplicably stood up. That's when I got curious; then Grant, Kane, and I went to Felicia's room."

Larry looked up from the notes he was taking—while attempting to eat a crispy fritter of goat cheese and foie gras—asking, "What happened at the party?"

I detailed how Glenn had fabricated the party in hopes of softening the encounter anticipated with Felicia. Grant and I listed the names of the ten people who were present in addition to the catering staff. I attempted to reconstruct the specific conversations that transpired from the point of Felicia's arrival until her stormy departure.

Larry asked, "So Felicia's attitude was confrontational throughout?"

"From the outset," I affirmed, "and she never let up. At one point, she even reminded Glenn that she could be 'surprisingly vindictive.' Glenn showed great restraint; he was civil if, at times, cynical. His emotions got the best of him only when Felicia called him a 'prissy control freak' and threatened to burn down the Dirkman house in order to sell the land. Throughout her visit, she seemed to be egging him on, using the catchphrase 'I thought you'd never ask.' "

Larry blew a soft whistle. "Tell me everything you can about that gin bottle."

"Glenn played bartender, hoping to set a more cordial tone for the evening. He'd set up a drinks table in the living room so the liquor would be close at hand. Kiki and I were having martinis, which Glenn mixed for us and presented in oversize birdbaths of rustic Mexican cobalt glass. Spotting these, Felicia was interested in having the same. Glenn realized he was out of gin, so he left for a moment, returning with a fresh bottle—the brand in the blue bottle, same as you found in the hotel."

"Did you see him break the seal and open the bottle?"

Grant and I exchanged a wary glance. I told Larry, "I wish I could say otherwise, but no, he had already opened the bottle when he returned to the living room. He was bouncing the cap in his hand."

Larry summarized from his notes, "So Glenn poured Felicia's drink from a blue bottle, then served it in a cobalt-blue glass. Felicia, not accustomed to gin, said it tasted like perfume. She had a couple of drinks, then left in a huff, taking the bottle with her, at Glenn's suggestion." Larry looked up to ask me, "I don't suppose anyone else had a drink poured from that bottle before she took it?"

"No, Larry. Kiki and I were the only other guests drinking gin, and we'd had enough by the time Felicia arrived."

"Any other details I should know regarding the bottle?"

"In fact, there *is* one additional detail." I leaned forward in my chair, telling him, "I'm not suggesting you should make anything of this, but when Glenn gave the bottle to Felicia, he wiped it with a towel first. I assumed the bottle had gotten wet while he was mixing drinks."

Larry shook his head while adding this point to his notes.

Other patrons had arrived for dinner by then, so we could not speak as freely as before—and I did *not* want to become the rumored source of gossip that D. Glenn Yeats had murdered his ex-wife. My friendship with the man, to say nothing of my job, would be in serious jeopardy. More to the point, I simply couldn't believe that Glenn had been involved with Felicia's poisoning. Still, the circumstances were compelling. I didn't envy the investigative task that lay ahead for Larry.

Our main course arrived, allowing us to focus on food for a few minutes, rather than Felicia. We all agreed that Fusión still fully lived up to its buzz. With the arrival of more guests, the dining room grew more convivial; by the time we had finished our entrées, it was noisy enough that we could again openly discuss the evening's main topic.

Grant told Larry, "I hardly need warn you, bro—you'll be playing with fire if you decide to go after Glenn Yeats."

"*Tell* me. But I've got very little else to work with right now."

"Now, let's put everything in perspective," I told both of them—the calm voice of reason. "Even if we assume Felicia was poisoned with antifreeze, it's too early to conclude the antifreeze came from Glenn. It's available everywhere, I understand, even here in the desert."

"Correct," said Larry. "Short of finding a half-empty jug of it stowed in Glenn's liquor cabinet, I'd have a tough time proving, even circumstantially, that he switched antifreeze for gin in that blue bottle."

"What's more," I noted, "Glenn had no motive to *kill* the woman. Sure, there was bitterness between them, and Felicia had made vague threats about burning the Dirkman house, but Glenn's not the type to go off half-cocked and resort to cloak-and-dagger techniques to settle a score with his ex-wife. He'd simply assign a roomful of lawyers to handle the predicament."

Grant nodded. "That's Glenn."

"Good point," Larry allowed. "But if not Glenn, who else would harbor motives against Felicia here in the desert? I mean, she's from LA."

I posited, "Though she drove here specifically to visit Glenn last night and confront him about the house, she's spent a fair amount of time here. I know of at least three people in her local circle of friends—Peverell Lamonte, Lark Tutwiler, and another woman named Adrienne Coleman. And don't forget Felicia's son, Dustin Cory. He accompanied her on this visit, and if you ask me, there's something slippery about him. He deserves some extra scrutiny."

"Agreed," said Larry, making a list of all the names I had mentioned. He asked me for contact information on Peverell, Lark, and Adrienne.

While supplying what details I knew, I also considered that, from any objective standpoint, Paige Yeats had also harbored motives against her reviled stepmother. Paige had been at Friday night's party, and I had seen her Saturday morning at the hotel. She had carried a bulky canvas tote bag and was on her way to visit Felicia. I realized, however, that by the time of Paige's intended visit, Felicia was already dead, so I concluded that these thoughts about Paige were not worth voicing to Larry. They would only draw his suspicions back to the Yeats family, while my instincts led elsewhere.

Karissa offered dessert, and though I was tempted to indulge in the Armagnac ice cream (having discovered on previous visits that the unlikely concoction tasted much better than it sounded), we all declined, opting for espresso instead.

The demitasse looked absurdly petite in Larry's hefty hands. Sipping, then setting the cup back in its doll-size saucer, he noted, "The legal conditions surrounding the Dirkman house seemed to be the central point of contention between Glenn and Felicia. What do we know about those arrangements?"

"Everything," answered Grant. "I helped with those arrangements. I'm no lawyer, but I've had a hand in many of Glenn's real-estate dealings since he moved to Nirvana. The trust, with its covenants and restrictions, is complex, and it's been a while since I've reviewed the particulars. But I'd be happy to check my files and get back to you."

"Great," said Larry. "I'd appreciate any background I can get." Searching for a meeting time, he and Grant settled on eleven o'clock

Monday morning at the Desert Museum of Southwestern Arts, the campus museum where Kane worked and where Grant presided on the board of directors.

Stirring a cube of sugar into my coffee, gently clanging the cup with a little silver spoon, I noted offhandedly, "My Monday-morning workshop is over by eleven."

Grant laughed, telling Larry, "I knew there'd be hell to pay if I suggested we meet any earlier."

Larry turned to me. "Care to join us?"

With a coy grin, I slurped the froth from the top of my espresso. Setting down the cup, I answered, "I'll try to work it in."

Grant leaned to tell me, "You've got a mustache, doll." Then he dabbed my upper lip with his napkin.

When we stepped out of the restaurant to the sidewalk, twilight had long turned to darkness, but the heat had not yet followed the sun beyond the horizon, and the temperature still hovered near a hundred. Oddly, after a couple of hours conversing and eating, huddled in a decor dominated by chrome, leather, and glass, the hot night felt fresh and exhilarating.

"Let me get that," said Grant, taking Larry's parking stub. "It's the least I can do—you really shouldn't have popped for dinner."

"But I invited you," Larry reminded him.

I said, "Thank you, Larry. It was wonderful. Glad you suggested it."

Grant gave the tickets and some cash to the valet, then joined Larry and me at the curb. "So," he said, patting his brother's back, "what's on tomorrow's agenda? Joining the family in San Diego?"

"Nah"—he hesitated, shaking his head—"I'll spend most of the day at the department. I need to get cracking on this case. Besides . . ." But he didn't finish the thought.

Larry was often hard to read, especially compared to Grant, whose emotions were so effusive, but I sensed he'd been particularly taciturn that evening, almost evasive, whenever the conversation had drifted to his personal life.

Grant sensed this too. He asked, "Something wrong, bro?"

There was no one near us on the sidewalk. At that moment, there wasn't a car moving in the street. Standing beneath a vast, starry sky, we seemed to be alone in the universe.

With a quiet sigh and a measure of relief, Larry said, "You'll hear about this sooner or later, so it might as well be now—and from me."

This didn't sound good.

"Hayley and I are on the rocks these days. Actually, it goes back quite a while."

Grant asked, "The career thing again?"

"Yeah." Then Larry explained to me, "Hayley has never been entirely supportive of my police career—the odd hours, the perception of danger, the slim likelihood of what she calls 'real advancement in the world.'"

"Gosh, Larry, I'm sorry. I've never met your wife, but that seems rather unfair of her."

Philosophically, he noted, "We each have our own perspective. No two people share exactly the same dreams, and ours have drifted in different directions."

Grant surmised, "I don't suppose the golf-course deal helped the situation." He was referring to a promising mountainside golf-course development in which both he and Larry had invested a few months earlier. When the deal crashed, both ended up getting only pennies on the dollar. For Grant, it was win some, lose some. But for Larry, it was a serious blow to savings that had been earmarked as his kids' college funds.

"No," said Larry with a tone of weary understatement, "that little boondoggle didn't help at all. Hayley saw the financial loss as further evidence of something she's suspected for some time now."

It was none of my business. I really couldn't ask the question. But Grant could and did. "What does Hayley suspect, Larry?"

With a hapless grin, he told us, "She's beginning to think she settled for the wrong man."

PART TWO

role reversal

8

Though I was grateful Larry had felt sufficiently comfortable with me to unburden himself with disclosure of his domestic woes, the story of trouble with Hayley had ended Saturday evening on a melancholy note. Granted, we had indulged in a lengthy discussion of the poisoning and probable murder of Felicia Yeats—no upper, by any measure—but news of Larry's travails had struck me with a sadness that was far more personal. Clearly, the guy was hurting, and because he was a friend, I shared his dejection.

Neither Grant nor I talked to him on Sunday. We felt it best to let him go about his stated plan of catching up on police business at his desk. If he wanted to phone, we reasoned, he would. But he did not. So I tried not to dwell on his marital issues, focusing instead on the mystery surrounding the untimely death of Felicia Yeats.

It was all over the news on Sunday, both because the poisoning was so bizarre and because the victim was Glenn Yeats's ex. I was relieved to note that neither the papers nor the television newscasts had learned of Friday night's cocktail party, so the public had no reason to see Glenn himself in a suspicious light—at least not yet.

Monday morning, I awoke to a new week and resolved to set aside the disturbing developments of the weekend. My workshop was meeting from eight till eleven, and my students deserved my undivided attention. Crime solving would have to be back-burnered for a few hours.

Driving my short commute from home to campus, I marveled, as always, at the natural beauty that surrounded me at every turn. Even now, in the depths of summer, the ruddy mountains, the cloudless sky, the stands of ancient palms and endless rows of oleander, these everyday sights never failed to renew my spirits, as if showing me the world through fresh eyes.

Arriving at the main entrance to Desert Arts College, I was reminded as well of the genius of I. T. Dirkman, who had designed all of the buildings in this collective testimonial to mankind's loftiest aspirations. Dedicated to the arts, the campus itself was not only artistic, but art, by any measure.

I counted myself lucky indeed to play a role in this noble venture—inspiring young minds and preparing talented, eager learners to take their place in the next generation of artists—so I appreciated, once more, the commitment that had been made by D. Glenn Yeats and the unflinching faith he had shown in me. Surely this was not a man who would stoop to the base devilry of murder.

Parking in my prime spot in the faculty garage, I left the car and crossed the circular campus common, approaching my theater. The sight of its soaring lobby windows always thrilled me, instilling in me the awe of a pilgrim approaching a cathedral. Though I could have easily slipped backstage from a service door in the garage, I preferred to take the longer route and "do it right," striding toward the front of the building under an open sky, entering through the main doors, and progressing through the lobby to the auditorium and finally to the stage itself—my sanctuary, a holy of holies that never failed to inspire me, to remind me of my purpose in life.

"Morning, Miss Gray!"

"Good morning, Morgan," I shouted to one of the stage technicians who had spotted me from a catwalk as I made my way down the aisle from the rear of the auditorium.

Most of my students had already gathered onstage, where we typically began our sessions seated in a circle of folding chairs. At the sound of my voice, they all turned, acknowledging my arrival with waves and greetings.

Dropping a satchel of papers on my director's table near the front row of seats, I continued toward the stage apron and climbed the short flight of rehearsal stairs that had been positioned far right. Approaching the group, I sensed an inordinate level of energy for the early hour. When Paige Yeats and Thad Quatrain broke away from the others and rushed forward to talk to me, I understood that the buzz infecting my workshop had nothing to do with theater and everything to do with dramatic developments of a less artful, more sinister nature.

Paige gushed, "We heard all about it!"

"Unbelievable," said Thad. "I mean, we were *there*—at the hotel on Saturday—and just a little while later, *you* discovered what happened to Mrs. Yeats."

Soberly, I reminded them, "There are still a great many unanswered questions. How is your father taking the news, Paige?"

The young woman gave an indifferent shrug, a gesture that came across as decidedly adolescent. "Pops is okay with it, I guess. He didn't say much."

Saturday afternoon and all day Sunday, I had been expecting to hear from Glenn. Though I was relieved he didn't phone (I didn't want to spell out for him that the circumstances of Felicia's death had cast him in a light that was, at best, unflattering), I also found it curious that he wasn't quick either to pump me for information or to reproach me for wading into another unsavory situation that might reflect badly on the school.

I asked Paige, "When did he find out about it?"

"Not till last night. Some detective called."

Strange, I thought. How could it take over a day for Glenn to learn that his ex-wife had died? I told Paige, "But it was big news—still is."

"*I'll* say. Thad and I heard about it Saturday night, from Kane Richter, when the three of us went to that concert together. Then, after I returned to the house, I saw it on the late news."

Astonished, I asked, "And you didn't tell your father?"

She explained, "I *would* have, naturally, but he wasn't around. Pops got worried that Felicia might try something drastic with the house in Santa Barbara, so Saturday morning he called the architect, that weird Dirkman guy with the goofy glasses, and they both drove out to the coast to check on the house. He didn't get back till last night. I wasn't home—Thad and I went out for something to eat—but the detective's call was waiting for him."

Cynthia Pryor wandered over from the rest of the group. "Miss Gray? Is it true—*you* found the body? It's just like what happened during *Laura*."

Scott chimed in, "Too cool!"

Other students voiced similar expressions of enthusiasm.

Oh, Lord. The previous winter, while mounting the school's first main-stage production, *Laura,* I had indeed had the misfortune of stumbling upon the corpse of a wealthy art collector who had lent a valuable clock for the stage setting—with the unfortunate aftereffect that my cast lost their focus during the precious final week of rehearsal. When the murder was finally solved, we pulled the show together, but just barely.

"Now, listen, people," I said, clapping my hands, feeling a bit schoolmarmish, "what happened on Saturday has nothing to do with our work here today. The matter is now in the able hands of the police, and it concerns none of us. So let's get busy."

My little speech, I knew, was a patent lie. Paige's stepmother had been killed, and I had discovered the body. What's more, Paige's father, who had built not only the theater in which we stood but the entire college, had been cast in a dubious light by factors that I hoped were nothing more than circumstance. Felicia's death, therefore, was a matter of legitimate concern to all of us in general and several of us in particular, but since I was eager to *teach* my students, rather than waste time gossiping and speculating with them, I chose to ignore our obvious involvement with the case, dismissing it as a paltry detail.

."Today," I began, strolling to the center of the circle of chairs, "we'll continue our exercises in the principles of stagecraft, using the *Rebecca* script as a starting point, a source of inspiration."

"Miss Gray?" asked Cyndy Pryor as she and the other students gathered around me. "When this workshop first met, you mentioned you were considering *Rebecca* for production next fall. It seems we've been working with the script more and more. Does that mean you've made up your mind about it?"

With a soft laugh, I acknowledged, "It does. Just last Friday, I decided *Rebecca* will make a wonderful season opener for next year's bill.

Those of you who are enrolled in the DAC program can start looking at the script with an eye toward auditions."

Predictably, my announcement created a momentary stir as the students began comparing notes, wondering who might be cast in the prime roles of Maxim de Winter, Mrs. Danvers, and the never-named second Mrs. de Winter, the ingenue bride who succeeds Rebecca as lady of Manderley.

"Let's clear our minds," I told them, referring both to last weekend's murder and next fall's auditions. "Time for our usual warmups—vocalization, projection, and enunciation."

They knew the drill. Forming a line at the edge of the stage, they waited for me to descend the stairs to the auditorium floor and make my way up one of the aisles. From the back of the theater, I turned to them and began leading them through a familiar series of vocal exercises. First we sang vowel sounds, progressing from low-pitched to high-pitched, soft to loud. Then we recited some stock sentences, working on raw volume. And finally we tackled tongue-twisters, stressing exaggerated enunciation.

This regimen produced the intended effect, getting everyone, myself included, focused on the task at hand. These drills had come to signal that our time together had officially begun.

"This morning," I said, strolling down the aisle toward them, "I want you to explore the concept of role reversal."

"Oh, no . . . ," said Scott with comic trepidation. "Does that mean the guys have to play *women* again?"

"No, Scott. You got your kicks last time. Today I'm going to assign two scenes from the *Rebecca* script, dividing the group in half. Working with your assigned scene, you're to study it as scripted and then, as you did last Friday, prepare an improvised version of the scene in which you speak only the imagined subtext."

"Sure, Miss Gray," said someone, "but where's the role reversal?"

"After you've all finished," I explained, "the two groups will switch scenes, with everyone playing a different role."

"Okay, got it," said Scott. The others nodded that they understood as well. Whether they also understood that auditions for the fall production had now begun, I could not say.

"Please take a look at your scripts," I told them as I moved to the director's table and pulled my own script from the satchel I'd placed there. Having dog-eared two pages, I told everyone, "First, take a look at page thirty, beginning with Frith the butler's line, 'Excuse me, sir, can I speak with you a moment?' This is the scene in which it's discovered that the young Mrs. de Winter has broken a valuable china cupid and hidden the pieces. *Improvising* this scene, I want Scott to play Frith, Cyndy to play Mrs. Danvers, Thad to play Maxim de Winter, and Paige to play his young bride."

The four named actors found their places in the script and retreated to a quiet area backstage where they could prepare their scene.

Thumbing to the back of the script, I told the others, "Turn to the bottom of page sixty-seven, please, where Mrs. Danvers asks Maxim, 'You wish to see me, sir?' This is the scene near the end of the play in which Rebecca's ne'er-do-well cousin, Jack Favell, attempts to blackmail Maxim." When my students found the spot, I assigned the roles of Jack, Maxim, Mrs. Danvers, and Mrs. de Winter. "Nick," I said, addressing the youngest student in the group, "since there are five roles in this scene instead of four, I'd like you to take the role of Colonel Julyan with both groups."

These five students then went to work in another area backstage, well removed from the other four.

As they would need a few minutes to prepare their scenes, I sat at the director's table and emptied the remaining papers from my bag. Organizing my notes for the rest of the week's classes, I was soon immersed in my planning.

But my thoughts were nipped with a jolt when one of the backstage doors opened, admitting a blast of sunlight, then closed again with a reverberating thud. Hurried footfalls clomped from the left wing, accompanied by the jangle of armloads of bracelets. "Claire, darling!" said Kiki, appearing onstage, "may I interrupt for a minute?"

"You already have," I noted sweetly.

"Sorry, love," she said, pecking her way down the stairs and beelining for my table, "but I just *had* to touch base with you before heading over to Glenn's office."

I patted the seat next to mine. "What's up?"

"Well," she said, flumping into the crimson cushions, "you've done it again."

"I admit, it's become something of a disturbing pattern."

"Have you talked to Glenn about it?"

"No, and I suppose I can't put it off much longer. I have an eleven o'clock meeting with Grant and Larry at the museum; I thought I'd pay Glenn a visit after that. Did you say you were headed for his office?"

"My *dear*," said Kiki, flopping a hand to her bosom, "it was positively *untimely*, his phone call on Saturday morning. There I was, lolling in bed with Irwin, and—"

"Who?"

"Irwin—I. T. Dirkman—you know, the architect."

"Yes, Kiki, I know him quite well. At least I thought I did."

"It's seems we hit it off on Friday night, or perhaps it was the liquor—"

"Surely the booze," I agreed.

"And, well, nature took its course, and we ended up at *my* place." She leaned near, confiding, "He's not much in the sack, and it *won't* happen again, but I suppose the experience gives me a certain amount of bragging rights."

"I suppose."

"And then *Glenn* called."

"What did he want?"

"Irwin. He called I. T.'s cell phone, wanting to rush right over to Santa Barbara. Glenn picked him up fifteen minutes later. When I saw them off at the curb, Glenn mentioned he needed to see me this morning—wardrobe issues."

"Good Lord, Kiki. What *have* you gotten yourself into?"

"It seems my comment at Friday's party struck a resonant chord. Unless I'm mistaken, he wants me to help *dress* him."

"Either that or he feels the theater needs a new wardrobe mistress."

Kiki's fingers shot to her lips. She mumbled, "I hadn't thought of that."

Though I found it doubtful that Glenn entertained notions of replacing Kiki, I enjoyed making her squirm. What are friends for? I reminded her, "Only one way to find out—and it's best not to keep him waiting."

"You're right, love. I need to dash." She pecked my cheek, rose from her seat, gathered her things, and shot up the aisle. The jangling stopped when the lobby doors closed behind her.

Shuffling my papers on the table, I called backstage, "Are we ready?"

Both groups appeared from the shadows. "Ready as we'll ever be," said someone. "Who goes first?" asked someone else.

"Uh"—I thought for a moment—"let's do the blackmail scene."

So the five actors arranged a few chairs onstage while the other four moved aside to watch.

I inserted a fresh legal pad in my clipboard and gathered a few pencils. When all was quiet, I told them, "Whenever you're ready."

The girl playing Mrs. Danvers gave the opening line to Maxim: "You wish to see me, sir?"

I reminded her, "Subtext only, please."

She nodded, rephrasing, "What the devil does my lord and master want now?"

"Good," I interjected.

And they were off and running.

I listened intently for a few minutes, enjoying their efforts as well as the humor that invariably arose from the subtext. I made a few notes, but then set down my pencil as my attention began to drift from the stage. I hoped they didn't sense it, but these five students constituted my "B group." While all of them were enthusiastic and dedicated, I knew from experience that none had the raw potential for likely success in building a career in acting. They would receive the best possible training while entrusted to my tutelage, but realistically, there was only so much I could do.

My assessment was not intentionally harsh. I thought of everyone in my program as a friend, as someone who shared a deep passion and respect for theater, someone whose future mattered to me. But no one's best interest would be served by overconfidence in goals that could simply not be attained. At some point, I knew, each of my students would take me aside and ask for an honest appraisal of his or her chances. Then, when bluntness was sought, I would give it. For now, we could enjoy together the exploration and the dream.

When I heard a round of applause from the other students, my A group, the ones with greatest potential, I realized the B group had finished their scene.

Snapping out of my thoughts, I said, "Very nice. Well done, everyone. Are you beginning to understand how subtext—of our own invention—can provide deeper insight into the meaning of the written script? Now let's give the others a chance. Let's see what they can do with the broken-cupid scene."

So Thad, Paige, Scott, and Cyndy took the stage, rearranging a few chairs while the other students moved off to watch. With the exception of Paige, all of my A group would be enrolled with me again for the fall semester, and I had little doubt they would each win a prized role in our production of *Rebecca*. Readying my notepad, I asked, "Shall we begin?"

Portraying Frith, the butler, Scott asked Thad, portraying Maxim, "Excuse me, sir, can I speak to you a moment?" Then, snapping his fingers, Frith rephrased, "Sorry to bother you, but you're not gonna *believe* what just happened."

Maxim planted a hand on his hip. "How many times have I told you, Frith? It's not 'gonna,' but 'going to.' Don't be so hopelessly middle-clahhs. We're the de Winters; this is Manderley. We have *standards,* for God's sake."

"Yes, sir. Sorry, sir. But it's Mrs. Danvers—she's on a rampage again."

Paige, portraying the young Mrs. de Winter, piped in, *"Again?"*

"Yes, madam. It seems one of the servants has broken one of the household treasures—a priceless cupid figurine."

"Oops." Mrs. de Winter turned away, biting a nail.

"Worse yet," said Frith, "the scalawag didn't own up to it, but hid the broken pieces in a desk drawer, wrapped in paper."

"Outrageous!" bellowed Maxim.

"Yes," echoed Mrs. de Winter, "outrageous!" Then, with a sugary voice, she added, "Would you excuse me, Maxim, dear? I really must run along now—I have menus to plan, flowers to arrange, and all manner of assorted whatnot to attend to." She started to move off-stage.

But she was cut short by the entrance of Mrs. Danvers, portrayed by Cyndy. With crossed arms and stern features, she asked, "Running along, madam? Why the rush? *Hiding something?* Hmm?"

"I'm sure I don't know what you mean."

Mrs. Danvers mimicked her mistress in a snide, childish voice: "I'm sure I don't know what you mean."

Maxim stepped in. "Now, see here, Mrs. Danvers. I don't appreciate your taking that tone with my beautiful, if somewhat naive, young bride."

Mrs. de Winter threw her arms around her husband. "Oh, *thank* you, darling! I love you ever so much."

Mrs. Danvers told him, "I'm sorry, sir. But unless I'm mistaken, Mrs. de Winter has some explaining to do."

And the scene played on, a delightful re-creation of one of the most memorable encounters in the script. I joined my students (the other five) in laughing openly at the comic melodrama that emerged from the spoken subtext.

I also noted on my clipboard that Thad and Paige made an attractive, believable couple as Mr. and Mrs. de Winter, though Thad simply looked too young for the role that everyone associated with Laurence Olivier in the Hitchcock film; I would face this challenge when casting any college actor in the role. As the scene ended, I joined the others in hearty applause.

"Most impressive," I told everyone. "I didn't take many notes. There was really no need, as I think you've already learned the lessons of this exercise. Next: role reversal. Let's take a short break; then each group will work with the other scene."

After I assigned their specific roles, some of the students wandered off to visit vending machines or washrooms. Others hunkered over their scripts, preparing their new roles. Thad, always the most earnest of the group, came down from the stage to spend a few minutes with me; Paige followed him.

"It'll be a great show," Thad told me. "Do you know the production dates yet?"

I eyed him askance. "Not thinking of leaving town, are you?"

He laughed. "*No,* Miss Gray. I just want to make sure Mark and Neil have the dates. They'll want to be here." He was referring to his "two dads" in Wisconsin.

I gave him the dates, then said to Paige, "If you're not too busy in LA, you should plan to come see the show."

"I'd like that," she said, sounding wistful. "Actually, I'd like to be *in* it, but—you know, other plans."

"I know." I assumed Paige's mild despondency was rooted in the events of the past weekend, so I added, "It was troubling, to say the least. Try as I may to focus elsewhere, my thoughts keep coming back to it."

Paige's brow wrinkled. "Back to what?"

"Well, Felicia's death, of course."

"Ohhh . . . that. Sure, Miss Gray."

"When I saw you at the hotel on Saturday, you said you were hoping to get some details of what went wrong between Felicia and your father. It sounded as if you were open to a rapprochement with the woman."

Paige considered this for a moment. "I'm not sure what I expected. Point is, it never happened."

Thad shook his head. "Poisoned—with *antifreeze.* How awful. I mean, how could you trick someone into drinking the stuff?"

I explained, "Detective Knoll said that in some poisonings, the antifreeze is masked in a colorful beverage, like Gatorade."

"Yech."

"In any event," I told Paige, "I'm sorry you didn't get to talk to Felicia that morning—woman to woman."

"At least I tried. I went to her room, but she didn't seem to be in. No one answered the door—guess we know why."

"Was the 'do not disturb' sign on the knob?"

"It was. But she'd invited me, so I knocked anyway, several times. I wasn't up there more than a minute or two; then Thad and I left the hotel."

Thad shot her a skeptical look. "I was waiting for you longer than *that.*"

"Whatever." She gave his arm a playful slap.

He told her, "Come on. Let's work on our next scene."

Then they excused themselves, joining Scott and Cyndy to confab offstage.

Within a few minutes, everyone was ready to begin again. I announced, "We'll do the blackmail scene first. Places, everyone."

Thad, Paige, Scott, and Cyndy arranged the stage, joined by young Nick, who would repeat the role of Colonel Julyan. The others settled around to watch. I shuffled my notes, prompting the group, "Whenever you're ready . . ."

Mrs. Danvers, portrayed by Paige, said to Maxim, portrayed by Scott, "It's been a rough day and a hellish night, but I am at your service, as always. What can I do for you, Mr. de Winter?"

Maxim told her, "Your old friend is showing his true colors again. I warned you before—Jack Favell is *never* welcome here at Manderley, yet here he is, making the most ridiculous demands."

Through pinched features, Mrs. Danvers said, "I'm sure I don't know what you mean, sir."

Jack Favell, portrayed by Thad, told her, "Ya see, Danny, it's like this. There seem to be some serious questions about the circumstances of my dear cousin's death, and I think Maxim is responsible for more than he'd like us to know. Even while Rebecca was still alive, Maxim never liked me, and now he expects me to keep quiet. Fat chance. Unless . . ."

Colonel Julyan said, "Favell, mind your tongue. You've had other brushes with the law. Do you think I'm deaf to your veiled threats of blackmail?"

Jack assured him, "Nothing 'veiled' about it, old man."

An anguished young Mrs. de Winter, portrayed by Cyndy, said to her husband, "Maxim, dear, whatever are they talking about? The threats, the implications—we all know how Rebecca died. The inquest proved it."

"*Did* it?" snarled Mrs. Danvers. "You're fools, the whole lot of you. *None* of you really knew Rebecca, not at all, not the way her dear, dear Danny did. She was perfect—*perfect!* And here you are, bickering over something so trivial as blackmail. She's laughing in her watery grave, Rebecca is. And she'll laugh all the louder when she sees you scamper from the flames like frightened, pathetic mice."

"I say, Danny, that's tellin' 'em." Jack turned to Maxim. "Now, then, in the mood to negotiate?"

As the scene played on, I took numerous notes, but two of them I circled.

First, Thad was a natural as the glib Jack Favell, who could be played younger than Maxim. Come fall, I wouldn't need to think twice about casting Thad in this sleazy, slippery role.

Second, Paige was magnificent as Mrs. Danvers, but unfortunately, she would not be available for DAC's production, as she would be returning to school in Los Angeles.

Two additional observations struck me, but I did not commit them to paper.

First, watching Thad as Jack, Rebecca's cousin and secret lover, I couldn't help thinking of Dustin Cory, Felicia Yeats's playboy son.

Second, watching Paige as the psychotic Mrs. Danvers, I couldn't help recalling Felicia's threat to burn the Dirkman house.

9

A few minutes before eleven, I dismissed my class, reminding the students that our workshop would meet again as usual on Wednesday. I asked them to reread the entire *Rebecca* script before then, as we would continue to use it as the basis for our next workshop project.

Gathering my things, I left the theater through the lobby and emerged into the full midday sun that glared from the limestone paving of College Circle. The vast plaza was empty at that hour. Even the lush landscaping, with its fountains and palms, was unable to lure students or faculty out for a stroll in the rising summer heat. I alone crossed this man-made oasis of stone and trickling water, surrounded by the dramatic shapes of campus buildings and the craggy silhouettes of mountains beyond.

A roadrunner darted in front of me, skittering across the pavement and jumping up to the seat of a bench. From that vantage point, it cocked its head, surveying the whole plaza but keeping a wary eye fixed on me. I laughed. When I had first arrived from New York, each time I saw a roadrunner, I reacted as if I had spotted a unicorn. Now I barely noticed the outlandish creatures, which had become a common feature of my adopted surroundings.

Straight ahead rose the facade of the Desert Museum of Southwestern Arts, newest of the campus buildings, dedicated the previous December. Like my theater, it was designed by I. T. Dirkman, but the two buildings were inspired by complementary aesthetics. While the style of the theater was fanciful and lyrical, the museum was simple and austere, a neutral canvas that neither embellished nor detracted from the art displayed within.

Opening one of the glass doors to the museum lobby, I was assaulted by a blast of frigid air as the day's heat blazed at my back. I felt like a leaf caught between two immense and opposing climatic forces, sucked into a vortex I was powerless to resist. When the door closed behind me, the galactic battle ended as abruptly as it had begun, leaving a crop of goose bumps on my bare arms. The lobby was as deserted as the plaza had been—a broiling Monday morning in July held little allure for the art-starved, I reasoned—so my lonely footfalls reverberated from the polished floor as I made my way from the front doors, passing the main galleries, and continuing back to the office area.

"Good morning, Claire," said Iesha Birch, the museum director, who was stepping from her office and into the hall. An exotic woman (the word *arty* sprang to mind) in both features and dress, she had an ageless face and straight dark hair pulled back in a giant knot. Her garb that day was a smock and pants of crude, rumpled muslin sporting fluorescent-colored embroidery at the wrists and ankles. A primitive breastplate of hammered tin hung from her neck like a gong. Her feet shuffled toward me on a pair of Tibetan leather sandals with straps so thin they disappeared in the cracks between her toes.

Meeting midway in the hall, we paused to extend hands and hook fingers, not quite formalizing the greeting with a shake.

"You're looking for Grant," she said. Though the statement was true, it struck me as odd in its delivery, neither offering guidance nor asking whether I needed it.

"I am," I replied, sounding equally oblique. "I'm meeting both Grant and his brother, Larry—have they arrived?"

Shaking her head in the negative, she said, "Grant's here, in the conference room with Kane." I took this to mean that Larry was still expected.

"Thank you, Iesha." I moved onward to the room at the end of the hall. Behind me, Iesha's sandals slapped the floor as she made her way toward the lobby.

"Hey, doll!" said Grant, rising from his seat at the conference table as I entered the room.

Kane seconded, "Hi, Claire. Welcome to my domain."

Grant cuffed his young partner's shock of tawny blond hair, telling me, "Listen to the kid—he lands an assistantship in the museum's publicity office, and he sounds like he owns the place."

"Good morning, guys," I said warmly, giving each a hug. On the white wall behind them was hung an overscale oil painting depicting the rape of the Sabine women. In its ornate, gilded frame, the yellowing masterpiece was almost shockingly incongruous with the museum's aesthetic mission to preserve and promote southwestern arts. Inherited as part of a windfall from a prominent local collector, the painting—along with several others of its period—had been relegated to decorating the building's austere offices. I asked, "Am I early?"

"Nope," said Grant, tapping his watch, "right on the button. But Larry is running a few minutes late, so Kane and I decided to catch up on some lingering business." Spread out on the table was a mishmash of paperwork.

With a comical sigh, Kane explained, "Wedding plans."

I offered, "Well, don't let me interrupt. I can wait out front."

"Nonsense." Grant pulled out a chair for me. "Milady is always welcome, even when discussing the most intimate minutiae of our private lives."

"Now, *there's* an offer I can hardly refuse." I sat, joining them at the table.

"Sorry," said Kane, "but Grant's exaggerating."

"Moi?"

Kane ignored Grant's theatrical protest, telling me, "We were just going over the guest list—again."

"Ah. No surprises, I hope."

"Nothing we can't handle," said Grant. I'd ceased trying to interpret his various grins, smirks, and double entendres—they were a language known only to himself.

Kane struck a line through the list. "So I guess my parents won't be there. It's not as if they weren't invited; we made every effort."

"We did." Grant squeezed Kane's arm. "At least your sister's coming."

Kane nodded. "Sure, Alyssa will be here. She has no problem with it."

I ventured to ask, "There's a problem with your parents?"

"They're up in Oregon. It's a long haul."

But it's your *wedding,* I felt like saying.

Picking up on my concern, Grant amplified, "Kane's mom and dad are fine with the gay thing. He came out to them before he moved to California. It's the commitment ceremony they can't quite accept."

"But why?" I asked, mystified. "I'd think they'd be delighted he's found the happiness and security of a committed relationship. What's the hang-up—religion?"

Kane flashed Grant a smile while telling me, "Uh, no, they're both pretty open-minded that way."

Grant added, "The hang-up is age—specifically, mine."

"Ahhh." I knew from previous discussions with Grant that there was a good possibility he was older than either of Kane's parents.

Grant continued, "I'm sure they must think of me in the worst possible light. In their view, I'm some lecherous old chicken hawk preying on their little boy."

Kane grinned. "Once they meet you, they'll know better."

"Hope so. We'll have to make a point of paying them a weekend visit sometime soon."

"Whenever you feel up to it."

Larry Knoll stepped in from the hall. "Sorry to keep everyone waiting—running a little late today."

"*Really,* bro," Grant said with a sniff. "Our time is precious."

I eyed him askance. "Since when have *you* punched a clock?"

"It was just a figure of speech," he assured me as we all stood, greeting Larry with a round of hugs.

Kane gathered his papers and closed his file, telling us, "I'll give you guys some privacy. I need to get busy at my desk. Besides, murder's just not my thing."

"Yeah," said Grant, whirling a hand blithely, "it's such a downer.

Think of Felicia last Saturday—now, *that's* what I call 'having a bad day.' "

"Let's show a little respect," I reminded him, "if not for the woman herself—we barely knew her—at least for the tragic circumstances."

"Sorry, doll, just trying to inject a humorous note. But I know— I really should learn to lay off the wisecracks."

"Yes," said Kane, kissing Grant's cheek, "you really should." Then he moved to the doorway, wishing us a productive meeting. Stepping out, he closed the door behind him.

As the three of us settled around the table, I asked Larry, "Busy morning?"

With a soft laugh, he answered, "For the dead of summer, the week's off to a brisk start. I paid a visit to Glenn Yeats in his office— that's why I'm late."

My eyes widened with interest. "And . . . ?"

"First things first." Larry pulled the pen and notebook from his inside breast pocket, asking Grant, "Were you able to review the covenants regarding the Dirkman house?"

"As promised," said Grant, pulling a folder from his briefcase and opening it on the table. "I had duplicates of everything, filed with Glenn's other real-estate documents in the Nirvana sales office." He tapped the papers in front of him. "It was an unusual arrangement, but at the time of the divorce, it seemed to keep everyone happy."

I recalled my housekeeper's observation that Felicia had not been a happy woman. "If she was happy with the settlement," I noted, "it didn't last."

"That's for sure," said Grant. "She was hell on wheels Friday night."

My eyes drifted to the painting behind him. The plump Sabine beauties wore frozen expressions of overwrought horror—and nothing else—as armor-clad warriors plucked them up and carried them off on rearing, snarling steeds. They were having a bad day, the Sabines, but unlike Felicia, they were not entirely unhappy about it, as revealed by the glint in their eyes, trained upon the oily physiques of their muscular abductors.

Larry cleared his throat. "The covenants?" he asked, reminding us of our purpose that morning.

Grant summarized, "Felicia owned the house and had use of it for life, but she was restricted from selling it or making substantial changes to it. We've already covered that, but I wasn't sure of the rest. I think you'll find this of interest." He paused for dramatic effect.

"Well?" I asked, sounding too eager.

Larry gently prompted, "I'm listening, Grant."

"Upon Felicia's death, the restrictions are lifted. The house will now pass, unencumbered, to Felicia's designated heir."

Larry and I looked at each other with arched brows. "Unless I'm mistaken," I said, "that means the house now belongs to Dustin Cory."

Larry noted, "The victim had no other children, so that's a reasonable assumption. I don't know if the terms of her will have been revealed yet, but if not, I imagine it won't take long."

"Dustin will see to that," I thought aloud.

Larry told his brother, "Thanks for digging up the details, but it turns out, it wasn't necessary. When I met with Glenn Yeats this morning, he gave me the same information."

Grant rolled his eyes. "And who do you think enlightened *him*? After you phoned him last night, he phoned *me*. He was at the house in Nirvana with Dirkman, and they were both in such a lather, I drove right up there."

I asked, "How did Glenn react to the news about Felicia?"

Grant chose his words carefully. "He was surprised, but far from grieving, and I can't say I blame him. I mean, we met Felicia. She was a real pisser."

Larry fingered his chin. "Not upset, eh?" He jotted something in his notes, which I assumed did not reflect well on Glenn.

In Glenn's defense, I suggested, "People react to sudden loss differently. You've told me that yourself, Larry. We can't assume Glenn feels no distress over Felicia's death just because he wasn't overtly upset."

"Oh, Glenn was *plenty* upset," Grant assured us.

"See?" I gave Larry a sharp nod, crossing my arms.

"Uh-uh-uh," clucked Grant. "Glenn wasn't upset about Felicia. He was upset about the covenants. He'd forgotten that the restrictions on the Dirkman house would be lifted upon Felicia's death, with ownership passing to other hands. Both he and Dirkman lamented—quite emotionally, I might add—that the house is no longer 'protected.' They were downright bitter and almost comically fearful that it would be razed and sold for the land. Talk about a couple of sob sisters . . ."

Larry wondered aloud, "Is it just a consequence of his accumulated wealth, or was Glenn Yeats always so coldhearted?" Larry underlined something in his notes.

"Now, hold on," I told him. "You weren't inside Glenn's *mind* last night, and neither was Grant. We have no knowledge of his personal history with Felicia, and we're in no position to judge his emotional priorities. In fact, if we take his cool reaction to Felicia's death at face value, he appears *less* suspicious, not more so."

Grant's eyes slid toward Larry. "I tried to warn you, bro. Milady's theatrical perspective on criminology can be a tad offbeat."

Larry suppressed a smile, asking, "Exactly why, Claire, does Glenn's cool attitude make him less suspicious?"

"Because"—I flipped my palms—"Glenn's passionate concern to preserve the Dirkman house, considered by many to be a work of art, should in itself be sufficient to clear him of suspicion of complicity in Felicia's death. The house remained *protected* only during Felicia's life-time."

"But"—Grant raised a finger—"Glenn had forgotten that detail of the covenants. If not, he was doing a damn good acting job last night when I reminded him of the facts."

Curses, I thought. "Still, his driving passion—his motive, if we must use that word—was protection and preservation of the house, not some deep-set, hell-bent scheme to rid the world of his ex-wife." With a sputter of laughter, I added, "With antifreeze, no less—it's preposterous."

Larry reminded me, "*Somebody* didn't find it so preposterous. Tricking Felicia into drinking antifreeze was no practical joke; it was murder."

"Apparently," I allowed, "but all my instincts point away from Glenn."

"And all the circumstantial evidence points directly toward him. This case isn't open-and-shut, far from it, but objectively, Glenn is the most promising suspect—with motive, means, and opportunity."

"He *didn't* have a motive," I repeated. "He wanted to protect the Dirkman house, and now that Felicia is dead, anything goes."

Larry turned to an earlier page of his notes. "But Felicia made an implied threat that she would *burn* the house. For anyone passionate about its preservation, that would provide a clear motive for immediate action. We've barely scratched the surface of all this, but I can't help feeling that the whole landmark hoo-ha could be a clever fabrication on Glenn's part to cover some deeper motive against Felicia. For starters, I'm curious to learn more about the other terms of their divorce, which made headlines with its titanic settlement."

I insisted, "Glenn's not 'about' money."

"Funny," said Larry, "I thought Glenn Yeats was *all* about money—he's one of the richest men in the country."

Grant seconded, "He's right, doll."

"Look how much Glenn has *given,*" I said, making a gesture that encompassed the meeting room, the museum, and the campus beyond.

Larry nodded. "Philanthropy is a wonderful thing. And when it comes to giving, few are so generous as Glenn Yeats. But remember, such gifts are *his* decision, *his* to bestow. The settlement with Felicia was *not*—she took him to the cleaners and very likely bruised a huge ego unaccustomed to losing. Who knows what sort of lingering resentments Glenn may have felt?"

Though I didn't voice it, I had to admit, at least to myself, that Larry had raised a compelling and unflattering point—Glenn's control issues.

"What's more," said Larry, "when I visited his office this morning, Glenn sure didn't *act* innocent. The guy is normally self-confident to the point of being smug, but he was shaken and defensive when I informed him that the circumstances of Felicia's death had cast him under suspicion."

"Who wouldn't be?" I muttered.

Larry sat back in his chair. "Look, I'm anything but eager to take on Glenn Yeats—and all he stands for—in a murder case. But I'm sworn to follow the evidence wherever it leads, so I need his cooperation if he hopes to be exonerated. Claire, you seem to have a way with him, and—"

"A *way* with him?" piped in Grant. "Milady has the doting billionaire wrapped around her little finger. Or is it her *ring* finger?"

Shushing Grant, I told Larry, "Yes, I have Glenn's ear, but when it comes to police matters, he's always insisted that I keep my distance. I doubt I could be persuasive in influencing his cooperation with your investigation, one way or the other. He has legions of lawyers on staff for the express purpose of building an impregnable wall of protocol between him and even the slightest whiff of trouble."

"Still," said Larry, "I hope you'll try. If you could solicit Glenn's direct, personal cooperation in getting to the bottom of this, both he—*and I*—may be much more pleased with the ultimate resolution of the case."

Perhaps I was feeling more flattered than sensible when I replied without hesitation, "Sure, Larry, I'll try."

"Uh-oh," said Grant, leaning toward his brother. "There'll be no stopping her now. Your sidekick has a tendency to get carried away."

Carried away in the literal sense, I noticed, was one of the Sabine women, whose demure kicks of protest proved futile as she was hoisted by one of the warriors onto the rump of his stallion. Her blushed white skin formed a virginal, amoebic blob against the glistening expanse of black horseflesh.

Larry said, "Let's review, Claire. If your instincts lead away from Glenn Yeats, let's discuss the motives of other possible suspects."

"Dustin Cory" popped from my lips. "Sure, he's the victim's only child, so we can presume he's the most bereaved. At the same time, we presume he's Felicia's sole heir, and unless I'm mistaken, she's worth considerably more than the Dirkman house. Inheritance is always a tempting motive."

"Agreed," said Larry. "When the terms of Felicia's will are made public, I'll know if anyone besides Dustin warrants scrutiny. Other than inheritance issues, what other motives could relate to Felicia's death?"

"The house in Santa Barbara was at the center of the conflict that was roiling when she died, so the house may well have played a role in what happened. Yes, if we follow that reasoning, the circumstantial evidence points strongly to Glenn, but remember, he wasn't the only one with an interest in the disputed house. Both I. T. Dirkman, the architect, and Peverell Lamonte, director of the Southern California Conservancy, were passionately committed to preserving the house. And Peverell, by the way, was the last person known to see Felicia alive. He drove her—*and* the gin bottle—back to the hotel from Glenn's party."

"I talked to him by phone yesterday," said Larry. "His story was consistent with what you've already told me, and he agreed to supply fingerprints, saying they should match the second set on the bottle—he carried it from the car for Felicia, fearing she would drop it. Like Glenn, Peverell reacted to Felicia's death with surprise, but with deeper concern for the future of the house. Logistically, of course, he would have had the opportunity to switch the contents of the gin bottle—if Glenn or someone else had not already done so. I'll be following up with him."

With a nod, I said, "And that brings us to Lark Tutwiler, the woman Grant and I met at lunch on Saturday. She was a friend of both Peverell and Felicia, having introduced them. She groused about having been stood up by Felicia, but otherwise, I have no reason to find Lark suspicious. It's just that, well, I hate to say it, but I got an uneasy vibe from the woman."

"*Not* very scientific," said Grant in a tone of mock disapproval.

"Maybe not," said Larry, "but don't underrate instinct. Any number of high-profile cases have been cracked by investigative vibes."

I had also been having uneasy vibes about Paige Yeats's visit to the hotel on Saturday, and I felt it was time to mention this to Larry, if only to raise the issue and then dismiss it.

But before I could voice this lingering concern, Larry continued, "I reached Lark Tutwiler on the phone yesterday, and we talked quite a while. Turns out she and Felicia haven't known each other all that long, maybe a year or so. They met on the charity circuit in Los Angeles and have visited back and forth."

Grant asked, "How did Lark react to the news of Felicia's death?"

"She'd heard about it by the time I called, so the shock, if there was any, had already worn off. She expressed sympathies for her friend, but with little emotion. What upset her most was the 'rising tide of crime in Rancho Mirage.' I assured her that while Felicia's death was highly regrettable, it was also a bizarre, isolated instance that did *not* signal the onset of a murder spree."

"Let's hope not," I mumbled, recalling each of the four corpses I'd encountered in less than a year.

Larry added, "Lark and Felicia, having both divorced rich husbands, were not only friends, but also occasional travel companions. Most recently, they spent a week at an exclusive spa called Los Pinos. It's near Idyllwild, the artsy community located up in the mountains just beyond the Coachella Valley. Lark reported that Felicia, uncharacteristically, spent much of that time by herself, raising Lark's suspicions that she was there for a romantic tryst with someone."

"How delicious," cooed Grant. "The plot thickens."

I nodded. "Exactly what I was thinking."

Larry closed his notebook and returned it to his pocket. "It's an intriguing angle, I admit, and a direction worth investigating. So I plan to drive up to the spa tomorrow morning, have a look around, and try talking to a few people."

"A secret lover," Grant thought aloud. "A deadly game of lust gone awry."

I told Larry, aside, "And he accuses *me* of being overly theatrical."

Larry stood. "Even if Felicia did visit a secret lover at Los Pinos, I can't imagine how that person would have any connection to the antifreeze in Glenn Yeats's gin bottle. Still, there's a lot at stake, so I'm trying to keep my mind open to *any* possibility. Claire? Can I count on you to have a word with Glenn?"

I stood, checking my watch. "I'll pop in on him right now. I ought to be able to catch him before lunch."

Grant rose as well. "I hardly think he'll be dashing out to McDonald's."

"I *meant*"—I grinned—"I wouldn't want to interrupt whatever plans he may have."

"Speaking of lunch," said Grant, "anyone care to join us? Kane and I thought we'd pop down to the corner."

I reminded him, "I'm going to see Glenn. Thanks, though."

Larry said, "Sorry, Grant. I need to run—other plans, down valley."

As the three of us gathered our things from the table and began moving toward the door, I hesitated. "Larry?"

"Hmm?"

"About tomorrow morning. My workshop doesn't meet on Tuesday, and the drive might give us a chance to catch up on any—"

With a chuckle, he told me, "I *wondered* how long it would take you to ask."

Under his breath, Grant said, "*I* didn't."

Larry asked me, "Did you think it was coincidence that I scheduled the visit on one of your nonteaching days? I *am* a detective, you know."

"Then you don't mind if I tag along?"

"You needn't even ask, Claire." He paused before adding, "Truth is, I've come to enjoy your company."

Grant studied his brother for a moment, then turned to me, bug-eyed.

On the wall behind him, one of the Sabines wore the same expression as an invading warrior hurled her to the ground at his feet.

Honest to God, she was looking up his tunic.

10

Walking across College Circle from the museum, I didn't even notice the heat. I wasn't pondering the metamorphosis of unicorns into roadrunners. Rather, I was weighing Larry Knoll's casual declaration, "I've come to enjoy your company." Not a loquacious sort, Larry wasn't prone to speak in riddles or metaphors; he spoke his mind plainly. Was I imagining things, or had he just expressed an interest in me that went beyond crime solving?

Entering the administration building, my thoughts were nipped by a blast of arctic air that bested even that in the frosty confines of the museum. I had often wondered whether Glenn Yeats suffered from an abnormally high metabolism, burning off calories so fast that he felt perpetually fevered. It was a reasonable explanation for the bone-chilling aura that always emanated from his suite of offices, permeating the entire building.

The administrative hallways reflected a design motif I. T. Dirkman had imposed upon the entire campus—circularity. While the plan was sensational on paper, sending breathless critics scrambling for their thesauri in search of higher and higher accolades, in reality the curving halls were disorienting and counterintuitive. It had taken me weeks to find my own office without retracing my steps, a futile exercise that had imbued me with a deep appreciation for the age-old tradition of designing buildings on a grid.

Rounding another hall, approaching the very epicenter of campus—in both the literal and figurative senses—I saw the twin mahogany doors that protected the lair of our school's founder and president. Stepping near, I grasped one of the knobs, opened the door, and braced myself for the colder air within.

The waiting room, with its deep carpeting, luxe appointments, and art-adorned walls (*real* art—pedigreed paintings by masters known to all), was vacant, as usual, on that late Monday morning. I always found it strange that D. Glenn Yeats, a man of enormous wealth and influence, didn't have scores of suppliants waiting in his outer office, begging for but a few precious seconds of his time. Wryly, I decided there was no shortage of would-be callers; they had simply never made it to Glenn's office, lost forever in the circular maze of hallways. Some, I feared, had frozen in their tracks, buried in the permafrost, never to be found.

"*Ms. Gray,*" gasped Tide Arden as I entered. Striding out from behind her desk, she looked distraught and fidgety, not at all her usual efficient, pulled-together self. "I was *so* hoping to see you. You've got to *help* him, Ms. Gray."

"Help Glenn?" I asked, baffled not only by her urgent tone, but also by her long, bare dark legs and arms, which showed no sign of goose bumps. In her miniskirt and leather halter, she had seemingly acclimatized to her boss's wintry habitat. I, on the other hand, was wishing I'd brought a sweater.

"That detective, Mr. Knoll's brother, was here this morning. He left about an hour ago, and I think Mr. Yeats may be in *trouble.*"

"Did you hear what they discussed?"

"Not all of it, but enough to understand that the topic was Felicia Yeats. She's *dead,* you know."

"Yes, I heard." My tone of understatement arose from distracted thoughts, not facetiousness. "Did Glenn ask to see me?"

"Well, no," she allowed. "He's been rather tied-up with something, but I know him well enough by now, Ms. Gray—you're *needed.* This way, please?"

She didn't phone inside. She didn't buzz, check, or knock. Instead, she delicately grasped my wrist with her knobby, mannish hand and led me forthwith to the door of the inner sanctum, which she swung open with authority, marching me inside. "Ms. Gray is here," she announced. "I knew you'd want to see her, Mr. Yeats." And she slipped out again, closing the door.

"Claire, dear," said Glenn. "What a surprise. I was just thinking about you."

He doubtless was surprised—but he didn't appear to have been thinking about me. Standing in the center of the room in blue silk undershorts, he was surrounded by a contingent of haberdashers with various garments draped over their arms or spilling from bags and boxes. Orchestrating this makeover was Kiki Jasper-Plunkett, sleeves rolled up, a pencil planted in her hair. Glenn stood directly in front of his sprawling semicircular desk, which was raised on a dais like an altar. Behind it towered a curved, concave wall of travertine marble in which were embedded row upon row of computer monitors, their flickering screens reflected in the polished granite desktop. Taken as a whole, the scene in which I suddenly found myself looked like a bizarre melding of *The Wizard of Oz* and *The Emperor's New Clothes.*

"*Dah*-ling!" said Kiki. "Weren't you taught to knock?"

"But, uh," I sputtered, "Tide—"

"Nonsense," said Glenn. "You're *always* welcome, my love. Join the crowd." The clothiers and tailors, some half dozen of them, who had swung their heads toward the door upon my entrance, went back to their business, snipping off tags, marking hems, stretching measuring tapes along various segments of Glenn's torso.

With slow, uncertain steps, I moved into the fray, telling Kiki, "It didn't take you long to get *this* project off the ground."

Glenn said, "I'm not sure I like being referred to as a 'project.'"

"Oh, but you *are,* darling," Kiki told him. "You represent one of the unique challenges of my career. And I assure you, it's a labor of love." She blew him a theatrical kiss with one hand while snapping the fingers of another, ordering one of the minions to assist Glenn into a mole-colored pair of gabardine trousers.

"Nice," he said, zipping the fly. I had to agree—they looked good on him.

"Jacket!" yelped Kiki, pointing to another minion, who scrambled to help Glenn into a tweedy-silk sport coat of an odd color that was neither sage nor sand but somewhere in between. Though he looked unnaturally brutish wearing the jacket without a shirt, its color and texture perfectly complemented the hard sheen of his gray slacks.

Kiki was truly in her element, and I was impressed by the transformation that was beginning to take place under her direction.

Though Glenn seemed distracted (hard to say whether it was the sartorial flurry that surrounded him or the murder case that had nudged into his life), he engaged me in a bit of small talk, asking, "Is everything running smoothly with your workshop?"

"It is," I assured him. "We have a fine crop of young talent in training for next season." Then I remembered: "Oh, by the way, I haven't told you yet. I'm glad you suggested I consider the *Rebecca* script. The students have been doing a marvelous job with it, and I think it's well suited to our resources. So I've decided—we'll put it on next year's bill. In fact, I'll open the season with it."

Glenn nodded as he listened. Then, through a sly grin, he told me, "I knew you would."

He was not, I realized, being smug. He was telling me plainly, bluntly, that he had calculated my response before submitting the script to me. He was telling me that he had decided the script should be produced at DAC and that he had known exactly how to elicit my consent, by suggesting the script as "an idle thought—take it or leave it."

Was this merely the mark of someone who had a solid grasp of commonsense psychology? Or did it verify the accusation of his late ex-wife, that he was a prissy control freak who would stop at nothing to ensure that his will be done? Felicia's unflattering assertion was probably overblown, but it contained at least a kernel of truth—a sizable nugget, no doubt—and I was growing firmly convinced that I would soon need to quash, unequivocally, Glenn's patient but persistent overtures of romance.

"Ughh!" he snarled, tossing aside a silk handkerchief that one of the minions was attempting to fluff in his breast pocket. While the gesture was intended as a manly display of impatience, Glenn's ferocity lost its punch as the pink hankie fluttered to the floor like a feather drifting on the breeze.

"Is something wrong?" asked Kiki. "I assure you, Glenn, no well-dressed man would leave the house without a coordinated pocket square."

"Out!" he blustered. "Everyone!" Then he clarified, "Well, not you, Kiki. And Claire is *always* welcome."

The minions scampered to gather their things—scissors, tape measures, and such—backing toward the door, bowing and scraping. Tide, having heard the outburst, opened the door to accommodate the minions' retreat, then closed it again, leaving Kiki and me with Glenn, surrounded by the rumpled heaps of His Majesty's new clothes.

"Shopping's a bitch," I told Kiki from the side of my mouth.

"Ain't *that* the truth." She laughed merrily.

"Truth be told," said Glenn, "I enjoyed it, as far as it went. I think we made some real progress today. Thank you, Kiki."

"Thank *you*, Glenn. But I know—a wardrobe makeover can be extremely stressful. Sorry if it got out of hand."

"It's not the *clothes*," Glenn said with a touch of exasperation.

I told Kiki, "Unless I'm mistaken, it was Larry Knoll's visit, not the haberdashers', that rattled Glenn."

"You know about that?" he asked.

I nodded. "I just met with him."

Glenn breathed a weary sigh. "Ladies," he said, "where are my manners? Please, do sit down." He gestured toward one of the sofas arranged in a U in front of his desk.

Kiki and I sat together, sinking into the buttery leather cushions.

Glenn sat in the middle of the opposite sofa, facing us. "Yes, Larry's visit took me totally by surprise this morning. When he phoned me at home last night, I was shocked by the news, certainly. I assumed his call was merely a courtesy. But when he showed up this morning, here, to explain the circumstances of Felicia's poisoning—and the apparent connection to the bottle of gin I gave her—well, these developments are disturbing, to say the least."

"To say the least," I echoed. "Glenn, pardon a question that may seem tactless, but when you left the living room Friday night for a fresh bottle of gin, where did you get it?"

"At the service bar in the catering kitchen. The liquor stock is stored in the cabinets beneath the counter."

"Had the bottle been opened?"

"No, I broke the seal myself. Didn't you see me remove the cap?"

"Sorry, but when I saw you return to the living room, you'd already opened the bottle, bouncing the cap in your free hand. That's Grant's recollection as well."

"Peachy. And Felicia was the only one to drink from that bottle. And then I *offered* for her to take it."

"Actually," I reminded him, "she asked to take a drink with her, and *then* you offered the whole bottle."

Shaking his head, he muttered, "Christ . . ."

"I must say," burbled Kiki, "when Felicia asked for 'one for the road,' little did she know how far it would take her."

I patted Kiki's knee. "You're not helping, dear." Returning my attention to Glenn, I asked, "Why did you wipe down the bottle with a towel before giving it to Felicia?"

"It was *wet*."

"Ah . . . ," said Kiki, "the perfect host."

Both Glenn and I gave her a steely gaze.

"But I mean it," she told me. "Everyone knows Glenn Yeats as the consummate businessman, the genius of the software industry. But you and I, *we* know him as a real person. And among his many endearing attributes, he is indeed the perfect host."

With a soft smile, Glenn said, "That's sweet of you, Kiki. I appreciate the kind words. But the truth is, if I were in Detective Knoll's shoes, I'd feel pretty confident I could wrap this up fast."

"*He* doesn't," I told Glenn. "Yes, Larry feels the evidence currently in hand points strongly in your direction, but it's all circumstantial. He doesn't want to take on the Yeats empire unless he has to. That's why I'm here, Glenn. Larry asked me to solicit your complete cooperation with his investigations—it's the best bet you have for exonerating yourself quickly and cleanly."

"Sure, fine. Why wouldn't I cooperate?" Glenn seemed truly baffled by the request.

I explained, "You have a tendency to distance yourself from conflict, which is perfectly understandable for a person in your position, but in this instance, it may not serve your best interests."

He raised his right hand, pledging, "I'll make myself fully available to the investigation, if that's what you recommend. After all, I have nothing to hide."

"Of course not." I mustered a smile.

He leaned forward, elbows on both knees. "I hope you both understand, I hope you *believe,* that I had no role whatever in Felicia's death. Remember, my top priority in this conflict was preservation of the Dirkman house. Now that Felicia is gone, who knows what'll happen to the house? But I had no bone to pick with her, not personally."

"Except," said Kiki, "on Friday night, Felicia made a veiled threat to burn the Dirkman house. We all heard her, Glenn."

He nodded. "And I suppose, from Detective Knoll's perspective, that gave me a motive to take action quickly."

I conceded, "Larry made that observation. But think about it— Felicia didn't voice her threat until late in her visit, long after you'd opened the gin bottle."

Glenn snapped his fingers. "That's *right.* I don't mind telling you, Claire, this whole business has really rattled me. Imagine—me, Glenn Yeats, scared. But I am. This could have a devastating impact on the software stock, the college, you name it. Good God, look what happened to Martha Stewart. But I'm completely *innocent,* and I hope you'll work with Detective Knoll to prove it. I'm man enough to admit it, Claire—you're damn good at this, and I need your help."

Well, well, well. Wasn't *this* a turnaround? During my previous brushes with mysterious death, Glenn had been quick to lecture me on the imagined dangers and questionable propriety of my involvement. He had found it unseemly for me to assist those investigations, fearing I might somehow sully the reputation of the school. He had cautioned me to leave such matters in the hands of the police, claiming concern for my safety—which made me bristle. I had found his paternalistic attitude both condescending and sexist, a clear warning that he was not a suitable candidate for romance, despite his wealth and his wooing.

But now, when Glenn found *himself* the victim of circumstance, he was only too quick to dismiss his previous concerns, flatter my sleuthing skills, and practically beg for my involvement. It was a tempting notion to refuse flat out, to throw his arguments back at him, or at the very least to make him squirm. I would take no pleasure, though, in playing games with him, and more to the point, I already *was* involved with the case, at Larry's bidding. Glenn's plea, therefore, struck me not as hypocrisy, but as icing on the cake of vindication.

Leaning back, stretching my arm along the squeaky leather of the sofa, I said with an air of ennui, "Perhaps I can help."

"Oh, I'm *sure* you can," Glenn said with wide eyes and an intent gaze. "Larry's a busy guy. He'll welcome any time and assistance you can offer."

Fussing with a hangnail, I noted, "I'll have to work it around my classes." Though I had not intended to play games with Glenn, I was doing exactly that—and enjoying myself immensely.

He said through a sheepish grin, "The workshop is *only* three mornings a week."

"Plus preparation, which is considerable. Still, that leaves me plenty of time to concentrate on Felicia, which I'm happy to do."

"Excellent." He rubbed his hands with satisfaction.

"In fact, I'm already scheduled to ride along with Larry when he follows up on a new lead tomorrow morning."

Kiki turned to me. "How delicious, darling!"

"Really?" asked Glenn, pleased as punch. "Where?"

With a barely perceptible shake of my head, I answered, "I really can't say—violation of procedure, you know." I had no idea what I was talking about.

But Glenn bought it. "Of course, my dear. Didn't mean to pry."

A gentle rapping drew our attention to the door, which then opened. Tide stepped inside, saying, "Excuse me, Mr. Yeats, but it's well past noon. If you won't be needing me for a few minutes, I thought I'd run out and get your lunch."

He rose. "Splendid idea, Tide. Thank you. My usual will be fine."

"Will your guests be staying?"

Glenn turned to Kiki and me. "Ladies? Join me? Big Macs, anyone?"

"No, thank you, love," said Kiki, rising, smoothing the wrinkles from her lap. "I have other plans."

"I can't stay either," I told him, also rising. "Thank you, though."

Tide said, "I'll be on my way, then." She began to leave, but stopped, popping back inside. "I spoke to the minister. Wednesday morning is fine. So he's booked." And she left.

Glenn moved to his desk and typed a word or two on his keyboard, making note of something, presumably the minister. (What was that about?) Looking up, he asked vacantly, "Is it just me, or is it getting cold in here?"

I blurted, "It's *freezing.*"

"Ah." He typed a few more keystrokes, and something rumbled within the bowels of the building. Instantly, the chilly draft grew a few degrees warmer. With a chuckle, he fingered the lapels of his sport coat, saying, "I like the new look, but it'll take some getting used to." His nipples were erect, a pair of purple pebbles studding his bare chest.

"Uh, Glenn," said Kiki, "you're supposed to wear a *shirt* with it. Because of all the fittings, we didn't bother."

"Ohhh," he said, enlightened. "I was wondering."

What a nerd. Kiki really had her work cut out for her. She and I exchanged a glance, deadpan, then moved toward the door.

"Uh, Claire," said Glenn. "Your workshop ends at eleven, correct?"

I nodded. "Monday, Wednesday, Friday."

"This Wednesday, I'm holding a brief memorial service for Felicia up at the house. She had some friends in the area, and I thought they'd want to pay their respects. The actual funeral will be later, in Santa Barbara or Los Angeles, after the coroner has released the body. That's up to her son."

Kiki asked, "See? What was I saying? Glenn *is* the perfect host."

I smirked. "Felicia might dispute that. She showed up for a cocktail party and ended up in an urn."

"She won't *be* there," Glenn reminded me, "in an urn or otherwise. She's still at the morgue."

"Yes, Glenn, I understand. I was being glib. Sorry."

He shrugged. "No need to apologize. Anyway, the minister is booked for eleven, so if you dismiss your class a few minutes early, you'll have no trouble arriving on time. Bring Larry too, of course."

"You're the boss."

But I couldn't help feeling that the hastily arranged memorial was little more than a transparent display of false sympathy from Glenn. If it was intended to underscore his innocence in Felicia's death, it was a plan that could backfire.

Moving from behind the desk, Glenn stepped to Kiki and me, then put his arms around us. "Who knows?" he asked, his voice barely above a whisper. "The killer could be among us that morning." Both his manner and his tone were curiously melodramatic.

I wondered, Is he acting?

If so, why?

11

Though we weren't going far—the drive would take about an hour—my Tuesday-morning excursion to Idyllwild with Larry Knoll had the feeling of an adventure into uncharted territory, promising a complete change of scenery from the desert setting I had called home for the past year.

In Palm Desert, Larry turned off the valley's main thoroughfare, Highway One-eleven, and aimed his unmarked white police cruiser up a long, continuous rise of Highway Seventy-four, taking us out of town and into the foothills of the San Jacinto Mountains, which border the Coachella Valley to the southwest. "This is known as the 'scenic route' to San Diego," he explained. "You can also take interstates *around* the mountains, but some prefer to drive it the old-fashioned way, on a two-lane road that winds its way up and *over* the mountains. This road is also called the Pines to Palms Highway."

"How poetic."

"It's beautiful," he agreed, "but sorta scary."

I was sure he was exaggerating.

"Once we get beyond this straightaway, the road narrows and gets much steeper; then it's hairpin curves all the way up to Idyllwild."

While his reference to hairpin curves raised a note of caution, I reasoned that these would be more harrowing to the driver than to the passenger, so I settled back to enjoy the changing landscape, having little doubt that Larry's wheelsmanship would be up to the task.

Though the driver proved both confident and competent, the passenger soon learned that her smug self-assurance was premature. My knuckles blanched as I gripped the seat with my left hand, the door handle with my right. The valley floor began to descend from view, and with each switchback, my window was filled with alternating sights—a sheer wall of rocky rubble as the inner lane hugged the mountainside, then a panorama of the faraway San Bernardinos as the outer lane skirted the brink. On these outer swings, my position in the passenger seat was far more torturous than Larry's; from the middle of the road, he was not forced to look directly over the precipice, and all the while, he had the wheel to hang on to. Me, I could only claw the vinyl upholstery, grit my teeth, and try to sway the direction of the car with my own feeble body English. There was no slowing down for the turns. With cars ahead of us and behind—and no passing allowed—we had no choice but to stay with the flow as we zigzagged ever higher.

"Let's stop a minute," said Larry.

"Huh?" With my heart racing and my palms sweating, I could barely find my voice.

"There's a scenic lookout just ahead. Great view, and we can let some of this traffic get ahead of us."

I croaked, "Fine with me, Larry."

As we rounded the next turn, the road widened sufficiently to accommodate perhaps a dozen parked cars. A rustic sign touted the view and elevation. A smattering of tourists gathered near the edge of the observation area, separated from the precipitous drop by only a split-rail fence and a few pay telescopes. A car was just leaving, so Larry signaled and braked, then parked in the vacated space.

Opening the door and stepping onto terra firma, I not only breathed easier, but noticed at once that the temperature had fallen. It was a hot July morning under full sun, but compared to the desert below at sea level, the air at four thousand feet felt downright balmy.

"I wonder what's going on," said Larry, pinching his brows as we walked to the lookout.

Now that he mentioned it, I noticed that the gathering of people seemed intently focused on something as a group. They didn't mingle or meander, pointing this way and that. They didn't even peep through the telescopes. They stood as one, saying not a word, peering just beyond the fence. Larry quickened his pace; I scooted to catch up. Joining the others, we instantly understood their silent fascination, which we now shared. Only a few feet away, on the other side of the fence, stood a hang glider preparing to launch himself over the valley.

A young man in neon-hued spandex was outfitted with a harness beneath broad, brightly colored nylon wings—a human kite, sans tail. A steady breeze blew around the mountain from the west; an updraft rose with the heat from the desert below; the effect of both could be seen in the wings as they tipped and bulged. His shoes flexed on the pebbled surface of his granite perch as he studied an instrument that clicked and whirled, mounted in front of him on the harness. He stood in this manner for several minutes, eyes fixed on the meter. No one said a word, which seemed to amplify the whoosh of the wind, the clicking of the meter.

Then, when the instrument conveyed something apparent to no one else, he left us. He didn't leap or dive or even jump. Rather, his feet seemed to act as hands, gently pushing him forward. He disappeared from view for a horrifying moment, then rose on the updraft and soared out before us. A wave of vertigo plummeted from my stomach to my groin as the onlookers joined in quiet, awed applause. He rose even higher, suspended by nothing. Far below, to the right, sparkled the surface of the Salton Sea; to the left were the gridded roadways of my adopted hometown; beyond it all was the San Bernardino range, rippling in the waves of heat.

Someone said, "He could ride those currents for hours, if he's lucky." I wondered, And what if he's not?

The little crowd began to disperse, some of whom, I now understood, were friends of the glider, acting as his crew. They piled into a van, which had apparently transported the winged contraption, and headed down the mountain to meet their thrill-seeking colleague upon landing. I hoped they would find him in one piece.

Walking me back to the car, Larry asked, "Had enough excitement?"

"You weren't kidding about those turns. Yikes."

With a soft laugh he told me, "Most of those are behind us now. We're going up another thousand feet or so, but the rest of the route is much flatter."

He was right, I soon discovered, after we got into the car, waited for some traffic to clear, then continued on our way. Not only was the road flatter, but it now traveled over some low crests, rather than hugging the sides of the mountain. It was a different world, strewn with boulders and pines. While its beauty was distinct from that of the desert below, the alpine landscape was formidable in its own way, with very few signs of habitation along the way.

This portion of our trek proved relaxing and enjoyable, and we soon found ourselves gabbing like sightseers on a tour bus, except that our conversation centered not on the local flora and fauna, but on murder.

"I'm more and more intrigued by this new angle," said Larry, glancing over at me from the wheel. "If Felicia had a secret lover, why was it a secret?"

"Good question—she was a 'free woman.'"

"Exactly. So if there was a need for secrecy, maybe something fishy was going on, and if so, the lover may have had something to gain from her death."

"But how would he spike Glenn's gin bottle with antifreeze?"

Larry grinned. "Let's first determine if there *was* such a person. Then we can worry about connecting the dots."

I had to admit, "The secret-lover scenario makes as much sense as any other. We each have our reasons for hoping Glenn Yeats is *not* the culprit. The only other possible suspects we've mentioned are Felicia's son, I. T. Dirkman, Peverell Lamonte, and Lark Tutwiler."

Larry nodded. "I spoke with Dirkman and Lamonte yesterday afternoon, and they both strike me as long shots. So does Lark Tutwiler; I reached her by phone, but haven't been able to meet with her yet. I did have another meeting with Dustin Cory, the victim's son, but didn't learn much. The terms of Felicia's will weren't known yet; I have a hunch that could tell us plenty."

While Larry summarized his various meetings, I was thinking about having seen Paige Yeats at the hotel on Saturday morning, about her contention that she had spent only a minute or two at Felicia's door, about Thad Quatrain's retort, "I was waiting for you longer than *that.*"

Interrupting my thoughts, Larry said, "Now, then. Tell me all about your theater workshop."

It was an odd request, coming from Larry, and a seemingly abrupt change of topic. Was he actually asking me about Paige, who was enrolled in the workshop? Did he sense there was something I hadn't told him? Was he psychic?

He explained, "It's still a ways to Idyllwild, and it seems we're always talking about *my* business. So tell me a bit about yours."

Happy to take Larry at his word, I told him, "The workshop allows me to lavish some intensive training on a handful of students who'll return to the program in the fall, plus a few others enrolled at other schools. Paige Yeats, Glenn's daughter, is in the latter group."

"Small world. But Felicia wasn't her mother, correct?"

"Correct. Paige's mother is Madison Yeats, Glenn's *first* wife."

Larry recalled from his notes, "Paige was at the cocktail party on Friday. How did she and Felicia get along?"

"Their relationship was strained, naturally, but they hadn't seen each other in years. Felicia tendered an olive branch that night, suggesting they should meet the next morning and get to know each other better."

"But it never happened," Larry thought aloud.

"No, apparently not." I was about to explain how their planned heart-to-heart was a near miss, but Larry preempted my telling of this detail.

He asked, "Will the workshop put on a play at the end of the summer?"

"No, we're not rehearsing a show, but we've been working with the script of *Rebecca,* which I've decided to produce in the fall."

"Ah, great flick. Hitchcock, right?"

"Yep, an early one, 1940. The stage play had its American premiere a year later. Both were based on Daphne du Maurier's 1938 novel."

Larry glanced over at me, asking through a squint, "What about the fire—how do you handle *that* onstage?"

"You don't." I laughed. "That's one of two major differences between the film and the play. At the end of the play, Mrs. Danvers doesn't burn the estate; she just leaves." Alluding to the burning of

Manderley, I recalled Felicia's similar threat on Friday regarding the Dirkman house, as well as Paige's reference to "scampering from the flames" during her portrayal of the crazed Mrs. Danvers during Monday morning's workshop session.

Larry noted, "Saves wear and tear on the set, I guess."

"And how."

"And the other major difference?"

"First, some background: Well into the story, we learn that Maxim de Winter didn't love his late wife, Rebecca; in fact, he hated her for her haughty ways and her promiscuousness. When she found out she had developed an incurable cancer, the vain Rebecca decided to avoid the hopeless ordeal that lay ahead by tricking Maxim into killing her, telling him that she had been impregnated by her rakish, ne'er-do-well cousin, Jack Favell. Hearing this, Maxim was of course enraged, and in the play, he relates how he confronted Rebecca on a stormy night, shot her, and set her body adrift in a boat, which he scuttled and sank."

Listening to these details, Larry said, "But in the movie, I don't think Rebecca's husband shot her."

"Bingo. The decency standards of the times wouldn't allow Laurence Olivier as Maxim de Winter to murder his wife and get away with it, even though he was 'killing a dead woman,' so to speak. Therefore, in the film—we see it in flashback—when Maxim confronts Rebecca, they quarrel, then struggle, and she falls, getting a fatal conk on the head. Maxim disposes of the body in the boat, and the rest of the plot details are the same, with Jack trying to blackmail Maxim because he assumes Maxim murdered Rebecca."

Larry said, "You've obviously given some thought to analyzing both the play and the film. Over the years, I've seen the movie a few times, and I've always felt it raises an issue that it never really resolves. What about the lesbian angle?"

I assured him, "My students are equally intrigued—and titillated—by that notion. No question, Mrs. Danvers was obsessively devoted to Rebecca; by any definition, she loved the younger woman. And because we know that Rebecca saw Mrs. Danvers as her confidante, we can assume the love was reciprocal. Did that love include intimacy? In those days, such a relationship would've been deemed not only depraved and evil, but unmentionable. My hunch is, yes, the author meant for us to assume the 'worst' about Rebecca and Mrs. Danvers."

Larry grinned, staring ahead through the windshield—doubtless envisioning the "worst" that Rebecca and Mrs. Danvers could dish up in his mind's eye.

But then he frowned.

"What's wrong?" I asked.

"Oh, nothing." His tone was evasive. "Just a thought—the problems at home."

"Your home?" Trying to lighten the moment, I added, "Guess you weren't referring to the problems at Manderley, the de Winter home."

"I was, sort of. I was referring to both. Granted, what we're going through in the Knoll household isn't nearly so *dramatic* as the conflict between Rebecca and Maxim, but Hayley and I share some of the same root problems."

I couldn't resist asking, *"Hayley's a lesbian?"*

Larry laughed so heartily, he had to slow the car. "Uh, no, not unless I missed something."

"And you *are* a detective."

His laughter waned as he told me seriously, "Unlike Rebecca, Hayley isn't promiscuous or sneaky or mean-spirited. But I've come to realize that she does share an indifference for her husband that sometimes verges on contempt."

"I'm sorry, Larry."

He shook his head, either dismissing my sympathy or thinking of something else. "Rebecca had no kids, but Hayley and I do—two of them. The situation is worse for them than it is for me."

Words failed me. I could only repeat, "I'm sorry."

"She's a good mother. And I try to be a good father. But together . . ." He didn't finish his thought.

At a fork in the road, a sign pointed us to the right. "We're getting close," said Larry, turning.

A few miles beyond, we entered Idyllwild, a charming village with a permanent population of some three thousand. Larry had described it as "arty," and I saw what he meant. In addition to the expected gift shops, galleries, and inns, the community boasted an arts center, an arts foundation, an arts academy, and a private high school for the arts. During our visit, an extensive summer workshop was in session, with programs in writing, dance, music, and theater, as well as the visual arts—all held "under the pines," as promotional banners phrased it.

"I should stop for gas," said Larry, pulling in to a quaint little station with a tall, peaked roof shingled with shakes; it could have been plucked from the bygone memories of my youth. Though Larry hopped out of the car to fill the tank, a uniformed attendant came over to lend a hand, washing the windshield. I opened my window to enjoy the fresh mountain air and listen to Larry's conversation with the attendant. The car didn't take much gas; it seemed Larry's main reason for stopping was to ask directions to the resort.

Stacked in a pyramid near one of the garage bays, next to an old-fashioned Coke machine that looked like a red refrigerator, was a display of plastic jugs containing windshield washer and antifreeze. I said to the man with the squeegee, "It must get cold up here."

"You bet, lady. Sixty inches of snow last winter." It was hard to believe we had driven only an hour.

Within a couple of minutes, Larry had paid for the gas and we were on our way again, headed out of town.

Traveling a narrow road, we burrowed deep into the cool shadows of a dense woodland where the smell of pine was so intense, it seemed artificial. Instinctively, Larry slowed the car as the turns came quicker and sharper. Rounding another bend, we were greeted by an ornate, elegant sign (totally at odds with the rustic setting) announcing LOS PINOS SPA AND HEALTH RETREAT. Hanging beneath it, cut in the shape of an arrow marking the turn, was a smaller sign that bore the unwelcoming admonition PRIVATE DRIVE, GUESTS ONLY. Taking the turn, Larry told me, "We're expected. I phoned ahead for a lunch reservation."

"La-di-da."

The long driveway finally emerged from the cover of trees into an immense clearing that allowed an overall view of Los Pinos. Far bigger than I had imagined, the compound of stately white buildings, with their pillars and verandas, looked more like an Old South plantation than an exclusive mountain getaway in California. Tennis courts and swimming pools dotted the rolling, manicured lawn.

The drive led directly to the largest building. As we passed a low, discreet sign announcing RECEPTION, I muttered, "If I'd known, I'd've dressed." I wore khaki slacks, a crisp white blouse, red canvas espadrilles, and a shiny red belt.

Turning to me with a warm smile, Larry assured me, "You always look great."

As we stopped under the porte cochere, two doormen darted to the car and opened the doors for us. Larry gave his name, adding, "We're here for lunch, but my friend and I are wondering if there's someone who could show us around first. We may want to book a stay on our next visit."

"Excellent. If you'll step inside, sir, our concierge will meet you." The doorman gave Larry a ticket for the car, then turned and said something into a cell phone.

Larry escorted me across the driveway, up a few stairs, and through the doors to the main lobby. As we paused to take in our surroundings, a lean, distinguished-looking man in a dressy gray uniform stepped in our direction, smiling. He asked, "Mr. and Mrs. Knoll, I presume?"

"I'm Larry Knoll"—they shook hands—"and this is my friend Claire Gray."

"My, what an unexpected pleasure. *Welcome,*" he gushed. I wasn't sure if he was a theater buff or if he was effusively friendly to every visitor. "I'm Hebert, and I'll be happy to show you the property before you dine with us today." The brass name tag pinned to his lapel repeated HEBERT, but I couldn't tell whether that was his first or last name, so I felt uncomfortable addressing him at all.

Hebert did most of the talking. Strolling us through the lobby and out the back doors to a formal garden, he began his spiel: "Los Pinos combines cutting-edge nutrition, detoxification, and diagnostics with world-class spa treatments in a luxurious setting available only to the very few."

"Detoxification?" I asked. "Do you mean that in the New Age sense, or in the substance-abuse sense?"

"Both," he assured us with a knowing nod.

"How's the food?" Larry asked.

"Superb. The cuisine at Los Pinos is second to none, and I daresay it's the reason we have so many return visitors."

Larry scratched behind an ear. "I mean, I've seen spa menus before, and—"

"We have that," Hebert acknowledged, "and I'm sure it's up to Los Pinos standards. But I couldn't agree with you more, Mr. Knoll— I much prefer 'real food,' and Los Pinos has based its reputation on fine dining."

I asked, "Can you get a drink—a 'real drink'?"

"Absolutely." Hebert grinned. "Now let me show you around."

As expected, it was all very impressive. We saw the various dining facilities, several guest rooms, and a private cabin. We toured the spa itself and learned details of the treatments offered. Classes were available covering everything from nutrition and weight training to yoga and Pilates. The athletically inclined had their choice of tennis, swimming, golf, hiking, and trapshooting. The lower lobby of the main building, as well as a Disney-style "main street" on the grounds, offered expensive little shops of every description—clothing, jewelry, antiques, resort souvenirs, cosmetics and spa supplies, kitchen gadgets, fudge. A separate building on the property housed a clinic.

"In case the guests have too much fudge?" I asked.

"Yes," Hebert explained, "there are doctors on staff for any guest emergencies that may arise, but Los Pinos took the concept a step further by establishing a first-rate diagnostic clinic right here on the premises. As a result, the resort has become a popular destination for corporate meetings, which can include medical workups for the companies' top executives."

"Ah," I said. "Killing two birds with one stone."

"I suppose so, yes. But most of our guests simply come to be pampered for a week or two."

"Who could blame them?" I asked airily.

"Certainly not I," Hebert said with a restrained chuckle. Directing us back to the main building, he asked, "Is there anything else I can do for you before lunch?"

"I was wondering," said Larry. "Do you have an office where we might talk privately for a few minutes?"

"Of course, Mr. Knoll. If you'd care to discuss the possibility of a future booking, I can supply all the information you'll need—and make the reservation, if you like." He escorted us to the main lobby, then turned us down a hall and through an office door, which he closed behind us.

"Please have a seat and make yourselves comfortable," he offered, sitting behind his desk. A window behind him, high on the wall, framed a sunny view of pines and sky. Tapping a few keys on his computer, he asked, "Are you interested in a particular week? I'm afraid we have no openings for a month or so, but autumn is lovely here and not so crowded."

"Hebert," said Larry, leaning forward in his chair, "I didn't mean to mislead you, but I'm afraid there's been a misunderstanding. I'm not here to book a vacation. I'm a detective with the Riverside County sheriff's department." He reached inside his suit coat, pulled out a leather wallet, and flipped it open, showing his badge. When he returned it to his breast pocket, his jacket opened sufficiently to reveal the glint of gunmetal from a holster.

Hebert sat silently for a moment, looking dismayed, which didn't surprise me. But then he turned to me, looking flat-out betrayed, which did come as a surprise. Planting a hand on his hip, he said, "And I suppose *you're* not Claire Gray."

"But I am."

Larry assured Hebert, "Yes, this is Claire Gray, the director. We're friends, but this isn't a social visit. I'm here on police business. There's been a murder in Rancho Mirage, and I'm afraid the victim was a recent guest at Los Pinos."

"Oh, dear." Hebert fingered his lips, minimally concerned, as if he'd just learned that a chambermaid had neglected to leave a mint on someone's pillow.

"It happened last Saturday at the Regal Palms Hotel."

Hebert's brows arched. "A fine establishment."

"Yes, but I'm afraid the poor lady was poisoned there—she was Felicia Yeats."

Hebert snapped his fingers. "Yes, I heard about that. She was the ex-wife of that computer guy. You say she had also stayed at Los Pinos? I don't recall her visit."

"We've heard she was here during the last week of June."

I leaned forward, telling Hebert, "We also have reason to believe she may have been here for a romantic tryst. If she had a secret lover, we hope to identify him. He may be able to shed some light on the case."

The concierge raised his hands in a slow-down gesture. "I'm afraid, Miss Gray, that Los Pinos has strict policies with regard to the privacy of its guests. And I'm certainly not about to speculate on who was sleeping with whom." Harrumph.

"Hebert," said Larry, the voice of reason, "this is a murder investigation. I could get court orders; there could be publicity. But I doubt that either of us wants to horse around with that. All I'm asking, at this point, is whether you can confirm that Mrs. Yeats stayed here last month."

Hebert sat back and thought for a long moment. The word *publicity* was doubtless ringing in his ears. While it has often been noted that there's no such thing as bad publicity, a murder investigation seemed a likely exception to the rule. He told Larry, "I suppose there's no harm in confirming whether the woman in question was registered here."

"I thought not," said Larry, offering a genial smile.

I was tempted to add, She couldn't possibly object. But the comment struck me as glib, so I kept it to myself.

Hebert nudged his chair closer to the desk and went to work on his computer, tapping away, calling up various screens. He checked with Larry, "The last full week of June, correct?"

"I believe so, yes." Larry pulled out his notebook and flipped through a few pages, nodding.

Hebert paused, studying the screen, then frowned. He tapped a few keys and studied another screen. Then another. "Nope," he said at last. "No one named either Felicia or Yeats was registered at Los Pinos in late June—or anytime during the last several months."

"You're certain?" I asked.

"Absolutely, Miss Gray. There's no record of anyone by that name having stayed here."

I wondered aloud, "Maybe a false name?"

Larry looked skeptical.

Hebert explained, "Our guests almost always settle their accounts with a credit card. A few write checks. Either way, it's unlikely she could have registered under a false name."

Larry looked up from his notes. "If she *was* here, she may have come with another woman, Lark Tutwiler." He spelled the last name.

Hebert got busy on the computer again. "Ah!" he said, peering at us over the terminal. "Mrs. Tutwiler was indeed registered during the last week of June—Sunday to Sunday."

I suggested, "They could have stayed in the same room."

"Yes, but that doesn't appear to be the case. Our records don't indicate that anyone was registered with Mrs. Tutwiler, and her account for the week—meals, spa appointments, and such—reflects charges for her alone."

Larry added, "I doubt if Felicia shared a room with Lark because Lark told me she saw very little of Felicia during their stay."

"The only other possibility," said Hebert, "is that Mrs. Yeats stayed in some other guest's room. Our policy is to register everyone in the hotel, but we're not naive. Couples here for an assignation aren't likely to volunteer every detail, so we don't press the issue."

"And if that was the case," Larry surmised, "we're at a dead end."

"I'm afraid so, yes. If she was staying here as someone's 'secret companion,' they've succeeded at eluding us. I have no way of deducing who might have played host to Mrs. Yeats—if she was here at all."

Larry closed his notebook and slipped it inside his jacket.

"I'm sorry I couldn't be more helpful," said Hebert, sounding distinctly relieved that he'd turned up nothing.

"We appreciate your time. Thank you." Larry handed him a business card.

Hebert returned the courtesy, passing Larry one of his own cards. "If you're ready for lunch, I'll alert the dining room to expect you. I want to make sure Miss Gray gets a special table—you too, Detective."

We thanked him, rose, and left the office.

Hebert made good on his promise. When we arrived at the main dining room, the maître d' greeted me as a celebrity—well, a minor one—before escorting us through the room and out to the terrace, where he seated us at a prime table draped with white linen and sporting huge damask napkins of shocking pink. In the shade of an ancient pine's long, graceful boughs, we overlooked a rolling green bluff that might have been the edge of the world.

As the maître d' backed away, two waiters stepped forward, one presenting menus, the other placing before each of us a frosty crystal champagne flute, filled to the brim. "Compliments of the hotel, Miss Gray," he said with a bow of his head. "Enjoy." And they both disappeared.

Larry and I suppressed a laugh. He said, "I should take you out more often."

I raised my glass. "Don't mind if you do."

He touched his glass to mine; the gentle clink was lost in the pervasive birdsong. We sipped. The bone-dry champagne tasted deliciously cold and refreshing as the bubbles slid past my tongue.

Sharing my reaction, Larry had barely set down his glass when he lifted it again for a second mouthful.

With a crooked grin, I asked, "Off duty this afternoon, Detective?"

He wobbled his head. "I can bend the rules now and then."

"Be my guest."

He swallowed a third sip. "I might have to ask you to drive back."

Though I assumed he was joking, I played along. "Happily. I know the way now. Piece of cake."

"You realize, of course, the trip *down* is even more tense than the ride *up.*"

I choked on my champagne. *"It is?"* Lifting the pink napkin, I dabbed a stream of bubbles that trickled from my nose.

"You bet it is. On the way down, you feel as if the car is *falling* into those curves." With a tone of understatement that sounded more serious than amusing, he added, "It's not pleasant."

I downed a hefty slug that emptied half my glass.

One of the waiters returned, recited some specials, and took our orders without writing them down. As for drinks, both Larry and I opted to switch to iced tea, thanking the waiter for the champagne as he removed the flutes.

After a pause, I asked Larry, "Wild-goose chase?"

"Our trip today? Hardly. Hebert's information was anything but conclusive, and it throws into question Lark Tutwiler's story about being here with Felicia. That raises some interesting possibilities, don't you think?"

Nodding, I reasoned, "If Felicia *wasn't* here, why did Lark say she was? And if Felicia *was* here, why the cloak-and-dagger tactics?"

"Exactly. Point is, I need to talk to Lark again. And knowing where to turn next, that's what I call progress." Pushing his chair back from the table, he asked, "Would you excuse me for a moment? Lunch will take a few minutes, and I'd like to phone in to the department."

"Take your time, Larry." With a contented sigh, I added, "I'm just enjoying the weather—what a marvelous break from the heat."

With a wink that sufficed as a brief farewell, he rose from the table, unclipped the cell phone from his belt, and wandered from the terrace to the open grounds.

Watching him move about, immersed in his conversation while stooping to pick up a pine cone, which he tossed idly in one hand before pitching it precisely between two trees and into the scrub, I was struck by an observation that took on the weight of revelation. Larry, I suddenly noticed, was a handsome man. Not only handsome, but attractive—in the literal sense that I found *myself* physically attracted to him.

Whoa. Where was *that* coming from? For nearly a year, I had known him as a friend. More to the point, I had known him as the brother of my best friend, Grant Knoll. Because Grant was gay, I had found it easy to connect with him, finding companionship without the potential for messy emotional entanglements, let alone physical ones.

Was that truly the allure I had felt in Grant, or had I been kidding myself? Was it possible that, all along, I had wanted more than Grant's friendship? Had I developed a pathetic crush on a man I knew I could never have? Having accepted, at least intellectually, that Grant was off-limits as anything other than a loving friend, was I now projecting my frustrated desire toward Larry? Had he become a stand-in target for my feelings toward his brother?

These feelings were not only confusing, but troubling, especially in light of my recent knowledge that Larry, a straight but married man, might soon become available.

Walking back to the terrace, Larry returned the phone to its belt clip and approached the table with a broad smile. Sitting across from me, he laughed, shaking his head. "Imagine that."

"Oh? An amusing development at headquarters?"

"Nah, nothing happened there. I was just thinking. Remember when we arrived at the hotel this morning? Hebert thought we were . . . well, a *couple*."

I grinned. "An innocent mistake."

Larry repeated, "Imagine that."

When Larry mused, "Imagine that," I didn't feel he was pondering a future with me, though it was easy to put such a spin on his comment. Rather, he seemed to find it funny that anyone could mistake us for a couple. I couldn't decide which of these two possible attitudes was more troublesome, so I masked my confusion by joining him in a chuckle.

Setting aside this nascent dilemma (I needn't—and couldn't—resolve it there at lunch), I enjoyed my meal under the pines with him, indulging in conversation that rarely strayed from the mysterious circumstances of Felicia's death. Odd, isn't it, that murder could qualify as a topic for pleasant table chat?

As Larry had predicted, that afternoon's drive down from Idyllwild was even more tense than the morning's drive up, but it wasn't only the accelerated momentum of the hairpin turns that goosed my anxiety. I was still mulling the meaning of "Imagine that."

Wednesday morning, I dismissed my workshop students about a half hour early, as I needed to be on time for Felicia's eleven o'clock memorial service, to be held at Glenn Yeats's Nirvana estate. Paige Yeats, who was in my class, would also attend the ceremony at her father's home and pay her respects, though she clearly felt little grief that Felicia was gone. Thad Quatrain would accompany Paige, a pattern that was becoming routine; attending the memorial with Paige had not been a spur-of-the-moment decision, but had been planned, as Thad was dressed more like an adult that morning and less like a college kid. Kiki, who was at the theater during our workshop session, would accompany me; though it was the dead of summer in the desert, she wore black bombazine.

"You're looking very, uh . . . *funereal* today," I told her as we got into my silver Beetle and pulled out of the faculty garage. With her hat and veil, it would have been more accurate to say she looked like a beekeeper.

"Thank you, *dah*-ling." She knew no greater compliment than being told she was correctly costumed for the role at hand.

Zipping across the valley floor to Glenn's mountain, we spoke of this and that, barely mentioning Felicia. Kiki kept steering the conversation back to our planned production of *Rebecca,* and I was grateful to be reminded of my true, current mission in life—student theater, not crime detection. Kiki's interest, naturally, centered on the show's costuming. "The masquerade scene should be great fun."

Glancing over at Kiki, I noted, "The crazed Mrs. Danvers won't be much of a challenge—your mourning getup suits her perfectly."

"You think so?" Kiki laughed merrily, then leaned toward me, touching my arm. "As long as we're on the subject of costuming, what do you think of Glenn's wardrobe makeover?"

"From what I've seen, it looks promising."

"*Promising?* My dear, it's gone swimmingly!"

"Do forgive my faint praise. I should have known—swimmingly, of course."

She paused, then gave me a broad wink that was visible even through the black netting of her veil. "I think he likes me."

"*Everyone* likes you, Kiki. Who wouldn't?"

She shook her head. "I mean, I think he *likes* me." She gave another wink.

Laughing at her presumed joke, I said, "I hope you're right—that would get him off *my* back."

"Impossible," insisted Kiki. "Glenn absolutely *adores* you. Even when I'm alone with him, he speaks of little other than you."

"I'm sure you're exaggerating." At least I hoped she was.

After passing the security guard at the gates to Nirvana, we sputtered up the winding roadway, all the way to the top, where Glenn's dramatic, angular I. T. Dirkman house rose from the mountainside, a man-made outcropping of granite and glass. Turning the final bend of the entry drive and pulling into the courtyard behind the house, my whimsical little car was greeted by two uniformed parking valets who helped Kiki and me out of the vehicle (my egress was unremarkable, needing little assistance, but Kiki—with her hat, veil, oversize purse, and yards of silky bombazine—presented another challenge altogether, requiring my valet to pitch in and help hers).

I asked one of the car parkers, "How many are attending today—any idea?"

"We've parked two dozen cars, ma'am, and the gatehouse phoned up to say more are on the way."

By late morning, the temperature had already topped a hundred, even at the breezy height from which Glenn's home overlooked the valley. Crossing the courtyard to the house, I wondered aloud, "Where will Glenn put everyone, in the living room? It's far too hot to be outdoors."

Stepping inside the house, we were greeted by waiters bearing trays of slim, elegant champagne flutes, ours for the plucking. Tide Arden strode about with her acrylic clipboard, keeping track of the arrivals. Acknowledging Kiki and me, she said, "Mr. Yeats is asking his guests to assemble on the terrace for the service."

"But the heat—" I began to protest.

"Everything's taken care of, Miss Gray." Tide gave me a reassuring smile, then moved to the door to greet the next arrivals.

Aside to Kiki, I asked, "How, pray tell, does anyone, even Glenn Yeats, 'take care of' the weather?"

Kiki shrugged. "He probably bribed God." Then she sipped her champagne.

I did likewise, strolling with Kiki across the vast living room toward the open wall to the terrace.

Stepping outdoors, joining the crowd, I braced myself for the heat but was stunned to find that the air was cooler there than it had been indoors. "Do you believe it?" asked Larry Knoll, stepping up behind us. "It's *air*-conditioned—the whole damn patio."

Sure enough, glancing around, I saw that the stone parapet, which delineated the edge between the terrace and the canyons below, was interspersed with large rectangles of metal grillwork that I had previously assumed to be ornamental. Now I understood that these grills masked industrial-size ducts that spewed chilled air when needed. I muttered, "Only in California . . ."

"Good morning, Detective," said Kiki. "What a perfectly pleasant surprise—seeing *you* here, of all people." She offered her hand as if expecting him to kiss it.

He shook it. "Claire invited me. In fact, so did Glenn."

"Ahhh, I get it," she said, attempting to tame her fluttering veil in the play of the icy breeze. "Hoping the murderer might make a guest appearance at the memorial for the deceased—is that it?"

Larry allowed, "It could happen."

"But this is anything but a typical funeral," I noted. Surveying the terrace, I asked, "How does this work?" I understood that Felicia would not be present—in either a coffin or an urn—but I had assumed there would at least be a framed photo of the woman. In fact, there was nothing whatever to invoke the memory of her.

"How does this work?" repeated Larry. "Perhaps my brother can answer that."

Grant Knoll was crossing the terrace in our direction, nodding greetings to various guests, looking very much in charge. "Morning, doll!" he told me, stepping into our circle. Giving me a light kiss, he also pecked Kiki's cheek and shook his brother's hand.

"Everything under control?" I asked. As director of the Nirvana sales office, Grant frequently helped Glenn by coordinating with the catering staff from the Regal Palms Hotel, as he had done at the previous Friday's cocktail party. A morbid irony struck me—both that event and today's had been cobbled together because of Felicia.

Grant checked his watch. "Everything's on schedule. The service begins in ten minutes, at two past the hour." He added, "Glenn's a stickler for precision."

I asked, "Where *is* our gracious host?"

"Dressing. Or talking with the minister. They'll come out to the terrace together when the music begins." A string quartet, seated between two date palms at the far end of the pool, discreetly tuned their instruments.

"Don't tell me—Glenn plans to deliver the eulogy." The previous autumn, just before the opening of school, a faculty member's wife had died under tragic circumstances, and Glenn had hosted a similar memorial at his home, stealing the show by turning his eulogy for the woman into a shamelessly transparent promotion of the new college.

Grant shook his head. "None of that, thank God. Glenn claims he can't bring himself to muster even a sympathetic word for Felicia, so he's leaving everything in the hands of the minister—some generic 'reverend.' Tide dug him up somewhere."

Larry scratched behind an ear. "Damnedest memorial *I've* ever heard of."

"Not even a *picture* of Felicia." Kiki sniffed.

Grant shrugged. "Glenn claimed he didn't have one. So he and the reverend plan to stand together in front of the fireplace, using it as a backdrop. If you squint just right, it looks a bit like an altar." Grant was referring to one of two gargantuan fireplaces, one of them in the living room, the other, its twin, out on the terrace. On many a cool night, I had contemplated its flames, reflected in the black surface of the swimming pool.

A waiter pranced by with a tray. Grant snapped his fingers, stopping the tuxedoed server in his tracks. Grant set his empty champagne glass on the tray, helping himself to another. "Ladies?" he offered. But we were fine. Larry was drinking water.

"Let's see, now," I said, gazing through the shifting pattern of guests who milled about. "Who's here?"

"Everyone who's *anyone*," said Grant with a flick of his wrist. Then, dropping the camp, he told us, aside, "If you ask me, it's a fairly seedy-looking crowd—hardly one of Glenn's A-list affairs."

"*We're* here," I told him with mock umbrage. So was Grant's young partner, Kane Richter, who gabbed with Paige and Thad near the edge of the pool. In addition to Tide Arden, other DAC staff included Iesha Birch, the museum director, and perhaps a dozen faculty who had been pressed into service, lured by the prospect of drinks and lunch.

Dustin Cory, Felicia's son, arrived just then with Peverell Lamonte, director of the architecture conservancy. They acknowledged us briefly while heading across the terrace to join I. T. Dirkman, who gazed out over the parapet.

"Interesting," I said.

"What?" asked Larry.

"Dustin and Peverell—either they happened to arrive at the same time, or they're 'together' this morning. I'm not certain whether they were formerly acquainted."

The other guests were largely unknown to me, perhaps distant friends of Felicia from her charity circuit. Grant knew virtually everyone, providing names that meant little to me, though a few sounded familiar as retired chairmen of various well-known companies.

Tide and a herd of waiters began moving among us, asking us to congregate along the edge of the pool. Grant excused himself, needing to check on the kitchen staff. Larry, Kiki, and I settled near the back of the crowd, a better vantage point for keeping an eye on the entire proceedings.

A late arrival—a woman with frosted blond hair—appeared from the house, snapped up the last glass of champagne from a waiter's tray, and zipped across the terrace, joining Peverell with Dustin and I. T. Dirkman.

She looked familiar; then it clicked. "That's Lark Tutwiler," I said to Larry.

"Do tell. I've been trying to get ahold of her since yesterday afternoon, but haven't been able to reach her. If you'll excuse me, I'd like to—"

But he was interrupted by the string quartet, which struck up a festive little baroque march, signaling that the service had begun. Under his breath, Larry told me, "I'll catch her afterward."

All eyes turned from the musicians as a side door from the house opened and out stepped Glenn with his generic reverend. He really did hunger for any opportunity to strut in public, even at his own home, and today he strutted in a sampling of his new wardrobe, somber and tasteful in gray, not black. I leaned to Kiki. "You simply *must* teach the man to wear socks."

"That's next on my list," she assured me.

The reverend wore a dark suit, a gray shirt with a band collar, and a liturgical stole of deep, mournful purple. The stole's design was a bit much, with embroidered doves and whatnot, lacking the simple dignity that would have been more appropriate for such a minimal memorial. He carried a black book that looked too small for a Bible. He and Glenn took their places in front of the fireplace, across the pool from the gathered onlookers.

The strings segued from their sprightly march to something more ponderous and stately, which sounded like a hymn without words. After a verse or two, they stopped.

"My friends," said Glenn (who had not planned to speak at all, but was apparently unable to resist the temptation), "thank you for making time today to join in remembering my late wife, Felicia. I've invited the Reverend Hornsby to officiate and to offer words of wisdom and consolation. Reverend?"

"Thank you, Mr. Yeats. Though I never had the pleasure to meet Felicia, I know she was loved by all present." And he was off and running, delivering a canned eulogy that was polished from repetition, but stumbling each time he was required to insert Felicia's name.

I listened with respect and attention for a few minutes, until the gist of his message grew as threadbare as the clichés that peppered his sentences: a daughter of the church, the bosom of God, his shining countenance, a holy city, life everlasting, and on and on. As these platitudes flowed from his lips, I struggled to shoo from my mind an unfortunate image that stood in stark contrast to our collective purpose. Backdropped by the behemoth outdoor fireplace, framed by the cold black hearth, the Reverend Hornsby appeared to be standing at the gates of the furnace of hell.

Some in the crowd hung on his every word—or did a convincing job of appearing to do so—while others had lost interest more quickly than I had, marveling at the scenery, studying the magnificent house, or indulging in whispered conversations with companions. While everyone present bore scrutiny, two groups of guests intrigued me most.

Lark Tutwiler seemed so distracted, I wondered why she was there at all. Hobnobbing with Peverell Lamonte, she covered her mouth to gab with him, fussed with her hair, and tried in vain to signal a waiter for more champagne. Dustin Cory joined their conversation, injecting a few whispered comments while checking his watch and shuffling his feet, as if he feared he might be late for a golf game; in fact, his chipper outfit of jaunty pastels suggested golf, lacking only the cleated saddle shoes. Rounding out this group was I. T. Dirkman, whose signature dark suit and black-framed glasses seemed especially apropos to that morning's gathering. Though he didn't speak to his companions during the service, he was equally removed from it, concentrating on the roofline of the house while sketching something in a small notebook he had pulled from inside his jacket.

The other group of guests who drew my attention consisted of the young people—Kane, Thad, and Paige. They were better behaved than most of the older guests; both Kane and Thad displayed a maturity that belied their years, paying their respects to a woman who had played no role whatever in their lives. Paige also listened in dutiful silence, but her emotions were far more difficult to read. Felicia had indeed played a role in her life, which had doubtless been magnified in Paige's mind as a mortal affront to both her mother and herself. Why, then, did a tear now streak down her face? I blinked. Had I imagined the glistening drop that appeared from the corner of her eye, brushed away by her index finger the moment it reached her cheek?

My gaze later drifted back to Lark, who had grown curiously silent. Rather than gossiping with Peverell or fidgeting with her champagne glass, she now stood erect and motionless, peering through the crowd. Though I tried to determine who was the target of her stare, I could not. Had she recognized someone—perhaps one of the ladies from her charity luncheons? Or was it a man who looked familiar because she had seen him at Los Pinos in late June?

"My friends," said the Reverend Hornsby, closing his black book, "the words of the psalmist have offered us comfort in this time of grief, and I have made my best, if feeble, effort to praise the spirit of the woman whose passing we mourn today. However, I did not know Felicia, while most of you did. At this point, therefore, I would like to invite all present to share with the rest of us their memories of Felicia Yeats." With a soft smile, the reverend paused.

An uncomfortable wave of anxious surprise rippled through the crowd. I daresay none of us anticipated being called upon to participate in such an active way. Some of the guests stared at their feet; others muffled coughs. No one volunteered.

Reverend Hornsby turned to Glenn with an expectant arch of the brows, as if to suggest Felicia's ex-husband should get the ball rolling.

Glenn responded with a quick, subtle, but firm shake of the head.

"Uhhh . . . ," said the reverend, looking about the crowd, deciding which victim to pounce upon next, "I understand that Felicia's son is among us today. Perhaps he could share with us some recollections of being dandled upon his loving mother's knee."

Dustin Cory looked like a deer caught in the headlights. As all eyes turned to him, he stammered, "I, uh, haven't prepared anything. I'm afraid I'd rather not."

"Of course, Mr. Yeats," said the reverend, who had not been coached in the family's mixed bloodlines. "Memories can't be forced, as they are from the heart." Then he waited.

As long seconds passed, it became apparent we were not to be let off the hook until *someone* said *something,* so finally, I. T. Dirkman cleared his throat and proclaimed, "She was a good woman."

A few in the crowd seconded, "Here, here!"

Reverend Hornsby folded his hands in prayer, intoning, "Amen."

The quartet struck up a lively anthem.

Glenn turned to the reverend and shook his hand.

Then Glenn asked the crowd, "Anyone need a drink? God knows, I do."

13

Despite the solemn purpose of our gathering, the luncheon reception following the memorial had a distinctly festive air. Once Glenn Yeats had concluded the service with his declaration that the bar was open, the crowd broke into lively chatter, praising the terseness of the ceremony. No one seemed much in mourning over the loss of Felicia, including her friends Lark and Peverell and even her own son, Dustin. As Reverend Hornsby removed the purple stole from his neck, everyone's attention shifted from the afterlife to a priority that was decidedly of this world—jockeying to get a fresh drink in hand.

"What'd you think?" asked Larry, strolling Kiki and me to one of the bars.

"Honestly?" I hesitated. "I think this whole affair is an overly generous gesture by Glenn, who had no apparent affection for Felicia. I'm sure he feels that by hosting this hoo-ha, he'll garner a measure of sympathy and the presumption of noncomplicity in Felicia's poisoning. But it's a plan that could easily backfire."

"And how," agreed Larry.

"But you must admit," said Kiki, "Glenn *looks* marvelous today."

"Yes," I allowed, "your makeover is progressing swimmingly." Watching Glenn work the crowd, I realized that he did seem more comfortable in his own skin—and less geeky in his new clothes. At that moment, he was pumping I. T. Dirkman's hand and slapping his back, doubtless thanking the architect for his pithy eulogy.

Corks were popping and ice was rattling at two bars that had been set up, one near the outer edge of the terrace, the other just inside the living room. Lines had formed at both, and we found ourselves in the shorter of them, moving closer to the interior bar. Kiki leaned to whisper to me, "Some *people,*" noting a woman who had abandoned the longer line and nonchalantly cut in ahead of us. Even from behind, I easily recognized the frosty hairdo. It was Lark Tutwiler.

"Thirsty?" I asked over her shoulder.

"Why, *yes,*" she said turning. "It seemed we were standing there for *hours,* didn't it?" Then she recognized me, sort of. "Didn't we, uh . . . ?"

"We did, in fact." I reintroduced myself, "Claire Gray."

"Of course, my dear. What a *dreadful* turn of events on Saturday. I understand it was you who *found* poor Felicia."

"Actually, it was the maid."

Just for the record, Kiki added, "But Claire put her up to it."

I introduced Lark and Kiki, then told Lark, "And this is Detective Larry Knoll. I believe you've met on the phone."

"Enchanted, Detective." Lark began to offer her hand, but just then, the bar opened up, so she turned and ordered a screwdriver, "easy on the OJ, please."

Kiki and I ordered kir; Larry made do with ginger ale. When we were served, Kiki flipped the gauzy black veil over her wide-brimmed hat and excused herself, wending her way into the crowd. Larry asked Lark, "Could we chat for a moment, Mrs. Tutwiler?"

"Certainly, Detective." Her enthusiastic tone suggested that a police interview would perk up an event she had anticipated to be hopelessly dull.

Larry suggested, "Let's sit down." Everyone else was still standing, so we had our pick of the various seating groups in the expansive living room. We settled in three club chairs at a small table near the huge fireplace.

"Cheers," said Lark with a toothy smile, lifting her glass as she dropped an elegant little handbag on the limestone floor.

More somberly, I toasted, "To Felicia."

Larry and Lark seconded my sentiment. We tasted our drinks, then set the three glasses on the black granite tabletop.

Testing the waters, I said, "I'm sorry for your loss, Lark."

For a moment, she looked genuinely confused by my comment. "Ah. Thank you, Claire. I feel terrible for Felicia, but the truth is, we weren't what I'd call 'real' friends—just a couple of middle-aged divorced gals on the same social circuit."

Leaning toward Lark, I asked quietly, with a sympathetic smile, "Then why are you here today? Why even bother?"

Without hesitation, she blurted, "I wanted to get a look at the inside of Glenn Yeats's *house*. Christ, it's fabulous! *N'est-ce pas?*"

"Can't argue with that."

Turning more serious, she elaborated, "And I wanted to pay my respects to Felicia—of *course* that's why I'm here. She visited the desert now and then, and we came to know each other by attending many of the same charity luncheons. Eventually, I introduced her to Peverell. But otherwise, we weren't all that close."

"Yet," noted Larry, "you traveled together."

"The one trip to Los Pinos, yes. I recommended the spa, and she agreed to meet me there during the last week of June. But we arrived separately and left on our own. As I told you on the phone, Detective, I ended up seeing very little of her during our stay. We had only a few meals together, and I never ran into her during my spa treatments. By the time I left, I was feeling a little put off." She lifted her glass and sipped the screwdriver, which contained so little orange juice it was barely yellow.

Larry nodded, recalling the details of her story. Then he told her, "Claire and I took a drive up to Idyllwild yesterday and had lunch at Los Pinos."

Lark lunged in my direction, touching my hand. "Isn't it *wonderful?*"

"Indeed."

Larry continued, "We spoke to the concierge about Felicia's visit, and it turns out they have no record that she was ever at the hotel."

Lark's features went blank. "But that's impossible. She was there. I saw her—off and on."

I said, "We don't doubt your word, Lark." I didn't mention that we had no reason to believe her either. "It's just that the hotel has no room account for Felicia. I assume she wasn't staying in *your* room, correct?"

With a crooked grin, Lark reminded me, "We weren't *that* close."

Larry said, "So we figure she must have been staying with someone else."

"Now, *that* makes sense." Lark gave a knowing nod. "Felicia and I occasionally confided in each other, but she was tight-lipped at Los Pinos—never shared stories of what she did with her evenings, or even her days, for that matter. I got the distinct impression she was shacking up with someone, if you'll forgive the indelicate expression."

I asked, "Did she have that . . . certain glow?"

"Not really, but that's Felicia, never the giddy sort." Lark fingered her lips, pausing in thought. "Now that you mention there's no record of her being there, something makes sense."

Larry and I glanced at each other, then turned to Lark.

She explained, "Several times, I asked Felicia for her room number—in case I needed to reach her to make plans or whatever—and she always had some lame excuse for not giving it to me. One night, for instance, when I asked at dinner, she said she couldn't remember the number, even though she could walk to the room 'blindfolded,' she said. So she checked her key card, but the cards don't show the room numbers, for security reasons. I gave up trying. She always ended up phoning *my* room to confirm plans."

Larry said, "As I'm sure you understand, a great deal could hinge on this next question: Do you have any idea who Felicia might have been spending her time with at Los Pinos?"

"Not a clue," she answered at once.

"Lark," I said, "earlier, during the memorial, I noticed you staring through the crowd at something or someone. I wondered if perhaps you had recognized someone, possibly from Los Pinos."

"I was staring at someone?" She blinked. "God, I don't recall doing it." She laughed. "I was probably just trying to catch a waiter's attention." With a wink, she tapped the rim of her glass. "Oh! I see they're serving lunch." She rose, plucking her purse from the floor.

Larry and I rose as well. He asked her, "I wonder if you might find time when we could talk again—say, tomorrow afternoon? I have some research in the works, and I'll have follow-up questions."

"Certainly, Detective." Her voice seemed to sparkle. "Anything to accommodate the law. You're welcome to visit me at home in Indian Wells. When should I expect you. Two-ish?"

"Two o'clock is fine; I have the address from our phone interview. Thank you, Mrs. Tutwiler."

She grinned. "Do call me Lark. I insist."

"I'll do that. Thank you." But he didn't.

With a coy nod, Lark excused herself, moving off with the crowd to graze at the buffet table. Larry's bent smile acknowledged her flirtatiousness. And my own pinched features (I could feel the tension around my lips) hinted that I had reacted to the flirtation as a personal affront. I mused, "Imagine that."

"Hmm?" asked Larry.

"Nothing." I smiled. "Care to eat something?"

"Sure. May I join you?"

"I was hoping you'd ask." And we made our way to the buffet.

Glenn always treated his guests lavishly, and that day's lunch was no exception, but because he routinely used the hotel's catering staff (and because I'd been entertained at his home so often), the selection of foods had a predictable sameness. The giant shrimp, the sliced rare tenderloin, the perfect sauces and sublime vegetables—I picked at all of them with the jaded weariness of a pampered monarch.

Nearing the end of the buffet line, I turned with my plate, wondering where we might sit, when Peverell Lamonte mirrored my motions, emerging from a second line of guests that moved in the opposite direction. "Ah, Miss Gray," he said. "There you are. I saw you earlier and was hoping we could catch up." Then he recognized Larry, who followed me through the line. "Hello, Detective. I trust that the case is progressing to your satisfaction."

Vaguely, Larry answered, "We're making some headway."

Then Dustin Cory appeared from behind Peverell. "Well, now," he said, seeing the rest of us, "the gang's all here." Carrying a large plate of food with both hands, he nearly spilled it on himself while turning his wrist to check his watch.

"Late for a tee time?" asked Larry.

"Nah, I'll make it. Besides, always time for lunch."

I said, "Larry and I were about to sit down. Would you gentlemen care to join us?"

"With pleasure," said Peverell.

"Why not?" said Dustin.

Larry caught my eye and gave me a discreet wink, approving of my setup, which would allow some further, informal questioning of Peverell and Dustin. Peverell had been the last person to see Felicia alive, leaving his fingerprints on the blue gin bottle, while Dustin, as the victim's son and next of kin, presumably had the most to gain from her death.

"How about over here?" I suggested, stepping to a pair of chaises longues near the shady end of the pool. The seat cushions were long enough for Larry and me to sit next to each other on one chaise, while Peverell and Dustin arranged themselves on the other, facing us, taking scrupulous care that their hips not touch.

Spreading napkins and plates on our laps, we began to partake of the luncheon. A waiter came by to take drink orders.

After a few offhand comments about the food (which was, as always, flawless), I mentioned to the men across from me, "I noticed that the two of you seemed to arrive together today. I wasn't even aware that you'd met."

"We hadn't," said Dustin with a snort of a laugh. "But this week, we've seen quite a bit of each other—right, Monty?"

Peverell Lamonte reacted with a flicker of disrelish for Dustin's use of the nickname, but he took it in good humor, telling me, "Let's just say that unexpected tragedy has a way of bringing people together."

"Yeah," said Dustin. "Police, lawyers, reporters—you name it."

Forking a piece of tenderloin and swirling it through a puddle of béarnaise, I asked idly, "Lawyers?"

"Well, sure. Now that Mom's gone, the estate has to be settled."

"Ahhh, of course. I hadn't thought of that. It must be terribly complicated."

Larry lifted his napkin to his mouth, trying not to laugh at my ditsy-broad act.

"Actually," said Dustin, "it wasn't complicated at all. I was Mom's only heir."

"You got everything? My, my, my. I suppose congratulations are in order, though that seems rather cold—under the circumstances."

"I hear ya. But thanks. Yes, I got it all."

"That includes the house in Santa Barbara, I presume?"

Dustin glanced at Peverell and exchanged a quick smile before responding, "Yeah, I got the house."

The waiter reappeared, bearing our drinks on a tray. I had ordered more kir, Larry more ginger ale. Dustin and Peverell took brown cocktails with cherries in them, which gave the oddly contrasting impression of being too potent and, at the same time, too childish. Peverell drank a tentative first sip, then set the glass on the terrace near his feet. Dustin ate the cherry first, dropped the stem on his plate, then took a solid gulp of the drink. Liking what he tasted, he set down his plate and held the glass between his knees with both hands.

"Nosy me," I said. "I hope you don't mind my asking, Dustin, but I'm curious. Do you have the same concerns about the Dirkman house that your mother had? Felicia voiced some privacy issues regarding the austere design."

"Never bothered *me,*" he said with a shrug. Then he paused. Looking to Peverell, he asked, "Should we tell them, Monty?"

Both Larry and I were now on full alert.

Peverell nodded, then told us, "This will be public knowledge very soon, and you may find it of interest. We have some *most* exciting news."

Larry asked, "Should I be taking notes?" He reached inside his jacket.

"If you care to, you're welcome to. Here's the long and the short of it: As Dustin said, he's Felicia's sole heir and has inherited the Dirkman house. Upon her death, the covenants restricting sale or modification of the house were lifted. By the terms of Felicia's will, the house now goes to Dustin, but with the stipulation that he immediately sell it to the Southern California Conservancy for Homes of Historic Interest. So the SCC will purchase the house at a previously agreed-upon price, which was negotiated some months ago, when she requested our lawyers' assistance in modifying her will."

Dustin groused through a smile, " 'Previously agreed-upon price'— you're getting it cheap, Monty."

Peverell allowed, "It might have fetched more on the open market, but the price is well above the value of the land alone, which is considerable. What's more, the house will now be fully protected and preserved, with the SCC as its steward. It's a win-win. The conservancy gets what *it* wants, and *you,* Dustin, get a substantial windfall, neat and easy."

"Yeah, I do," said Dustin, taking a big, happy slurp of his cocktail. Under his breath, he added, "And the timing couldn't be better. All's well that ends well."

"Oh?" I asked with a naive lilt. "You had some pressing need?"

He wagged a hand. "Not really. I sorta phrased that wrong. It's just that I've had some unexpected business expenses lately, and this'll take the pressure off."

Larry flipped back through his notes. "What line of work are you in, Dustin? I'm not sure we covered that during our previous discussion."

"It's a little hard to describe—involves venture capital. I'd prefer to leave it at that." He drank the remains of his cocktail.

When previously questioned, Dustin had been similarly evasive about his occupation. I still had to wonder: Was Dustin merely a playboy with no real job and a load of debts? Or was he actually involved in some sort of speculative business, a venture that sounded potentially shady?

Glenn Yeats strolled over to us with I. T. Dirkman in tow. "Everyone having a good time?"

With a disapproving smirk, I reminded him, "It's a *funeral,* for God's sake."

Grinning, he reminded me, "No, it isn't, not technically. It's a tribute to the memory of my dear ex-wife." The remark seemed intended more for Larry's ears than for mine.

Larry stood to greet Glenn and the architect, adding, "The big news must come as a comfort to both of you."

Glenn turned to Dirkman, who returned his quizzical stare.

Peverell said, "Dustin and I have been waiting to catch these two gentlemen together, thinking they deserved to share the moment."

Through a squint, Glenn asked warily, "What moment?"

"*Well,*" said Peverell, setting down his plate and standing to explain, "the terms of Felicia's will are now known. The Santa Barbara house has been inherited by Dustin, but with the stipulation that he immediately sell it to the SCC. Gentlemen, your worries are over. The future integrity of your landmark specimen of contemporary residential architecture is now assured—in perpetuity."

Dirkman's hand shot to his mouth as he gave a happy gasp. "What an astonishing turn of events! I had *no* idea of Felicia's plans. Did you, Glenn?"

"No, I didn't," he said, sounding not entirely pleased.

I asked him, "Is something wrong?"

"Felicia could have saved us all a lot of anxiety if she had simply told us her intentions."

I stood, crossing my arms. "Her intention was surely *not* to die on Saturday. The provisions of her will were part of a long-range plan, irrelevant to her recent complaints regarding the house."

"Whatever," said Dustin, rising, tired of the whole business. Tapping his watch, he said, "If you'll excuse me, I have a tee time."

"In *this* weather?" I asked.

"No problem. That's what Gatorade is for."

I knew of at least one other use for it.

Dustin shook hands with everyone, thanked Glenn for hosting his mother's memorial, and left.

Taking his cue from Dustin, Peverell also decided to leave, thanking Glenn, then telling Dirkman with a congratulatory handshake, "Mission accomplished. While Felicia's untimely passing is tragic, at least we have the comfort of knowing that the Santa Barbara house is now in good hands." He turned to me. "Good day, Miss Gray. Always a pleasure." Then Peverell left the terrace, departing through the living room.

Stepping Larry aside, I told him, "Peverell Lamonte was the last to see Felicia alive. He was also privy to the terms of her will."

"Duly noted," said Larry. The phone on his belt vibrated. "Excuse me," he said, flipping the phone open and strolling over to the parapet to take the call.

Which left me standing alone with Glenn. "You're scowling," I told him.

"That Felicia. She's exasperating."

"She's dead."

"It's so *like* her—this was obviously meant to embarrass me."

I gave him a questioning look of blank astonishment.

"Think about it," he said. "Sure, I feel a measure of relief that the Dirkman house is now protected and out of reach of her crazy schemes, but the house is now thoroughly out of *my* control."

"So what? It'll be preserved by the SCC. That's exactly what you wanted."

"But now *she* made it happen. Don't forget who built that house."

"Glenn, I'm sorry to say it, but you're sounding downright peevish, And trust me—it's not becoming." His attitude was far worse than unflattering; it was a perverse manifestation of his deep-seated control issues. His ego not only irked me, but also nudged me toward the firm conclusion that I could never truly love him, let alone wed him.

His posturing was so outrageous, I had to wonder whether he was putting on an act. But why would anyone paint himself in such a negative light? Struck by a possible explanation, I nearly choked. The only reason Glenn would deliberately portray himself as a jerk would be to forestall the suspicion that he was something worse. I had just said to Glenn that the issue of the house had been resolved exactly as he had wanted; what I had not said was that Glenn had gotten his way so quickly because of Felicia's untimely death. Was he attempting, through a false display of peevishness, to prevent those dots from being connected? Or was he simply an egotistical ass?

"What's the matter, my dear?" Stepping near, he placed his hands on my shoulders. "You're looking flushed. Are you warm? I can turn up the air-conditioning."

"No need for that," I said through a crooked smile. "There'd be ice on the swimming pool."

Considering the prospect, he suggested, "We could have a skating party."

"And we could stoke up the fireplace and toast marshmallows."

"Your wish is my command." He signaled a waiter.

"*Glenn*—you wouldn't."

"Just joking about the ice skating, but I do need a drink."

"Ah." Even after a year, I still found his humor hard to read.

"Hey, Pops. Great party." Paige Yeats approached us with Thad Quatrain. She carried a tall glass of something clear and icy, garnished with lime. He carried a tiny plate heaped with the gigantic shrimp.

"I'll take that, young lady." Glenn pried the tonic from her fingers. "Thank you." Tasting it, he added, "You need to be careful with gin—it's deadly." They laughed.

It was a dim joke and in questionable taste, but because I wasn't laughing, Paige felt compelled to explain, "Felicia's martinis got the best of her."

Thad winced. "Let's try to be nice about it, okay?"

Paige hesitated. "Sure, Thad. For you, I'll try to cut Felicia some slack."

Glenn peered over my shoulder, through the crowd. Waving, he broke into a broad smile. "Would you excuse me?" he asked us. "Need to say hello to someone." And he stepped away.

To Thad, Paige continued, "I'll try to cut Felicia some slack—even though she was the bitch who wrecked my mother's home."

"She's gone now," I told Paige.

"It's over," said Thad, putting an arm around Paige's shoulders.

She nodded. "I know. It was terrible, what happened to her. But I can't quite bring myself to feel sorry she's gone. What she did can never be undone. I'll probably get over it, someday. But my mother— she *never* will."

Time heals all wounds, I was tempted to say. But the remark was not only insipid; it was ill informed. I had never even met Madison Yeats, Paige's mother, who perhaps had borne Felicia a greater grudge than anyone else. More to the point, I had no rational basis for assuming that time would ever heal Madison's wound, inflicted by Felicia. There were some things that some people could simply never forgive.

Thad tried to change the subject. "I enjoyed our workshop this morning, Miss Gray. Even though the session was cut short, I think the whole class is really starting to click with their improvisations."

"I'm glad you sensed that, Thad. I did too. I keep returning to the *Rebecca* script for a purely practical reason—we'll be producing it in the fall—but I've discovered that it makes *sense* to use a single script as inspiration for all of our ongoing exercises. It's a technique I'll use again."

"It sure helped that you asked us to read the entire script again. It'll be a great show. I can hardly wait to get going on it next semester." Then he reined his enthusiasm. "Sorry, Miss Gray. I didn't mean to presume you'll cast me, but—"

"Thad," I told him with a wink, "don't sweat it."

"Thanks, Miss Gray. There are so many terrific characters."

"There really are," said Paige, entering our conversation. "And they're not just characters in the sense of stereotypes."

"Right," I said, "they're flesh-and-blood. They're complex, each of them, with histories and motives and destinies."

"Motives and destinies," reflected Paige. "If you think about it, Felicia and Rebecca had a lot in common."

Intrigued by Paige's notion, I asked, "How so?"

Without hesitation, she replied, "They both got what they deserved."

I had expected something deeper and more analytical, but Paige's statement struck me as harsh and shallow—a cheap shot in the guise of profundity. Choosing my words carefully, I hoped to steer her to the same conclusion and encourage her to contribute to the discussion with greater intellect and less spite.

But my noble intentions to mentor and educate were waylaid by the damnedest sight.

As I gazed across the pool, my jaw sagged. There, near the water's edge, sat Glenn and Kiki, sharing the cushion of an oversize ottoman. Having broken away from the rest of the crowd, they were lunching together, feeding each other from their plates like doting teens at a malt shop.

Kiki had said earlier of Glenn, "I think he *likes* me."

Had her assessment been not self-flattery, but fact?

Was I really to be let off the hook so easily?

14

On Thursday afternoon, a few minutes before two, Larry picked me up at home in Rancho Mirage and drove us down valley through Palm Desert to Indian Wells, which many considered the most enviable address among the various desert cities. The community's lofty reputation was due in large part to a handful of exclusive country clubs within its borders, all boasting astronomical housing prices. Within one of these walled and guarded enclaves resided Lark Tutwiler.

Pulling up to the gatehouse, with its grand fountains and stately rows of date palms, Larry lowered his window and identified himself.

"Certainly, Detective," said the guard. "Mrs. Tutwiler is expecting you." He gave us a map, using a yellow highlighter to trace the winding route to Lark's home, which seemed to be in a prime location, abutting the golf course.

When the gate wheeled open for us, Larry drove through, handing me the map so I could navigate. The turns came more quickly than I would have guessed, as the scale of the map was deceptively sprawling. In truth, the housing struck me as too dense, with only slivers of land separating one palatial residence from another. Most were of dramatic, modern design, but without the telltale sameness that marks cookie-cutter developments. Nothing had been chosen out of a book—as in "We'll take the plan three–B, plus guest casita, delete the wet bar." No, each of these homes had been custom-designed by an architect of the owner's choosing.

From the street, Lark Tutwiler's home presented a simple facade that was both elegant and reserved, not unlike the woman herself. The stone walls and tinted windows gave no hint whatever as to what lay within.

Parking at the curb, we got out of the car, and I was struck not only by the renewed assault of the afternoon heat, but by the eeriness of the streetscape. There was no other car in sight, as if we had landed in an artificial village, a movie set with houses that had only front walls and nonfunctioning doors that led nowhere. Nor were there any other people in sight, not even a gardener to tend any of the fussy landscaping. Walking from the street to Lark's front door, I heard a sound—a sign of life, though it seemed mechanical. Turning, I saw a security vehicle, a glorified golf cart, as it puttered through the intersection of the next side street. The driver was hidden behind dark windows.

Stopping along the walkway, I told Larry, "They really keep an eye on things." My voice was hushed, lest I disturb the peace.

"The crime rate in these places is virtually nonexistent."

"Yeah," I said skeptically, "but that's because they bury their dirty secrets."

He laughed. "You're in an unusually conspiratorial frame of mind today."

I laughed as well. "Just being melodramatic. But you must admit—this whole setup is pretty weird. Where *is* everybody?"

"It's summer, Claire. Most of these houses are empty."

As proof of his assertion, we were surrounded by absolute silence, save the low, dull roar of unseen air conditioners. When we walked the remaining steps to Lark's front door, our footfalls on the concrete seemed to reverberate under the blue plaster dome of a synthetic sky.

Extending from the roof of the house, a cantilever sheltered the door, hiding it under an oblique shadow, which appeared both welcoming and foreboding. Drawn to the darkness, we paused to let our eyes adjust; then Larry pressed the doorbell button. The door itself was a large, thick panel of rippled glass. The distorted patterns of light from the other side shifted as someone approached.

When the door opened, a Mexican housekeeper greeted Larry by name. She dressed much more formally than Oralia, in a snappy maid's uniform, suggesting she might be live-in help. (This notion was reinforced by the absence of a parked car that might have been hers.) She first offered us water, a typical courtesy in the desert during the torrid months. When we declined, she said, "Mrs. Tutwiler is expecting you, Detective. This way, please?" She wasn't sure who I was or what to make of me.

We were led straight through the living room—very stark, white, and classically modern—to a set of glass doors that opened to a rear terrace.

Stepping outdoors, I paused to take in an expansive view of green fairways and the mountains beyond. While the streets leading to the house had felt cramped and claustrophobic, the effect from the rear of the house was just the opposite—luxuriously open and ruggedly pastoral. On that late-July afternoon, no golfers had ventured out, so Lark Tutwiler reigned solo over the entire majestic domain.

Reclining on a lounge chair near the end of a cobalt-tiled swimming pool, she wore a black bathing suit of one-piece design that was strikingly immodest for a middle-aged woman at an appointed meeting with a police detective. Shaded by palms and a huge modern umbrella consisting of a flat disc of stretched fabric, she sipped something blue-green from a tall glass; it looked curiously like antifreeze. Her hair and makeup were perfect, and though the temperature was well into three digits, her bronzed and oiled skin showed nary a trickle of sweat. At her side was a low table, where an icy pitcher of the blue drink stood at the ready, along with a second glass, empty. "Paloma," she said, "it seems we'll need an extra glass."

"Sorry to intrude," I said, stepping forward with Larry.

"*Nonsense,* Claire." Lark gave a low chortle, peeping over the top edge of her sleek wraparound sunglasses. "Delighted to see you again. Please, join me here in the shade. The heat's not too bad; in fact, it's quite pleasant." Easy for her to say—she was wearing next to nothing.

Larry said, "Thank you for making time for us, Mrs. Tutwiler."

"Now, *please,* Detective. I asked you before—do call me Lark."

"Certainly." But he didn't.

After a moment of awkward hesitation, she said, "Forgive me if I don't get up." With a pout, she added, "I just got settled."

So Larry and I sat in two chairs near her. But even in the circle of shade, it was still damn hot, and I felt myself instantly break into a sweat. Larry donned a pair of sunglasses from his pocket; I squinted. Paloma returned with the third glass and a crystal bucket containing more ice. She filled the two empty glasses, handed them to Larry and me, then left.

Peering at the glass in his hand, Larry asked, "Is it alcoholic? I'm on duty."

"*Barely,*" Lark assured him with an exaggerated wink. "Just a drop or two." She raised her glass to us in a casual salute.

It was too hot for dithering, so I readily took a gulp of the blue concoction, not caring what was in it. Swallowing, I made two discoveries: it was deliciously cold and fruity, and it contained enough booze to waste a frat boy at a toga party.

Larry took a taste, then set down his glass.

With a tiny sigh, Lark said, "So tell me, Detective—are you making any progress? Have you figured out why Los Pinos has no record of Felicia's stay at the hotel? She *was* there, you know. I *saw* her."

"I'll take you at your word," said Larry, opening his notebook and paging through it, "but the hotel's registration records are a dead end."

"Oh, dear," she said airily. "Case closed."

"It's not that simple," Larry assured her. "Many other aspects of the case are under active investigation."

"Really?" Big smile. "Such as what?" She leaned back, stretching, as if her amusement that lazy afternoon were the sole purpose of Larry's visit.

He told her, "That's how I'm hoping you can help me, by sharing whatever background you came to know of Felicia, her family, and her friends."

Lark set down her drink. "Felicia and I ran into each other at a few charity lunches, which is how we met. We had dinner now and then. I really don't know terribly much about the woman."

I noted, "You introduced her to Peverell Lamonte. Tell us how that came about."

"Well, *Peverell,*" she said, primping. "Such a charmer, isn't he? I met *him* on the charity circuit as well. So cultured and well mannered—he makes a nice armpiece, I'll hand him that. When Felicia mentioned all the problems she was having with the Santa Barbara house because it's considered a landmark, I was sure that Peverell would like to meet her because of his work with the conservancy. Let's just say I put two and two together."

Larry asked, "Has he thanked you? That introduction really paid off."

Lark looked confused. "What do you mean?"

I asked her, "Haven't you heard? The conservancy got the house."

"Already?" She slipped off her sunglasses. "That was fast."

Larry explained the terms of the will, concluding, "So the conservancy is buying the house from Felicia's son, Dustin Cory. It seems everyone's happy, even the architect."

I didn't point out that not *everyone* was happy. Glenn Yeats's peevish behavior had defied explanation.

Mulling Larry's statement, Lark wondered, "Everyone was happy? Even Dustin? That's good, I suppose." She put her sunglasses back on.

Larry asked, "You're surprised that Dustin is happy?"

"Not that I *know* the man; I met him only yesterday at the memorial, and briefly at that. But his mother did speak of him now and then. She claimed to be worried about him."

"Did she say why she was worried?"

"Not Felicia. She divulged very little, even though she made a point of telling me she appreciated my friendship. She kept private matters private—except for her loathing of Glenn, of course."

"Did she openly express hostility toward him?"

"Oh, she hated him," she said matter-of-factly, flipping a wrist. "It ran *much* deeper than the house issue, and it didn't take much liquor to get her talking." At the mention of liquor, Lark noticed the absence of a drink in her hand. Reaching for the glass on the table, she swallowed a hefty slug of the icy blue cocktail.

"As I understand it," I said, "Felicia rarely drank."

"Correct." Lark wrinkled her nose. "Felicia would sometimes take a few sips of wine with a meal, but that's all it took to send her on a rant about Glenn." Lark paused, thinking of something. "It's odd, isn't it, that Felicia died from drinking? Too much gin—let alone antifreeze— it's so unlike her."

I conjectured, "She wasn't quite herself that evening. It was stressful for all concerned."

Larry said, "Tell me about her rants against Glenn."

"Well." Lark sat up, swinging her feet to the ground, leaning toward Larry—giving him a good gander down her cleavage, which seemed the purpose of her move. "In a nutshell, Felicia felt Glenn was domineering. Sure, he was fabulously wealthy—a genius, some would say—but he seemed to feel that entitled him to rule the lives of everyone close to him."

"In other words," I suggested, "she thought he was a control freak."

"Exactly!" Lark turned, showing me most of her boobs (*something down there wasn't real*). "As a matter of fact, Claire, she called him a 'prissy control freak.' "

I told Larry, "Felicia used those very words Friday night."

He asked Lark, "Did these rants stop at name-calling, or was she specific about her complaints?"

Lark trained her bazookas on Larry again. "Yes, she was specific—in a *vague* sort of way, if that makes sense. While they were married, Glenn scrutinized Felicia's spending, disapproved of her friendships, kept tabs on her mail and her phone bills, and generally kept her under his thumb. After they were divorced, he still did everything in his power to keep control. The restrictions on the house were a typical example, but that was just the tip of the iceberg. He meddled in car leases, tax escrow payments, bank accounts, you name it."

"Incredible," I said with a soft shake of my head. Lark had confirmed my worst suspicions about the man who hoped to win my heart. At least, I assured myself, his aggression was nonphysical.

"And *then*," added Lark, "there were the fights and the threats."

"Fights?" asked Larry, looking up from his notes.

"You know, screaming matches. It happened all the time while they were married. But the threats went a step further. Once, he threatened to take away her car, and another time, he ordered the staff not to let her leave the house. Felicia had spunk, though, and could dish it right back. Her favorite way to needle him was threatening to break some of his precious art objects. Once, she gloated, she actually did it, smashing a Chinese porcelain figurine—she said it was priceless."

"Really?" I couldn't help thinking of the broken cupid in *Rebecca*.

"At least that's what she *said*, though frankly, I felt she was exaggerating."

Larry frowned. "Bragging about something like that—it's playing with fire."

Again I thought of *Rebecca*. Felicia had threatened to burn the Dirkman house, as Mrs. Danvers had burned Manderley in the Hitchcock film.

Sitting up straight, Lark stroked the icy surface of her tall glass, then dabbed her cold fingertips across her forehead. (I did the same. It helped.) She said, "It makes you wonder about Glenn Yeats, doesn't it?"

"What about him?" asked Larry.

"Felicia's stories may well have been inflated, but where there's smoke . . ."

The unspoken source of the smoke invoked thoughts, once again, of *Rebecca*.

Lark continued, "I don't know if Glenn ever locked Felicia in the house, and I don't know if she ever retaliated by destroying his artwork, but one thing's for sure—they didn't get along. And the common thread that ran through *all* of Felicia's stories was Glenn's obsessive need to control her life. So it makes you wonder: What makes a man like that tick? How could a smart, independent woman like Felicia fail to see his darker side before being snared by his money? And what was it like for his first wife?"

"Madison Yeats," I said.

"Ah, yes. That's the name."

"Did Felicia ever talk about Madison?"

"Several times. Felicia never met Madison, but she expressed interest in having a talk with the woman, which I found perverse. I mean, what would they do—swap war stories? And what did she expect to find out—that Madison had also learned the hard way that wealth alone is no guarantee of a happy marriage?"

I felt the need to defend Glenn on this point, explaining, "Madison and Glenn married while the software empire was more a dream than a reality, so back then, she couldn't have married him for the money.

He's always been a man of ideas and vision. Some women find that enormously attractive."

"Really?" asked Lark, incredulous. "God knows, *my* ex had neither ideas nor vision."

I assumed the guy had had money, but I refrained from asking what else had attracted Lark to him.

Dismissing thoughts of her ex, Lark continued, "Felicia also spoke of Glenn and Madison's daughter, Paige. Despite her sneering, I got the impression she might have wanted to know Paige better—the daughter she never had, perhaps."

"Or maybe," Larry suggested, "she felt guilty about being the 'other woman' who'd broken up Paige's home."

"That's possible, but Felicia seemed far more concerned about the emotional aftermath of her own marriage to Glenn. I doubt if she had any deep regrets for the effect she'd had on his previous marriage."

As Lark and Larry discussed Felicia's attitudes toward marriage—her own and others—my thoughts were stuck on Lark's notion that Felicia had thought of Paige as the daughter she'd never had. Recalling Friday night's party, I was struck that Felicia's behavior toward Paige was conspicuously civil, even friendly, in comparison to her attacks on Glenn and her sniping with others. She had gone so far as to suggest that she and her stepdaughter should meet, alone, to get to know each other better. Paige, on the other hand, had referred to Felicia as a bitch before her arrival and had challenged her on several points of conversation, showing little interest in the proposed private meeting. Then, Saturday morning, Paige did indeed show up at Felicia's hotel, and at Wednesday's memorial I had glimpsed the young woman shedding a tear.

Something didn't add up, but I was reluctant to explore my confusion with Lark and Larry, as it would suggest I was harboring murder-minded suspicions of Paige. Like her father, she had felt a good deal of bitterness toward Felicia, but neither father nor daughter struck me as sufficiently motivated to kill the woman. Nor did I believe that either could be capable of such a heinous act.

Larry was asking Lark, "And her name, please?"

"Adrienne Coleman. I've known her for several years—can't even remember how we met—but we keep bumping into each other."

I remembered the photos of Adrienne in Saturday's newspaper, pointed out by Oralia, who kept house for both of us.

"Recently," said Lark, "during Felicia's visits from LA, she began joining Adrienne and me at our luncheons. On several occasions, we rode together."

"Carpooling?" I asked.

Larry gave me a facetious grin.

"Something like that, yes. Good for the environment, I suppose." Lark poured herself another full glass from the pitcher, then topped mine up as well (Larry had barely touched his). She explained, "I had great hopes for us, thinking we'd make a fun threesome, but Felicia and Adrienne never quite hit it off. Ultimately, Adrienne told me she didn't care for Felicia and asked not to be included in future outings with her."

"What was their problem?" asked Larry.

"Minor annoyances. Whether it ran deeper, I never knew. And now, with Felicia out of the picture, I guess it doesn't matter."

"No, I guess not," said Larry, but he asked for Adrienne's phone number.

Lark supplied it from memory, adding, "There was one peculiar incident—a fund-raiser for ALS, I believe."

Larry asked, "Lou Gehrig's disease?"

"Yes. There was nothing peculiar about the luncheon itself, the charity, or the speaker—they all blur after a while—but there was an unusual incident at the table involving Felicia. Dessert and coffee had been served, and the speaker, some bigwig doctor, was droning on and on, dry as dirt. He was losing his audience, and many of us had simply stopped listening, preferring to gab with each other. Adrienne and I were leaning together, chatting about her new hair-dresser, who'd just moved from San Francisco and opened a fabu-lous salon—it's decorated in a monkey motif, with an open bar. Anyway, the noise level in the hotel ballroom was rising, but there was nothing *we* could do about it, so we talked a little louder. *Then,* if you can believe it, Felicia actually leaned over and *shushed* us! 'That's very rude,' she told us. With a false smile, she added, 'Can't we just listen?' Well, needless to say, the etiquette lesson did *not* sit well with Adrienne. It was the next day when she asked me to nix the threesome."

I asked Lark, "Was Felicia generally so prim and proper? She didn't strike me as the sort."

"Lord, *no*. She could gossip with the best of us and had a *wicked* sense of humor. But we all have our off days, and that's what I tried telling Adrienne."

Larry asked, "Have you talked to her since Felicia's death?"

"Of *course*, Detective. The phone lines have been positively *buzzing*."

"How did Adrienne react?"

"She was horrified, naturally."

Larry paused, paged back through his notebook, then closed it. Standing, he said, "I appreciate all your time. This background could be helpful."

Lark fumbled to don a pair of sandals, then stood as well. "You don't have to rush off, do you?"

"Actually," I said, rising, setting my drink on the table, "it's gotten terribly hot. I think we should be going."

She suggested, "We could move inside . . ."

"Thank you," said Larry, "but I have no further questions. And I do have other calls to make."

She sidled up to him, her sandals scuffling across the hot pavement. "If anything comes *up*," she said suggestively, "you know how to reach me."

When we had said our good-byes and Paloma had seen us through the house, closing the front door behind us, Larry paused on the sidewalk to ask me, "What'd you think of her?"

"I think she was hoping to spend some time alone with you this afternoon."

He laughed. "Then I'm doubly glad you tagged along."

"What'd *you* think of her? Her story, I mean."

"I'm not sure. There was a lot of scattered detail, some of which might be useful. But the question we still haven't pinned down, absolutely, is whether Felicia was actually at Los Pinos when Lark said she was." He jerked his head toward the street. "Let's cool off the car. I need to make a phone call."

We walked to the car, got in, and left the doors open while Larry started the engine and cranked up the air conditioner. I watched a roadrunner hop from a garden wall and make its way across Felicia's lawn. The poor thing looked as bedraggled by the heat as I felt—his gait was more of a shuffle than a run, and he looked more like a skinny brown chicken than a fabled unicorn.

When we thumped the doors closed, Larry pulled out his wallet, checked a business card, opened his cell phone, and punched in a number. A moment later, he asked, "May I speak to Hebert at the concierge desk?"

Gazing through the windshield, I noticed that it framed a view of the San Jacinto Mountains, and unless I was mistaken, I saw the same slopes we had climbed on Tuesday, driving up to Idyllwild and the resort where Hebert had mistaken Larry and me for a couple.

"Yes, Hebert," Larry was saying into the phone, "this is Detective Larry Knoll. I wanted to thank you for your assistance the other day and to let you know that both Miss Gray and I appreciated the extra attention at lunch. It was very good of you. What I'm wondering now, Hebert, is whether you could help me with some additional research. This regards the question of whether Felicia Yeats actually stayed at Los Pinos in late June. You've already determined that if she was there, she didn't pay for anything by credit card or check. I know this may seem like a long shot, but could you ask your bookkeeping department if *any* hotel guest has recently settled an account with cash? Great, you've got my number, and I'll wait to hear back from you. Thanks so much, Hebert."

Larry closed his phone and turned to me. "It's an intriguing notion that Felicia was at Los Pinos for a secret romantic rendezvous, but we can't simply take Lark at her word and base the investigation on an assumption. That would be an unacceptable leap of faith."

Peering at one of the distant mountains, I spotted the ridge where we had watched a hang glider step calmly from the edge of a cliff.

That, I mused, had been a leap of faith.

PART THREE

subtext

15

"Read between the lines," I told my class on Friday morning. "That's the nature of subtext—the true thoughts behind the spoken words. Sometimes, this imaginary dialogue complements and amplifies the text of the script; other times, it contradicts the text and conveys irony, humor, or deceit. In either case, it guides the actor in interpreting the text mentally and in inflecting the lines vocally."

"In other words," said Scott with a dopey smile, "subtext is our friend."

The other students groaned.

"Yes, Scott," I lectured patiently, "subtext *is* your friend. This concept isn't new; we've been working on it all summer, along with exercises in improvisation and role reversal. But today we'll sharpen our focus on subtext, taking our inspiration, once again, from the *Rebecca* script."

Cynthia Pryor asked, "When do we get to read the actual lines, the real dialogue?"

"Not till fall, I'm afraid—when auditions are held for the production."

"No fair," said Paige Yeats with a good-natured pout. "I won't be here."

Thad Quatrain mimicked her pout, patting her hand. Though Paige was not enrolled in my degree program, Thad was, and it was increasingly apparent that neither looked forward to their coming separation at the end of our summer session.

"Now, now," I consoled Paige with feigned sympathy, "I'm sure you'll find ample amusement in your film classes in LA." To my way of thinking, theater was the real deal, while movies were a second-class derivative, an entertaining distraction. My attitude was well known to my students.

Paige flashed me a grin. "Touché, Miss Gray."

"Claire, *dah*-ling," said Kiki, who whisked across the stage just then with an armload of costumes, "your defense of the legitimate theatuh is admirable, but you should save it for the great unwashed. With these kiddies, you're preaching to the choir."

They all laughed.

So did I. "Point taken, Kiki."

Her heels clacked the stage floor as she made her way to the wings, then stopped. Dropping the costumes onto a heap of others that were piled in a bin, she began checking them against an inventory list. The jangle of her bracelets drifted through the vast space and dim shadows of the empty theater like distant sleigh bells—an odd illusion, given the intense heat and blazing sunshine that buffeted the building's exterior.

My students sat on folding chairs, surrounding me onstage in a loose circle. I told them, "Let's work with the closing scene of the play, in which the young Mrs. de Winter comes into her own as the new lady of Manderley. No longer the blushing, awkward ingenue, she becomes the 'strong one,' inspiring her husband, Maxim, to ignore the anticipated local gossip about Rebecca's death and to cancel their plans for an extended second honeymoon." Opening my script, I said, "Turn to page seventy-one, please."

They did so. I continued, "We'll begin with the last line on the page, where Mrs. Danvers asks Maxim if anything else will be required of her. As before, we'll divide the class into two groups, each of which will improvise the scene in subtext only. First, let's have Thad play Maxim, with Paige as his young wife, Cyndy as Mrs. Danvers, and Scott as Frith, the butler." Then I assigned the same four roles to students from my B group.

With a clattering of chairs, the two groups separated and reassembled offstage—one right, the other left—to study the script and to plan the framework of their improvised scenes.

Stepping to the stage apron, I was about to descend the stairs to the auditorium floor when Kiki bustled up behind me, asking, "Got a minute?"

"For you, love? Anytime."

She followed me down the stairs and settled with me at the director's table. Bursting to tell me something, she fidgeted with her hair, straightened the shoulders of her blouse (sort of a peasant smock of nubby muslin died a shocking shade of peacock blue), then crossed her arms and leaned close to me, announcing, sotto voce, "He invited me to dinner."

"Who?" Though I could easily guess.

She confirmed my hunch: "*Glenn*. I'm telling you, things are heating up."

I reminded her, "Glenn hosts many dinners. I wouldn't read too much into it."

"Claire," she said, placing her fingertips on my arm, "it's at *his* place, tonight—Friday, the start of the weekend—and according to Tide Arden, it's 'dinner for two.'" She gave a meaningful nod.

"His *secretary* invited you?"

"Well, you know Glenn—he's a busy man. But you must admit, 'dinner for two' has certain . . . overtones."

"Yes," I admitted, though my voice was laced with skepticism, "I suppose it does. Did Tide mention any pretext for the dinner?"

Kiki sat back, hands on hips. "Why would he need a 'pretext' for dinner?"

"I mean, was there any stated purpose, or did it have the flavor of a rendezvous, a date?"

"Well," Kiki recalled, finger to chin, "Tide did say something about Glenn wanting to discuss his wardrobe makeover—it's an ongoing effort—but come on, there are many ways to call a meeting other than proposing a cozy dinner at home."

I doubted that dinner at Glenn's would be "cozy." Neither the stark design of the sprawling house nor the presence of tuxedoed caterers would contribute to an evening of snug intimacy. Still, in Kiki's mind, Glenn would doubtless dismiss the staff and then cook for her, asking her to lick the spoon and spice the pot as they absentmindedly trashed the kitchen. I saw no purpose in disillusioning her by invoking reality.

With an earnest gaze, Kiki said, "I hope you don't think I'm poaching your man, dear."

In truth, I didn't know what to think.

I thought Kiki was overestimating Glenn's interest in her. I thought she wasn't poaching because I had never thought of Glenn as "my man." I thought I would welcome the opportunity to sidestep Glenn's romantic overtures. I thought Kiki should be far more cautious in getting chummy with Glenn, as he seemed to have control issues with the women in his life. One thing I didn't think, but *knew:* Glenn would rue the day he ever tried reining the irrepressible Kiki.

"I think you should go for it," I told her.

"Really?" she asked through a wicked smile. Then her features fell.

"What's wrong?"

"Well, I haven't dated in years. It's been ages—*eons,* darling."

"What about I. T. Dirkman? Your tumble with Irwin wasn't back in the Stone Age; it was last weekend."

"Oh, *that.*" She rolled her eyes. "That was hardly a date. That was the consequence of too much liquor."

"Tonight, it's just dinner," I reminded her, "and you have a pretext, the makeover. If the evening turns into a date, it needs to be his idea, not yours."

Nodding, she mused, "Or at least let him *think* he's calling the shots."

"Exactly. See, Kiki? Those dry years haven't left you inexperienced, but wiser."

She crossed her arms. "Dry years? You make me sound like a withered crone."

With a laugh, I assured her, "No more withered than I."

She laughed as well. "I won't even *attempt* to respond to that."

"Fair enough. Point is, Glenn Yeats is a handful. Do what you want, but do it with open eyes."

"I'm a big girl," she said with an uncertain smile. "I can handle myself."

"Oh, I'm sure you can. But it's easy to be blinded by Glenn's wealth, to say nothing of his power, fame, and influence. You wouldn't be the first to fall under his spell. Look at poor Felicia. She—" I stopped myself, not knowing where my own words were headed.

"She *died*," said Kiki. "Worse yet, she was poisoned. You're not saying . . . ?"

"Don't be silly." I gave a lighthearted chuckle, but it wasn't convincing. "I merely meant to say that Felicia married for money, which netted her an unhappy marriage and, ultimately, divorce." I couldn't help wondering whether her relationship with Glenn had also led to her death, but I didn't voice that question.

I didn't need to. It was on Kiki's mind as well. Dismissing it more deftly than I could have, she joked, "Well, one thing's for sure: no gin tonight." She stood.

"You'll fill me in tomorrow?"

"Of *course*—if I live to tell about it."

"Now, stop that. Are you headed backstage? Let the kids know we can begin."

"Sure, love." She blew me a kiss and strutted off.

Sorting a few papers on my table, I pondered the words that had flowed so spontaneously from me: Kiki wouldn't be the first to fall under Glenn's spell. Look at poor Felicia. She—

"All set, Miss Gray," said Thad, walking onstage with his group.

"Wonderful. Take a moment to set the stage, and the others can come down to watch. Remember, subtext only, beginning with Mrs. Danvers's line. I'm ready when you are."

While Thad and his colleagues arranged a few chairs, the B group filed down to the auditorium and I readied my clipboard for notes.

Cyndy cleared her throat and squared her shoulders. Speaking as Mrs. Danvers, she asked, "May I be of any further service to you, sir?"

Thad, playing Maxim de Winter, asked in return, "Tonight, Mrs. Danvers? Or are you inquiring about the future?"

She lifted her nose and looked away, indifferent. "Both, I suppose."

"Then the answer, *I* suppose, is neither. I shan't be needing you tonight, and sure as Shinola, I shan't need you tomorrow."

"Well, *really.*"

Playing Frith, the butler, Scott piped in, "I say, guv-nuh, that's tellin' 'er good!"

"Oh, *yes,* Maxim," squealed Paige as the young wife, "I think it's ever so clever and forceful of you to take the upper hand in this matter."

"Like a *man?*" asked Mrs. Danvers. "Is that what you're trying to say—your husband has at last displayed the typical signs of his pathetic gender?"

"Hardly," said the wife. "Well, not exactly. I do wish you wouldn't be so quick to put words in my mouth. It's not very charitable of you."

"Charitable?" asked Frith. "Why, that old battle-ax pulls the wings off butterflies just for a laugh. I've seen her eat *pins* for breakfast. I've seen her—"

Maxim interrupted, "That's enough, Frith." Turning to Mrs. Danvers, he asked, "So you find my gender pathetic, do you?"

She sized him up for a moment, then laughed. "Yes, I do. I have *always* found your gender pathetic—you wear it so poorly. And rest assured, Rebecca was thoroughly unimpressed. You never knew how to *please* her, Mr. de Winter. No one did. Only her dear old faithful Danny held the key to her heart—and her womanly pleasure."

"Mrs. Danvers, *please,*" said the wife. "We're English. Our sensibilities are quite delicate. I wish you wouldn't go there."

Frith told Maxim, aside, "I wouldn't mind hearing a bit more."

"Frankly, ol' boy, neither would I"—Maxim slapped his servant's back—"but the missus . . ."

"The missus, indeed," said Mrs. Danvers, sneering. "Manderley has had but one true mistress—Rebecca—and that will *never* change, not so long as I'm here."

"Then perhaps," said Maxim, "you should start packing."

"I shall. Straightaway! And by morning I'll be gone. Without Rebecca, Manderley is but rubble and ashes. Do you hear me? Ashes!" And she left the stage in a whirl, cackling.

Frith said, "That sounded like a threat, guv-nuh."

Maxim scratched behind an ear. "Probably nothing. But do me a favor, will you, Frith? Hide all the matches."

"Very good, sir." The butler bowed, then left.

The young Mrs. de Winter skittered to her husband, wrapping him in her arms. "Oh, Maxim, at last we are rid of her!" Under her breath, she added, "She was *such* a shrew."

"Rebecca seemed to like her." Maxim grinned.

She touched a finger to his lips. "Enough of *them*, Maxim. Now it's just us. We have so many happy years ahead of us."

"Oy." Maxim sat, thumping his forehead. "What about the gossip? The circumstances of Rebecca's death will have tongues wagging for a fortnight. Did I kill her? Did she *trick* me into killing her? Was she really pregnant with her cousin Jack's child? Or was she so smitten with Mrs. Danvers that she would never have carried *any* man's child?"

"Oy, is right." Maxim's wife plopped down next to him.

"We have but one choice, my dear. We must leave this place. We shall pack tonight and go far, far away. We shall have a long holiday, a second honeymoon, a *proper* honeymoon, and go back to Venice. Remember how you loved Venice?"

The young wife thought for a moment, took a deep breath, then stood. Planting her hands on her hips, she said, "No, Maxim. Manderley is your home, and now it's *our* home. We shan't be run out of here—not by Mrs. Danvers or by memories of Rebecca or by the ignorant sniggering of boobs and yokels."

"Boobs and yokels?"

"Yes, my darling." Her gaze drifted upward, into the full stage lights.

Maxim stood. "You . . . you've changed. You're not afraid anymore."

"We have each other, my love, and together, we've nothing to fear."

She and Maxim wrapped each other in a full, swooning embrace. Their passion played convincingly, and while I judged both Paige and Thad to be fine young actors, I had a hunch their evident affections had been rehearsed outside of class, requiring little dramatic artifice. Despite my initial casting notion—that Thad would make a fine Jack Favell and Paige was a natural as Mrs. Danvers—I now realized they were equally well suited for the leading roles of Mr. and Mrs. de

Winter. Pity, I reminded myself, that Paige would not be available for either role come fall.

Thad then stepped out of the role of Maxim, announcing with a simple bow, "Curtain."

Kiki had watched from backstage and now burst into applause; her bracelets clattered like a rickety machine thrown into high gear. Seated in the auditorium, the B group joined in the clapping, as did I.

"Not bad," I said over the noise. "Everyone onstage, please."

As I mounted the stairs and joined the others, Cyndy said, " 'Not bad'? That's rather faint praise, Miss Gray."

"Not bad at all—better? Actually, you did a marvelous job with it, all of you. Your invented dialogue showed considerable insight into the meaning of the script, both in terms of its surface language and in terms of the embedded, overarching plot. That's no small accomplishment."

"*And,*" said Scott, "it was funny."

"We had a few laughs," I allowed, "but the lesson is this: to play the scene in subtext, you needed not only to understand the plot and the roles, but to *become* the characters, inventing their dialogue from *their* points of view, in real time." With a chortle, I added, "I had *no* idea that the loyal, subservient Frith was so lascivious. Thank you, Scott, for enlightening us."

"Righto!"

"Let's take a short break," I told everyone. "Then we'll see what sort of spin the second group can bring to this scene."

Most of the students moved away, gabbing of this and that; some of them studied their scripts. Thad remained onstage, with Paige, telling me, "I *love* this play." His grin was infectious. "I'm really getting into it, as if you couldn't tell."

"I could tell," I assured him. "You're presenting me with some difficult choices."

"Oh. Sorry, Miss Gray." He meant it. He sounded genuinely apologetic.

I laughed. "I *meant,* Thad, that I'll have a tough time casting you—you'd be perfect in several roles."

He positively beamed, and my affection for the unassuming kid from Wisconsin grew all the deeper.

Paige said, "I like the script too, but it's a shame there's no role for Rebecca herself. I mean, she was in the *movie*."

I explained, "Movies tend to be more literal. In the play, it's a wonderful dramatic device, having everyone constantly talk about Rebecca, a character who's never seen. While the second Mrs. de Winter, who's there in the flesh, doesn't even have a *name*."

"Yeah, that's cool, I guess." With a crooked smile, Paige added, "The more I think about it, the more I'm convinced—Rebecca and my dear, departed stepmom, Felicia, had a lot in common."

I hoped Paige would now demonstrate some depth of thinking in her life-imitates-art analogy.

But she reached the same shallow conclusion as before: "They both got what they deserved."

Her unvarnished rancor for her murdered stepmother was disturbing, to say the least, forcing me to wonder—seriously now—whether she could possibly have been responsible for what had happened to Felicia. Recalling Paige's visit to the Regal Palms Hotel on Saturday, I was struck again by the canvas tote bag she had carried. Specifically, I was curious about the bulge in the bag. Could it have been a jug of antifreeze or windshield-washing fluid? Had Paige somehow managed to switch the contents of the gin bottle? The timing didn't make sense, as Felicia had probably died before Paige's arrival, but nonetheless, I couldn't shake the notion that there might be some connection between the visit, the bulging tote, and the poisoning.

I was uncomfortable even considering such a possibility, as I wanted to convince myself that neither Paige nor her father could be capable of such a crime. What's more, I had come to feel nothing but pure affection for Thad Quatrain—as a student, a protégé, and a thoroughly likable young man—so I hoped, for his sake, that his blossoming romance with Paige would not be dashed by the discovery of deadly, vindictive mischief.

Thad was saying something, and I was about to give an absent-minded response, when Tide Arden, Glenn Yeats's executive secretary, burst through one of the auditorium doors, silhouetted by a blast of daylight from the lobby windows. "Ms. Gray!" she said with breathless urgency, loping down the aisle; if her tight leather miniskirt had hitched any higher on her long legs, she'd have risked baring more than her emotions.

All heads turned as she approached.

I asked, "Yes, Tide?"

"It's for *you*, Ms. Gray. I thought I should rush right over." She held a cell phone aloft. Arriving at the stage apron, she reached up from the auditorium floor to hand it to me.

Stepping downstage, I crouched to take the phone, asking, "Is it Glenn? Does he need me?"

"*No*, Ms. Gray. It's Detective Knoll. He phoned the office, asking if I knew how to reach you. I thought it might be *important*." She appeared so exhausted, I feared she might drop.

As all eyes had now turned to me, I thought it prudent to absent myself. Assuming Larry had phoned to report some breakthrough on the case, I retreated to the relative privacy of a shadowy area backstage, well removed from Kiki's costume-sorting project. Nestling the phone to my ear, I asked quietly, "Larry?"

"Hi, Claire." He laughed. "What's up with Glenn's secretary? I asked if there was a way to reach you at the theater, and bingo, there you are."

"Tide has a tendency to err on the side of earnestness. She must have transferred your call to a wireless phone; then she ran it halfway across campus to me. My class is on break right now. What can I do for you?"

I expected him to ask for background on a suspect or to divulge some intriguing tidbit from the coroner.

But no. He said, "What can you do for me? You can meet me for dinner tonight. How does that sound?"

I paused to think. "I, uh . . . have no other plans."

"Good."

"What's the occasion?"

"Nothing special—I mean, we have to eat, right? How about that place downtown, where we've been with Grant?"

"Fusión? I've always enjoyed it. Is Grant coming?"

"Nope. Didn't ask him."

"Just you and me?"

"Exactly."

16

I accepted, of course.

Larry's impromptu dinner invitation took me so much by surprise, I responded with a clumsy lack of grace that must have given him second thoughts about asking me out. Why, though, *was* he asking me out? We had shared working lunches before, but never dinner for two, so I couldn't help feeling that his proposed meeting that night carried overtones of a date.

The very notion was preposterous. I was thinking like a doe-eyed schoolgirl. Hell, I was thinking like *Kiki*—fretting over her lost dating skills in preparation for a rendezvous with Glenn Yeats that same evening. Kiki had already apologized to me for poaching my man, which I found both premature and unnecessary, but to her mind, the courtship had begun.

My thoughts of Larry were not at all in that frame of mind. Though I had recently discovered that I found him unexpectedly attractive, this revelation struck me as no more significant than a new dimension to our evolving friendship. What's more, I could easily dismiss this attraction as a groundless transference of the deep affection I felt for his gay brother, Grant.

My own rationalizations aside, I remained curious all day about the underlying motive for Larry's invitation. What was *he* feeling? Had he phoned merely because, as he had said, "we have to eat"? Surely not. The invitation both acknowledged my friendship and expressed his in return. But I couldn't help wondering if his feelings had begun to run deeper.

By six o'clock, I had grown so flummoxed, I could barely dress. Having pulled various outfits from my closet, I laid them out on my bed, attempting a mix-and-match. With an eye on the clock, I tried on this and that, breaking into a sweat (how charming). Checking each ensemble in the mirror, I scrunched my features in disgust, finding that each attempt made me look worse than the last. Finally, there was but one choice remaining, a nubby silk dress of vivid scarlet—old faithful.

I love red and generally wear at least a touch of it, reserving a full-blown splash in that color for special occasions, such as opening night at the theater, a dressy dinner, or any evening that carries romantic, or at least erotic, prospects. Justifying my flashy choice of attire on the premise of a dressy dinner (and nothing else), I stepped into the dress, managed to zip the back, then dabbed my face with water before sprucing up my hair and makeup.

Sometime after six-thirty, I was in my car, backing out of the garage, and heading up valley toward Palm Springs. As Larry would arrive from the opposite direction, logistics made it impractical for him to pick me up, so we had agreed to meet at the restaurant at seven.

Turning off Indian Canyon and spotting the pert little awning that marked Fusión's front door, I glanced at the Beetle's overhead clock and saw that I was ten minutes early. As I could barely remember the route I had driven, I realized that my thoughts had not been properly fixed on the road. In my eagerness to arrive, I had driven like a bat out of hell.

So I took my time pulling to the curb, chatting with the beefy car valet (college-age; tennis shorts; impossibly white, perfect teeth), tucking the parking stub in my purse, and strolling across the sidewalk to the door. I killed maybe a minute.

Since it was far too hot to linger outdoors, I entered the restaurant, planning to wait for Larry at the bar—not a bad idea, as a "quick one" seemed to be in order. To my surprise, the hostess informed me that Larry had already arrived, beating *me* by ten minutes.

As I strutted into the narrow bar, he rose from his stool. "We're early," he told me with a smile.

I offered a hug. "Seems we were both ready to get on with the evening."

"Yeah, guess so." Larry already had a brown cocktail sitting on the bar. He signaled the bald, brutish bartender, the one who wore nipple rings and a black leather vest, saying, "I believe the lady would like a martini."

I began to detail the particulars (how is it that such a pure, simple drink could have so many infinitesimal variations?), but the bartender stopped me with an amiable nod; he knew my formula by now. Pouring the gin from its blue bottle (which I was determined to disassociate with antifreeze), he mixed, shook, and poured the drink with a finesse that utterly belied his bad-boy biker appearance.

As Larry handed me the glass, I noticed he was wearing a red shirt (crisp cotton broadcloth, with an open collar) under his dark suit. The overall effect was decidedly more studied and stylish than his usual attire. "I like the shirt," I told him, then sipped the microscopic layer of ice from the top of my martini.

Sheepishly, he asked, "It's not . . . too much?"

"Hardly." I laughed. "Most handsome."

"I thought you might like it. I mean, *you* seem to enjoy wearing red."

I was surprised—and touched—that he had noticed, which could have stemmed from either of two reasons. Either he had been paying closer attention to my habits than I had realized, or my affection for red had become flat-out quirky and conspicuous. Willing to assume the former, I noted, "Then we match. Most thoughtful of you."

"That's what I had in mind." He touched his glass to mine, then sipped.

I wasn't sure what he meant. Had he had in mind to be thoughtful, or had he had in mind for us to match? Though his meaning was ambiguous, either option was pleasant enough, so I didn't pother over the alternatives.

He asked, "Care to sit down? Or we could go to the dining room."

"The night is young," I said with a dramatically wistful air. "Let's sit."

So he helped hoist me onto a barstool (no small feat, in my skirt and heels), and we sat gabbing for a few minutes, facing ourselves in the mirror behind the bar. Maybe it was Larry's matching dash of red, but I realized with a start that Hebert, the concierge at Los Pinos, had been right—we *did* look like a couple. Though Larry was forty-six, I wore my extra years well that night, and I daresay no one glimpsing us together would have sniggered at our pairing. In fact, the burly bartender seemed to sense we needed privacy; obligingly, he gathered a rack of glassware and carried it to the kitchen, leaving us alone.

At a pause in our small talk, I asked, "Anything new . . . regarding Felicia?"

Wrapping both hands around his glass, he allowed, "I've had a productive day of developments on the case."

Tantalized, I asked, "Such as . . . ?"

He grinned. "No hurry. We have all night to compare notes."

I was sure he had meant to say, We have all evening.

He added, "We can cover that during dinner."

An awkward silence fell over us. Felicia's death had dominated our conversations for a week, but Larry had now set that topic aside, reinforcing my impression that tonight's meeting was meant to be social. Feeling the need to say *something,* I asked, "And, uh . . . how are things at home, with Hayley?"

Shrugging off the troubles to which he had previously alluded, he explained simply, "She took the kids and the dog to spend another weekend with her parents in San Diego."

"Oh."

The bartender returned, asking, "Would you like to go to your table?"

"Sure," said Larry, "good idea."

As if summoned by telepathy, the black-garbed hostess appeared with menus and a tray for our drinks, then escorted us from the bar. Though the dining room was not empty that night (as it had been when we arrived with Grant the prior Saturday), the other patrons were few, at perhaps three or four tables. Since no music was playing, the room seemed hushed. All eyes slid in our direction as we entered and were seated. "Karissa will be right with you," said the hostess, leaving our menus before returning to her post in the small, dark lobby.

Larry and I sipped our drinks without speaking, letting the others in the room adjust to our presence as they resumed their quiet conversations. When we did speak, we instinctively conversed in whispers, adding a conspiratorial note to our rendezvous, which I rather enjoyed.

Larry paused, looking at me, then said, "I've rarely seen you so happy."

Was I smiling?

"Something obviously agrees with you tonight—must be that martini."

It was an astute observation. Something did agree with me that night, and while the martini played but a minor role in the experience, I allowed, "The bartender is indeed *masterful*."

Larry caught my allusion to the bartender's leather attire, and we shared a hearty laugh. All eyes were on us again, curious about the ruckus. The other diners apparently didn't know what to make of us, so they quickly returned their attentions to each other and their food.

Karissa appeared and recited a few specials—a change of practice from the previous weekend, when no specials had been offered. Perhaps the chef had made a marketing decision intended to attract more aggressively the slim summer clientele. The new policy seemed to be working, as we did not have the room to ourselves tonight.

Intrigued by Karissa's unusual offerings, I noticed a subtle but exotic blend of aromas wafting from the kitchen. Both Larry and I ordered without even opening our menus.

When Karissa left, I leaned forward, asking Larry, "Up for a little shop talk?"

He mirrored my position, answering quietly, "Sure, Claire."

"Any updates you can share with me? Did you talk to Adrienne Coleman?"

"I did, in fact. I phoned her yesterday after we visited Lark Tutwiler, and I met with her this morning." With a soft chuckle, he noted, "They're birds of a feather, Lark and Adrienne."

"I saw them pictured together in the paper. They *do* look alike."

Larry nodded. "But it's more than the look. It's the whole lifestyle, the charity circuit, the *attitude*. Not to say I found either woman condescending; both went out of their way to be helpful, even solicitous."

"Well, Lark was clearly on the prowl, if you want to call that 'solicitous.'"

"Lark's flirtations aside, I sensed an emptiness underneath. Same with Adrienne. They seem so adrift, with no purpose in life—other than to dress up and do lunch. We each play the hand we're dealt, but I couldn't help finding them both rather pathetic."

I understood. Larry wasn't judging the women with contempt, but with pity; they had aroused his sense of pathos. And in revealing these charitable feelings toward people who could easily be dismissed as vapid or unlikable, he also revealed the goodness of his heart. Though we were engaged in a discussion aimed at solving a murder, my thoughts drifted from the victim and her catty friends to the man who sat across the table from me. Larry, I was beginning to understand, was not just a stand-in for his gay brother, whom I loved platonically as my best friend. Larry, I discovered, was another man entirely, second-best to no one.

He was telling me, ". . . so Adrienne Coleman brought very little insight to the case, telling me nothing I hadn't already heard. She corroborated every detail Lark had told us regarding their tenuous friendship with Felicia, including the story of that little snit Felicia threw at the fund-raiser."

"Did you sense Adrienne and Lark had talked—compared notes?"

"Definitely. So they're hard to read. Are they just a couple of gossips? Or are they guilty of some sort of collusion?"

"What's your hunch?"

Larry turned the tables: "What's yours?"

"Well," I reminded him, "I haven't even met Adrienne, but as for Lark, she doesn't strike me as sinister. What would she have to hide? Other than being mildly miffed at Felicia for being so scarce during the time they supposedly spent together at Los Pinos, what possible *motive* could Lark have had to harm Felicia, let alone poison her? On top of which, as far as we know, Lark had no *opportunity* to do the deed. So the only point of suspicion regarding Lark is her claim that Felicia was at Los Pinos."

Larry gave me a wink. "Good summation. And while I can't claim to have solved the Los Pinos riddle definitively, I do have news on that front, and it's persuasive."

Karissa drifted by. "More cocktails?"

"Ah!" I touched the rim of my empty glass. "It does seem to have disappeared. Yes, please."

Larry seconded, "Another round, please."

As soon as Karissa was gone, I leaned forward on my elbows, asking Larry, "Well . . . ? What about Los Pinos?"

He slipped the notebook from his breast pocket and opened it on the table. "I heard back from Hebert, who checked with the resort's accounting department. Sure enough, during the last week of June, a guest calling herself Frances Gates settled her account in cash. This was so unusual, the desk clerk easily remembered the transaction and has given a general description of the woman, who could well have been Felicia."

"Frances Gates," I noted, "is similar to Felicia Yeats—a slight shift of persona. But why the subterfuge with either the name or the cash payment?"

Larry posited, "Perhaps Lark's theory was correct all along—Felicia was there for a secret tryst. That would easily explain why she concealed her identity."

I nodded. "But finding the guy, that won't be easy."

"Needle in a haystack," agreed Larry. "Felicia's boyfriend, if there was one, could have been anyone there that week. We've gone over the 'Frances Gates' account in detail, and it points to no connection with anyone in particular."

"What sort of charges were on her account?"

Larry listed, "The room charges, of course; meals; long distance; lots of spa treatments, including the hair salon; a standard two-day workup in the clinic; cosmetics and clothing from various resort shops; and a substantial charge, six thousand dollars, for a watch from the jewelry store."

"Hngh. She didn't travel cheap, did she?"

"Didn't have to, I guess."

I recalled, "Lark said she never ran into Felicia at the spa. Sort of odd, isn't it?"

Larry shrugged, pocketing his notes. "It's a big place. If they didn't book their treatments together, maybe they never crossed paths."

"Maybe."

Karissa returned with our drinks, followed by a waiter who presented our appetizers.

Larry and I touched glasses, tasted our cocktails, and were about to begin eating when we were distracted by two new arrivals who were being shown into the dining room. Looking in their direction, Larry asked, "Isn't that Dustin Cory, Felicia's son?"

"Right," I said, "and he's with Peverell Lamonte, director of the conservancy that's buying the Dirkman house from Dustin."

Spotting us watching them, they stepped over to our table, and we exchanged brief greetings. "My," I added, "what a coincidence."

"Not *really*," said Peverell with a soft laugh. "Fusión is one of the few good restaurants in the valley to remain open during the off-season. If not here, where *else* would we bump into each other?"

Dustin piped in, "Where the elite meet to eat!" He gave a loud har-har, the sort of backslapping golfer's laugh that would have played far better on the links than in the sophisticated confines of an elegant dining room. I winced as our fellow diners turned to flash us disapproving glances.

"Since you seem to know each other," said the hostess, "would you care to be seated at the next table?"

"Uh," said Peverell, looking flustered, "we'd rather not intrude, and in fact, we have business of our own to discuss. Perhaps over there?" He gestured toward a table at the far corner of the room.

"My pleasure, sir." And they were escorted away from us.

Lifting his fork, Larry grinned, mouthing, "Small world."

Under my breath, I said, "I was surprised to see them, but *they* seemed downright uncomfortable to find *us* here. Don't you think they're acting rather . . . secretive?"

Larry reminded me, "We're the ones whispering."

With a sputter of laughter, I picked up my fork, wishing Larry, "Bon appétit."

Savoring our first bites, we exchanged comments on the food, wonderful as always. Then Larry said, "I'm glad they didn't sit nearby. I was about to fill you in with some new background on Dustin."

I swallowed. "Oh?" I was suddenly far more interested in Larry's information than in the crispy cheese-thing that sat on my plate in a pool of lingonberries and lobster reduction.

Speaking quietly—though above a whisper—Larry told me, "Dustin is basically a playboy, as we've suspected all along, with no real job or career. Looking into his financial dealings, I've learned that he's been involved in numerous failed business ventures, moving from one risky project to another."

"Like a gambler addicted to high-stakes gaming."

"Good analogy. Most recently, Dustin entered into a partnership that marketed a fad dietary supplement, and—"

I joked, "Not antifreeze, I hope."

"No, nothing like that, just the typical zany, macrobiotic health-nut sort of supplement that comes in a brown bottle. Anyway, in promoting this product, Dustin made the supreme mistake of making specific medical claims—in print—that could not be backed up."

"Oops."

"Oops, is right. The FDA shut them down, and the partnership's bankers have called the loan for their operating capital, forcing personal guarantees and threatening a likely bankruptcy. Bottom line: Dustin has desperately needed a quick infusion of cash, and the sale of the Dirkman house gets him out of a very tough bind."

I set down my fork. "Sounds like a motive to me."

"Could be."

"Here's lookin' at ya, Monty!" bellowed Dustin to Peverell, raising a glass. This time the annoyed glances of other diners were directed at a table other than ours.

After exchanging a silent look of gratitude that Dustin had been seated at a distance, Larry and I enjoyed what remained of our appetizers. Sidestepping the murder and shifting to more pleasant topics, Larry asked me about the summer workshop and my plans for the fall production of *Rebecca*. When we had exhausted that subject, I mentioned Grant and Kane's commitment ceremony. "Tomorrow night at this time, the celebration should be in high gear."

Larry said, "It just occurred to me—we'll be having dinner together again tomorrow night. That's three times in eight days."

"Surely a record." I smiled.

"But unless I'm mistaken, we won't be seated together. I'm acting as, uh . . . 'best man' or whatever, so I think I'll end up at the head table."

"That's sweet of you, Larry, standing up for your brother."

"Hey, he stood up for *me* fifteen years ago. Fair is fair."

Larry's decency, his basic goodness, grew plainer by the minute.

During dinner (the main course surpassed the first, a pattern that had remained delightfully unbroken over the course of many meals at Fusión), our conversation again drifted back to the investigation and the various leads Larry had been exploring. "I'd say you've had a productive week," I concluded.

He set down his knife and fork, breathing a thoughtful sigh. "This case has presented plenty of tantalizing leads," he agreed, "but still, the most obvious suspect, by far, is Glenn Yeats."

"What about Dustin? We know he was pinched for cash, and his mother's death solved the problem."

Larry nodded. "Dustin had a feasible *motive,* all right, but we can't prove he had the *opportunity* to act on it. He said he went out on his own last Friday night, deliberately avoiding Felicia's run-in with Glenn."

I recalled, "He told us he went out on the town and stopped at lots of places, 'looking for action.' Started early, got back late."

"So I asked him to reconstruct an itinerary of the bars and clubs he visited that night. It was sketchy, but I followed up, and by and large, his alibi checked out. He tends to be loud and conspicuous; people noticed and remembered him. We already knew he wasn't at Glenn's cocktail party on Friday, and I now have no reason to believe he was anywhere near Felicia's hotel room later that night."

Fishing, I asked, "And what about Peverell? He got what he wanted, the Dirkman house, so he had a *motive* for Felicia's death. And as far as we know, he was the last person to see her alive, so he also had the *opportunity*. As for *means,* well, antifreeze is available everywhere, so virtually *anyone* had the means to obtain the deadly methanol."

"Correct," said Larry. "Peverell Lamonte presents some intriguing possibilities, and he warrants further scrutiny, which is already in the works. But the evidence we have in hand—that Felicia died of methanol poisoning, traces of which were found in the gin bottle given to her by Glenn Yeats—points very strongly to Glenn himself. If he was Joe Blow, if he was *not* the nabob he is, he'd be under arrest by now. I'm not ready to make such a move—yet—and I hope I don't have to. But I do know this: it's time for me to inform Glenn that it would look bad for him to leave town right now."

I was tempted to trot out other possible suspects for Larry's consideration, all of whom had harbored plausible motives against Felicia: I. T. Dirkman, the architect; Paige Yeats, Glenn's daughter; Madison Yeats, Paige's mother; and Felicia's secret lover from Los Pinos, if such a man existed. But these, I knew, were all long shots, mere "noise" in an investigation that had already come into focus for Larry, who was pragmatic enough to fear his own findings, but objective enough to recognize the inevitable.

Because I did not voice these thoughts, the suspicions and the suspects cluttering my mind were held at bay, and my conversation with Larry returned to the benign pleasantries of dinner in a fine restaurant on a Friday night.

We even had dessert. Then we lingered over coffee.

All day, I had fretted over the meaning of Larry's invitation: Was our "dinner date," in fact, a date? The question continued to drift through my thoughts during the pleasant two hours we spent at the table, but it was not until we left the restaurant that my question was clearly answered.

Stepping outdoors, we gave our parking stubs to the valet. Larry asked the kid, "Could you get Miss Gray's car first, please?"

With a nod, the valet trotted off, leaving us standing on the sidewalk.

"It was a wonderful evening, Larry. Thanks for asking me."

"Glad I thought of it. Thanks for making time for me."

"I had no other plans." As my words sounded more dismissive than intended, I added, "But if I'd had other plans, I'd have changed them."

"Really? For me?"

"Of course, for you."

The moment seemed right. Larry offered his arms for a parting hug, which I readily accepted. This had happened before. But then Larry lingered in our embrace, which had not happened before.

And then he kissed me.

No casual peck, it was planted squarely on my lips.

My Beetle sputtered to the curb; the valet hopped out.

Without another word, Larry helped me into the car and sent me driving off into the hot night.

17

Puttering in my kitchen on Saturday morning, I was interrupted by the doorbell. Grabbing a towel, I wiped my hands while traipsing through the house to the front door. When I swung it open, I found Grant Knoll waiting beyond the threshold. "What a pleasant surprise," I told him.

"I'm running absolutely *wild* this morning," he said, breezing inside, giving me a hug. Then he noticed the towel in my hand. "Hope I'm not intruding." Sniffing the air, he added, "Don't tell me milady is whipping up a cheesy little breakfast soufflé."

"You know me better than *that*," I said wryly, closing the door. "I was rinsing out the coffeemaker. But I could brew a fresh pot."

He flicked his hands. "Don't bother, doll. I'm plenty wired already— it's my *wedding* day, for God's sake, and there are at least sixteen *thousand* details that still need my attention." Justifying his hyperbole, he added, "I made a list."

"Then why are you here? Though you're always welcome . . ."

He blurted, "*What happened with Larry last night?*"

I had mentioned on Friday that his brother had invited me to dinner, and Grant had been no less intrigued than I regarding the nature of my night out with Larry. I informed him, "I got a complete update on the investigation."

Though Grant was prying for details on a more personal front, he was nonetheless intrigued. "Oh?" he said coyly. "What's up?"

"Let's sit down, love." My sixties-era living room had classically modern furnishings that included no conventional sofa. Instead, a long, chrome-legged bench with a black-leather-upholstered cushion served as the primary seating. Strolling Grant to the bench, I said, "There were background developments regarding Felicia's son, and we also have reason to believe that Felicia did visit Los Pinos last month, consistent with Lark Tutwiler's story." We sat.

Confused, Grant asked, "Felicia's son had something to do with Los Pinos?"

"Nothing at all," I said, shaking my head; at least I assumed there was no connection. I then told him the details of both Dustin's brush with bankruptcy and Felicia's secretive visit to Los Pinos as Frances Gates, who settled her account in cash.

Grant noted, "It sounds as if the suspect pool is expanding. On top of which, there's a new unknown—Felicia's mystery man at Los Pinos."

"My thoughts exactly, but your brother is growing more convinced that all the hard evidence is stacked against Glenn." Slumping, I added, "Larry plans to tell Glenn not to leave town."

Grant grimaced. "*That'll* go over like a ton of terra-cotta."

"And how. But it's Larry's investigation. He's the pro, so we shouldn't second-guess him."

"*You've* changed *your* tune." Grant crossed his arms, grinning.

"I beg your pardon?" Though I knew what he was driving at.

With a laugh, he reminded me, "You couldn't *wait* to get in on this—playing the sidekick and trotting out your theatrically based hunches. But now that Larry's hunting big game, you're afraid of the fallout and taking a backseat."

"Now, that's ridiculous," I scoffed. But I knew there was a sizable grain of truth to Grant's words. The thought that Glenn Yeats might have murdered his ex-wife—and the prospect of his arrest for the crime—was unnerving, to say the least. Not only was Glenn a prominent, influential, and generous member of the community, but he was also my employer, a man who had lavished me with professional respect and had made no secret of his romantic interest in me as well. He had recruited my assistance in clearing his name with the police, and now I was helpless—or reluctant—to dissuade Larry from following the evidence to its seemingly logical conclusion.

But what could I do? Though all my instincts told me Glenn could not have murdered Felicia, I couldn't prove otherwise, and the circumstances pointed persuasively toward his guilt. I could only place my faith in Larry's professionalism and hope that his remaining leads would steer the investigation elsewhere.

"Well," Grant was saying, "we're not going to solve the riddle of Felicia's poisoning here and now, but I know you have the answer to *another* great mystery."

I'd lost his drift. "Huh?"

He repeated his earlier question: "What happened with Larry last night? The *date*—I want the dirt." He fixed me with a piercing stare that assured me evasive replies would be deemed unacceptable.

"I'm . . . ," I stammered, standing, "I'm not sure where to begin."

Grant lolled backward, hands clutching his knees. "How about we begin with Hayley? Where was the *wife* last night?"

It was a direct question, so the answer came easily: "She took the kids to visit her parents in San Diego—again."

"Hmmm. Sounds like a pattern, a growing habit, an ominous trend—the wife's away. What, then, was the purpose behind Larry's invitation?"

"What *is* this—an inquisition?"

"You bet, doll." Grant stood. "So fess up."

I recalled, "Larry *said* he was inviting me because we 'had to eat'— simple as that. And it was self-evident that he wanted us to spend the evening together because he enjoys my company; I enjoy his as well. But"—I hesitated—"there *is* something else. Something 'happened.'"

"Do tell?" Grant's eyes widened with such interest, he looked like a cat who'd strayed upon a dozing mouse.

"Well, if you must know—"

"And I must."

"If you must know, the evening ended on an unexpected note, at least from my perspective, though I don't think it was entirely spontaneous on Larry's part. Grant, he kissed me."

Grant's stare faded as he closed his eyes, then opened them again— a slow blink. He'd expected more.

I amplified, "This was no quick good-night peck. It was the

genuine article, out on the sidewalk while we were waiting for our cars."

Grant rubbed his chin. "Sounds like a touching, tender moment."

"Oh, it was. But I sensed it was premeditated."

"With malice aforethought," added Grant.

"We needn't be melodramatic, dear."

"What'd he *say*?"

"Not a word. The car arrived just then, he helped me in, and I drove away."

"My, my, my—a hit-and-run. You know what?" Grant's analytical tone turned instantly manic. "I think it was just the opening salvo. *Yes,* doll—love is in the air!"

"Don't you think you're jumping the gun?"

"Hardly." Titillated beyond measure, Grant explained, "Larry is *not* the most demonstrative sort of guy. Why, for *him,* that little smooch is tantamount to swooping you up on his horse and riding off with you into the sunset."

Reminded of the brutish warriors who abducted the Sabine women, I thought it reasonable to point out, "Larry doesn't have a horse."

"Don't be so literal."

"You know what I mean: he's *married,* he's your *brother,* and it makes *no* sense whatever."

"Milady doth protest too much." With a grin, Grant asked softly, "Are you trying to convince *me* of something—or yourself?"

Stepping into his arms, I gave him a hug. "Gosh, Grant, who can tell? I don't know *what* to think."

With his chin on my shoulder, he said into my ear, "Then don't think about it. Let it cook awhile. Overanalysis has killed many a romance."

I stepped back. "But I don't think it *is* a romance."

"Then forget that word. Skip the labels. Let it play out."

"Oh, Grant"—I gave a quiet, wistful sigh—"you make it sound so easy."

He smiled. "It needn't be difficult, honest to God, Claire."

My eyes closed. "It's *always* been difficult. And I'm fifty-four."

Grant clapped his hands over his ears. "No numbers. *Please.*"

Stepping close, I took his hand. "Thank you, Grant. You're more than a friend. I love you."

"I love you too, doll." He gave me a peck. "But . . ."

"But you've got a wedding to tend to, I know. And you need to run along—those zillion details."

"I really do need to dash." He looked deep into my eyes. "You don't mind? Sorry to stir up a hornets' nest of emotions, then ditch you."

With a laugh, I strolled him to the door. "It's anything but a hornets' nest, and I'm not feeling ditched."

Opening the door, he reminded me, "Cocktails at seven."

"Shall I be fashionably late? Or will I miss the shrimp?"

"Bottomless shrimp," he assured me, "but I still think you might prefer to be punctual."

"Curtain at seven—I'll be there."

He gave me a hug, then stepped outside, closing the door behind him.

Without Grant's patter, the house seemed suddenly, eerily quiet. But his earlier words still hung in the silence: "Love is in the air."

Though I had dismissed his assertion as premature, I could not deny that my emerging feelings for his brother were not only unexpected, but exhilarating. I wasn't sure *what* was in the air, but I had a gnawing, and pleasant, suspicion that my life might soon change.

Spotting the dish towel I had left on the leather bench, I plucked it up and returned to the kitchen. Stepping to the sink, I turned on the water and finished rinsing the various parts of the coffeemaker, then dried them and reassembled the machine. Though Grant's proclamation that love was in the air kept tugging at my thoughts, I was also intrigued by something else Grant had said. Rather, it was a question he had asked: "Felicia's son had something to do with Los Pinos?"

Though I had assumed there was no connection between Dustin's brush with bankruptcy and Felicia's apparent fling at the spa, it now occurred to me that she might have told Dustin her reasons for planning the getaway to Los Pinos. Or she might have mentioned it to him after her return.

It was shortly past ten o'clock. I reasoned that Dustin was probably out of his hotel room by that hour, off for another round of golf before the heat of the day set in. Still, it was worth trying to reach him, if only to leave a message for him to return my call. I stepped to the kitchen phone, checked my book for the number of the Regal Palms, and dialed.

When the hotel receptionist answered, I asked to be connected to Dustin Cory's room, then waited as the phone began to ring, expecting to be transferred to his voice mail. On the fourth ring, however, the line connected, followed by a clatter as if the receiver had been dropped.

After a moment's silence, I asked with apprehension, "Hello?"

A man's voice, seemingly distant, muttered something unintelligible, but it had the distinct cadence of colorful obscenity. A clattering came over the line again, as if the receiver were being pulled from the floor by its cord. Finally, a low, groggy voice asked, "Hello?"

"Sorry to disturb you, but I was phoning Mr. Cory."

"Speaking. What time is it?"

"It's after ten, Dustin. This is Claire Gray, Detective Knoll's friend."

"Oh, uh, sure." He cleared his throat. "Guess I overslept."

I couldn't resist asking, "Out late with Peverell Lamonte last night?"

"Yeah." He started to laugh, then coughed. "Monty and I made a few stops after the restaurant." He grunted as if hoisting himself out of bed; then I heard him opening the curtains. "Jeez," he said under his breath, doubtless squinting at the assault of daylight.

"I can't blame you for doing some celebrating last night. It must be a great relief—selling the Dirkman house and getting those bankers off your back."

Without inflection, he agreed, "That's for sure." He wasn't fully awake yet; otherwise he surely would have questioned my knowledge of his financial problem, now solved. Speaking to no one, he said, "I need coffee."

I suggested, "Why don't you call room service? That is, after *we're* finished. If it's not too much trouble, I wonder if I could ask you a few questions about your mother's recent travels. It could help shed some light on how she died."

"Anything to help, Miss Gray." Though his words were genial enough, I could tell by their flat delivery that he was itching to hang up.

"This regards a trip she may have taken recently, but we're having trouble confirming the details. We believe she spent some time at a resort called Los Pinos, up in the mountains near Idyllwild."

"That rings a bell," said Dustin. "Yes, Los Pinos, that was it—about a month ago. Back in LA, Mom told me she was going away for a week, and as far as I know, she went."

I thought aloud, "Then Lark was giving us the straight story all along."

"Who?"

"Lark Tutwiler, a friend of your mother's who lives here in the desert. They arranged the trip together and met at the resort. Did your mother mention her?"

"No, I'd remember a name like that."

"What's strange, Dustin, is that the hotel has no record of your mother's visit, but a woman calling herself Frances Gates was registered that week and settled her account in cash. Lark saw very little of Felicia during their stay, making her wonder if your mother had set up a rendezvous with some man. I mean no disrespect to Felicia, but do you think it's possible she was there for a secret romance?"

Dustin exhaled a low, pensive whistle. "Now that you ask about it, before she took that trip, she told me she planned to meet 'a clever little man named Lester'—those were her words. I remember them because, when she said them, I couldn't quite imagine Mom with *any* guy named Lester."

"When she told you this, how was her mood?"

Without hesitation, Dustin answered, "Chipper. And that was unusual; Mom had been sulky for months, not that she's ever been what you'd call 'perky.' So I thought, This Lester must be a real stud." With a laugh, Dustin added, "Or maybe Lester has *other* assets. Maybe he's the hotel jeweler or furrier. The prospect of a major purchase always gave Mom a little lift."

I recalled that Frances Gates's hotel bill included charges from various resort shops, including the jewelry store, where she'd bought a pricey watch, so Dustin's theory had merit. Unfortunately, it didn't suggest a motive for this secret, sinister Lester to kill Felicia a month later.

"Miss Gray?" said Dustin. "Is there anything else? If not, I really do need to get some coffee ordered."

"Go right ahead," I said with a soft laugh. "Thanks for the background, Dustin. It's most helpful. And I hope you feel better soon."

He thanked me in return. Then we said good-bye and hung up.

While Dustin phoned room service, I phoned Larry Knoll. After a couple of rings, my call was shunted to voice mail. While electronic screening typically makes me bristle, in this instance I was grateful for it, as I did not wish, at that moment, to compare notes with Larry regarding the previous evening's dinner—and parting kiss. That discussion, while inevitable, would have to wait.

At the beep, I said, "Good morning, Larry. It's Claire. I just had a phone conversation with Dustin Cory, who essentially confirmed that Felicia spent the last week of June at Los Pinos. He said she planned to meet, quote, 'a clever little man named Lester.' Maybe our friend Hebert could tell you if there was a Lester Somebody registered that week. Or, according to Dustin, Felicia may have been referring to the hotel jeweler. Either way, I thought this might help. I'll see you this evening, Larry." I hesitated before adding, "And thanks, by the way, for last night. Everything was wonderful." Satisfied that my closing was sufficiently vague, I hung up the phone.

And the doorbell rang. A quiet Saturday morning it was not meant to be.

Traipsing from the kitchen and through the living room, I arrived at the front door and swung it open. Waiting outside were Thad Quatrain and Paige Yeats.

"Good morning, Miss Gray," said Thad. "Sorry to disturb you at home."

"But it's sort of important," explained Paige. "Mind if we come in?"

"Of course not." I gestured them inside. "Always a pleasure to see two of my favorite students. Would you care to sit down?" My voice was laced with concern, as I sensed their visit had something to do with Felicia.

Sitting on the leather bench with Thad, Paige set aside the same canvas tote bag she had brought to the hotel a week earlier; it now appeared all but empty, with no bulging contents.

I offered, "Can I get you something—iced tea, perhaps?"

"No, thank you, Miss Gray," said Paige. "Please don't bother."

Thad added, "We won't take much of your time. We just need to ask you about something."

I sat on the edge of the coffee table, twisting my torso to face them. "If it's about the investigation, I'm afraid I'm not at liberty to—"

"Heavens, *no*," said Paige with a laugh. "With my evil stepmom out of the picture now, I really haven't given the woman a second thought."

Thad touched Paige's knee, telling her softly, "I'm sure that's not true."

"Close enough." Paige explained to me, "Actually, we're here about school."

Logical enough, I thought, when students drop in on a teacher. Still, I felt a smidgen of disappointment that the topic had shifted from murder to the merely mundane. I asked, "What about school?"

"Well, *first,* Miss Gray, I wanted to tell you how glad I am that I followed Pop's advice and enrolled in your summer workshop. I was skeptical, especially about spending a summer in the desert, but he was right—it was worth it. I feel my acting skills have really benefited from your training."

I nodded. "You've come along beautifully. I'm happy to have you in the class."

She hesitated, took a deep breath, then blurted with wide-eyed enthusiasm, "So I'm wondering if I might *stay* in your class. I mean, do you think there might be an opening in the *real* DAC theater program? I'd like to enroll for the fall semester."

"What about your film work in Los Angeles?"

She bowed her head. "That can wait, Miss Gray. I need to concentrate on the basics and learn my craft first."

Correct answer. I grinned. "Well, I'll have to look into this, but I have a hunch some strings can be pulled." Hell, Paige's father had built the school. What's more, she was a promising young actress, and I had regretted the prospect of losing her. I admitted, "I've been giving a lot of thought to casting the roles of Mrs. Danvers and the young Mrs. de Winter in our production of *Rebecca*. Cynthia Pryor can't play *both* parts."

"I should say *not*," agreed Paige with good-natured rivalry for her classmate.

Thad laughed. "Uh-oh. I can just see you and Cyndy, scheming to do each other in before auditions. Broken brake cables, cyanide-dusted brownies, pianos falling from high windows . . ."

"Whatever it takes," said Paige, crossing her arms. "Mrs. Danvers is a role worth fighting for."

I reminded her, "But Mrs. de Winter is the larger role. She's the central character."

Paige didn't buy it. "She may be the lead, but let's face it, she's not very memorable. No, Mrs. Danvers is the prize. I'd *kill* for that role."

Thad winced, telling me, "She's exaggerating."

"Well, maybe a little," Paige allowed. With a giggle, she wrapped an arm around Thad and hugged him close. It was evident that her plan to enroll for the fall semester was motivated by her desire not only to study theater, but to remain with Thad.

I stood, telling Paige, "Let's not get ahead of ourselves. Auditions are some six weeks off, but if you're serious about enrolling, we need to get your application moving, and fast. Let's plan to meet in my office Monday morning before class."

"Perfect." She stood, hiking the strap of her tote over her shoulder.

Thad stood as well. "Thanks so much, Miss Gray. Paige has been torn between studying here or back in LA, but I think she's made the right decision."

I told him, "I'm *sure* she has."

Moving to the door with Thad, Paige said, "I appreciate your faith in me, Miss Gray."

It was an odd statement, overly formal and a tad presumptuous, but at that moment I was concerned not so much with her words as with her bag. "That tote," I said, stepping near for a better look at it. "I noticed you carrying it at the hotel last Saturday. I've been looking for something like that—for class papers and such. May I ask where you got it?"

She shrugged. "I've had it forever, as if you couldn't tell—it's looking awful ratty. Seems to me, it was a giveaway with something. Sorry I can't be more helpful. But, hey! Would you like to have it? I can manage with something else."

"Thank you, dear, it's most kind of you to offer, but I would never come between a woman and her favorite bag." Besides, as she had noted, it was ratty.

"If you change your mind, just let me know—though I can't *imagine* why you like it." Paige laughed, holding the scruffy tote at arm's length.

"It's just so . . . roomy," I explained. "For instance, at the hotel last week, I couldn't help noticing that your tote was, well, *bulging* with something. But you didn't seem to have any trouble lugging it around—whatever it was." I smiled expectantly. Though my words stopped short of asking the question, my inflection demanded an answer. Ah, the skilled artifice of a life in the theater.

"Now, what *was* that?" Paige asked herself, squirming some. "I can't quite recall—ah, sure, I know. I was carrying my running shoes that day, and yes, they *are* kinda bulky."

Thad's brow wrinkled. "We didn't go running that morning. It was too hot."

"But I thought we *might* go running." Her tone seemed to tell him, Play along with me here.

"Really? It never even crossed my mind, not in *this* weather."

"It doesn't matter," I said blithely. I already knew what I needed to know: Paige did *not* want to tell me what she'd had in her tote that morning.

Thad had driven her to the hotel on Saturday and waited for her in the lobby while she went to Felicia's room. On Monday, they had disagreed about the length of his wait. I wondered if there were valet records at the hotel that could clarify how long Thad's car had been parked.

"So," said Paige. "We'll see you tonight at the ceremony?"

I opened the door for them. "You bet. It's Grant and Kane's special evening. Wouldn't *think* of missing it."

They thanked me again for considering Paige's fall enrollment, we exchanged farewells, and they left.

As I closed the door, the phone rang.

Heaving a quick sigh—the morning had been an exercise in non-stop communication—I crossed the room to the pass-through bar from the kitchen and picked up the phone that sat there. With a note of annoyance, I answered, "Yes?"

"Claire? It's Glenn."

Good God. His daughter had departed only seconds earlier, and already he was checking to see if I had accepted her informal application to my theater program. Was he that transparently pushy?

No, actually. I had misconstrued the reason for his call. He told me, "Larry Knoll just paid me a visit—at home."

Though I knew the answer, I asked, "Not a social call?"

"Not at all. He was polite and reasonable—he's never been less than a gentleman—but he gave me an update on the investigation, and it's not looking good. He didn't come right out and say it, but he suggested that, 'under the circumstances,' it might look bad for me to leave town right now. Can you imagine? I'm under house arrest."

"Well, not exactly."

"Okay, I'm *virtually* under house arrest. Bad enough. I don't mind telling you, Claire: I'm growing more worried by the hour. This could really get out of hand. It already *has*. So I'm asking you—*begging* you—to do whatever you can to help move the case along and to steer Larry toward some other suspect, *any* other suspect. This has gone too far."

He paused, then added, "It's time to *fix* this."

18

Exactly how Glenn expected me to "fix" his situation was not clear to me. His pressuring to nail another suspect—*any* other suspect—went well beyond a plea for simple justice and sounded disturbingly like the desperation of a man with something to hide.

Though I was grateful for all that Glenn had done for me, my gratitude was not sufficient to inspire blind loyalty in return, so I did not consider, even for a moment, the possibility of steering Larry's investigation down a false path. I hoped to help save Glenn's hide, but only if it warranted saving. I assured him, "I'll do the best I can."

By evening, there were no new developments on the case. Though I hadn't yet spoken to Larry, we had played phone tag. Calling while I was out running errands, he had left a message that Hebert had found no record of a recent guest at Los Pinos—or a jeweler—named Lester.

Had our mystery man, Felicia's secret lover, also registered at the resort under a false name? If so, why all the subterfuge? More to the point, why and how would he kill Felicia a month later? Something in the emerging Lester plot didn't add up.

Such were my thoughts as I tussled over my choice of outfit for the night's festivities. Clearly, the red dress—old faithful—was out. Larry had seen me wear it the previous evening, and besides, it was too conspicuous for a wedding; I didn't want to upstage either of the grooms. So I ended up in a predictable summery pantsuit of cool off-white linen, jazzing it up with a short red-silk scarf knotted around my neck.

Shortly after six-thirty, I drove the few minutes to Palm Desert and picked up Kiki at her condo. She emerged from the front door wearing a simple but flowing gown of gauzy gold fabric, topped off by a long strip of silver lamé that wound through her hair and draped down her back—her idea of "toning it down" for a dignified event, apparently. Getting into the car, reeling in her train, and pulling the door closed, she asked, "What's wrong with this picture?"

I was reluctant to answer. "Why, your outfit is smashing, Kiki. As usual."

"No, love, not the dress. I mean, *us.*"

More curious than defensive, I asked, "What's wrong with 'us'?"

"Two single gals, well into their fifties, dressed to the nines, going out together on a Saturday night—to a wedding, no less. Catch my drift?"

I roared away from the curb. "Doesn't bother me in the least. Besides, we're just *riding* together. It's not as if we'll be joined at the hip all night."

Primping, Kiki cooed suggestively, "I certainly hope not. Who *knows* what may develop?"

I assumed she was referring to her prospects with Glenn Yeats. I thought it best not to advise her, not just yet, that Glenn might be dealing with issues far headier than romance this evening.

By the time I drove us back to Rancho Mirage and up the winding mountain roadway to the entrance of the Regal Palms, it was a few minutes past seven. Parking valets hustled to jockey the cars of arriving and departing guests at the busy hotel. As my Beetle was being driven away, Kiki and I stepped through the double doors to the main lobby.

A discreet sign on a stanchion, KNOLL-RICHTER CEREMONY, directed us down the long hallway toward the ballrooms. "This way, I guess," said Kiki. I already knew the way. Moving through the lobby and down the hall, we retraced the steps I had taken a week earlier, on the morning Felicia had died.

As we rounded a bend in the wide hall, the prefunction area came into view, and I saw that most of the guests had been prompt. The cocktail hour was already in full swing, and as planned, the space outside the ballroom had been outfitted with a bar and a grand piano; a soft, jazzy improvisation on a Cole Porter melody drifted above the chatter of the crowd. Waiters in tuxedos moved among the guests with trays bearing drinks and appetizers. Grant and Kane, wearing elegant new suits, dark gray, probably Armani, mingled as well.

Stepping into the fray, I caught the eye of the waiter with the shrimp, who immediately turned in my direction and offered his tray. I plucked an enormous icy specimen, set it on a napkin, and moved to another waiter, who offered wine. I took a glass of chardonnay.

Kiki leaned to ask, "Lost your appetite for gin?"

"Later, maybe. The night is young."

"*There* you are, doll!" Grant swooped over to me. "I see you found the shrimp."

Between bites, I told him, "I've been thinking about this all day." Giving him a quick kiss, I added, "Everything is lovely, as expected. But I'm sort of surprised to see you—I mean, out here, *before* the ceremony."

Hand on hip, he lectured drolly, "That's the *bride* they usually keep under wraps till the organ thunders. Kane and I were going to toss for the honors, but then we decided that neither one of us looks good in white lace, so we figured, what the hell, let's just join the party."

"Glad you did," I assured him.

Kane stepped over to us. "Good evening, Claire. Hi, Kiki." He kissed us both, telling us, "You look *great* this evening."

"Nah"—I hugged his shoulders—"*you're* the star tonight, the target of all these admiring eyes." Though he had always struck me as handsome and youthful, I had never seen Kane dressed so formally, which lent to his good looks a surprising new dimension of maturity. The disparity of his and Grant's years seemed suddenly irrelevant.

"Excuse me, duckies," said Kiki. "There's Glenn." She waved to him across the room. When he turned and waved back with a broad smile, she took off in his direction.

Watching this, Grant asked, "Is something going *on* with those two?"

I told him, "Kiki seems to think so. And I must say, she's done a remarkable job with Glenn's makeover. He's looking downright . . . presentable this evening."

"A marked improvement," Grant allowed.

Iesha Birch, director of the campus museum, strolled by with Tide Arden, Glenn's executive secretary. They stopped to greet and congratulate Grant and Kane. Tide stepped aside with me, asking breathlessly, "Will everything be all right, Ms. Gray? Mr. Yeats is beside himself. How could they *possibly* think he had anything to do with the poisoning? Why, he's the finest man alive." Her devotion was never less than slavish.

"Soon enough," I told her in a soothing tone, "this will all be sorted out." But I had no such knowledge, of course, and even less assurance that her beloved boss would not be implicated.

"He really needs your help," she said into my ear, giving my arm a fierce squeeze. Then she and Iesha drifted into the crowd together.

Someone tapped my shoulder from behind, saying, "Hope I didn't scare them off."

I turned. "Larry!" My inflection was entirely too enthusiastic, as if I hadn't seen him in a year, when it had been only a day.

"Hi, Claire." He smiled, offering a quick hug (but no kiss). He wore a dressy, well-tailored dark suit, a white shirt, and a silk tie sporting horizontal gray and silver stripes, its knot punctuated with a perfect dimple. All in all, he was looking unexpectedly stylish—or had my point of view changed? He asked me, "Quite the elegant to-do, isn't it?" To his brother, he added, "Not that I'd expect anything less from *you*, Grant."

"Shucks, bro, it's just a little ol' wedding."

"A little unconventional," said Larry, "but I'm proud to be a part of it."

"Me too," said the young woman at his side, beaming a warm smile. Was this Larry's wife, Hayley? I'd thought she was spending the weekend in San Diego. Then again, wouldn't she set aside their differences and make an appearance, if only out of respect for Grant?

Apparently not. Kane introduced me to the woman: "Claire, this is my sister, Alyssa Richter. She and Larry will be our two witnesses at the ceremony."

Alyssa shook my hand. She was older than Kane, perhaps thirty. "Under slightly different circumstances," she said, "I'd be the bridesmaid, but tonight . . ." We all laughed.

Grant asked her, "You'll look after my brother tonight?"

Larry good-naturedly informed Grant, "I'm not *that* much of a hick. I can handle a gay wedding."

"I *know* you can, bro. I merely meant, the two of you seem to be on your own this evening."

"And as the two witnesses," noted Alyssa, "we do make a logical pairing." Taking Larry's arm, she told Grant, "I'll be happy to look after him." And they strolled off together to get drinks.

I wasn't sure *what* to make of that. Alyssa was simply being playful; Larry, polite and genial. Still, I'd envisioned myself hobnobbing with Larry that evening, even if not seated at the same table. But I had no claim on him, so there was no point in dwelling upon—let alone voicing—the umbrage I felt as Alyssa dragged him off to liquor him up.

These unworthy thoughts were nipped by Paige Yeats and Thad Quatrain, who appeared through the crowd and joined us. Paige swirled her glass of wine, hoisting it like a trophy of adulthood; in her low-cut dress and heels, she looked well beyond her twenty years. Thad had no interest in alcohol. Instead, he chomped at one of the shrimp piled on a small plate he carried. When he offered me one, I gratefully accepted it and gnawed away.

Grant and Kane excused themselves, needing to circulate. So I engaged my two students in a bit of small talk, sticking close to Thad, pilfering more shrimp. We spoke first of Paige's intended enrollment, then of the event that had drawn us together that night.

With a contented sigh, I noted, "The surroundings couldn't be lovelier."

Thad agreed, "It's a beautiful hotel."

"Yeah," said Paige, "but it's a little weird being here, isn't it?"

"Hmm?" I asked.

"*You* know." Leaning forward, she told us in a stage whisper, "It's like returning to the scene of the crime." She smirked, looking decidedly adolescent in her evening dress.

Yes, a crime had been committed, and yes, we had returned to the hotel. But the expression she had used was typically said of the culprit—not innocent bystanders, witnesses, and wedding guests—so her lame little joke struck me as intriguing, if not humorous. I reminded her, "But we don't really know *where* the crime was committed—possibly here at the hotel, or possibly the night before, at your father's house."

"It was just a figure of speech, Miss Gray."

Thad gave Paige a soft smile. "Let's say we drop the murder for now. This is Kane's big night with Grant—it's all about happiness."

"Most sensible, Thad." I dropped a shrimp tail onto his plate. "A party is no place to stew about murder." But I was a fine one to talk. I'd been sizing up everyone in the room, wondering if the killer was among us, exactly as Paige had suggested.

She touched Thad's arm. "Yes, sweets—most sensible. Happy thoughts tonight, I promise."

They gabbed some; I listened, contributing a nod now and then. Addressing Thad as "sweets," Paige had chosen an innocent term of endearment, hardly passionate, but it signaled nonetheless that their relationship had progressed beyond that of chummy classmates. Their easy banter, their in-sync body language, made it only too evident that they had begun to share the same thoughts and to build the beginnings of what could become a shared future.

"Miss Gray?" said a woman with a clipboard. "So nice to see you again. I hope everything is to your liking."

Thank God she wore a little brass name badge—it was Crystal Conner, the hotel's events manager. I effused, "Your staff has done a *splendid* job. The Regal Palms certainly lives up to its reputation."

"*Thank* you, Miss Gray." She actually blushed; one would have thought I'd slipped her a hundred-dollar tip.

So I paid her another compliment: "This hotel is the perfect setting for Grant and Kane's vows. It's so . . . 'them.'"

"Isn't it, though? They're in the ballroom right now, doing some last-minute rehearsing with the celebrant."

I hadn't thought to ask Grant who would be officiating at the ceremony. As neither Grant nor Kane was religious, I doubted they would recruit a clergyman, nor had I spotted anyone fitting that description at the cocktail reception. Like everyone else, I would have to wait and see who would preside over their union. Glancing at my watch, I noted that the hour was drawing near.

"If you'll excuse me," said Crystal, "I need to check on a few details." With her clipboard tucked under an arm, she plied the crowd, heading toward the ballrooms.

As eight o'clock approached, there were few new arrivals. All the guests were gathered, drinks in hand, awaiting the main event. Some fifty in all, the group consisted largely of Grant and Kane's friends, some of whom I knew, as well as associates from the college, all of whom I knew, at least by name.

While chatting about something with Paige and Thad, I received another tap on the shoulder from behind. "Yes, Larry?" I said, turning with a smile.

"Larry? I guess you were expecting someone else. I thought you'd be glad to see me." It was Tanner Griffin, the young actor I had mentored (and loved), who was now living in La-La Land, making his first film.

"Now, *that's* an understatement. Of *course* I'm glad to see you." Handing my wineglass to Thad, I wrapped both arms around Tanner.

He returned the hug, nuzzling my cheek. "You look wonderful, Claire. I'm glad to see you too."

"When I talked to you last week, you hadn't even *heard* about the wedding."

He laughed. "I lied. I'd already received my invitation, and the guys suggested I should surprise you. So: surprise!"

I clutched him all the tighter.

When our initial flush of emotions had abated, Thad joined our conversation, saying, "Hey, Tanner, welcome back." They had appeared together in my first two productions at the college. "How's Hollywood? How's *Photo Flash*?"

"*Hollywood?*" asked Paige. Though she had not previously met and had probably never heard of Tanner Griffin, I had no doubt that his name would become a household word upon release of his first movie.

He filled her in on the background of the project, regaling us with his insider's tales of the filming, which Paige lapped up with eager, starry-eyed interest.

Noting this with a crooked grin, Thad asked her, "Not having second thoughts about transferring to Desert Arts College, are you?"

"Nope." She shook her head definitively. "If Miss Gray will have me, I'm in."

The music stopped, and the crowd instinctively hushed. "Ladies and gentlemen," said Crystal, standing in front of the doors to the smaller ballroom, "the time has arrived. May I ask all of you to step inside to witness this most special of milestones in the life to be shared by Grant and Kane."

As the doors slid open, the pianist began playing again, but his jazzy ditties were now replaced by something dignified yet joyful, probably Bach. Filing into the ballroom, we deposited our drinks on trays near the door (there would surely be more to come). Stepping inside, we were greeted by the same melody played on a second grand piano, perfectly synchronized with the first.

A week earlier, I had seen the room bare, but it had now been transformed into an elegant wedding chapel, replete with flowers, candles, and rows of draped chairs, all white.

Grant and Kane were already positioned on the dais in front of the wall of French doors that looked out upon the terrace and the mountainous view beyond; with the waning daylight, the sky had turned indigo, the peaks orange. Flanking Grant and Kane were Larry and Alyssa. In the center stood a middle-aged woman in a simple white dress; around her neck hung an ornate liturgical stole that reminded me of the one worn by the generic reverend at Wednesday's memorial service, except that his had been a maudlin purple, while hers was a merry gold brocade. All five of them nodded and smiled as the guests entered, quietly greeting many of us by name. They leaned to exchange comments with each other, sometimes laughing softly, signaling that the tone of the ceremony, while formal, would be anything but solemn.

Tanner and I took seats toward the back of the room, which offered an open view of the entire proceedings. Glenn made a beeline for the front row; Kiki joined him. Tide and Iesha sat among a group of other college staff, behind Glenn. Paige and Thad didn't venture far into the room, sitting near the door to the hall.

Outdoors, on the terrace behind the dais, other hotel guests occasionally wandered past, doubtless taking a stretch from their tables in the main dining room. Some smoked; others simply enjoyed the scenery; a few peeped through the windows into the ballroom, curious about the flicker of candlelight.

Tasteful printed programs (of Kane's design and making) were placed on each chair. Glancing through mine, I saw that the ceremony would end with a "handfasting." What, I wondered, had I gotten myself into?

When all the wedding guests were seated, the music stopped.

"My friends," said the woman in white, "my name is Sarah Standish. I am a civil celebrant, and it's my honor this evening to preside over the commitment ceremony of our loving friends, Grant Knoll and Kane Richter." Her words were polished and delivered with poise and clarity. I wasn't sure what a civil celebrant was, but she struck me as a good one.

She continued, "There is no traditional ritual, no set liturgy, for the commitment we celebrate tonight, so Grant and Kane have worked with me to invent a ceremony uniquely theirs, writing most of the words themselves."

I leaned to Tanner, whispering, "Get comfortable—this may take a while."

Covering a laugh, he shushed me with a nudge of his elbow.

After introducing Larry and Alyssa as the two grooms' witnesses, Sarah said, "Let us begin, quite simply, with Grant and Kane's exchange of vows."

The two men stepped to the front of the platform, facing each other. Grant spoke first. With a measure of humor, but forgoing his usual snappy patter and campy cracks, he professed to Kane his deep love and promised to stay with him forever, "come what may, through thick and thin."

Kane echoed the same pledge while thanking Grant for "a happiness I had never thought possible—till you entered my life." Speaking from the heart, Kane may not have been aware of the tear that slid down his cheek, but it escaped the attention of no one else present.

Grant choked back a tear of his own. In the front row, Kiki leaned her head on Glenn's shoulder. To the side of the room, Thad and Paige leaned together in each other's arms. And sitting next to me, Tanner reached over for my hand, which he held to his heart.

Grant and Kane exchanged rings, the same rings they had already worn for months. Then Sarah presided over a "ceremony of light" as the grooms and both witnesses touched the flames of small tapers to a large "unity candle."

"And now," said Sarah, "Grant and Kane will perform the ancient ritual of handfasting."

I whispered to Tanner, "Just when you thought you were on safe ground—"

Again, the elbow.

Sarah explained that handfasting was a rite of union that had descended from Scandinavia into old England, a sort of common-law marriage that involved the "fastening" of hands. Standing between Grant and Kane, who faced each other, she instructed them to join opposite hands. Doing so, their arms crossed at the wrists. She then removed the stole from around her neck and wrapped and knotted it around their hands. As a final fillip, she asked the two witnesses to add their hands to the bundle, which were then "fastened" as well. She incanted something that sounded vaguely Chaucerian, paused, then declared Grant and Kane united for life.

To the applause of the guests, she unwrapped the newlyweds, who indulged in a big, sloppy kiss.

Tanner turned to tell me, "There, now—back on terra firma?"

I grinned. "You're right. It was all quite touching."

But it was not quite finished. The grooms had spoken. Sarah had spoken. Now it was the witnesses' turns. Alyssa went first.

"A month or so ago," she said, "early on a Sunday morning, when my little brother phoned to say he was getting married, my skepticism bordered on disbelief. Sorry, Kane, but that is *not* the sort of news you unload on the unsuspecting before they've had their coffee. Then, as the details of the wedding became clearer to me, I was forced to wonder about this character named Grant. Happily, I've since discovered that my misgivings were totally unfounded . . ."

Listening to Alyssa describe her growing understanding and support of her brother's commitment to Grant, I recognized that I had shared the same feelings. Grant and Kane's unlikely but true love was a model of "normalcy," despite their shared gender and their disparate years. I wondered if I myself would ever find such happiness.

When Larry stepped forward to speak about his brother, I wondered if—just possibly—I was watching a man who would play a larger role in the unscripted scenario of my life.

He was saying, ". . . and it's traditionally the role of the best man to offer the first toast . . ."

Right on cue, a battalion of waiters entered the room, bearing trayloads of icy champagne flutes, filled to their brims. Larry paused as the waiters moved from row to row, while the guests, standing, passed the glasses to each other.

Outside on the terrace, several passersby had paused to look through the windows, sensing that our ceremony was nearing its festive climax. It was difficult to see their faces, backlit by the sunset and obscured by reflections in the glass, but three of the onlookers, hanging close together, seemed familiar to me. When they turned from the window and ambled on, I recognized them.

Peverell Lamonte, Lark Tutwiler, and Dustin Cory were taking a stroll together, doubtless arriving for dinner at the hotel. I had no way of knowing how or why the three of them had connected that evening, but seeing them, I realized we had established a quorum of sorts. Adding them to the guests attending the wedding, we now had present virtually everyone who had played any role whatever in the drama surrounding Felicia Yeats's death. In fact, I found it conspicuous that the only player *not* present was I. T. Dirkman, the architect whose house had been at the center of the controversy between Felicia and Glenn Yeats.

Then, glancing about the room as everyone raised their glasses, I noticed an empty chair next to Thad Quatrain. Paige Yeats had disappeared, presumably slipping out to the hall.

Larry said, "To my brother, Grant, and to his partner, Kane—may they share a long and happy life together."

"Here, here!" we chorused.

Everyone drank.

Over the rim of my glass, my eyes scanned the crowd.

19

Happy chatter broke out as the ceremony ended, and we all made our way to the adjacent, larger ballroom, which had been set up for the dinner reception and the dancing that would follow. We were greeted by yet another pianist, who had been joined by a harpist and two violinists. Like the room we had just left, this one also had a wall of French doors leading out to the terrace, and in front of these windows was the head table, which would seat the five members of the wedding party, all in a row, facing into the room. The other eight tables were round, each seating six.

I was flattered beyond measure to find that Grant and Kane had assigned me to the table nearest theirs; Tanner was given the seat to my left. To my right were Glenn and Kiki, looking very much like a couple. Completing our table were Thad and Paige, though Paige's whereabouts were still unknown. When asked about this, Thad replied with a carefree shrug, "It's a mystery to me—but then, *that's* Paige."

Once we had all found our places, most of the guests did not immediately sit, but mingled and talked, drifting to the bar for fresh cocktails, waiting their turns to congratulate Grant and Kane, who circulated through the room. They were truly in their element, surrounded by friends in a setting of rarefied elegance—the flowers, the table settings, the music, all were flawless.

But I couldn't shake the suspicion that our celebration was tainted by the presence of a killer. Catching Larry's eye, I beckoned him aside, and we stepped outdoors to the terrace. The air had yet to cool in the twilight; heat still radiated from the limestone pavers.

Glimpsing the grooms through the window, Larry said, "They're perfect for each other—who'd've thought?"

I couldn't help wondering if the same observation might apply to him and me. I nodded. "They're an unlikely pair, but sometimes that's exactly what draws two people together."

"Too bad Felicia's murder is hanging over the evening. It sorta puts a damper on things."

Laughter erupted indoors as Grant yelped at something, probably one of his own jokes. I assured Larry, "Your brother's spirits are not easily dampened."

"But I wonder how Glenn Yeats is doing. I can't imagine *he's* in a party mood tonight. God knows, I'm not." Larry didn't need to explain. It wasn't so much the murder that was vexing him; it was the unsavory prospect of arresting our powerful local billionaire.

"Tell you what," I said. "Glenn's at my table. I'll keep an eye on him and try to sound him out. Maybe we can come up with some overlooked detail that'll help put him in the clear. And did you notice? Lark Tutwiler and Peverell Lamonte are at the hotel tonight; I assume they're joining Dustin Cory for dinner. Who knows? Anything might develop—could be interesting."

"Interesting?" Larry laughed. "This is Grant and Kane's big night, remember. Whatever you're up to, let's not spoil the party."

"Wouldn't dream of it." I crossed my heart, then opened the top buttons of my jacket. "It's *hot* out here."

"No kiddin'. Let's get back inside."

And in we went.

Most of the guests were seated by now, as a crew of waiters had begun serving the first course, a chilled vichyssoise garnished with chopped chervil and cracked pepper—a fitting prelude to a late-July dinner in the desert.

"*There* you are," said Tanner, rising to help me with my chair. "We thought you disappeared."

"Me? Among the missing? Hardly." I gave an airy laugh, offering no explanation for my absence. Noting that Paige had joined the others at the table, I asked her, "Everything okay, dear? You seemed to disappear as well."

She was every bit as oblique as I had been: "Just needed to freshen up."

I couldn't press for details regarding her claimed foray to the rest room—not politely, anyway—so I turned to Glenn, asking, "Are you aware that Paige would like to continue her studies at DAC this fall?"

"What?" His features brightened, but he controlled his smile, as if skeptical of the good news. "Why, no, she hasn't said a word." Turning to his daughter, he asked, "Is this true, baby?"

"Right, Pops, if Miss Gray will have me."

I told Glenn, aside, "I'll get it taken care of on Monday."

"*Fab*-ulous!" said Kiki. "I've sat in on some of the workshops, and Paige will make a splendid addition to the program."

Glenn wagged a finger. "No special treatment, though. Paige needs to prove herself like any other student."

"I'd admit her in a heartbeat," I assured him.

Paige told him, "I'm really glad you convinced me to take the workshop."

Thad seconded, "So am I." He placed his hand over hers on the table.

Beaming, Glenn asked her, "And what about that movie career?"

"All in due time, Pops. I've got *work* to do first."

Thad said, "And you'll be doing it at the right school. Look at Tanner—after only a few months at DAC, he's off to Hollywood, making an important movie."

Tanner put his arm around my shoulder. "I had connections."

Kiki said, "Tell us all about it, love. Your film, *Photo Flash*."

Waiters began filling the first of our three wineglasses with a fruity white bordeaux as we tasted our soup and listened to Tanner. "Well," he said, "it's *nothing* like doing a play. The scenes are shot piecemeal, so it's hard to keep a sense of the whole story."

"And you never really memorize the whole role," I added.

"Right—memorize a scene, shoot it, forget it, and move on to the next. On the surface, film isn't as demanding as the stage, but it presents its own challenges. Since the process is still new to me, I have *no* idea how the finished product will turn out."

"It's a solid script," I said. Prior to Tanner's departure to begin filming, I had read *Photo Flash*—as had Kiki, Grant, and Larry—so I knew it contained the ideal role for Tanner's debut. "And with Gabe Arlington directing, the project will have plenty of creative vision."

Tanner snapped his fingers. "Guess what. Gabe decided to shoot several key scenes in *black and white*."

"Do tell," I said coyly. It was an idea I myself had promoted to the director.

"How very *arty*," said Kiki.

"So you see, Claire," Glenn lectured, "filmmaking need not be the entirely pedestrian craft you claim it to be." His tone was facetious.

I laughed. "Let's just call a truce on that topic."

Despite my plea, spoken only half in jest, we launched into a spirited discussion of plays versus films. As our soup course was succeeded by the hot appetizer—a delicate puff pastry brimming with lobster chunks and caviar—our conversation turned to plays that had been turned into movies. Before long, we were focused squarely on *Rebecca*.

Tanner said to me, "You must admit—the Hitchcock film is an all-time classic. The play is all but forgotten."

I agreed, "Hitchcock was a genius, and certainly, his *Rebecca* is definitive. Unlike live theater, film, by its nature, lasts. Once you nail it, it stays nailed. *But*"—I paused for effect—"it can never be improved upon, either. In the theater, each and every night we're blessed with the opportunity to reach new heights."

Kiki whispered, "Bravo, Claire."

"Ahhh," said Glenn expansively, "the gospel according to Claire Gray."

I must have grimaced.

"Sorry, Claire, if that came across as sarcasm. But I'm dead serious—you *know* you've always stood on a pedestal, at least in my eyes."

"*Really*, Glenn," I twittered. "I'm no saint. You mustn't exaggerate."

Dryly, Kiki agreed, "Yes, Glenn. You mustn't."

With his usual wide-eyed enthusiasm, Thad said, "That's why we're so excited about doing the play this fall. A revival of the stage version of *Rebecca*, with Claire Gray directing—it's, like, *history* in the making."

"It's worth changing schools for," agreed Paige.

Tanner told me, "It seems you have some high expectations to live up to." Leaning to kiss my cheek, he added, "And I'm sure you will."

I joshed, "I wish I shared your confidence." (In fact, I did.)

"Well," proclaimed Glenn, "I think it's a wonderful idea, to mount a production of *Rebecca*. We could establish a tradition at DAC of reviving the theatrical antecedents of great films."

I reminded him, "It *was* your idea."

"Oh?" he asked playfully. "Guess it was."

I ventured, "As great as the film was, I think we have a credible chance of besting it. We have the makings of a fine student cast, and the production values will be first-rate, but most important, we have a solid script, and in many ways, I think it's stronger than the screenplay."

"Except," Thad reminded me, "you can't burn the set at the end."

"Right, and without that closing spectacle, we need to rely on the inherent drama of the script, its characters, and their motivations."

Paige nodded. "And that's why you've had us working so much with subtext."

"Precisely."

Kiki set down her wineglass, now empty, asking me, "You really think the stage script is stronger than the screenplay?"

"On one point in particular—much stronger. The key difference, other than the burning of Manderley, is that Maxim de Winter, in the play, has *murdered* Rebecca, shooting her point-blank with a gun. In the movie, Hitchcock was hampered by decency standards, dictating that his hero couldn't get away with murder, so the backstory was revised—Max killed Rebecca by *accident*. Pretty lame, if you think about it. That single detail weakens Max's motive to conceal what happened, and it totally changes the dynamics of his relationship with his young bride. In the movie, she essentially bucks him up and helps him out of a tight spot. In the play, however, she reaffirms her love for a man who has murdered his first wife. Strong stuff."

Tanner nodded. "Max murdered Rebecca—it really does make a difference."

Kiki agreed, "Even though Rebecca was already, in a sense, a dead woman—because of her disease—Max didn't understand that she was using him to end her suffering. He willfully killed her."

Paige noted, "And I suppose it doesn't matter, in a legal sense, that Rebecca got what she deserved. I mean, she was a real bitch."

"Any way you slice it," I concluded, "Max murdered Rebecca."

Glenn had remained conspicuously mute during this discussion, picking chunks of lobster out of his pastry, forking aside the caviar, which he did not eat. Were the words *Max murdered Rebecca* ringing in his ears? Did they suggest analogous words, *husband murdered wife,* and by extension, *Glenn murdered Felicia*? Was he merely toying with the analogy, or did it threaten to bring something sinister to the surface—just as Rebecca's body had surfaced with the scuttled dinghy?

Paige too seemed lost in her thoughts. I recalled her earlier comment, made more than once, that Felicia and Rebecca had a lot in common—they both got what they deserved.

Tanner lightened the moment. "Don't forget poor old Mrs. Danvers. With all her sweet memories dashed, she was hell-bent on destruction."

"Hmm?" I asked, distracted.

Feeling her liquor, Kiki amplified, "Well, it's hardly a *secret,* darling. We all *assume* Mrs. Danvers was muff-diving, if you'll pardon the indelicate expression. Very likely, Rebecca was too."

Tanner and Thad burst into laughter.

"Good God," I mumbled.

Glenn leaned to me, asking quietly, "What's that, my dear?"

"Uh, nothing." I stood, placing my napkin on the chair. I asked the whole table, "Would you excuse me, please? There's something I need to take care of."

"Do hurry back, love," warbled Kiki while signaling a waiter for more wine.

Stepping to the head table, I caught Larry's eye. He excused himself from a conversation with Alyssa and the civil celebrant, then stood. Leaning close, I asked loud enough to be heard over the music, "Do you know how to reach Hebert, the concierge at Los Pinos?"

"Sure. What's up?"

"A new theory just struck me. It's probably groundless, but I'd like to check with Hebert."

Larry took out his cell phone, flipped it open, and scrolled through a list of numbers. "All set," he said, handing me the phone. "Whenever you're ready, press the button."

I thanked him, then slipped through one of the French doors and out to the terrace. Dusk had turned to darkness, and while the night air was still toasty, the intense heat of the day had dissipated with the waning light. A marble balustrade separated the elevated terrace from the deck of the hotel swimming pool and, beyond that, a sheer drop-off to the valley below. Overhead, the first few bright stars, probably planets, had winked to life near a crescent moon. No one else strolled the grounds just then, and I felt momentarily alone with an orderly cosmos. My heels pecked the stone pavers as I crossed the terrace, turned, and sat on the balustrade. Looking back through the windows, I saw waiters gliding through the ballroom, silhouetted by dancing candlelight. Then I lifted the cell phone and placed my call.

Hebert answered on the second ring.

"Good evening, Hebert. I'm so glad I was able to reach you on a Saturday night. This is Claire Gray—I'm a friend of Detective Larry Knoll."

He greeted me warmly, assuring me that no reintroduction was necessary.

After exchanging a few pleasantries, I got down to business: "I understand that Detective Knoll has already spoken to you about a guest by the first name of Lester who may have stayed at Los Pinos last month while 'Frances Gates' was there. Yes, I'm aware you were unable to identify such a guest. But I've had another thought, Hebert. Could you check to see if there was a guest with the *last* name Lester—or is there perhaps someone by that name on the hotel staff?"

Without even pausing to check, he was able to answer on the spot. It was the answer I had expected.

I asked, "Do you have that phone number?"

Hebert gave me the number.

I thanked him.

Then I placed the second call.

Some ten minutes later, as I was closing the cell phone, Tanner opened one of the French doors, saw me, and turned back inside to say, "She's out here." He then stepped out to the terrace, accompanied by Glenn and Kiki, Thad and Paige.

Noting that our table had been completely abandoned, I said, "Don't tell me I missed dinner. Has the dancing begun?"

"*No,* darling," said Kiki, moving near, her bracelets jangling in the quiet night. "Dinner hasn't been served yet; we're between courses. I got antsy."

Glenn added, "We wondered what became of you."

"Just needed to make a quick call." I showed them the phone.

Tanner asked, "Is everything all right?"

I answered vaguely, "Yes, I suppose so—in a manner of speaking."

Paige moved forward to ask me something, but she was interrupted by a shaft of light from the ballroom as one of the doors opened.

Larry stepped out to join us. "Well . . . ?" he asked me.

"I was able to reach Hebert. He was most helpful."

"*Hebert?*" said Kiki. "Who the hell's Hebert?"

"He's the concierge at Los Pinos, a resort visited by Felicia Yeats last month."

Paige groused, "I might have guessed this had something to do with her."

"I admit, the timing is unfortunate—with the wedding tonight."

Glenn raised a finger. "But the case *is* important. Innocent people have fallen under suspicion. We need to get to the bottom of this, and fast." He thumped his fist on nothing more substantial than thin air.

Bewildered, Thad asked, "Who do they think did it?"

Neither Glenn nor I was inclined to answer. We were saved the trouble when interrupted by Dustin, Peverell, and Lark, who made a noisy appearance from the main dining room, coming out to the terrace for some air. Dustin lit up a fat cigar.

"Looks who's here," said Peverell, spotting the rest of us.

"Is that Detective *Knoll?*" asked Lark, almost drooling at the sight of him. Her low-cut evening dress covered more flesh than her bathing thong had, but it still drew incredulous stares, exactly as intended.

"Well, the gang's all here!" bellowed Dustin. Har-har. "Didn't see you guys in the dining room."

Larry explained we were taking a break from his brother's wedding reception.

"What a pleasant coincidence," said Peverell, moving toward us with his friends. "May we join you in appreciating such a starry desert night?" The blackening sky had blossomed with a bright array of constellations, joining the moon and the planets.

"Of course," I told him. "In fact, I'm glad you're all here. We were just discussing a topic that I know you'll find of interest."

"Police work?" Lark asked eagerly, sidling next to Larry.

He backed off a step, explaining to Lark, "Claire was about to tell us something she's learned about Felicia."

"It's not just 'something,'" I assured everyone. "It's everything. I know who killed Felicia Yeats."

While my statement was not intentionally melodramatic, that's how it played: Lark and Kiki gasped; Dustin and Peverell turned to each other, sputtering disbelief; both Glenn and Paige looked suddenly ashen.

Larry moved to my side to retrieve his cell phone. As I handed it to him, he asked, "You *know* who killed Felicia?"

"Deductively, yes."

"And what, exactly, did Hebert tell you?"

"Actually, it goes back a bit further—to *Rebecca*."

"Who?" asked Dustin.

"The *play*," said Kiki, as if addressing a dimwit.

I explained, "My summer workshop has been studying the script of *Rebecca,* and it's escaped no one in my class that the play's plot, which centers on the death of Maxim de Winter's first wife, bears some uncanny resemblances to the mystery surrounding Felicia's death. It's as if art has imitated life—or vice versa. Coincidentally, the script was brought to my attention and promoted by none other than our college founder, Glenn Yeats."

All eyes turned to him. He asked warily, "What are you implying, Claire?"

"Nothing," I assured him. "I don't need to imply anything when the circumstances speak so strongly for themselves. Felicia was poisoned with methanol, traces of which were found in the blue gin bottle you gave her the night before she died. And then there's the running battle you had with her over the Dirkman house, which she threatened to burn that night. Taken as a whole, I'd say that's fairly strong evidence."

"I *know* it is," he said with quiet desperation, "but I didn't tamper with the gin. I opened the bottle fresh. *I didn't kill Felicia.*"

Larry tensed.

"No," I said to Glenn, "you didn't."

He looked more surprised by my words than relieved by them. "But then . . . ," he stammered, "why . . . ?"

I continued, "Even though it was *you* who had recommended the script, it was your *daughter* who first voiced the parallel to her stepmother's murder. More than once, Paige said, 'Felicia and Rebecca had a lot in common—they both got what they deserved.'"

"Miss Gray," said Paige, her voice tinged with panic, "I . . . I wish I hadn't said that. It was heartless, I know. I'm *still* trying to sort through my emotions. After all, Felicia did destroy my mother's home."

Glenn told her softly, "That's not entirely true."

Thad came to Paige's defense. "I'm sure she didn't mean what she said, Miss Gray. *No one* deserves to be poisoned."

I reminded him, "You yourself questioned how long you had waited for Paige in the hotel lobby last Saturday, disputing her claim that it was only 'a minute or two.' And this morning, when I asked about the bulge in her tote bag at the hotel, she said she'd been carrying her running shoes, which you also disputed."

Thad gave Paige a wary, questioning look.

"All *right,*" said Paige, "I admit I lied about the running shoes. But I *couldn't* tell Miss Gray what was really in the bag."

I asked, "Why not?"

She hesitated. "It was Gatorade, a big bottle of it, okay? During

Monday's workshop, you mentioned that antifreeze poisonings some-times involve Gatorade, and . . . well, I didn't want to raise suspicions about my bringing it to the hotel."

"Why *did* you bring it?"

"Because it was *hot* that morning. Like Thad said, it was too hot to run that day. Some people carry bottled water; I like Gatorade."

Larry asked her, "What were you doing at the hotel in the first place?"

"Felicia *invited* me, Detective. At the party the night before, she sug-gested a visit on Saturday morning. Even though I hated the woman, I never really *knew* her, so I thought—just maybe—it was time to hear *her* side of the story."

Glenn sighed. "I wish you had."

"As a kid, I felt nothing but bitterness. But now, I figured, we could at least . . . talk. Woman to woman."

Thad took Paige's hand. "I believe you."

Larry glanced at me, as if waiting for his cue to make an arrest.

"Paige," I said, "I also believe you." I told everyone, "She had noth-ing to do with Felicia's death."

"Well, *that's* a relief," said Kiki with an expansive gesture. "But I don't get it. You said Felicia's death had something to do with the *Re-becca* script. If not Glenn or Paige—who?"

Tanner crossed his arms, grinning. "Yeah, Claire. You've got all of us stumped. What are you driving at?"

I returned the grin. "Rest assured, the clue to solving the mystery of Felicia's death is planted in the *Rebecca* script. Paige saw a parallel—that both Felicia and Rebecca had gotten what they deserved—but there's at least one other parallel, one that's been overlooked. Until to-night, that is. Something was said at the dinner table, and then every-thing fell together for me. A quick phone call confirmed it."

Larry scratched behind an ear. "I don't mind telling you: I'm lost."

I reminded him, "You were sitting at a different table."

Kiki said, "*I* was at your table, love, and I'm *clueless.*"

"Really, Kiki? It was something *you* said that clued me." I ex-plained to the others, "So I borrowed Larry's cell phone and came out here to call our friend Hebert, the concierge at Los Pinos."

"Los Pinos?" said Lark. "That's the resort Felicia visited last month. I was with her."

"Yes, you were, weren't you?" I told everyone, "Earlier today, I phoned Dustin here at the hotel and asked him about his mother's trip to Los Pinos with Lark—"

Dustin interjected, "I didn't meet Lark till tonight."

Peverell explained, "I suggested we all have dinner."

Lark tweaked Peverell's cheek, baby-talking, "He's so gwacious . . ."

"Indeed he is." I continued, "Dustin told me his mother had mentioned plans to meet 'a clever little man named Lester.'"

"Yep," affirmed Dustin, "those were her words."

"Naturally, this gave credence to a theory Lark had previously suggested: the true purpose of Felicia's visit had been a clandestine rendezvous, a secret romance."

Dustin recalled, "Mom seemed way up before the trip, then way down afterward, so this guy must've been a disappointment."

"So it would seem. But Larry checked with the hotel today, and there was no 'Lester Somebody' registered during Felicia's visit. At the table tonight, it occurred to me that we may have had the name backward, so I phoned Hebert to ask if anyone with the *last* name Lester had stayed or worked there. And bingo—"

Everyone's brows arched expectantly.

"—Hebert immediately suggested one Anne Lester."

A moment of confused silence was followed by a round of dismayed chatter. Kiki blurted, "You mean, Felicia Yeats and Anne Lester were muff—?"

"Kiki," I shushed her, "enough of that."

"Felicia?" asked Glenn, incredulous. "I don't *think* so."

Tanner suggested, "Midlife crisis?"

Paige nodded. "So *that's* why she asked me to her hotel room."

Dustin squeaked, *"Mommy?"*

Larry, Peverell, and Thad said nothing, but exchanged titillated glances.

Lark wondered, "Just who *was* this woman—this Anne Lester?"

Larry reminded her, "Felicia registered under a false name. Maybe her friend did as well."

"*Yeah,*" said Dustin with sudden insight. Dropping his cigar to the stone floor and crushing it with his shoe, he crossed his arms, facing Lark. "Mom went there with *you*—didn't she, 'Anne'?"

"*What?*" shrieked Lark. "You think your mother and I were . . . were . . . ?"

I forewarned Kiki, "Don't."

Lark blustered, "But that's . . . that's *absurd*." Stepping close to Larry, she heaved her moonlit bosoms, saying, "*Really,* Detective, you can't possibly believe that a woman like *me* would have any interest in a woman like *that*."

Larry turned to me, slack-jawed, needing help.

I told the group, "There's a danger to jumping to conclusions, and you've all just done so. Lark isn't Anne Lester, and in fact, Anne Lester wasn't even a guest at Los Pinos. *Doctor* Anne Lester works there—in the diagnostic clinic."

As these words sank in, Dustin noted, "But Mom said she was meeting 'a clever little man.'"

I suggested, "She knew she had an appointment with Dr. Lester, who she probably assumed was a man."

Larry recalled, "Her hotel account, paid in cash, included a two-day workup at the clinic. There's nothing unusual in that; many hotel guests take advantage of the facilities for a routine checkup."

I assured him, "There was nothing routine about Felicia's checkup. I just got off the phone with Dr. Lester, having reached her at home. Naturally, she was reluctant to discuss any dealings she'd had with a patient at the clinic. But when I explained that the patient was Frances Gates, who had visited the clinic last month and had since become the object of a murder investigation as the result of methanol poisoning, Dr. Lester was distraught and told me the details of Felicia's visit. She said to tell you, Larry, that she would welcome your follow-up call."

"I'll do that," he said, taking out his notebook, "but go ahead—fill us in."

"Dr. Lester told me that the purpose of Felicia's visit was to obtain a second opinion regarding a troublesome diagnosis that had been rendered during a previous workup at another clinic, where she had apparently used the same pseudonym. Dr. Lester confirmed that Felicia had developed a case of Fanning's syndrome."

Everyone looked puzzled. Glenn said, "I've never even *heard* of it."

"Neither had I. The doctor described it as being related to ALS, but even worse and—thank God—much more rare. While diagnosis of ALS is a lengthy ordeal, a process of elimination based on developing symptoms, Fanning's syndrome leaves distinct markers in various blood tests that allow a fast and definitive diagnosis. The degenerative disease is untreatable and progresses rapidly."

Lark mumbled, "So *that's* why Felicia was so testy when Adrienne and I were gabbing at the ALS fund-raiser—she was trying to listen to the speech about research developments."

"I'm sure." Exhaling a somber little sigh, I further revealed, "Fanning's is such a hopelessly morbid condition, Dr. Lester confided to me that if she herself were to be diagnosed with the syndrome, she wouldn't hesitate to get her affairs in order and end her own life. While she never shared such thoughts with Felicia, she said it was apparent that Felicia had done her homework and fully understood the implications of the diagnosis. Felicia made comments that led the doctor to fear she was already contemplating suicide."

"Good God," said Lark, shaking her head. "No *wonder* the poor gal seemed so distracted that week."

"Dr. Lester tried several times to follow up on her 'Frances Gates' file, but Felicia had done a good job of covering her tracks. Given the circumstances and the timing, the doctor feels all but certain that Felicia took her own life."

Though clearly relieved, Glenn was also confused. "But the party," he said, "and the confrontation about the house, and the tainted gin bottle . . ."

I averred, "Felicia had apparently researched not only Fanning's syndrome, but also her means of escaping its ravages, settling on methanol poisoning. Antifreeze is available everywhere, so it's easy to obtain it, and it's therefore easy to make it appear that someone *else* could be responsible for deadly mischief involving the antifreeze. In this case, Felicia carefully set up a scenario that would lay the blame on Glenn. Consider:

"Her fussing about the Dirkman house struck me as trumped-up from the beginning and blown out of proportion, almost as if she were looking for an *excuse* to pick a fight with Glenn and have an open confrontation.

"What's more, Felicia was a teetotaler, yet at last Friday's party, she not only asked for a strong drink, but kept guiding Glenn's actions with the catchphrase 'I thought you'd never ask.' In effect, she instructed him to offer her a drink, to open a fresh bottle of gin, and then to send that bottle home with her.

"She even noted that Kiki and I were drinking our martinis from dark cobalt-blue glasses, and she asked for the same, knowing it would make it impossible for anyone to say with certainty, later, whether she had actually been drinking gin—a colorless liquid—at Glenn's that night.

"And when she sipped the first martini Glenn served her, she made the memorable comment that it tasted like perfume. She already knew antifreeze had a distinctive taste and smell; she had stored in her hotel room a deadly dose of it, which she would not only drink, but also use to contaminate the blue gin bottle."

Glenn tossed his hands. "I'm stunned. She even warned me that night that she could be 'surprisingly vindictive.' She was always a handful, but *this* . . ."

"Ughhh!" groaned Dustin; the loud, ugly noise seemed to shatter the quiet, respectful tone that had colored our discussion of his mother's death. "Why would Mom *do* such a thing? Why didn't she *tell* us about this illness? I mean, we could have helped her—or at least seen her through it, till the end."

"If I knew Felicia," said Lark, shaking her head, "your mother had *zero* taste for suffering."

"But to poison herself?" countered Dustin. "It's so . . . *extreme.* Why?"

I said, "I'm afraid *you* played a role in this, Dustin."

"Me?" he asked defensively. "I *loved* my mother."

"I know you did. But Felicia had three motives to end her life the way she did. Taken in total, they are, I believe, sufficient to explain her actions. One of those motives, Dustin, was to provide you with a cash windfall from the sale of the Dirkman house, which could not be sold during her lifetime. She understood your predicament with the FDA and your lenders, didn't she? And she understood that her death could save you from financial ruin."

Dustin made no effort to control the sobs that rose from within his jaded playboy's heart.

I continued, "The second motive, obviously, was to escape a hopeless battle with a vicious, untreatable disease."

"Just as Rebecca did," Paige noted quietly.

"Yes, and Felicia's third motive—I'm sorry to say this, Glenn—was to cast her reviled ex-husband under suspicion of murder. I don't know what happened between the two of you, but it left unhealed wounds sufficiently painful to give her perverse pleasure in plotting to make *you* pay for her self-inflicted death."

"And she damn near succeeded," said Glenn through tight lips. He showed no sign of remorse for the pain he and Felicia had caused each other, only bitterness for an aftermath he could neither predict nor control.

Kiki snapped her fingers. "The *Rebecca* script."

I nodded. Through a wan smile, I recounted, "At the table tonight, Kiki, you said that Rebecca was already, in a sense, a dead woman—because of her disease—and Max didn't understand she was using him to end her suffering. *That's* when I recalled that Felicia had visited the Los Pinos clinic, and that's why I left the table to borrow Larry's cell phone." Summing up the events of the past week, I said, "Pure and simple, Felicia's death was a suicide—but just like Rebecca's, it had a bizarre participatory twist."

Kiki chortled. "And here *I* thought it was my lesbian reference that had proved so insightful."

Larry closed his notebook. "It was an intriguing thought."

"It sure was," agreed Thad.

Tanner said, "I think we *all* bought in to that theory."

"Well, *I* certainly didn't," Lark told us.

Then she paused to preen her helmet of frosty-blond hair.

Larry said the case was essentially closed. "The evidence against Glenn was circumstantial, and the background from Dr. Lester—particularly her fears that Felicia was suicidal—leaves little reason to pursue the investigation as a homicide."

While Dustin was understandably shaken by this conclusion, he thanked both Larry and me for our efforts, then retreated with Lark and Peverell to the lobby bar. Perhaps the disturbing news about his mother could be softened by a snifter of good cognac.

Though I felt pleased with myself for solving the mystery, I resisted any temptation to crow about it. Tonight, after all, was a celebration of Grant and Kane's formal commitment to lifelong love. If congratulations were in order, if glasses were to be raised, I would gladly partake in the toasting as one in the crowd, not as the hero of the moment.

"Let's go back inside," I told the others. "Our dinner is surely cold by now, if it hasn't been cleared altogether."

"Who could eat *anyway*?" asked Kiki. "What a night!"

"I'm starved," Glenn assured her. "My stomach's been sour for days, but now I'm suddenly famished."

I suggested, "What happened out here, let's keep it to ourselves. Tonight's spotlight belongs to Grant and Kane and their future happiness—not the tragic details of a bitter woman's suicide."

Everyone agreed. We all filed back into the ballroom, save Larry, who remained on the terrace to phone in his findings.

Indoors, lively conversation filled the room, drowning out the dinner music. Most of the guests were finishing the main course, but our table, having been abandoned, had not yet been served. When we appeared from the terrace, a line of waiters beelined to our table bearing silver-domed dishes that were presented the moment we sat down.

"*There* they are," announced Grant from the head table. In a tone of good-natured reprimand, he asked, "*Where* have you kids been? We were ready to send out the dogs."

Glenn answered, "Claire was just tidying up some loose ends, some school business. I thought I'd give her a hand."

"It was nothing," I said. "We needed some fresh air."

Suspiciously, Grant wondered, "Then where's my brother? The best man seems to be missing."

"He'll be along shortly. He needed to make a phone call."

"Ahhh," said Grant wistfully, "the law never rests."

"Dinner looks *marvelous,*" I said, changing the subject. And our table ate heartily, feasting on a mixed grill of tenderloin, rack of lamb, and veal medallions.

Soon the main course was cleared from the other tables, and as dessert was being served, the understated dinner music turned upbeat, prompting Grant and Kane to rise and take to the floor for the first dance. They had clearly rehearsed this, as their swing routines were far too polished to be improvised. We awarded their slick moves with whistles, shouts, and enthusiastic applause.

When their performance was finished, they bowed in all directions. Grant mopped his brow, telling the crowd, "And I *swore* I wouldn't break into a sweat."

Kane feigned exhaustion. "There's no keeping up with *this* guy." Less than half Grant's age, Kane could easily have danced rings around his partner, but he lovingly let Grant revel in the limelight.

When the next dance number was played, Tanner turned to me, suggesting, "Shall we?"

"With pleasure." Dabbing my lips with my napkin, I rose as he helped with my chair. Joining several other couples, we stepped to the dance floor, found our rhythm, and became one with the music. It was a slower tune, allowing us to talk as we held each other close.

"I've missed you," he said.

With a tone of understatement, I assured him, "The feeling is mutual."

"But you were right."

"About what?"

"In April, just before I moved to LA, you said a phase of our lives was drawing to a close, but we'd always love each other."

"As loving friends," I reminded him.

"Yeah." He laughed. "And I thought those words sounded so chaste and proper. But now it makes sense. I'll always love you, Claire."

We missed a step as I hugged him tight. "And you'll always be in my heart. But a lifelong, live-in relationship—it was never in the cards."

"Still, the months we were together, they were some of the happiest of my life, certainly the most adventurous."

"*I'll* tell the world." As we resumed dancing, I had a thought. "Tonight—this is bound to run late, and it's a long drive to LA. Would you care to stay over?" I quickly added, "The guest room is vacant; it's yours for the asking."

"Awww, that's sweet, but I can't stay. I need to get back tonight—poolside brunch with the publicity people tomorrow morning. Thanks, though." He kissed the side of my mouth.

Someone's hip gave my rump a solid jolt. "*Sorry,* darling," said Kiki, twirling into view; Glenn clung to her as if he feared being jettisoned across the dance floor. "Would you mind *terribly* if I cut in?" Theatrically, she added, "This may be my last chance—ever—to dance with Tanner Griffin. Once his film is released, I fear his dance card will be forever filled." She sighed.

With a grin, I asked Tanner, "Do you mind?"

"Of course not."

Kiki leaned close, speaking into my ear, "Besides, I think Glenn wants to have a word with you." Dumping Glenn, she snatched Tanner from my arms and whisked him away without missing a twirl.

I noted, "That Kiki—she marches to a different drummer."

"And dances to a different tune—heard only by herself." Glenn watched her part the crowd with Tanner in tow. "I guess that's what makes her so . . . so *intoxicating.*"

Glenn's wistful gaze and fawning smile seemed to confirm Kiki's earlier contention that things were heating up between them. With a start, I thought of something, saying, "I almost forgot . . ."

"What, my dear?"

"Your dinner for two. Kiki said you invited her to the house last night."

"Word travels fast," he mused, delighted to be the subject of such gossip.

"Not that it's *any* of my business . . ."

"But it is," he told me, offering his arms. "Shall we?" And we began dancing with the others.

Warily, I asked, "Why is your dinner with Kiki any of *my* business?"

"Because you weren't there." Was he speaking in riddles?

Searching for safer ground, I said, "Congratulations, Glenn. The new wardrobe is smashing."

"Isn't it, though?" He spun me at arm's length to allow a better look at him. "She's a genius, that woman—a *genius.*"

Kiki?

I agreed, "A stunning transformation." Then again, it wouldn't have taken much to improve on the red pirate shirt he'd worn a week earlier.

Glenn pulled me close, hustling to recapture the rhythm of the music (though I felt we were now a half beat off, as if I were dancing with one leg in a splint). He said, "This is heaven—but so difficult."

Again the riddles. "Glenn," I demanded, "*what* are you trying to say?"

He repeated, "This is heaven." Then he elaborated, "Dancing with you."

"Then why is it 'so difficult'?"

"Claire"—he paused—"let's talk." And he led me off the dance floor just as Paige and Thad were joining the crowd.

As we passed the head table, I saw that Larry had returned. He momentarily withdrew from a lighthearted conversation with Kane's sister, Alyssa, to give me a thumbs-up, which I interpreted as a signal that the evening's police work had come to a satisfactory conclusion.

Opening one of the French doors, Glenn escorted me out to the terrace.

I quipped, "We nearly missed dinner. Now we'll miss dessert."

"This is important," he said, sounding concerned as well as earnest.

Echoing his concern, I asked, "What is it, Glenn?"

Strolling me out to the balustrade, he made a broad gesture toward the vista of valley lights beyond. "I've always taken a measure of personal pride in this community."

"It's your kingdom," I said, exaggerating only slightly.

He didn't dispute my statement. "But something has always been missing. Rather, *someone* has always been missing."

"Glenn," I said, touching his arm, "I've been enormously flattered by your faith in me—as an artist and as a person. You've given me the opportunity to shift the direction of my career and to reshape my life, long after growing satisfied that I'd accomplished every goal of my dreams." I shook my head. "How smug, how complacent, can one get? I'll never be able to thank you, Glenn, for teaching me there's always a next act, a next chapter, a new challenge."

With quiet sincerity, he said, "I don't expect your thanks. Having you here is reward enough."

I asked, "Like having a treasure, a porcelain goddess, on a pedestal?"

Through a soft laugh, he acknowledged, "Perhaps I laid it on a bit thick with the 'pedestal' reference, earlier, at the table. But I really did feel that way, once."

Trying not to sound too eager, I asked, "Has something changed?"

"Well . . . yes, Claire, something *has* changed. In fact, there have been unexpected changes on *two* fronts."

He was finding it so difficult to be direct, I decided to help him along. "Let me guess," I said. "Are we talking about Kiki?"

Looking into my eyes, he tried to gauge whether I was feeling affronted. When it became apparent there was no jealousy lurking behind my question, he grinned, then blurted, "Yes! We *are* talking about Kiki. She's been here a year—under my very nose, as it were—and it didn't click for me till *now,* this past week, that she's a captivating, enchanting creature."

"Don't forget 'intoxicating,' " I reminded him.

"What *fire*, what *gusto*," he gushed. "And it turns out, we share so *many* of the same interests."

He didn't specify their common interests, and frankly, I found them difficult to imagine. Certainly, Kiki shared Glenn's passion for theater, but so did any number of other faculty members. Beyond that, was he referring to Kiki's interest in his own wardrobe? Was he that superficial? If so, he and Kiki were a fair match.

Another common interest of theirs was I. T. Dirkman. Glenn had long admired the man's architectural talents, while Kiki had cut to the chase and bedded him. Presuming Dirkman was a shared interest that Glenn and Kiki had *not* discussed, I didn't inquire—but I was unable to control my wry smile.

"Your smile," he said, touching my lips. "I see that my confession doesn't come entirely as a disappointment. I could never forgive myself if you felt in any sense . . . jilted."

I wanted to tell him, *Au contraire*, I'm delighted to be let off the hook. But such honesty seemed imprudent; the man signed my paycheck. "Kiki is my oldest friend," I said, "and one of my dearest. I've rarely seen her so 'up'—and *that's* saying something. If the two of you are inclined to explore your possibilities, I wish you the best, truly." With a touch of theater, I added somberly, "I'll get over it, Glenn."

"Ah, Claire"—he wrapped me in a hug—"you're the most understanding woman in the world. This changes nothing at the college, you know. Rest assured, I'll always view you as my faculty's crown jewel."

"Still on a pedestal, eh?"

"In a sense, yes." He hesitated, then dropped his embrace. "Earlier," he explained, "when I said something had changed—on *two* fronts—one of those changes was Kiki, of course, and the other . . . well, the other was the pedestal."

Genuinely intrigued, I crossed my arms and backed up a step to take a good look at him. With a grin that conveyed affection as well as amusement, I said, "Tell me about the pedestal."

"I hope you won't take this the wrong way, but I've come to understand that some of my feelings for you were the result of infatuation."

"I understood that long before you did, Glenn."

He nodded. "Which explains why you were 'buying time' after I professed my love to you last fall."

"Yes, exactly." (Well, not exactly. It was my infatuation with Tanner Griffin, not Glenn's infatuation with me, that had been responsible for my foot-dragging. But that's another story.)

"This sounds corny as hell, but I had worshipped you from afar for years. One of the reasons I *built* DAC was to lure you here, to work with you. Accomplishing that, once you arrived, I set my sights even higher—a *life* with you. Yes, Claire, you were very much on a pedestal. And your reference to a 'porcelain goddess' was right on the mark."

"Not unlike the china cupid in *Rebecca*," I noted. "It was a priceless curio shattered by the arrival of another woman."

Glenn chuckled. "Let's not take this life-imitates-art business *too* far, Claire. It wasn't the arrival of another woman—in this case Kiki—who knocked you off your pedestal."

"Who, then?"

"Me. I myself did it. To my mind, you *were* a deity, a goddess of the arts, replete with all manner of romantic folderol. And for the past year, you kept bucking that image every time you got involved with a police investigation, which I instinctively discouraged. Until this past week. Finding myself in one hell of a fix, I encouraged—I *begged* you, Claire—to help me with your sleuthing skills. Once again, you triumphed, and this time, you saved my sorry, uh, butt."

"My pleasure, Glenn. Delighted to help a friend."

"And that's when you fell from my pedestal. Because your knack for crime solving is so inherently pragmatic and logical, my vision of you has been altered. While finding you no less 'artistic,' I now recognize you as more 'real'—and less an object of worship." He sighed. "Does that make *any* sense?"

I assured him, "It makes perfect sense."

"I do hope this won't harm our working relationship."

"Glenn"—I hooked my arm around his—"a good, stiff dose of reality can only *help* our working relationship. I predict a long and fruitful collaboration."

"Then let's get back to the party." He paused to give me a light kiss on the cheek before escorting me indoors.

Dessert had been served, and a few of the guests were already taking their leave, filing past the head table to extend another round of well-wishing. Most of the remaining guests were on the dance floor.

Kiki was still with Tanner, wearing him out, dancing up a storm; her bracelets added a percussive jangle to the upbeat tune being pounded out by the musicians. Thad was still with Paige, and they were dancing in each other's arms as if hearing a slow ballad.

Glenn noted, "They're looking decidedly romantic."

I wondered, "Puppy love?"

"They're not kids anymore, but not quite adults. Who knows?"

"Maybe they're just infatuated—an outgrowth of working in such close proximity this summer."

Glenn shrugged. "Or maybe it's the real thing. I can't say I'd object; Thad is a fine young man."

I squeezed Glenn's arm. "Come fall, I'll keep an eye on them for you." My sense of duty extended not only to Paige's father, but also to Thad's uncle, Mark Manning. How would *he* react when he learned that I had played some role in his nephew's budding romance—to a billionaire's daughter?

As Kiki and Tanner were still occupied with each other, Glenn invited me to dance again. We were about to do so when the music was stopped by the clanging of someone's spoon on a glass.

Oh, no, I thought, don't tell me we're to be subjected to an endless barrage of juvenile demands for the wedding couple to smooch—a trite convention that struck me as an embarrassingly lowbrow intrusion on Grant and Kane's elegant evening.

Imagine my surprise when I realized it was Grant doing the clanging. Larry, at his side, sat back with his hand over his mouth, looking chagrined.

When everyone's attention was directed at the head table, Grant announced, "My brother and best man, Detective Larry Knoll, has just informed me that congratulations are in order. It seems our dear friend Claire Gray has assisted him this evening in untangling yet another riddle of perplexing death. Out of respect for the family of the deceased, I won't divulge any details, but the upshot is this: there was no foul play, and Claire played a decisive role in bringing this sensitive investigation to a speedy close."

Kane stood next to his partner. They both raised their glasses. "Bravo!" said Kane. "To Claire," said Grant.

Larry and the other seated guests stood also. The guests on the dance floor turned to me. All applauded.

I wagged both hands, quelling the tribute. "Thank you, everyone, but I was simply trying to help my friends. Besides, tonight isn't about *me*." I was glad I hadn't worn the red dress, which would have lent a disingenuous note to my protest. I continued, "This is Grant and Kane's party, and as long as I have the floor, I want to wish them many years of love and happiness together." With a laugh, I added, "They're the model relationship, aren't they? This May-December gay duo is the most committed and 'normal' couple I know."

Everyone joined in laughter, applause, and a smattering of toasts.

With mock umbrage, Grant asked me, "Whataya mean, 'May-December'? Who do I look like—Spring Byington?" The guests of my generation laughed at his reference to the ancient sitcom *December Bride,* while the guests of Kane's generation exchanged quizzical glances.

Those who had planned to leave early had now left, so the members of the head table joined the rest of us on the dance floor as the pianist played the first notes of something soft and jazzy.

Thad and Paige were standing near Glenn and me. Before beginning the next dance, Paige paused to tell me, "Thank you, Miss Gray. Knowing the truth about Felicia and how she died . . . well, it leaves me with mixed feelings, naturally. But now, at least, I understand that she was human and had her own baggage to deal with. I don't think I could ever have learned to *like* the woman, but I do wish I'd gotten to know her."

Glenn told his daughter, "I wish you had too. Felicia had some faults—obviously—but in her own way, she was an extraordinary person. I can't imagine what she went through, dealing with the knowledge of that awful disease. Let's hope she's at rest."

Paige gave a soft nod. "Sure, Pops." Then she and Thad joined hands and drifted out among the dancers.

Just as they left us, Larry and Alyssa drifted near. Larry's dancing skills, I noted, were polished and confident. While it came as little surprise that Larry's brother, Grant, was exceptionally light in his loafers, I hadn't expected such adroit footwork from this nuts-and-bolts, just-the-facts-please homicide detective. He and Alyssa stopped to greet Glenn and me.

I told them, "Nicely done tonight. Your brothers are both fortunate to have such support from their families."

Alyssa quipped, "Yeah, well, always a bridesmaid . . ."

Glenn asked Larry, "May I cut in? I was hoping to connect with Kiki again, but first she was tied up with Tanner, and now . . ."

We followed his glance toward Kiki, who apparently had taken pity on Sarah Standish, the civil celebrant, who was alone that evening, and had asked her to dance. The two women waltzed across the dance floor, then stopped in unison, turned, and launched into an uncomfortably sensuous tango.

"Ah, Glenn"—I laughed—"you're going to have your hands full with *that* one."

He twitched his brow. "I'm planning on it." Then he turned to Alyssa. "Meanwhile, may I?"

Alyssa asked Larry, "Do you mind, Detective? I've never been propositioned by a living-legend computer tycoon before. It'll make a hell of a story someday."

Larry gave her a wink.

Glenn tendered his hand to Alyssa, then whisked her into the crowd.

Which left Larry and me standing alone together.

He offered his arms. "Shall we?"

"I was hoping you'd ask. You're surprisingly smooth on your feet." I stepped into his arms.

Spinning me into the crowd, he explained, "Grant taught me."

"You're kidding."

"Nope. I was in eighth grade; he was a junior in high school. My first 'big dance' was coming up. We had some dorky lessons at school, and I was nervous as hell. Grant to the rescue. He said, 'Just think of me as Big Sis.' "

"Who led?"

Larry laughed. "I've already told you far too much."

We danced without speaking for several measures, enjoying the music, each other's company, and the celebratory mood of the evening. He led me through a particularly elegant step. Impressed, I told him, "Big Sis taught you well."

A beat later, he said, "Thanks, Claire."

"No, I mean it: you're a wonderful dancer."

"That's kind of you, but I wasn't talking about dancing. I was talking about the case. You really did come through for me—*again*. This time, though, there was more at stake than simple justice. My career was on the line. If I'd arrested the all-powerful Glenn Yeats, which I was leaning toward, and he turned out to be innocent, which we now know to be the case, I'd've been demoted at best—or even booted out of the department. On the other hand, if Glenn actually *had* been guilty and I'd caved to pressure to handle him with kid gloves, I'd then be accused of dereliction of duty. Hardly a win-win. The only *sure* solution was *your* solution: prove someone else was responsible. And you did it, Claire—quickly and neatly."

"That's me—quick and neat."

With a chuckle, he noted, "I was skeptical at first regarding your 'theatrical perspective' on criminology, but I must admit, there's nothing artsy about it—it's thoroughly logical."

" 'Logical,' " I repeated. "That's the very word Glenn used tonight during a heart-to-heart on the terrace. He said my sleuthing skills were inherently pragmatic and logical."

"Then I'm happy to second the compliment."

"Ironically, Glenn didn't mean it as a compliment, not in his heart. By solving the case and helping him out of a fix, he said, I'd altered his vision of me. I'd become 'real'—and less an object of worship."

"That's nuts."

"That's *Glenn*. Anyway, I'm relieved his doting has crashed to a halt. The timing is right—Kiki seems more than willing to step in and tussle with his neuroses."

The timing was right for another reason, as well. Not only had Glenn found Kiki, but also, I had found Larry. I couldn't help wondering: Did my pragmatic and logical nature, which had proven something of a turnoff to Glenn Yeats, have the opposite effect on Detective Larry Knoll?

If so, he didn't tell me.

We danced several more numbers, and the party began to wind down. We chatted and joked, but our words carried little of substance. He was warm and affable to me the entire evening, but he offered no overt signs of affection—and there was no repeat of the unexpected kiss he had given me the night before at the restaurant.

If his feelings toward me were unclear, my feelings toward him were all the more muddied. At that moment, I couldn't even define the relationship.

Friendly, certainly. Interested, perhaps. But heated, not at all.

Besides, I reminded myself, he's a married man.

Kiki and Glenn finally connected on the dance floor, and when the evening's festivities were over, he asked her to leave with him. Giddy as a schoolgirl, she pulled me aside, saying, "I *told* you things were heating up, darling. It seems I won't be needing a lift." So I drove home alone.

Despite the late night, I awoke with the birds on Sunday morning and hopped out of bed, having grown accustomed to taking advantage of the day's early hours, before the heat would set in. In the year since my move, I had come to appreciate the serene beauty of dawn in the desert, with its play of light on the surrounding mountains, its birdsong, its metaphoric sense of hope and promise and new beginnings.

Shrugging into a light silk kimono, I tied the sash and padded barefoot out the front door to my driveway, where I retrieved a rolled copy of the *Desert Sun,* just delivered. While the Sunday edition was always the week's largest, its bulk was down considerably during the dog days, when tourism and advertising reached low ebb. Glancing at the dateline on the paper's masthead, I noted that it was nearly August—the desert's hottest days were still ahead.

Stepping indoors again, I went to the kitchen, where I removed the rubber band from the newspaper, unrolled it, and spread it on the counter. Not that I seriously expected a banner headline to trumpet that a high-profile homicide investigation had been cleverly solved the previous night, but I felt a measure of disappointment in finding that most of page one had been devoted to a think piece regarding political wrangling over Colorado River water rights. Realistically, I assumed the paper would contain nothing whatever regarding my role in unraveling the details of Felicia Yeats's poisoning. The mystery had been solved too late for the morning deadline, and because the bizarre death was now known to have been a suicide, not a homicide, there would be no sensational arrests.

Still, I decided I would take my time with the paper that morning, skimming through every page, just in case.

I found scant appeal in brewing a pot of piping-hot coffee—I'd be plenty warm later—so I opted instead for iced tea. Checking inside the refrigerator, I was pleased to confirm that Oralia had prepared a fresh pitcher during her last visit. Someday, I vowed, I would master her simple recipe, but fortunately, there was no need to fret over my culinary inadequacies, not at that moment, anyway.

Filling a glass with ice, I grabbed the pitcher and the newspaper, then headed outdoors to the pool. As the terrace was still in full shade, the early-morning temperature was comfortable, if not quite cool, so I left the kitchen door open behind me, figuring the house could use some fresh air.

I settled in my favorite spot, a cushioned chair and ottoman overlooking the pool and, beyond the garden wall, the undulating peaks of the Santa Rosas, radiant in the low-angled, golden light of sunrise. Arranging my glass and the pitcher on a small table next to the chair, I poured some tea, took a few sips, then spread the newspaper open on the ottoman and began paging through the front section.

As expected, there was nothing about Felicia Yeats, not even the sort of late-breaking story that typically gets wedged into some inside-corner space that had been occupied by an 'anytime' feature deemed expendable. I noticed several stories that could easily have been spiked—a pancake breakfast, a Q-and-A on toxic mold, a report of latest airport-use statistics. But then, they hadn't sought *my* editorial input, had they? I chortled at my imperious thoughts as I tossed aside the news sections and began browsing through the real-estate guide.

Lost in the fantasy world of guest houses, catering kitchens, and infinity-edged pools, I was not quite certain how much time had passed (though I was on my second glass of iced tea), when the doorbell rang. Rising from my chair and crossing the terrace, I was glad I had left the kitchen door open; otherwise I would not have heard the bell. I also felt a wave of apprehension. A visitor at such an early hour—on a Sunday, no less—was surely not the bearer of good news.

Passing through the kitchen, I glanced at the clock and noted that it was not yet seven. Quickening my pace, I zipped through the living room, reached the front door, grabbed the knob—hesitated—then turned it. As I cracked the door open, a thin shaft of sunlight sliced across the floor.

"Morning, Claire. Sorry if I woke you."

"Larry?" I swung the door wide open. "No, you didn't wake me. I was in back, reading the paper. What's wrong?"

"Not a thing." A soft smile confirmed that I needn't be alarmed. He wore the same clothes as the night before, and unless I was mistaken, he'd missed his morning shave. He asked, "May, uh . . . may I come in?"

"Of *course*, Larry, sorry. Glad you dropped by. But I must look like hell." Which I did.

"Don't be nuts—you're perfect."

I closed the door and walked him into the room. "Can I make you some coffee? Or how about some of Oralia's iced tea? It's far better than mine."

He wagged a hand. "No, thanks. I just got off the road. Had plenty of coffee during the drive—too much, in fact, so I'm feeling sorta wired."

I, on the other hand, was still waking up. Confused, I asked, "You've been on the road? Where were you?"

He suggested, "Let's sit down."

Whatever he had to say, it seemed important. And there I stood in a wrinkled bathrobe, with bed-rumpled hair. I hadn't even brushed my teeth. But Larry didn't notice. His eager smile conveyed that appearances didn't matter, that he had something timely on his mind. I gestured toward the leather bench, then sat next to him. "Now, then," I asked with mock formality, "to what do I owe the pleasure of this unexpected visit?"

He took a breath, exhaled, then began, "You asked where I've been. When I left the hotel last night, I started driving home, but along the way, I changed directions and headed over to San Diego. I needed to talk to Hayley."

With a note of apprehension, I said, "I hope you phoned first."

"Yeah"—he laughed—"I called from the car. If I'd appeared without warning on her parents' doorstep, waking her in the middle of the night, she wouldn't have been very receptive."

"Receptive to what?"

"To a heavy discussion, a discussion we've been avoiding for too long. Turns out, it did us both a world of good. We talked for *hours*, and we have a much better understanding of who we are and where we're headed."

"Well," I said philosophically (if not quite sincerely), "I'm glad you patched things up."

He gave me a quizzical look. "We didn't patch things up, Claire. We decided to split. We had a long heart-to-heart and, without rancor, decided we could never realize our dreams with each other. In short, we agreed to end the marriage."

I began to offer words of sympathy or support—I wasn't sure what to say.

But Larry cut me off. "It's *okay*, Claire. We're fine; we're good with it. Hayley will be happier, and so will I. We fully understand that I need to remain a strong presence in our kids' lives, but both she and I are now free to find love elsewhere."

Free to find love elsewhere—his concluding words had a poetic overtone, sounding almost cliché. These were not the sort of words that seemed natural to Larry, yet he had spoken them with ease. Through the trace of a grin, I asked, "Why are you telling me this?"

He reached for my hand and held it on his knee. "Last night, when you figured out how Felicia Yeats had died, you said that Glenn saw you in a new light. You were suddenly logical and 'real.'"

I nodded. "He was relieved that the mystery was solved and grateful for my role in it, but he lost his infatuation." Under my breath, I added, "Thank God."

"So it seems that both you and I are, well . . . 'free agents.'"

Playing dumb, I asked, "Isn't that a sports term?"

"I think you catch my drift." Larry cleared his throat. "Claire," he said, sitting up straight, acting downright prim, "I'm wondering if I may call on you—*socially*—in the future."

I studied him for a moment, broke into a smile, then tossed my arms around him, answering his query with a big, sloppy kiss—which he readily returned.

When we broke apart a few inches, he said, "I'll take that as a yes."

"Larry," I confirmed, "you're not only welcome to call on me; I hope you'll do it often. But, uh"—I slid a finger across his cheek—"do you suppose you could take care of that stubble?"

With a laugh, he stood. "Do you suppose Tanner left a razor behind?" It was an open secret that Tanner had lived with me before Hollywood beckoned.

I rose. "He did, in fact. But I wasn't asking you to shave *now.*"

"Actually, I'd like to. I'm sort of fussy about shaving."

"So is your brother. He told me it takes twenty minutes to shave properly. Can you believe it?"

Larry hesitated. "Grant taught me how to dance—*and* how to shave. I've never timed it, but twenty minutes sounds about right. He's certainly a perfectionist."

"And you're certainly his brother."

Larry raised a brow. "Is that a good thing?"

"That's a *very* good thing."

He snapped his fingers. "Hey, are you busy today?"

I shrugged. "My day's wide open."

"After I shave, as long as I'm here, I could fix breakfast for us. Hang out by the pool, maybe. Read the papers . . ."

"Larry, that's the sweetest invitation I've heard in a long, *long* time."

He reminded me, "It's *your* home. I invited *myself.*"

"Details, details . . ." I put my arm around his waist. "Let's get you set up in the guest bath."

As I strolled him toward the bedrooms, he asked, "By any chance, did Tanner also leave a T-shirt and some shorts? I need to get out of this suit."

I assured him, "We'll find something. Of course, you may end up in a towel."

"Whatever."

I guided him into the bathroom, found the razor and a fresh toothbrush, and told him, "Make yourself at home."

He gave me a hug. "Thanks, Claire. I will."

"While you're at it, I really ought to fix myself up." I primped.

"I already told you: you're perfect. Just wait for me by the pool. I'll be out in a minute."

"*Twenty* minutes," I corrected.

"Okay, twenty." He turned on the hot water.

"Larry?" I paused in the doorway. "I have a feeling some wonderful times may lie ahead for both of us."

"Funny. So do I." He winked, then began washing his face.

Slipping out of the bathroom, I pulled the door closed behind me and retraced my steps through the house. Walking through the living room, I felt Grant's presence; he had found the house for me and influenced its tasteful, vintage decor while solidifying his role as my best friend. Walking past the bar, I felt Kiki's presence; she had enjoyed a good many cocktails with me while revisiting our shared history, a friendship that stretched back more than thirty years. Walking into the kitchen, I felt Tanner's presence; he had been the focus of many a happy morning, standing at the counter, setting up the coffeemaker while articulating his passions for theater and his dreams of success. Finally, walking out to the terrace, I felt Larry's presence.

He was still indoors, but my instincts told me he would play a role in my life. Whether it would be a summer fling—or the real thing—I couldn't begin to guess. I knew, though, that something unexpected had clicked for us the prior Tuesday during our trip to Los Pinos. And now, only five days later, the implications of his overnight drive and his early-morning visit left little doubt that we would soon take our friendship to a different level altogether.

Strolling to my chair, I leaned to refill my glass from the pitcher of iced tea. The sun had crept above the roof of the house, and the surface of the pool danced with the languid play of light. In the distance, waves of heat had begun rising from the desert floor, which made the outlying mountains shimmer. I squinted. From a faraway precipice, a speck of black drifted into space, silhouetted by the bright sky, riding the heat waves to greater heights. It was a hang glider, possibly the same daring fellow we had seen on our drive to Idyllwild.

Inspired by his leap of faith, I set down my glass, loosened my sash, slipped out of the kimono, and dropped it on the chair. The stone pavers burned the soles of my feet as I moved to the pool. Stepping in, my feet felt momentarily icy, but the water was perfect, and without hesitation, I slid in deeper, up to my neck.

Lolling my head back, I watched a mockingbird dart and swoop from the fronds of a towering palm. It sang with abandon, spinning melodies out of thin air. Among the brilliant red bracts of bougainvillea that crowded my garden wall, a tiny finch cheeped and twittered while pecking at something in the foliage.

Then, from the corner of my eye, a shadow moved across the terrace.

Turning my head, I spotted a roadrunner as he scampered from the wall of bougainvillea toward the far end of the house. Hearing me splash the water, he paused to twist his head, looking back at me. Then he sauntered on, taking his sweet time.

This was no everyday, humdrum roadrunner—a skinny brown chicken with a long, thin tail.

No, I mused, this was a lovely specimen, rare and exotic.

On that hot Sunday morning in late July, I saw a unicorn in my garden.